THE END IS NEAR

THE END IS NEAR

Harry Ramble

Published by Ebb Press

Copyright © 2010 by Harry Ramble

All rights reserved. Published in the United States
by Ebb Press, LLC.

ebbpress.com
harryramble.com

ISBN: 978-0-9816502-2-7
Library of Congress Control Number: 2010933014

Manufactured in the United States of America
First North American Edition Published September 2010

For Abigail and Owen.
Treasure every day.

THE END IS NEAR

The first Angel of Death came to me on my seventh day here. My seventh conscious day, I should say.

I woke from a sweaty, haunted nap and there she was, sitting in the wooden chair by the door.

Napping is most of what I do here at the Hudson Maxim Long-Term Care and Rehabilitation Unit, since I emerged from five weeks of coma, minus my jaw and a lot of my face, my head a beanbag of buckshot. Napping and filling one notepad after another with hastily scribbled replies and requests.

"Well! Hi there!" the Angel of Death said.

I knew right away that this visitor was different from other visitors I've received since I awoke here. She was wearing a lime-green pant suit with matching lime-green, strap-buckle shoes. And a little hat. A round, lime-green hat with an orange band. Death's Angel was sitting very straight in the chair, an opened magazine in her lap.

I did what I usually do upon waking and finding someone in my room. I tried to say something. Something like, Who are you? I couldn't say anything though, because the lower part of my head now consists of a temporary prosthetic device, an elaborate enamel contraption bristling with drains and shunts and clamps and plastic tubing.

"My goodness," the woman said. "That all looks like it hurts. Does it hurt?"

I had retrieved my notepad from the bedside table and was looking around for the pen I usually keep clipped to its cover.

"I'm sorry," Death's Angel said. "I borrowed your pen." She closed her magazine, rose from the chair, and offered my pen to me. I saw that the magazine was, in fact, The Big Book of Word Finds.

I took the pen and pushed the nurse call button. Then I started writing. Death's Angel returned to her seat and watched me. She had a cherubic round face, a mole at the left corner of her mouth, and red hair tied back severely into a bun at the nape of her neck.

After a moment, a nurse entered the room, a young black guy with a lifter's build, a goatee, and a ribbon pin in the lapel of his nurse's coat, one of those ribbons commemorating this or that disaster or disease.

"What's up, Nathan?" He didn't look pleased. His name was Jordan. He wasn't one of my favorites.

I held up the pad. On it, I had written, Tell me you don't see this one.

This is my primary means of communication now. I write on the pad, hold it up for inspection, write on the pad, hold it up. I pointed at the chair Death's Angel was occupying.

Jordan didn't bother looking at the chair. "Come on," he said. "I've got forty-five minutes left on this shift. Save it for Shaniqwa."

I pointed again.

"He won't be able to see me," my visitor said. "They never do."

Fine, I wrote. Then I don't see you either.

"It's a chair, Nathan. It's just a chair." Jordan was looking around for something. "Why don't you watch some TV?" He lifted a remote from the foot of the bed and clicked on the TV.

Turn that thing off.

I can see, right away, that I'm going to have trouble distinguishing my notebook-scribbled communications to others from my unconveyed musings. I could put my written statements into quotes, as if I'd said them. But I don't really say anything, do I? Not aloud, as others do. I think what's required is a new form of notation. Let's try this:

Turn that thing off.

No, maybe not. Little stars give this account a kind of Girl's First Diary feel, I think. Like any minute I'm going to start dotting my i's with hearts. Hang on.

Turn that thing off.

How about that, huh? From now on my notebook communications to others will be in blue, everything else in black. For your reading convenience. So let's get back to our first Angel of Death.

"But you do see me," she said. "Some people see me and some people don't. The ones who see me, I think, must be closer to me and farther from them." I should point out here that the Angel of Death doesn't call herself any such thing. She calls herself Estelle.

No. Fuck you. And your little friend, too. The girl in the pinafore who keeps running around painting blood on the walls.

Jordan had clicked off the TV and was watching me write. "Enough with the girl already, Nathan. There's no girl."

"Oh, that sounds scary. I haven't seen anything like that," the Angel of Death said. "That could be your imagination. You never know with some of these medications."

And you're not, right?

"What? Imaginary?"

"Alright, Nathan." Jordan was backing toward the door. "You want to do this the hard way, we can do it the hard way."

I was looking at Death's Angel. The problem with her was that she was nothing like my previous otherworldly visitors. She looked as substantial as Jordan. She possessed quite a bit of finely realized surface detail. Her eyes were painted up like a cartoon peacock's; her lips were a happy crimson bow of enthusiasm. She was no wispy hallucinatory fragment. She looked like a young housewife. Granted, a housewife who did her clothes shopping at some mod-hippie-era Sears or Montgomery Ward. And she had handed me a pen. This pen. The one I'm writing with.

What do you want?

"I guess I could be imaginary," she said. "But to be perfectly honest, I don't feel imaginary. I feel as real as ever."

I should also say here, in the interests of full disclosure, that I had been having some problems, earlier in the week, with my medication. With the morphine, specifically. Nurses and orderlies without faces. Odd, flickering images of people, moth-fluttering in a kind of half-light, rising up through the floor, walking through the walls. A bad episode with the chicken pot pie on, I think, Wednesday.

It's no secret. It's all documented in my chart. As are the doctors' successful efforts at correcting these problems. Tinkering with my dosages. Medicine isn't as precise a business as some would hope.

"I'm getting Croate," Jordan said. "I'm sick of this. You can work it out with her." He left the room.

"Well, he's no ray of sunshine, is he?" The Angel of Death rose from her chair again and peered at something on the bedside table. Then she approached and exchanged her Big Book of Word Finds for the untidily stacked, rubber-banded sheaf of paper, about an inch thick, that had been lying there. She went back to her chair and started peeling back the tops of the first pages, glancing at them. "He wouldn't last a day in my line of work."

Your line of work?

"I'm a stewardess. Well, I was a stewardess. For NAL."

NAL?

She looked up and grinned. "National Airlines. Airline to the playgrounds of the world. You wouldn't catch me back-sassing a paying customer."

The sheaf of paper was a transcript of my suicide journal. A court-produced copy of the blood-fouled original found by state troopers and local police next to my shotgun-ventilated body, after they'd stormed into the auto-parts store where I was holding my two remaining hostages. My lawyer, a shiny-suited legal beagle provided for me by the state of New Jersey, gave it to me.

A lot of people are familiar with some of the contents of that journal. Excerpts of it were picked up by the local newspapers here, printed as poignant evidence of my deranged frame of mind, before and during the "Standoff in Sussex." Even the national news services picked up bits of it, I've been told.

The transcript is officially Exhibit C in an ongoing criminal trial, State of New Jersey v. Nathan Huffnagle, that originated with charges filed against me by one Felicia Fowler. Felicia was the woman I released first among my hostages, unthreatened and unharmed, early in the "Standoff." She is also, paradoxically, the most vengeful of my four "victims," and the only one to file charges of any sort against me.

But I'm getting ahead of myself, aren't I, Death?

Beginnings within beginnings, ends within ends. I have to keep it all straight.

"Some of us have a theory about why we're here." Death's Angel was still thumbing through the transcript.

Us?

"People like me. Like you. People stuck in the middle."

Oh no you don't. Jordan can see me. You're the one he can't see.

"I don't know why they can see you. Or, since they can see you, why you can see me. It happens sometimes, but it's very confusing. Every time I think I have it figured out, something new comes up." She looked vexed. "What was I saying?"

You have a theory.

"Right! I do!" She beamed at me, her dramatically made-up lashes fluttering. "It must be something we've left undone. Something we have to finish. What else could it be?"

Could what be?

"The reason we're here, silly. Stuck in the middle."

In the middle? You mean dead. Are you dead?

She looked pained. "I don't like to think of it that way. I like to think of it as, well, stuck in the middle."

Well speak for yourself. I'm clearly not dead, despite my best efforts.

To illustrate my robust corporeality, I thumbed the nurse call button again.

"But you can see me. Usually, people who can see me—"

Die?

"No. Get stuck. Are stuck. In the middle."

All I can say is your thing isn't here. Whatever it is you're looking for. Unless it's in your Big Book of Word Finds. You can take that with you.

"There's no need to be mean," she said, sitting up even straighter in her chair. "I don't know what my thing is yet. I might not even have a thing. It's just a theory. But you have this big . . . letter."

If I had known dying was going to be this entertaining, I'd have died a lot sooner.

"I'm glad you're entertained. But all of this is no joke to me, I can tell you."

How did you die?

Her brow furrowed and she looked away. "I don't know."

Maybe it was a plane crash.

"Well now, I think I'd remember that."

So you're just wandering around.

"I've met some very nice people."

We looked at each other for a freighted moment. I really don't have enough face left to convey much in the way of expression, but if I did, you might have said that I watched my visitor apprehensively.

If you're a figment of my imagination, you can go away now.

She didn't answer this.

All I wanted to do was die. And then, thinking about it, I wrote, *I'm not up for any kind of afterlife thing.*

The Angel of Death laughed, a raspy, earthy horse laugh from someone who clearly laughed a lot. "I wasn't either!" she said. "Believe me, it takes some getting used to!"

Why can't you just die? Like everybody else?

"My point exactly! That's what I mean about something left undone. It's not like the halls are packed with people neither here nor there. There's hardly any of us at all!"

There's more of you?

"It must be something we have to finish. Or set right. Or something."

Who else is here?

"Well, you for one. And me." She popped up out of her chair and extended a hand to me. "I'm Estelle, by the way."

I took her slim little hand. It was cool, and light, but certainly not so much so as to seem otherworldly. She had stewardess's hands.

"There are a few others, too. I'm sure they'll be by."

Oh, no. I'm on a suicide watch. Visitors restricted. I can't just be having people come by. Especially dead people.

The Angel of Death—oh, alright, Estelle—had returned to her chair. She was thumbing through the transcript again. "The thing is, you have this letter. It's a suicide letter, isn't it?"

I like to think of it as an editorial statement to the world about life as I knew it.

"Aren't you fancy? Is it finished?"

As much as it could possibly be. Given the hectic pace of events toward the end there.

She leaped up again and abruptly deposited the sheaf of paper into my lap. "You should finish it! This could be your thing!"

Trust me. This is not my THING.

"Well, then, I just don't know." She picked up her Big Book of Word Finds from the bedside table and clutched it to her chest. "Maybe we don't have anything. Maybe there is no rhyme or reason." She arranged her face into a sorry little pout. "Still, it's nice to have company, at least. Some of the others here aren't big talkers, you know."

I was afraid to even touch the transcript in my lap. I knew perfectly well the pathetic drivel I'd written weeks before, back in June, looked even more pathetic in its second incarnation as court evidence. There's a lot of bushwah in it about the sanctity of truth and the tyranny of lies. All of which didn't prevent the journal itself from being packed to the gills with lies. Lies and self-deceptions and empty sarcasms of the sort that I'd thought were amusing when I'd also thought that my sorry life was someone else's fault.

If I'm going to be visited by hallucinations or ghosts of Christmas past or whatever, I hope they're all as pretty as you.

"That's very flattering," Estelle said, still looking sad. "Thank you."

I wasn't much of a magnet for hot chicks before I blew my head off. You have an interesting fashion sense.

"Fashion sense?" Estelle said. She drew herself up in her chair and looked at me sternly. "Have I mentioned I'm married?"

Your outfit. It seems a little

But Estelle wasn't paying attention to my notebook now. "I guess I mean I was married. Almost two years. Tom was a pilot. Is a pilot." She held up her ringless left hand and tugged at the base of her ring finger. "They don't like us to wear rings, wedding rings, on the flights. It gives passengers the wrong idea.

They want us all to be, you know," she shrugged deferentially, "sky bunnies, I guess."

I set aside my notebook and lifted the transcript in my lap. I peeled back the last page. To the last nine words I'd written.

"I'm kind of hoping, if I have a last thing, something that I have to do," and here I looked up as her voice began to waver, "that it isn't my ring, you know?" She grinned weakly. "Because where would I find it here?"

I didn't know the answer to that, and I looked politely away, back to the transcript.

The last full entry in my suicide journal is dated June 30th, 12:15 am. The last nine words of the journal, however, were written twenty-four hours later, in the first hour of July 1st. I scrawled them in the stock room of A&B Auto Parts, as my hostages, the two that remained of the original four, lay sleeping in a heap of foam packing peanuts on the other side of the room. I wrote them just before jamming the cold twin o's of shotgun barrels beneath my chin and reaching out for the trigger with a trembling fingertip.

It was all for nothing. There's nothing to say.

When I wrote those words, all I wanted to do was die. And I was thinking, how hard could dying be? People are doing it every day. For the most part, without even trying.

I started to reach for my notebook, to say something else, but I saw that Estelle was gone.

That was two days ago.

It was all for nothing. There's nothing to say.

If there are any truer words about my life, about the human endeavor itself, I'm sure I don't know them.

§

THE END IS NEAR

I wasn't going to do this. Leave a suicide note.

People in my position, in extremis, as it were, often delude themselves with the notion that they have something special—or necessary—to impart, at the end. As if the last moments of life were some grand stage and the mere proximity of death might confer some great wisdom.

But what is there to say, really? Not much, in most cases. Why am I killing myself? For the same reason anyone does, I guess. The less said, the better.

Tonight, though, that changed. My simple suicide has become a murder-suicide. Before I kill myself, I'm going to confront Randy Trent with his crimes of long ago. Then I'm going to kill him. I may torment him a bit in the days leading up to that confrontation.

That's why I'm writing this tonight, instead of being dead. That's why you're reading this.

This journal—for it's no mere suicide note, it's a whole suicide journal—is intended to document my actions leading up to my death. And to present the reasoning behind them.

Note the verb. Present. Not justify. Not excuse. Because, believe me, there's no excuse for what I'm about to do.

This journal is addressed to the Lake Lenni Lenape police, who'll want to know how I did what I did. And it's addressed to the family and loved ones of Randy Trent, who'll want to know why.

So. Why have I decided to harass and kill Randy Trent? Why did my elegantly simple suicide become a more messy and complicated murder-suicide?

It's a long story. So I'll start with the facts of this night and work backwards. And sideways and forward.

Here's what happened.

I was finishing a last glass of beer in the Sail Inn. Or a next-to-last glass of beer, I hadn't decided yet. I was raising a silent toast to a life poorly lived, a life squandered, preparatory to going back to my late mother's derelict, barren house and snuffing myself as unobtrusively as possible.

That's when I heard it. A voice from my past.

"Hey, Brittany! I remember when you used to love me!"

It was a distinctive voice, a raspy growl with a rough, ruined edge to it, like a starter motor stuttering ineffectually on a cold winter morning. It was a clout to the ears. It was the carefree, careless bray of the bully. The call of someone accustomed to getting his own way in everything. The voice of someone used to living at the expense of others. Used to using people up. It sent a chill up my spine, as they say in paperback thrillers. I looked up and there he was.

It was Randy Trent. He was leaning on the bar, an empty beer pitcher in his hand. He was hectoring a barmaid, calling out across the length of the bar to her.

The sight of him, the sound of him, triggered a fight-or-flee response in me so long dormant, I'd forgotten it existed. It was like a genetic marker, lodged deep in my DNA, emerged from some long benign dormancy to give my heart a good, swift kick. I hadn't seen Randy Trent, hadn't cringed at the sight of him, in more than twenty years.

The past has been much on my mind these days, since my mother died—a week ago this morning—and I returned to tidy up her house, the house I grew up in, for the realtors. I'd like to say that I wouldn't have recognized Randy Trent so instantly in a different setting, out of the context of this shitty bar in this shitty town we both grew up in. But I don't think that would be true. Some people make a mark on you, for better or for worse, and you don't forget.

"In your dreams, Trent. In your dreams." Brittany the barmaid took the pitcher and went to fill it at the tap.

So I didn't have long to second- and third-guess my initial impression. It was confirmed right away. I was looking at Randy Trent.

After Brittany exchanged his empty pitcher for a full one, Randy Trent turned from the bar and his hard gray eyes fell on me, stopped by what must have been an odd expression on my face.

"Yeah?" Randy Trent said. "You got a problem?"

Twenty-some years is a long time. People change. I don't think I look anything like the pale, slight, narrow-shouldered, long-faced boy I once was. Two decades and more of mostly sedentary pursuits have caused me to grow redder, riper, and rounder, like a berry, while stress and bad habits have pulped and tenderized every square inch of my surface.

But Randy? He looks very much the same to me. It may be that his physical attributes are elemental like prime numbers or fractions reduced to their lowest terms. He was always this way: long-jawed, heavy-browed, with big hands and feet. Pale with deep-set eyes. There's something stiff about his face that resists warmth or expressiveness. His ears have no lobes; the lower planes of his ears line up directly with the lines of his jaw, giving him a simian quality. His nose has two distinct facets—out, then down—vaguely Native American in aspect. He's big, over six feet tall. Even as a teen, he seemed a man among boys. His features seemed already set, with nowhere else to go. Today, his belly might be a little bigger, his eyelids a little fleshier, his hair grayer and shorter. That's about it.

Cold. That's the first word that always comes to mind when I think of Randy Trent.

"No," I said, and then, "Not me. I've got a smile for everybody I meet." And I smiled.

I don't know what I expected from Randy. Surprise, anger, contempt. Something. At the very least, I expected him to recognize me.

But he didn't. Instead, he watched my big, goofy grin grow wider, a cross, put-upon expression settling on his own face. "What's that supposed to mean?"

"Nothing," I had to say. And it was true. He didn't remember me at all.

Randy grunted and carried his pitcher of beer back to the table he was sharing with two women and another guy. Back to his unexamined, untroubled, unshadowed life. The easy life of the bully.

And that set me to thinking.

About things, and why they are the way they are.

About the unfortunate irony of encountering Randy Trent, of all people, on the last night of my life. About how utterly unsurprising—how fitting, even—it was, that I should be killing myself against the backdrop of another prosperous, carefree day in Randy Trent's life. Killing myself—discreetly, unobtrusively— even as Randy Trent, the architect of my childhood despair and mortification, lifted another beer with his plainly admiring friends.

I watched Randy Trent for a while. Randy looked happy. So did his friends. The girl Randy Trent was with looked happy to be with him. She was very pretty. She was of some Asian descent, her cheekbones high, her blunt haircut sleek and shimmering and black, her eyes large and lively above a tiny lipsticked mouth, her laugh a sudden, surprised-sounding bark. She might have been thirty or so, maybe less. She seemed too solicitous of his regard, too self-consciously aware of his presence, to have known him for long. She looked like a girl on the make.

And why not be desirous of making Randy Trent? If this Randy Trent was much like the Randy Trent I knew twenty-some years ago, he had a lot going for him. An easy, offhand way of breaking things, of breaking people. A rough and charming sadism. A simple happiness derived from humbling the weak, the shy, the fearful. There's something in a man who knows that life is unfair and shabby and demeaning and brutal, and delights in it, that women find reassuring, attractive. I know, I've seen it myself. All my life.

I watched Randy for quite a while. I watched myself in the mirror behind the bar, huddled, alone, over my last beer.

And that was it. That's when I stopped playing by the rules. How do they say it now? I "went over to the dark side." I became a "rogue operative." See? Even the language is sexy.

That's when I decided to harass and kill Randy Trent.

I mean, why not? What had reason and civility, fair play and good manners, empathy and restraint ever done for me? Nothing, that's what.

Why should I die alone? Why should I die like a sheep, while this brutal thug lifts a glass of cheer with his adoring friends? Why shouldn't I take this bully with me? This bully whose reign of terror cast a shadow over my youthful life that—let's be honest—exists to this day?

Why not? I'll never have a better chance.

Oh, don't worry, loved ones of Randy Trent. I don't expect you to understand. That's not the purpose of this communication.

Blame me, of course, for what's about to happen to him. Blame Fate, too. With a capital F. For surely Fate must have had something dire in mind for your beloved Randy, when she swept him into my path at such a perilous juncture, mere moments before I would have sheepishly pulled the plug on myself.

Tough luck, indeed.

I've given myself an eight-day stay of execution. I've given myself a reprieve until June 30th, my birthday. I've made a new plan.

And I want to clarify something here. I'm no old hand at harassment. I've never stalked anyone before. I've never tormented anyone. Unlike Randy Trent, I've never made someone's life miserable just for the sheer sport of it. I've certainly never killed anyone before. These are all first-time additions to my job jar.

Read on, officers of the law, loved ones of Randy Trent.

Read on in these journal pages and you'll find my reasons for everything I'm about to do.

Maybe you won't like my reasons. I'm prepared to accept that. But I can promise you this. My reasons for killing Randy Trent will be at least as good, at least as valid, as his reasons for tormenting me, all those years ago.

And now, to get things started, I'll give you a reason. My first reason.

It's a reason the Randy Trent I once knew would surely have understood and appreciated. Here it is.

Because I can. That's why.

Because I can.

§

I have to admit, Estelle's visit didn't change much about what I was doing with my time here at Hudson Maxim. I slept a lot. I watched hospital TV. I made an effort to keep my notebook-scrawled thoughts to myself around Jordan and Dr. Croate. Probably, I was hoping that I was simply losing my mind and that I would be able to take an essentially passive approach to the onset of derangement.

But it's true, what they say. You can't cheat Death.

Today, Death sent me a Waitress.

She was a not unattractive redhead, fortyish, a bit frowzy, lean and backlashy like a green willow branch, with pale blue eyes and a bent snub of a nose that looked like it might have been broken once or twice. She was wearing a green apron with a white frill, a green cloth visor, and a name badge. The badge said *Hi, I'm* in flowing script and, beneath that, in handwritten block caps, BETTY.

Death's Waitress wasn't taking any orders, though. She was issuing them.

"For a writer, you sure don't do much writing, do ya?"

Am I supposed to be writing?

"You're supposed to be doing whatever it takes to get from Point A to Point B. Didn't you hash this all out with what's-her-name? The flight attendant?"

Estelle. She calls herself a stewardess.

"Right. So? Writers write. Stewardesses . . ." she waved her hand vaguely, "steward. We've all got our job to do."

I don't want to write anymore.

"Oh, please. So you're going to, what, watch Judge Judy all day?" Death's Waitress was sitting in the chair by the door. She reached into a canvas bag by her feet and produced a bundle of knitting. "Cry me a river, Mr. Creative Person."

I'm not a creative person. I'm an ad writer.

I crossed out the *'m* and replaced it with *was*.

"My son's the same way. Nine parts whining, one part creating."

He's an ad writer?

"He's a painter. Have you ever been to the Florida Central Power & Light home office?"

I shook my head.

"Well, if you had, you'd've seen one of his paintings. Twenty feet high and forty feet across. Fills the whole atrium, practically. It was commissioned by the president of the company himself."

Can I ask you a personal question?

Death's Waitress looked at me, a heap of fuchsia yarn-knots in her lap, her knitting needles poised. "You can get to work, Mr. Creative Person."

Are you supposed to be dead?

She started knitting, needles ticking busily through the fuchsia fuzz. "I'm going to pretend you didn't ask me that."

Sorry. I'm just curious.

"Where I come from, a man doesn't just up and ask a woman intimate questions."

I watched Betty knit for a while. She had mastered a perfect economy of movement, so that the knotted rows seemed to boil up and out of her nearly motionless hands. I wondered what she was knitting, and for whom. What with my current physical state, a lot of questions that I might normally ask go unasked simply because I can't be bothered writing them out by hand. Some questions, however, must be asked.

Why are you here?

"Because there's a chair here." Knitting one, purling two. Lips pursed. "And because I have work to do. As do you, I believe."

Is this some kind of Seventh Seal thing? Because I'm really not up for that.

"Seventh Seal?"

Bergman? Chess board. The plague? Death has this

"Save it for your book club, mister. I'm talking work. We all have work to do. Work is what we are. Work is what gets us from here to there."

Again with the work. Is this Estelle's THING thing? The reason we're here? We never got to the bottom of that.

Betty glanced at this, written at the bottom of the next-to-last blank page in my notebook, and let it pass, unremarked upon. I resisted the urge to hit the nurse call button again. I've pretty much exhausted the goodwill of the nurses on the day shift.

Can I call you Betty?

"You can call me queen of the county fair, if you'll just get to work. This is very important, you know."

WHAT is important? Writing more of this crappy journal? You've got to be kidding me!

"Do you have a better idea? It doesn't look like you're in any position to start building an ark."

Are you being funny?

"Why don't you just start where you left off?"

Because I left off at the end!

"Can't be the end if we're still here. Maybe what it needs is less fancy-pants poetry and a little more truth."

Truth, Betty? You want to talk about truth?

"Don't get snippy with me," Betty said. And then, "You got a problem with the truth?"

I'd scribble you a short thesis on objective and subjective reality, Betty, but I'm running out of paper here.

"You can save the philosophy nonsense for your egghead friends, Mr. Creative Person. The truth is, the truth ain't nearly as hard to pin down as some people would have it. Sometimes it's staring you right in the face. It might be painful to live with, but it's there all the same."

I don't have any egghead friends.

Betty just looked at me. Sternly.

I've already tried to write the truth, Betty. I made a mess of it. Truth may not be my medium.

And that was it. I had used the last blank page of my last notebook. I've ordered more. Nonessential supplies aren't always immediately forthcoming for those of us without health insurance. Eventually, Betty balled up her knitting and left. Through the door. She didn't just disappear or poof or anything. That was a few hours ago. Long enough for me to scribble the foolishness above.

I'm writing this on the backs of the pages of my suicide journal transcript. And boy do I have writer's cramp. How did everyone do all this damned writing, before computers? I can't remember.

Pick up where you left off. That's what Betty suggests.

Is that what you want, whoever you are, out there? Is it okay if I call you Death? Does Betty speak for you?

I left off where I left off—on June 30th, the morning before the actual taking of hostages—for a couple of reasons. One, because hostage situations are time-consuming and filled with distractions. And two, because the journal no longer served any purpose. I wrote the journal to tell the truth, as I knew it. And I wrote it to explain why I was stalking Randy Trent with the intent to kill him.

I knew pretty soon after taking my hostages that I'd failed on both counts. I never did get to the truth. And I knew, by the evening of June 30th, that I wasn't going to kill Randy Trent. That I wasn't going to kill anyone but me.

Readers of my journal might be mystified as to why I didn't kill Randy Trent. I certainly seemed like I was going to, at the point where the journal ends. But I had my reasons.

I'm not going to be coy about them, either. There are no secrets here, Death. If you're looking for hard-won truths, truths lodged in deep, secret hiding places, you've got the wrong guy. The truths of my life are self-evident. They're right on the surface for everybody to see. There are no artful subtexts here, Big Guy.

I didn't kill Randy Trent because, quite simply, he had beaten me again. Beaten me in a manner more devastating than he could ever have managed, all those years ago, with his taunts, his contempt, even his fists.

He beat me by becoming a better person than I was. That was the final indignity.

So I scribbled nine words beneath my neatly laser-printed entry for June 30th, 12:15 am, and then I peppered my brain pan with buckshot.

It was all for nothing. There's nothing to say.

Nine words of the truth, as I saw it.

THE END IS NEAR

Not enough for some otherworldly agents, evidently. For some glorified toll-takers at the gates of the eternal void.

You want more, Death? I'll give you more. You can have all you want.

The truth is, I pretty much suspected I was wrong about everything, even as I was kicking open the door to A&B Auto Parts, a shotgun tucked under my left arm, a pistol in my right hand. Wrong in my assumptions about Randy Trent. Wrong in blaming anyone else but me for the dismal outcome of my life.

Maybe I had hoped to find out differently, in confronting Randy Trent. Maybe I'd hoped Trent would confirm my worst—my fondest—imaginings, under pressure. Or maybe I really believed, as I'm sure I've stated somewhere on the other sides of these pages, that one injustice could cancel out another, and tip the scales back to even. More likely, I'd merely hoped to muddle my way through the way I always have, to complete my fool's errand of havoc and violence and vengeance on the sheer strength of self-deception and forward motion.

But havoc and violence and vengeance are the refuges of the strong, not the weak. And I'm the weak. Oh boy, am I the weak.

So here's the rest of the "Standoff in Sussex," Betty. The rest of the story, Death. You too, Estelle.

Memo to Death—If you're expecting something different, feel free to let me know. Maybe you can send Death's Busboy around to deliver the news.

§

June 22nd, 5pm

If you're reading this, loved ones of Randy Trent, then your Trent is very likely dead, as am I. If that's the case, you'll have some grievances to air. Let's get them out in the open now, before we go on.

You think it's unfair that you've been deprived of your Trent by some crazed suicidal killer.

Okay. Unfair to you, perhaps. I'll grant you that.

But unfair to Trent? No, I don't think so.

What, after all, constitutes just punishment? Where, exactly, does fair punishment cross the line into cruel and unusual punishment? Are the punishments inflicted on me by Randy Trent—unprovoked punishments which, in a very real way, blighted my youth and my adult life—less cruel and unusual than those I'm choosing to inflict upon him?

I don't think so. I, at least, had a worthy motive. Revenge.

Randy Trent did it for nothing. He made my life a living hell because it amused him. Because he had nothing better to do. Because he could. Because he was safe from retribution. My capacity for it, anyway.

And now I'm getting even. Why? Simply because I can. Because I have nothing better to do with the last eight days of my life. Because I'm beyond retribution.

That's one of the great things about being dead. It's a perfect getaway.

But what about us, you say, the aggrieved family and friends?

Tough luck, I say. Next time, choose your loved ones better.

Am I being harsh? Well, I used to have empathy. I used to sympathize with the plights of others. I commiserated with buddies down on their luck, girls mistreated by their guys, the misfortunate, the downtrodden. I got teary-eyed at sad movies. I signed petitions. I donated to the World Wildlife Fund.

I cared about things a lot. I cared to a fault. And look what it got me. Nothing.

Not anymore, bucky. You're on your own, now.

I only hope I can bring the same unreflective, vicious, hoodlum glee to the task of killing your Trent that he brought to making my life hell.

Okay, what else?

Oh, right. What kind of guy, you say, goes around brooding over adolescent insults and humblings that happened half a lifetime ago?

What kind of guy plots mayhem and murder based on some stupid playground shit from over twenty-five years ago?

This frigging Nathan Huffnagle must be some kind of addled, self-pitying crackpot. He must be the national poster boy for arrested development.

Well, you're absolutely right.

There. Feel better?

Actually, this seems like a good place to introduce myself. To start explaining my motivations. To tell you who I am.

Who is this crackpot, Nathan Huffnagle?

To answer that question, I think I'll show you around this house I'm occupying right now. My mother's house, the house I lived in when Randy Trent was my mortal enemy.

Would you like that? A tour of the house?

A guided tour?

Sure you would. Come on.

As I tap this out on my laptop, I'm sitting at my mother's old kitchen table, the battered formica-topped centerpiece of countless Huffnagle skirmishes, nursing a mild hangover with aspirin and Rolling Rock beer.

But let's move now, from the kitchen to the dining room. Don't worry, we'll come back to the kitchen later.

I grew up in this house, as I've said. No, I wasn't born here. I moved here with my family—father, mother, sister, and brother—when I was ten. The house was brand new, then. It isn't brand new anymore. It's seen better days.

So has my family. In fact, in what must be something of a statistical anomaly, four of those five Huffnagles are now dead, if you count me. My father, my mother, my brother, and me. All dead, four different exits. Only my sister Sherilyn remains to tell the tale. And I haven't seen or talked to her in almost twenty years. She could be dead, too, for all I know.

Here we have the dining room.

That's what it was called in the builder's floor plan, although the Huffnagles did very little group dining here. The Huffnagles did very little group anything. I can remember Sunday dinners here, Huffnagles huddled apprehensively around a rickety dining room table. False cheer, false little politenesses. Lengthy silences. The sound of chewing. At first we gathered here most Sundays, then just major holidays, then we abandoned the practice altogether. Toward the end, my father was rarely around; my mother ate standing up at the kitchen countertop, when she ate at all. My sister, brother, and I fended for ourselves. Spaghetti, pancakes, breakfast cereal, lettuce sandwiches. Whatever was around.

That dining table is still here, in this room. Somewhere.

A lot of families have what they call a "junk drawer." A drawer in the kitchen or family room where unclassifiable odds and ends go. Our family had a junk room. This is it.

It wasn't this bad when I lived here. After we stopped eating together, the table collected junk; stacks of newspapers and magazines grew on the chairs. The sideboard cluttered up with dead plants, catalogs, and unpaid bills. Cast-off clothing and the leavings of scores of half-finished household projects were pushed under the table and into the corners. But you could still walk into the room and pass through it into the living room. It wasn't impassable.

Now, the junk has piled up to the ceiling and engulfed the table and sideboard entirely. A folding screen, stretched across the entryway to the living room, gave the junk a foothold across that side of the room and soon the junk reached the ceiling there, too. There's a door in the opposite wall that's completely obstructed by junk. Just as well, since it leads outside to what was once a small wooden porch and steps down to the side yard. The porch and steps rotted away years ago; no one bothered to replace them. Walk around the side of this house and look up and you'll see a door suspended ten feet off the ground, no exterior access to it.

What is all this stuff? The byproduct of laziness, mostly. The crap that most people bag and leave at the curb twice a week. The crap that normal people—people concerned with appearances—impose order on, tidy up, give away, throw out. The whole house isn't like this. Not at all. My mother didn't save this stuff on purpose. It just piled up and this room turned into a kind of big closet.

So let's backtrack through the kitchen and enter the living room the other way.

Quite a difference, eh?

The living room is bare, but for a spring-sprung Barcalounger, an old-style folding TV tray, a footrest, and a newish 17-inch Samsung TV. The rest of the furniture—a rotting couch, a rocker, a collapsed chair—is in the basement. The TV would have been the only new addition my mother made to the house in, oh, fifteen years, I'd say. In the Huffnagle house, when a big-ticket item—a couch, a dishwasher, a garage door—broke or wore out, it stayed broken and worn out. It wasn't fixed or replaced. Small-ticket novelties and decorations and gimcracks ascended to the rafters, but big-ticket items were, somehow, too daunting to be realistically considered. The Huffnagles suffered from a failure of imagination in that way.

The TV works, though there's no cable. Sometimes I can tune in police radio chatter, down by channel two on the dial.

Not much else to see here. There's nothing on the walls, just a long dark stain where the top of the couch used to be. In here, you can see that the screen drawn across the dining room entry is a cheap folding thing with ersatz Chinese dragons printed on it. It bulges dangerously into the room, barely restraining the rising tide of junk behind it. There are no plants hanging from the hooks in the ceiling above the picture window, my mother's patience with plants having evaporated long ago. There are no curtains in any of the windows, just a couple of battered, flimsy shades. My mother must have reached a point where she just didn't have anything to hide anymore.

My mother was a couple months short of her sixty-seventh birthday and in not particularly poor health. She was at the courtesy counter at FoodKing, cashing a check, when she collapsed. A stroke. She lingered for three days in the hospital, never regaining consciousness. I spent most of her last day by her bedside.

She's buried in a big Catholic cemetery in Tuxedo Junction, New York. Next to her sister, who died, unmarried and childless, some thirty years ago. There's an empty plot next to my father's grave in Locust Knoll Cemetery here in Lake Lenni Lenape. It had been intended for my mother, until she bought the one next to her sister. And that's where she is.

I say that a stroke got her, but the truth is, my mother gave up on life a lot earlier than her faulty cardiovascular plumbing gave up on her. She was bushwhacked by two climactic events in Huffnagle life—the deaths of her husband and son—and never really recovered. Her last two decades were spent living check-to-check off my father's life insurance and Teamster pension, bedroom-slippering around the house, avoiding bill collectors, mouthing mild pieties, fabricating a fanciful alternative Huffnagle family history, and watching TV. Oh, and beating me out life's back door.

Here's an odd fact. If my mother had lived for a few more weeks, your Randy Trent would have been safe. I would have killed myself in my Hoboken apartment, rather than here in my childhood home. I never would have run into Randy Trent in the Sail Inn. There's Fate again, stacking the deck, rigging the game.

Let's move on. Back through the kitchen and down a short hall. Past a room on the left, the bathroom, to a second door on the left. I shared this room with my brother for six years. Until he moved downstairs, into the unfinished basement. I had the room to myself for one year, my seventeenth year, and then I was gone, too.

My brother Thomas played sports, had friends, and generally spent as much time as possible out of the house. After completing eighth grade, he went to the county vocational/technical school and drifted ever further away. He learned a valuable trade—something to do with fluid-regulating machines and computers, some new and profitable interface between the two—and married. He liked to keep busy, my brother. And he liked people. He was a joiner. He was a real go-getter.

My brother, who thought college was a place for lazy people to hide for four years, was married at eighteen, had a son at nineteen, bought a house at twenty, and made more money in his twenty-first year than I would ever make in a year in my life. And then he died.

Late one summer night in 1989, he came upon a leaking oil truck, pulled onto the shoulder of Route 15. My brother was a volunteer auxiliary policeman, so he did what volunteer auxiliary policemen do. He radioed the police station, set out some little triangular reflective markers, and started directing traffic around the truck and the spill. When the cops arrived, my brother was a long stripe of gore on the road. He'd been mowed down by a drunk driver. Dragged over a hundred feet, I was told. I was impressed by the number of people who came to his funeral. He liked people and they, evidently, liked him.

This is the bunk bed I slept in, the only bed I ever had as a kid. Thomas moved one just like it downstairs. Toward the end of my time here, the soles of my feet would touch the footboard as the crown of my head pressed the headboard. I got out just in time. This is the little pine desk I scribbled and typed at, night and day. This is the bureau my brother and I shared. If I tried to pull out one of its cheap, pressboard drawers, it would fall apart, just like when we were kids. On the walls here are my brother's posters of his sports heroes of the day. My mother never took them down.

Let's cut, caddycorner across the hall, to my sister's old room.

Nice shade of blue, eh? Sherilyn picked it out. It looked relatively benign on its little sample tile. It was only later, as the last brush strokes were being applied to the room, that it assumed its true character, this deep ultramarine blue of the vasty deeps. Davy Jones' Locker, we called it. My sister kept it this color. She was stubborn that way.

Sherilyn was twelve when I left for college. The girl I left here was loud and insolent, round with baby fat, and quick to cry at insults both real and imagined. When I returned five months later, for winter break, that girl was gone. She had been replaced by a tall, shy, long-haired beauty who rarely spoke, never ate. On the occasions when she did speak, she spoke in a whisper. The metamorphosis was astonishing. They were two completely different people. What I know about this second person is mostly inferred from circumstances.

I know she must have been dying to get out of this house, already abandoned by my brother and me. And my father, too. Unaccustomed to beauty, she seems not to have known what to do with hers until it was too late. Her first boyfriend was a shady, long-faced manic depressive with a jealous streak and few marketable skills, remarkably few even for this no-future town. Their breakup was followed by stalking episodes and a restraining order.

Sherilyn married the second boyfriend, a quiet, intensely religious repairer of home appliances and electronics. Maybe his abiding belief in God made him seem less dangerous. He did, at least, have a marketable skill. His name was Jacob or Caleb, something like that.

I can remember their wedding, a grueling, three-hour, extended-service affair with a full roster of optional readings and arcane devotionals. I remember the rehearsal dinner that was held here, the future groom nervous and grim, my sister gamely silent, the groom's family appalled at the state of this house. My mother rented folding chairs and set them up in the living room; the shabby, broken living room furniture was moved to the basement. Afterward, no one ever moved it back.

Within three years, Jacob/Caleb's religiosity escalated into an all-encompassing mania that consumed his little appliance repair business and his prospects here in town. So he packed up the appliance repair truck with wife and belongings and headed out to, I think, Montana. A religious commune of some sort. That commune, that cult, vanished without a trace a few years later. So did Jacob/Caleb and my sister. As I've said, I haven't talked to her since.

The walls here are a mosaic of girlish passions—pasted-up magazine photos, mementos of school and social events, glitter-and-paste crafts, self-conscious artwork and cards and notes. Sherilyn's bed is made; her dresser is strewn with my mother's stuff. My mother slept here in later years, after everyone was gone.

The room next to it is empty, wall-to-wall. There was furniture in it once—my parents' bed, his-and-hers dressers, a mirror in the corner—but that's all gone now. My mother had it hauled away. This room isn't characterized by a presence at all, but by an absence. The absence of my father.

In the early years of our life here, my father worked odd hours, nights and Saturdays. They paid better, he said. And we needed the money. He'd come home in the early morning hours, be in bed as we readied ourselves for school, and be gone, headed back to work, when we returned.

Later on, my mother got a job, too, and my father transferred to a regular nine-to-five shift at the shop. Soon, though, my father took a room in the city where he worked, east of here, and stayed there during the week. Ostensibly, he did this to be closer to his job, to avoid the fifty-mile, rush-hour commute each way. But really he did it to be further from us.

Years before this, in the very beginning, we Huffnagles lived in an apartment in urban northeast New Jersey. My father, newly discharged from the army, shook off a bad period of drinking and general wildness, learned the commercial printing trade, and devoted himself to a dream, a dream of moving us to a house in the country. It took ten years of saving to build that house. On summer weekends, he drove us into the woods of northwest New Jersey, so we could walk through the scrub and trees of our undeveloped lot and then swim in the waters of Lake Lenni Lenape. On the day after my tenth birthday, we bid farewell to our apartment-building neighbors and moved into our dream house in the country.

That's when the trouble started. My father, as it turned out, was a one-dream man. And his dream, achieved, proved too small somehow, too meager, to hold his attention for long. My father emerged from his ten-year devotion like a man waking from a trance. We would catch him looking around, dazed, wondering, perhaps, what he could have been thinking, walling himself up in this shabby country castle with a wife he only now suspected he didn't like much, and three children he barely knew. He'd sit in a wrought-iron chair on his sparse and weedy front lawn, a newspaper folded, forgotten, on his knee, and look around. Puzzled.

My father, a man of very, very few words, wouldn't have told us any of these thoughts. He didn't have to. We sensed them. We knew.

THE END IS NEAR

After ten years on the wagon, my father returned to drinking. He returned to it with a vengeance, like a man making up for lost time. At first, he confined it to his rented room and the bars of Fort Lee, near his job. He'd return to our house on weekends looking wan and pained and fidgety. Sober, but desperate to escape on Sunday night, back to his room.

Very soon, his drinking leaked into our lives, the way serious, dedicated drinking will, staining everything around it. There was trouble at work, phone calls from my father's workplace that my mother took, tight-lipped, shaking her head and making one-word replies. He would arrive at our house on Saturday morning, not quite sober, and disappear for mysterious stretches of time. He would become oddly garrulous and touchy-feely with us, then retreat into angry, silent funks.

Beer showed up in our refrigerator, in our house where alcohol had never been before. Flasks of liquor, cheap vodka and bourbon, materialized in odd places, tucked in a toolbox in the shed or behind the hot water heater in the basement. Strange new friends came calling. Scruffy, disreputable people who kept late hours. They came calling for my father, a man who'd had, until then, very few friends to speak of. My mother wouldn't let them in the house, refused even to speak to them. After a few spectacular, shrieking, wall-pounding fights with my father, she stopped speaking to him, too.

The entire descent, from unhappy, unremarkable family man to sunken-eyed, furious, helpless wastrel, took less than a year. From the autumn into the early spring of my senior year in high school.

One weekend, he didn't show up at all. The next, either. His absence went uncommented upon by my mother. The third weekend, he showed up. Or rather, a leering, disheveled, shitfaced scarecrow bearing a passing resemblance to my father showed up. Somehow, my mother convinced him to leave. I don't know how. He packed a few random, inconsequential items—a steam iron, some cans of soup, a framed print that had hung, unnoticed, on the wall in the living room for years—into a vinyl carryall and left.

The next morning, there was a call from the Fort Lee police. They needed our help in removing my father from their city. My mother took me along, literally grabbing me by the shoulder and pushing me into the car. It was time I grew up, she said. That's all she said.

When we arrived at the Fort Lee police station, my father wasn't there. He wasn't under arrest, the helpful cops informed us. It was merely time for him to go. There had been complaints from proprietors in town. The cops would take us, my mother and me, to where he was.

We could see, right away, that this was all great fun for these Fort Lee cops. They were enjoying themselves.

We followed the cops—four of them in two cruisers—in our car to a round-the-clock tavern called Pete's Peek-In, a barely legal enterprise on the outskirts of Fort Lee, above the abandoned waterfront docks of Weehawken. When my mother asked for help in getting my father out of the bar—she surely didn't want to go into a shithole bar by herself, at eleven o'clock in the morning—the cops refused. Pete's, they said, smirkily, was a rough place they usually steered clear of. I still don't understand, to this day, why the cops treated us the way they did. Maybe it was their obscure, misguided way of getting back at my father. I don't know. The cops waited in their cruisers across the street.

My mother sent me in. Another part of growing up, I guess.

My father was the only customer at the bar. The bar was a big rectangle surrounding a rack of booze bottles and a well for mixing drinks. A single heavyset bartender was polishing ashtrays by the cash register and a Hispanic kid about my age, seventeen, was loading packs of cigarettes from a box into an open vending machine. The shades were drawn up at all the windows, letting in shafts of daylight that spotlighted random circles of profound filth on the floor and walls. My father was at the opposite side of the room, slumped on the bar, watching me stand in the entrance. He had, I remember, a messily scabbed-over cut on his forehead. He looked gray, ill.

After about twenty minutes of nothing much—my father rambling one-sidedly, me foisting off the drinks he was attempting to buy me—my mother came in. She asked my father to leave the bar, to come home with us. She told him the cops were outside. My father looked her over and agreed.

We got him into the car. We managed to drive a short distance, maybe a few blocks, the two Fort Lee squad cars right behind us, escorting us out of town.

My father was sitting in the back seat, looking at his folded hands in his lap. Then he looked up at me, watching him from the front passenger seat. He smiled an impish grin and raised a finger very slowly to his lips, shushing me, as if I were about to say something, as if we were complicit in some naughty secret. Then he reached forward, buried both hands in my mother's hair, and ripped her head back, while howling a rapturous, anguished howl of fury.

Our car hopped the curb before my mother managed to somehow get it into neutral or park. My father was hauling her back by her hair, over the front seat, and screaming a torrent of vitriol into her ear. He was, he said, going to kill her. Right now. She would see. We'd all see.

What was I doing? I wish I could say. I haven't the slightest idea. Maybe I was trying, feebly, to defend my mother, to beat my father back. Maybe, but I doubt it. Probably, I was just sitting in the front passenger seat, watching the last, pathetic remnants of our family life vanish in front of my eyes.

All four doors of our car seemed to fly open at the same time. Two cops grabbed my father, one grabbed my mother, and one picked me up and threw me free of the car. When I scrambled back to my feet in the roadside dirt, I saw that my father hadn't given up his intentions, regarding my mother. The cops ended up dragging both my father and mother from the back seat of the car, my father still wrapped to the elbows in my mother's hair. The cops beat him with their clubs until he let go.

My mother had not uttered a word, a single sound, in all this time. When she was free, she stood up, shakily, crazy-eyed, and tottered stiffly back to the car. She got in, put the car in gear, and drove it off the sidewalk. The car rolled to a stop in the road and idled for a while—a full minute, at least—before I realized she was waiting for me. Three of the doors were still wide open. I went around, shutting them, and got in.

My father, meanwhile, was giving the cops all they could handle. In the end, it took all four of them to wrestle him to the ground.

As we were driving away, I turned and looked back through the rear window of the car. The four cops were methodically, efficiently beating the living shit out of my father. I watched until they were too small, too far away, to see.

I never saw him alive again.

Oh, no. He wasn't beaten to death by Fort Lee cops. Nothing as dramatic as that. In fact, he was released some time later, when my mother refused to press charges against him. I'm not sure how domestic violence is handled now, but back then you could cut some corners, absent formal charges. My mother may have had a restraining order placed on my father, though I never heard about it. My father never came back to the house. He telephoned a few times. My mother had the phone disconnected.

Six months later, in October, my mother received a visitor. She still hadn't reconnected the phone. I was away at my first semester in college. My father's body had been found in a tenement courtyard in Manhattan's Lower East Village. He'd been beaten unconscious, robbed, and left to choke to death on his own vomit.

My mother identified his body, made the few arrangements for burying him. There were no services. We weren't a religious family and, by then, my father no longer occupied a place in our lives or, presumably, our hearts. In fact, I didn't hear of his death until Thanksgiving, when I returned from school for the break. My brother had already moved out of the house. My sister? She had gone mysteriously silent.

Looking back on the whole episode, I scarcely know what to add to the words I've written above. His descent was so steep and sudden, it was like a single, sharp blow to us. He had never been happy, and then he was crazy, and then he was dead. It must be true what they say, that some people harbor within themselves the seeds of their own destruction, their own fiery immolation, predestined and unalterable. And this, too: Some people just won't abide moderation. They're all of one thing, and then they're all of another.

Okay. So.

Ready for the kitchen?

The kitchen, as you can see, is where I spend most of my time. I keep the sum of my worldly belongings here. This laptop that I'm writing to you on. My printer. A big box of envelopes, paper, and office supplies left over from my freelance ad writing. Some microwaveable goodies, keeping the beer company in the fridge. And an opened suitcase with some clothing in it.

Yes, that's it. I'm traveling light, here at the end of my life.

There's a table. A chair rescued from the garage. A single plaque on the wall, above the table. God Bless This Home. That dishwasher worked for a few years, then broke down. It was never fixed. There's a bottle opener on the counter, a fork and knife set out on a dish towel.

The pantry is empty, the shelves bare. But if you step inside and look closely . . . see? There? On the door jamb? Right there. The obligatory hashmarks denoting the heights of growing children. Look closely. See?

Dates and heights and names, ascending from Sherilyn, 3'11" to Nathan, 5'4 1/2". A few entries for Thomas, my brother, as well. Every house has one of these irregular little growth charts. Right?

The Huffnagles' chart dates back to a time in the very beginning, a brief time when we would have been filled with hope, with optimism and team spirit, with simple awe for what we must have felt was the start of a good life for all of us.

It just didn't work out that way.

Oh, now, don't cry.

Sometimes things don't turn out for the best. Not every ending is a happy one.

Ask your cherished bully, Randy Trent. He knew.

Anyway, now it's left to me to unload this ramshackle wreck of a house on someone else. Though it obviously isn't worth much. Not even as a "handyman's special." And it wasn't just our slovenly maintenance that destroyed it, either. The builders built it as cheaply as they could, never using four nails when two or even one would do. Even the design was odd—a sort of upright, featureless rectangle on two floors, with the first floor a bare claustrophobic entry walled off from an unfinished basement, and the second floor as I've described it, with that afterthought of a porch hanging off the side of it. More of a barracks than a house, really. It looks nothing like the other split-level ranches on the street.

My mother died without leaving a will, so a sizable portion of whatever this house is worth will go to the state of New Jersey and/or the federal government. The rest will be held in trust for my sister, if she's alive and if anyone can find her. I've already had the realtors through, each wandering the rooms and clucking like distressed pigeons at the shoddy workmanship, the neglect, the waste of resources. The land is worth quite a bit, they say.

THE END IS NEAR

§

Alright, what did Betty say? Start where I left off.

That's what death—or Death—wants, right?

So let's start here.

As I walked into A&B Auto Parts, packing a shotgun and a pistol, all hell was breaking loose. This state of affairs had nothing to do with me or my entrance.

Randy Trent was standing behind the counter, holding an air filter in both hands, clasping it to his chest, looking unhappy. "I am not screwing Alice," he said.

In addition to the shotgun and pistol, I was also carrying a rough cotton twill bag, its handles slung over my shoulder. I set the bag down by the door.

It was about three-thirty on Monday afternoon, June 30th. I had originally planned to make my entrance in the morning— about ten am or so—but I'd been up very late the night before and I just couldn't get started. As it was, I was lucky to get to the shop before it closed.

Randy was talking to a tallish, attractive woman with long curly black hair. She was wearing a kind of wrap-around slinky dress, fire-engine red, and heels, an unusual outfit for a visit to an auto parts store on a Monday afternoon. She was facing Randy, leaning forward over the counter, her back to me. I knew this woman, Felicia, from the Sail Inn crowd. And from her amateur film work. She was one of Randy's girlfriends.

"Fuck you," she was saying. "Then whose car was outside your apartment at eleven-thirty last night?"

"You were outside my apartment at eleven-thirty?"

"No, I wasn't outside your apartment at eleven-thirty." I've already described Felicia in my first account, on the other sides of these pages, so I won't be rehashing any of that content here, for the benefit of omniscient and/or otherworldly beings. Death, you're up to speed , right? But I will say that Felicia is the kind of woman you might describe as "lovely," but not "pretty." Does that make sense? Anyway, she has a commanding presence. She had balled up her fists and was staring Randy down with what must have been an expression of fierce disdain. "What do I look like? Some kind of pathetic stalker?"

Which was, of course, exactly what she was. I would know, being some kind of pathetic stalker myself. Pathetic stalkers both of us, our stalking paths had already crossed a few times, by then. I'd encountered her most recently the night before, in the Sail Inn. She'd been looking for Trent. Apparently she'd found him.

By now, PJ, the stock clerk and third occupant of the shop, had noticed me standing there, between a rack of motor oil liters and a shock absorber display. PJ was a tall, gangly kid with a flattop haircut, jug ears, and huge hands and wrists. He seemed unsure what to do or say about my presence in the shop. My armed presence. Or reluctant to interrupt Randy and Felicia.

"Then how do you know there was a car in front of my apartment?"

"A little fucking bird told me, okay? And you can be damned sure if I had been outside your apartment at eleven-thirty, which I would have had every right to be, as your goddamned girlfriend, I would have been at your front door, crashing your little fuck party.

"I certainly haven't gone through life making a big impression on people. I don't know why I'd thought that this day, the supposed last day of my life, would be any different. But I had. That had been the point, after all. To make a big impression.

"As it is," Felicia was saying, "I strongly suggest you see a doctor. Because, from what I hear about this tramp Alice—"

"I am not fucking Alice."

"—from the guys in that supermarket she works in, you are at risk of having your dick fall off, from some kind of disease."

"Felicia, she's a pharmacist, for god's sake. A perfectly nice, respectable . . . pharmacist. And I am not fucking her."

"How nice for her. A pharmacist. Easy access to antibiotics must come in handy."

I should have been saying something dramatic to Randy and Felicia here, barking orders and waving the pistol. But that stuff doesn't come naturally to everyone. I know that now.

"Were you in my apartment the other day?" Trent was saying. "Did you sneak in and flood my place?"

"Did I . . ." Felicia looked shocked. "You son of a bitch. No, I did not sneak into your place."

Untrue. She had. Snuck into his place. Just before I snuck into Randy's place.

"And stop trying to change the subject. Whose car was outside your apartment all night?"

"There are a lot of cars outside my apartment. It's an apartment complex. Other people live there, too." Trent, finally, was looking over Felicia's shoulder, recognizing my presence in his shop. "And it wasn't all night."

"Then there was a car. You admit that there was a car." Felicia turned around and gave me a contemptuous glare. "Oh, terrific. You again. What the fuck do you want?"

"It was Colleen," Randy said. "It was Colleen's car."

"This is a hostage situation." I tossed the pistol into the bag at my feet and raised the shotgun, pointing it first at Felicia, then at Randy. "Put your hands up where I can see them." That seemed like the right thing to say.

PJ raised his hands and started sidling backwards toward the door to the stock room. Felicia, though, turned back to Trent, slowly, an incredulous look on her face.

"You sick fuck," she said. "You're fucking your ex-wife?"

"Look," I said. "I don't want to hurt anybody."

"I am not fucking Colleen," Randy said.

"Well, mostly anybody," I corrected myself.

"And you, you wormy little psycho," Felicia spat venomously at me, "you can just wait your turn, loser."

Loser. That hurt. Even here, entered upon the presumed last day of my life, I had to be subjected to unwarranted abuse. Even packing an arsenal, I was finding respect hard to come by. I took a step further into the room. Just as I did so, the front door opened behind me, the bell tinkled, and someone else entered the shop. I saw Felicia's eyes slide from me to the new visitor. Her expression of contempt, if anything, only grew.

"Well surprise, surprise," she said. Sneered. "The little pharmacist herself."

I turned. It was Alice, a petite, third-generation Chinese-American girl whom I also knew from the Sail Inn crowd. She was a pharmacist. She was another of Randy's girlfriends.

"What's going on?" Alice said, looking, not at me, but at Randy.

"Go stand with the others," I said, pointing with the shotgun to Randy and Felicia.

I saw that PJ was gone, slipped out through the stock room.

Alice wasn't moving. She was holding a plastic shopping bag with something bulky in it. "What's going on?" she said again.

"Let me guess," Felicia said to Alice. "You're making a prescription delivery."

That's when I fired my first shot. It was the first time I'd ever fired a gun.

§

June 23rd, just before dawn

Good luck all around today.

Good luck for you, Miz Trent and Boy Trent. And good luck for me.

Yes, that's right, Miz Trent and Boy Trent. I know who you are now. No first names yet, but I'm working on it.

It looks like my job is going to be even easier than I could have suspected. Such is the quality of my luck, now that I'm dead.

Your good luck, Miz Trent and Boy Trent, resides in the fact that you've been moved off center stage, remote from the unpleasantness to come. You probably won't know a thing until it's over.

There are sixteen Trents in the Sussex County phonebook. Two Trent, R.'s. And one Trent, Randall. The Trent, Randall is a listing in Waverly, a prefab strip-mall town huddled around the nexus of Interstate 80 and several local highways, about ten miles from here. The address, 37 Circle Drive, #3D, suggested one of the anonymous beehive garden apartment complexes that have been springing up and fading into instant shabby disrepair in that area for decades. I would have called the number, just to cross it off the list, had I not recognized the address for one of the Trent, R.'s.

16 Reese Trail.

Not a half-mile from this house I grew up in. I remembered the Trent house well, a white, ceramic-shingled house, oddly tall and narrow, almost like a rowhouse lifted from some city street and dropped here in the middle of the woods. Standing on tiptoe on its half-acre, conserving space, as if anticipating an influx of similar rowhouses that never arrived.

All those years ago, Randy lived there with his mother. An older woman even then—fifty, at least—she had never married; she worked as a nurse in the local loony bin. That loony bin, Greyling Hospital, is closed now, after what seemed like decades of news "investigative reports" exposing its wretched conditions and patient-care atrocities. Her name, I still remember, was

Vivian. She was a small, round-faced woman with untinted gray hair—a rarity then, among the mothers of Lake Lenni Lenape's teens—who, like my mother, kept to herself, far removed from town and school life. On those rare occasions when she appeared in public, she was always dressed in one of her nurse's uniforms with matching nurse shoes.

I can remember it being rumored—maliciously, in whispers—that Randy's dad was one of the Greyling lunatics. Whispered by kids braver than me.

Vivian would be almost eighty now, if she were still alive. I tried to picture her, still ghosting about in her nurse shoes, in that broken-shingled, tiptoed house, but I couldn't see it. I couldn't picture Randy Trent still living there, either, though the Trent, R. listing suggested otherwise.

What kind of life would Randy Trent be living in that house? Would he have brought a wife to it, raised kids there, little thugs and thugettes in miniature? The girl he was with in the Sail Inn, the Asian-American cutie-pie, hadn't looked like any kind of wife. Little more than half his age, for starters, and far too frankly admiring of Trent. A girlfriend on the side, perhaps. Maybe he was divorced. A lifelong bachelor myself, it hadn't occurred to me to look at his hands for a ring, the way a married man might have.

But let's start at the beginning.

Yesterday afternoon, I stopped at a hunting and fishing supply outlet and bought myself a spiffy camouflage jacket, a pricey pair of binoculars, and some bug spray. The first two items were extravagances for this one simple task I had planned. But hey, I can afford to do this right.

Credit cards can be a joy, when you're dead. Especially when you're dead and have no heirs or dependents to fuss about. Already this month, I've far outstripped my meager budget and maxed out my credit cards with purchases and cash advances. Probably, even now, red flags are going up in the consumer-surveillance departments of Capital One and Citibank. Too late, though. Too late.

I'm packing a bankroll and I've got things to buy.

The hunting and fishing outlet, like many such stores, had a community bulletin board bristling with business cards and index cards, offering services and items for sale. I looked at the cards offering weaponry—hunting rifles and shotguns represented by gnomic, obscure signifiers like Mossberg 500 Combo, GP 100 357, and Woodside 12 Gauge 28". Each card, I noticed, had some variation of the phrase Must have valid FID on it. I plucked a couple of the more childishly scrawled cards from the board and left.

Staking out a house in Lake Lenni Lenape is both easier and more difficult than it would be in most neighborhoods. On the one hand, a stranger walking these streets—curbless, sidewalkless "Trails," where undeveloped, wooded lots still outnumber houses two-to-one—will attract notice, if there's anyone around to notice. On the other hand, there's plenty of cover to spy from. As it happened, I was lucky on both counts. I encountered no one during the half-mile walk to the Trent, R. home. And the lots opposite the Trent house are still undeveloped, due to a deep gully and steep, rocky rise beyond the gully. Fifteen minutes after leaving my mother's house, I was nestled in the scrub atop the rise, camouflage-jacketed, engaged in a bug-spray battle with the mosquitoes, and training my binoculars on the front door of 16 Reese Trail.

No one was home. A half-hour later, at about six o'clock, a late-model Jeep Cherokee pulled into the unpaved driveway and a woman got out. She was forty-or-so and short, gone a little ruddy and thick through the hips, though not unattractively so. She had long black hair tied in a pony tail and an inward-toed way of walking, like a geisha girl in the movies.

You, I presume, Miz Trent.

I got a bit of a scare when you went to the front door, opened it, and a German shepherd bounded outside. The dog made a beeline across the street and raced right up to me, barking and circling. You'd already gone inside, though, and the dog settled down almost immediately, rubbing against my legs and looking up at me hopefully. When it had determined that I had no snacks and didn't want to play, it wandered off, back to the house. Eventually, the front door opened and the dog slipped back inside, my presence our little secret.

And I waited some more. Until seven, when you arrived, Boy Trent.

I heard you, your motorcycle's engine keening on the uphills, rumbling and farting on the downhills, some moments before I saw you. And then there you were, accompanied by a friend on another motorcycle. You both rolled to a stop before the house, straddled your idling bikes, and gave your throttles the obligatory, purposeless twists into high gear required by youth and testosterone.

When your friend removed his helmet, however, I saw that he was a she. She lifted her helmet and a gorgeous length of auburn hair spilled out. She tugged it back and arranged it with unmistakably girlish movements and rose into a hip-slung stance above her bike.

Thirty years ago, the boys rode the motorcycles, and the girls, if they were present at all, sat off to the side, knees hugged to their chests, waiting patiently for the guys to tire of showing off for each other and talking engine talk. But times have changed, as I hear it, and the girls do boy things now; they play baseball and tinker with tech hardware and form rock bands.

The world's a better place. And not just because I'm no longer part of it.

You, too, had a surprise for me, Boy Trent. You shrugged off your motorcycle helmet and all the years fell away. You're the mirror image of your dad, as he was then. Cold and gray-eyed and pale-cheeked, thick-chested and blocky, possessed of that same ominous gravity and chilly indifference your dad used to radiate like an open icebox on a summer day. A glittering iceberg, wickedly adrift in the shipping lanes, just like your fucking dad.

I watched you through the binoculars, entranced. There were subtle differences. Your blond hair is buzz cut in today's style, while your father's was shoulder length in deference to yesterday's fashion. And tattoos. All the kids have tattoos now. In our day—mine and your father's—tattoos weren't cool. They were something Uncle Rocky had, something he'd gotten during a drunken shore leave in Manila. And the places you kids get them! That one on your neck, the black widow spider, that must have hurt, huh? Even the girl had one, revealed at the small of her back by the cropped black shirt she was wearing. An eagle? A phoenix? Something with wings.

At first, I assumed she was your girlfriend. My middleaged mind, leaping to outdated conclusions about a boy and girl alone. What else could they be up to? But when she left, there was no touching or kissing. She just tugged her helmet on, waved, and roared off. Just a buddy, on her way home. You wheeled your bike into the ramshackle detached garage and went into the house, leaving me to consider the cyclic nature of life, circles inside of circles.

The sun dipped toward the hills ringing the lake valley behind me and the bats came out, flitting through the trees and feeding on the hordes of mosquitoes that were feeding on me. The cicadas and tree frogs went berserk, shrieking in full jailbreak mode. The twilight deepened gradually. Very, very gradually, on this second longest day of the year. At about eight-thirty, a few lights came on in the house. A TV flickered bluely in an upstairs window. Your bedroom, Boy Trent? Yours, Miz?

Lacking programmed entertainment, I sat in the luminous half-dark and entertained myself with memories. When you're dead, memories are all you have, and my recall was particularly keen last night, jump-started by the sight of that house, the former den of my enemy, and by the sight of you, Boy Trent, a mirror reflection from my past.

I remembered other times, other waits.

I was a great one for waiting, in my youth. A real keeper of vigils. I was that kind of boy. Patient, unobtrusive, unassuming. Indifferent to small indignities like wasted time and doomed pursuits.

Even in puppy love, I was content to wait at the fringes. In my junior year of high school, I fell in love with a girl. Her name was Terry. Short for Teresa. She existed on the border between plain and pretty—a tall, narrow-chested, freckled girl, with straight blond hair that hung in bangs over her forehead, a little snub nose that twitched and crinkled, just like a bunny's, and a hipshot, slouchy way of standing that was surely intended to de-emphasize her height. She was a specific kind of girl, and widely known for it in our high school. In fact, she was so widely known for it that even I knew of it. She was a girl who "put out."

I think I must have fallen in love with her simply because she, on occasion, would take time out from her busy, fascinating life to belittle me, in a not unfriendly manner. Though we were on two different tracks through high school—me on my "honors program" track, she on a general or "vocational" track—we shared two classes. A typing class and a U.S. history class.

The typing class was a haven for dull-witted, hair-chewing girls already anticipating their futures as secretaries. Terry, though, was a 'tweener, brighter than the vocational crowd, but not focused or disciplined enough to aspire to college. I was in the typing class because I'd already exhausted our small school's tiny roster of "elective" courses, and because I harbored some dim thought of becoming a journalist. For some reason, I'd thought a basic knowledge of touch-typing might prove helpful in such a career.

THE END IS NEAR

I was one of only three boys in the class. In most settings, I tended to be invisible, a shadow presence at the periphery. In the typing class, though, I couldn't help but stand out, first because of my gender, and second, because of my odd proficiency at typing. I discovered, right away, that I was a natural touch-typist. In no time at all, I was typing eighty, ninety words a minute, with no errors, while my hair-nibbling classmates were fumbling along, dogged by errors, at thirty words a minute.

Terry thought both my typing skills and my stolid, self-effacing silence were funny. She would make a point of bringing my typing feats to the attention of the class. "How did you do, Nathan?" she would call out, at the conclusion of an exercise. I would look up into her falsely earnest gaze and look away, dumbstruck. She would applaud the work of others, only to conclude, mock sadly, "though you're no Nathan." Eventually that phrase, "You're no Nathan," became the catch phrase of the class. Even the teacher picked it up. And I—graceless, charmless—sat in red-faced silence and endured.

Soon, to my horror, Terry's needling carried over to our U.S. history class, a "straight" class with real students who had been content to ignore me, until then. Caring as little for U.S. history as she did for typing, Terry would raise her hand and flub the answer to some easy question. Then she would turn in her seat and spear me with a deadly look, counterfeit wide-eyed curiosity, and ask, "What do you think, Nathan?"

My history classmates thought this was hilarious. They probably couldn't decide which was funnier, that two such disparate social circles—loser/geek and prole/wild child/slut—should suddenly overlap at this one point, or that I existed in their class, in their lives, at all.

I responded to this good-natured abuse predictably. I fell in love. I began to shadow Terry around, taking note of her daily schedule. It didn't take me long to determine likely times and places where I might arrange "chance" meetings. The most likely, and safest, time was after school, after Terry was released from detention and, having missed the buses, would sometimes walk home alone. Terry, like many smokers, could count on after-school detention virtually any time a teacher decided to raid the girls' restrooms. Which was fairly often.

On days when I knew Terry had detention—the same fifteen or twenty kids had their names called over the PA at the end of every day—I would hide in the woods in a spot along her route home and wait for her to pass by.

Yes, Boy and Miz Trent. Just as I was hiding in the woods above your house, last night.

Why was I hiding in the woods? Because I was working up the courage to meet Terry on the road. To engage her in conversation. Beyond that, I hadn't dared to imagine.

I'll spare you the full account of that first encounter, Boy and Miz, except to say that it went well, in its clumsy, overheated way. Better than I'd had any right to expect. Terry seemed as amused by me in an after-school, one-on-one situation as she did in the public life of the classroom. Our conversation, such as it was, consisted of Terry making ironic observations about me and me enduring them with all the reserve of an ecstatic puppy. It was probably perfectly apparent to her that I was in love. And though there was most likely nothing she could do—or wished to do—about this fact, she wasn't unkind to me.

I floated in a fog of wonderment and joy for three full days, until I could manage another "chance" meeting. I remember that it felt like a whole new world had opened up before me, a world in which it might be possible to co-exist with Terry, to talk and laugh and be with Terry, on almost equal terms.

In the midst of our second conversation, Terry as bemused with me as before, I heard the distant rumble of a motorcycle. As it grew louder, I knew, with the unerring prescience of the downtrodden and doomed, who it was, riding that motorcycle.

The bike eased up behind me, rumbling ominously, and came to a stop. I turned. It was Randy Trent.

He was straddling his mud-spattered dirtbike, arms folded, coatless and wild-haired on that chill spring day. No one wore motorcycle helmets in those days, Boy Trent. He twisted the throttle, then cut the engine.

"So what do we have here? Secret meeting, looks like."

No one responded to this, and Randy looked from Terry to me to Terry again, seemingly delighted. "Love, true love," he said.

"Fuck off, Trent," Terry said. "We're talking here."

We. We're talking. My heart soared, though I knew my situation was hopeless. Terry and I, we made up a we, in her mind. For now. For one precious moment. We.

"Yeah? Why's that? You two need privacy?" Getting no answer to this either, Trent turned to me. "What I tell you about leaving your mousehole, Nathan?"

He'd told me that if he ever saw me out on the street, I'd be one sorry-ass faggot. That my dick-sucking face would be feeling the heel of his boot. That I'd best tug my jism-stained bedsheets over my head and hide, if I knew what was good for me. And etcetera.

"You know what I think? I think maybe you got some ideas about maybe sticking your needle dick into Terry here. Am I right?"

What could I do? I knew from experience that if I tried to flee, as embarrassing as that would be, Trent would run me to ground in fifty paces. Likewise, hitting him first was out of the question. Trent had half a foot and fifty pounds on me, and wasn't very meticulous about the rules of fair fighting. So I stood there and gaped like a fish.

"What's the matter? You tired of fucking your hamsters? You think you're gonna get yourself some real gash?" He swung a leg over his bike and propped the bike on its kickstand. "You gonna help him out, Terry?"

"Fuck you, Trent. Why don't you go find some greaser monkey your own size to pick on?" Terry, no stranger to taunts, was used to giving as good as she got. Which was more than I could say.

Trent grinned and threw a companionable arm around my narrow shoulders, turning me so that we both faced Terry. So that we almost appeared to be united against her.

"Fuck me? Again? Don't you ever get enough, honey?"

"Fucking creep. Let him go." Meaning me. Let me go.

"Creep, huh. That's not what you were calling me a couple of months ago, in the CYO parking lot, was it, Terry?" He hugged me tighter. "You should see little Terry here suck dick, junior. She really aims to please. Don'tcha, honey?"

Terry stepped forward and smacked Trent, hard, across the face. I struggled to get free, but Trent's grip only tightened across my shoulders. I could feel him radiating dangerous good humor.

"She's a real eager beaver, with a cock in her face. Don't waste a drop, neither." He gave me a shake, like shaking a ragdoll. "Tommy Flanagan says you assfuck, too. That true?"

Terry was holding her hand to her chest, as if she'd hurt it on Trent's face.

"Lemme save you some trouble here, Nathan. Terry here'll fuck anyone. Already has fucked just about everybody, the way I hear it. But she ain't fucking you." He suddenly snagged a hand in my hair and jerked my head up. "See that pretty mouth? Every swingin' dick in Lenape High's been in that hole. Except yours."

It would be difficult for me to piece apart the anguish in my heart at that moment. To lay bare for you, Miz and Boy, the many different assaults being made on my heart and mind. Trent lifted my head and forced me to look into Terry's eyes as he said these things. I was a virgin, obviously, still sufficiently shy and unworldly enough to be wincing at some of the ugly epithets above. He both humiliated me with these words and, somehow, made me complicit in them, as he said them. He had the torturer's genius for inflicting pain, Trent did.

"And your dick'll never be in it, junior," Trent was saying. "Because no whore, not even Loose Lips Terry here, would fuck you." He shook his head. "Nope. Never happen."

"Let him go, Trent." Terry's bunny face was set in a mask of stoic sufferance. Her face told this simple story: she'd been in spots like this before, and survived it those times, too. That was the difference between Terry and me. She was a swimmer. I was a drowner. "Go home and help your mom try to remember which one of those Greyling loonies is your dad."

Trent grinned and nodded at this.

"I think it's cute, little no-nuts Nathan here hoping you'll fuck him. He must've thought, as long as you're fucking every guy who asks for it, you wouldn't mind doin' him, too." He turned to me, his eyebrows raised in a pantomime of polite interest. "Is that what you were thinking, Nathan?"

I started to struggle again and suddenly I was on my knees, my face viced between the blacktop and one of Trent's knees.

"Maybe if you ask nice, she'll do it." Trent's voice was steady, easy, conversational. "So ask nice." He applied more pressure to my head. I could hear something, my neck, my skull, creaking. I was still struggling, but it was pointless. My soul was already dead. "Ask Loose Lips, will you please suck my little needle dick." I felt his hand encircle the back of my neck, expertly seeking the pressure points there. "Ask."

I wrapped my arms around Trent's boot and tried to topple him, but it was like trying to tip a statue.

"Loose Lips. Will you please ..." Trent dug thumb and fingers into the sensitive pouches between shoulder and neck, "... suck my ... little ... needle ... dick." Calm, remorseless. "Say it."

Lights were exploding before my eyes. I couldn't breathe.

"Will you ... please ..." I didn't have breath enough to say more.

"No, no, no," Trent said. "You wanna address a lady by name. Say, Loose Lips, will you please—"

I heard Terry's shoes on the road gravel—crunch, crunch, crunch—then I heard a soft thump above me and a gasp. Trent released his hold on me and fell over sideways.

"Fuck," he said, almost sadly.

And I was free. I stumbled up and I ran blindly, careening off the road and into the roadside scrub. I fought through a thicket of creepers and pricker bushes and turned around. Trent was on both knees then, hands cupping his crotch. Terry was already gone. I started to make my way up the hill above the road.

And that was it. In the year and a half that followed, I never again looked Terry in the eye. I think she must have avoided me, too, though I can't be sure of it. Viewed from afar, she seemed like much the same person she'd been before—a wild child, a prole, a specific kind of girl. But her gentle taunting of me was over, and I never shared another class with her.

This still hurts me today as much as it did twenty-some years ago. When I think of it, my chest still constricts, my heart flutters, my face twitches, as if it had happened this morning.

Does this surprise you? Do you think that's an exaggeration, Miz and Boy Trent?

Do you?

And so.

At about nine o'clock, full darkness had thrown its cloak over me, in my station above your house, Miz and Boy. And it began to occur to me that Randy Trent might not be coming home. At ten o'clock, I gave up. I had to. I'd run out of bug spray.

I went to the Sail Inn, where, not surprisingly, I found Randy. Either he no longer lived with you, Miz and Boy, or he was an extraordinarily low-key, hands-off hubby and dad. I wouldn't have bet against either explanation.

He was eating his dinner alone, at the bar, and watching a baseball game on TV. He didn't appear to be in the jovial mood he was in two nights ago. People would stop and exchange a few words with him on entering or leaving the bar, or getting a pitcher refill, but Randy seemed intent on his dinner, the game.

There was one woman—a frown-lined divorcee, already looking chronically tired and old at, maybe, thirty—who was making a valiant effort to engage him in conversation, over the course of three trips to the bar for drinks. Finally she succeeded, pulling a barstool nearer to Randy's and entering into a long tale that required a lot of amazed looks on her part and touching of his shoulder. Randy slid his dinner plate away and attended to the woman's tale, occasionally glancing over her shoulder at the ball game.

I sat on a barstool at the other end of the bar. And watched. And waited. I saw that Randy does not, in fact, wear a wedding ring.

I didn't have to wait long. Eventually, the woman's tale came to an end and the barmaid brought Randy's check. Randy started making the fidgety movements of someone wanting to go, but trying to be polite. I left the bar first, so I'd be prepared to follow him in my car.

At first, comically, I followed Randy at quite a distance, skulking at least a block behind, almost losing him in a couple of places. Then I reconsidered the situation and cruised right up behind him, at times only a car's length behind.

Because really, what was Randy supposed to think? That someone was following him?

Life isn't like a detective drama on TV. People aren't dusting the doorknobs for fingerprints; they aren't checking the rearview mirror and employing evasive driving techniques. In real life, people are oblivious. They don't suspect a thing.

When we got to Randy's place, I all but pulled into the spot next to him in the lot and got out with him. And where were we?

Where else? 37 Circle Drive, #3D. Randy had a garden apartment in a development called, depressingly, The Dominion at Waverly Acres.

He was divorced. Or separated, at least. Hence the women attending to his every movement. Any unattached, uncommitted guy not currently in prison is a catch, out here in Buttfuck Nowhere, New Jersey.

Randy got out of his truck, a gleaming-red Ford F-250 with all the options, and let himself into his apartment. The kitchen light went on behind dingy red-checked curtains.

It occurred to me that now there was another Trent boy at 16 Reese Trail, being raised by another working mom on her own. Just like all those years ago. I wondered what Randy made of the cyclic nature of life. I wondered if he was surprised at himself, disappointed in himself, for creating the same sort of broken home he himself had grown up in. For perpetuating the cycle of absent fathers. On June 30th, I'll have to ask him.

I pulled out of the lot and drove, slowly, around the complex. It was a huge complex, covering what seemed like square miles and flowing seamlessly into other developments with similarly depressing names.

It didn't take me long to find what I was looking for. The roads of Waverly, like those in Lake Lenni Lenape, are littered with vehicle-mangled animal carcasses. I found a stomach-turning sample of roadkill, a mashed squirrel the size of a fox, and returned to Randy's apartment.

After a short time, not five minutes, Randy's lights went out. I crept up to his door and wedged the dead squirrel into his mailbox.

§

THE END IS NEAR

I was surprised at the roar, the kick, of a shotgun blast.

The gun practically leaped out of my hand. The buckshot punched a good-sized hole in the plaster above my head, raining powder and debris on me.

Felicia finally shut up, though. Alice had yelped and dropped her shopping bag, her hands flying up to her mouth. She was still standing like that, her eyes wide, her hands over her mouth.

"I said move," I said. "Over there. With the others." I waved the barrel of the shotgun toward the counter, where Randy and Felicia were standing.

Alice dipped at the knees and retrieved her bag, then started moving toward the counter. We listened to Alice's shoes scrape across the gritty tiles as she shuffled across the room.

"I have something to say," I said, in the new, ear-ringing silence.

"Jesus fucking Christ, Nathan," Randy said, looking put out, "you can't fire a shotgun in here. You'll hurt somebody."

I lowered the shotgun until it was pointing at Randy. His blackened right eye looked a lot better than my blackened left eye, though we'd looked like mirror images of each other five days before, when we'd received our respective clouts to the eye.

"That's the plan," I said. "In a nutshell."

"I knew it," Felicia said bitterly, throwing up her hands in disgust. "I knew it. I knew he was a whack-job freakout waiting to happen. I knew it the first time I saw him." She looked in exasperation at Randy. "Did I tell you or what?"

"What are you talking about, Nathan?"

"I'm talking about today's itinerary, Randy. I'm talking about some unfinished business we have. Me and you."

"Me and you." He seemed guardedly surprised at this. "Have I pissed you off in some special way I'm not aware of, buddy?"

"Yes, Randy. You have."

"Okay. How's that?"

I took a step back and hefted the shotgun in both hands. A shotgun's heavier than you'd think. Heavier than it looks in the movies, anyway.

"You know, I don't know which pisses me off more," I said. "The fact that you ruined my life for fucking sport," I pointed the shotgun at Randy's head, "or the fact that you can't even remember doing it."

"This is what happens! You see? This is what happens when you treat a desperate, creepy loser like a normal person. This." Felicia waved a dismissive hand at me. "You see it on the news every day."

"That's enough, Felicia," Randy said. "Stay out of this."

"Don't you watch the fucking news?"

"No. I don't." Randy wasn't taking his eyes off me. "Okay, so we got some issues to iron out, it looks like. Okay." He set the air filter he'd been holding on the counter. Cautiously. "But there's no reason we gotta involve the girls in this, right?"

"There isn't?" I swung the shotgun from Randy to Alice, who seemed to be eying the distance back to the front door. Alice yelped again. Gratifyingly, I must say.

"So why don't we let the girls go powder their noses and me and you can lock horns on this, see if we can't get to the bottom of things."

I pretended I was thinking about this. "That would be the fair and reasonable and generous thing to do. Wouldn't it?"

Randy blinked at this, as if reconsidering. "Just common sense," he said in a more careful tone of voice. "So whaddeya say?"

"What do I say? I say . . . I'm moved by your call to a shared sense of fair play, of justice. Here I am, advocating senseless violence, the unprovoked harassment of blameless innocents, and you're lobbying hard for kindness and compassion for all. Randy, I'm really moved."

Randy's brow furrowed. "I guess."

"But tell me this, Randy. When did senseless violence and sadism go out of style? Huh? How did I miss that? Because it seems to me, it used to be all the rage. Thirty years ago, it was a scream. Everybody was doing it."

"You're losing me, Nate."

"I guess I am, Randy. Why? Because I'm behind the times. Leave it to me to embrace stupid, vicious, unthinking cruelty, after it's lost its cachet. After its day is gone. But that's me all over, isn't it? Forever out of step with the current fashion."

"You're talking in riddles, Nate. I think I need a clue, here."

"Fuck you, Randy."

Randy chewed on this awhile, then said, "I thought we were friends."

"Friends, Rand?" Leaning on the last word, sarcastically. "Well, we're not. We're really not."

"Okay." Nodding at this, gamely. "I'm sorry to hear it."

"Randy!" Felicia barked, her patience at an end. "Will you fucking do something? He's pointing a gun at us."

"Chill out, Felicia. We're just talking here." Randy still hadn't moved his eyes from me. "I don't know what sort of chip you got on your shoulder, but I know this. I know nothing bad has to happen here. Okay? Nothing bad has to happen."

"Is that your considered wisdom on the subject, Randy?"

"I'm just sayin', ain't nothing happened here we can't all walk away from. You might want to take a moment to think on it."

Ah, Death, my reticent friend. Is this all you want? Really?

Of course, you know and I know what I should have said here. I'd come to a fork in the road. This was my big chance to do the right thing. To redeem myself.

I should have said this: Sure thing, Randy, let's let bygones be bygones. I'll set aside my petty grievances and rise above my flawed personality, my embittered worldview. I'll grow as a person. Let's be friends, neighbors, teammates on the A&B softball team.

That's what I should have said. But I didn't. Why? Because I was a pigheaded imbecile bent solely on vengeance and self-destruction.

If that's the truth you're looking for, if that's the Easter egg of wisdom hidden in the tall grass of my ignorance, than you're welcome to it. Just give me a sign, Death, and I'll stop writing, right here.

No? Okay, then.

Here's what I said instead.

"You know what, Randy?" I said. "You don't know shit. You don't even know who I am."

§

June 23rd, late afternoon

Well, I've done it. I've embarked on a life of crime.

There's no turning back now.

Law enforcement representatives, sharpen your pencils. This part will be of special interest to you.

My first crime, you ask? Breaking and entering.

My second? Petty theft.

At about ten o'clock this morning, I walked up to Randy Trent's garden apartment door and slipped my expired Hoboken library card between jamb and knob.

People—two Indian men out walking, a kid tucking handbills under the wipers of cars in the lot, an Indian mother with swaddled baby, a kid bringing buckets of soapy water out to his vintage Chevy parked at the curb—watched without apparent interest as I fiddled with the card and pawed at the knob. After a minute or so of this, the door popped open.

THE END IS NEAR

If Trent had been the kind of guy who double-locked his door, I would have had to smash a window. I doubt even that would have gotten a rise out of his neighbors, though. I've lived in crappy apartments long enough to know one of the first laws of apartment life. The closer you live to your neighbors, the less you want to know about them. The less you want to become involved in their affairs.

I entered Trent's apartment and closed the door behind me. I looked around.

Jesus, no wonder the guy's at the Sail Inn all the time. Breaking into Trent's apartment was like breaking into a bus shelter.

There was nothing there. An easy chair, an entertainment center, and a TV in the living room. An old-fashioned rolltop desk and chair in the dinette off the kitchen, a bed and a night table in the bedroom. Some shirts and two suits in a closet, two open suitcases with clothes spilling out of them, a pile of dirty laundry four feet high in a corner. Boxes heaped along two walls of the living room, filled mostly with binders of business records. Food trays and cartons piled in the sink, pizza boxes on the little back porch. That was it.

Randy Trent's place tells a story I've heard before. I know it intimately. It's a story of a man who is "between situations." About a man who has reached the end of one thing and has yet to start the next thing.

I was surprised to see it. I mean, my Hoboken place was no Better Homes and Gardens showplace either, but I'm also penniless and without future prospects, well into the epilogue of my plotless life story. I'm killing myself in seven days.

What's Trent's excuse?

Something else I'll have to ask him before I kill him.

Anyway, barren as it was, it made the job of collecting what I needed very easy. Credit card numbers were there for the picking, printed on the dozens of credit card records jammed into pigeonholes in the rolltop desk. I took a book of his checks from a box on the kitchen countertop, though I doubt I'll need them. Randy even had an address book, an old-fashioned ledger with pages and handwritten entries, sitting conspicuously beside his old-fashioned land line.

I looked through some of the boxes of business records. Their contents all pertained to an operation called A&B Auto Parts. Randy Trent, esteemed local businessman. Who'd have thought? As a reward for my due diligence, I found a company credit card, a MasterCard with expiration date 06/12, in a box marked Important Stuff.

On my way out, I browsed Trent's tiny entertainment library, his little clutch of DVDs. Trent watches the crap you'd expect him to watch. Formulaic cop-buddy movies, movies starring martial arts fighters and former stand-up comics, movies starring Harrison Ford. He did, however, have The French Connection, Papillon, and, incongruously, The Last Emperor. I took those.

He also had two recordable DVDs, one with a little row of girlishly drawn hearts on the adhesive label, another with a row of X's and O's, girlish kisses and hugs, inked on its label.

I took those, too.

§

I'm having a little trouble with the staff here.

I guess this is as good a place as any to mention that my account of Estelle's visit is the abridged version. My conversation with her is recorded verbatim, as nearly as I can remember it. As is the bit with the nurse call button and Jordan.

I just left out a bit toward the end, before Estelle left. She didn't really leave suddenly, for no apparent reason. That would hardly be like her, would it? No, she left when Jordan returned with Dr. Croate.

In retrospect, the button thing was a mistake. I admit that. As was my insisting to Dr. Croate that an Angel of Death was sitting right under her nose.

Since then, I've noticed a significant beefing up of the round-the-clock surveillance that attends me. And now, today, Dr. Croate has returned with more bad news.

Dr. Croate, the primary doctor assigned to my case, is a pretty woman, just the sort of leggy young thing that once appeared in music videos for hard-rock songs about lascivious lady doctors. Long, shapely legs hardly defeated at all by opaque white hospital stockings and sneakers. Long, curly, black hair scrambled atop her head. Striking olive eyes. She's not very lascivious, though. In fact, Dr. Croate's a lot more tired-looking than those music-video lady doctors. More dour, too.

"You're still experiencing hallucinations?"

She was standing at the foot of my bed, scanning my chart, and looking even more tired and dour than usual.

I'm still receiving visitors.

"Mmmm-hmmm. The flight attendant again?"

Stewardess. And no. A waitress, this time. Waitress Betty.

"Is she helping you die, too?"

Indirectly. Providing spiritual guidance and encouragement, mostly.

Dr. Croate grunted and leafed through some pages in the thick medical folder devoted to me and my various maladies. "Even the table servers won't come in on our side. I keep hoping one of your ghosts will try to talk you into living."

They're not ghosts. And they're not mine. They work for Death.

"Right. You said."

You must hear a lot of paranormal fiddle-faddle, in your line of work.

She closed the manila folder and clasped it before her. "I get my share."

Any waitresses?

"No." She thought about it. "Sickbed visitations by angels, by saints, by dead relatives. Out-of-body experiences. The welcoming white light at the end of the tunnel. That kind of thing."

Ever see any of that yourself?

"No."

Ever have any reason to believe any of it was true?

"No. They're hallucinations. With clinical causes. In your case, lingering brain trauma from a self-inflicted gunshot wound, severe depression, rapidly escalating blood toxicity levels, and your medication. Or some exotic combination of the four."

I don't mind that you don't believe me. The way I see it, you'll find out for yourself, soon enough.

"Oh? When I die?"

I thought about Death and Dr. Croate going one-on-one. I would have grinned, if I'd had a mouth.

"We need to talk again, Nathan. About your situation here."

What? If you can write warily, then that was a warily written *What?*

"We're going to turn the camera back on."

No! No camera. You promised.

We have our own unit-within-a-unit here at Hudson Maxim. We being those of us who have demonstrated a capacity and willingness to indulge in self-harm. The rooms in the Observation Unit have all been suicide-proofed for our safety. No exposed pipes, bars, or sprinkler heads that we could hang ourselves from. No sharp edges or breakable objects. No pillow cases or bed sheets. The blanket on my bed is a rectangle of stiff, sturdily quilted nylon, impossible to roll or fold, that is called, forthrightly enough, an anti-suicide blanket. The chair I've mentioned before, by the door, is bolted to the floor. Even this pen I'm writing with is a clever little thing, too soft and blunt and flexible to plunge into my throat. And then there's a camera, behind an opaque square of plastic mounted near the ceiling at the opposite side of the room.

"Video surveillance was discontinued, contingent upon your making progress. But we're not really seeing that, are we?"

I'm progressing fine!

"Not according to Dr. Singh."

I was surprised to hear this. I'd thought my sessions with Dr. Singh, the psychiatric case worker assigned to me, were going fairly well. I'd thought he liked me, that we had a similar, dry sense of humor. Although perhaps I had been projecting Dr. Singh's own indefatigable cheerfulness onto the sessions as a whole.

What did Dr. Singh say?

"Certainly all this talk of death and death's angels isn't a positive sign."

I can't sleep with a camera on me.

There are three levels of surveillance here at Hudson Maxim. The first and least invasive involves half-hourly peek-ins by hospital staff. Sometimes a staffer will enter the room and ask me a few questions while jotting notes on a clipboard-mounted sheet of paper. Mostly, though, it's simply a visual check, carried out by an orderly or a security guy, to verify that I'm not in the process of trying to kill myself. Although how I would manage to achieve this feat in this room, short of strangling myself to death with my own hands, I don't know.

"Maybe we'll catch one of your angels on tape."

If I say they're hallucinations, can we leave the camera off?

Level Two is video surveillance combined with half-hourly visual checks. Level Three, horrifically, requires an actual, physical person, an orderly or nurse, stationed in your room with you at all times.

"On the subject of hallucinations, I'm reducing your dosages again."

Again? Why?

"Because they're doing you more harm than good. We can't keep pouring pain killers into you if you're incapable of metabolizing them. Your blood toxicity levels were sky-high when you got here, and they're getting worse."

You said they were stabilized.

"I said we expected them to stabilize. But they haven't. Your liver's overtaxed. From your liver's point of view, you've picked a remarkably bad time to require extensive surgery and medication."

I want to keep my dosages as they are. I'm tough as nails. I've always been. My system can handle it.

"Your system couldn't handle a chocolate-covered doughnut."

I want my medication.

"Nathan, I need you to start thinking realistically about your situation."

Why is everything taking so long? When is my reconstructive surgery scheduled for?

"It's not, Nathan. It's not scheduled. You know that. You know what we're up against here. We've discussed this."

When am I getting out of here?

"We've talked about that too, Nathan."

Oh yes, we have. It's true. We have.

I'm in a fix here. It's no secret.

Dr. Croate talked some more, though I wasn't really listening. I was thinking back on my conversation with Estelle, the first Angel of Death.

It must be something we've left undone. Something we have to finish.

Fucking hell.

Look, Death. I'm doing the best I can here, you know?

§

THE END IS NEAR

Lose weight and look great the easy way! Without dieting! Without doing a single sit-up! Without sacrificing the foods you love! Without depriving yourself in any way! Order your 30-Day FREE-trial copy of Feast Your Way to Fitness today! Find out just how easy it can be to snack and relax your way to a slimmer, trimmer you! Order now!

How does a man know when he's reached the end of the line?

The words above look like a pretty reliable indicator to me.

They're the last words of my advertising career. The last underlined word. The last exclamation point.

I'll surely be dead before I receive payment for them—payments to freelance writers being notoriously slow—but what the hell. After a life untidily lived, at least I'll be able to say I left a clean IN basket.

I have only to seal these words—and 1,500 more just like them—in an envelope and drop the envelope in the FedEx box in town and I'm out of the advertising business, after twenty years. I could deliver these words in person, but nobody at the Pendleton Press wants to see me in person.

I'd like to say that I'm leaving the advertising business of my own volition, the way I'm leaving life, but it wouldn't be true. The truth is, I'm leaving the advertising business after a long, painful, humbling descent down the ladder of professional prestige, the kind of freefall that moves decent people to avert their eyes.

I worked at the Pendleton Press, the last rung on the ad writer's ladder, for almost two years. A year and a half on staff, as senior copywriter, then another six months in a "freelance capacity." The Pendleton Press is a publisher of a particular type of health, self-help, and professional books. It sells these books through direct-mail advertising. More specifically, it sells these books by appealing to the absolute worst instincts of people in desperate situations. Chronically ill people. Maladjusted control freaks. Lonely people. Venal people. Bitter people. Stupid people.

These books and their appeal can be summed up in the headlines of the flimsy, low-quality brochures and letters used to sell them. Get People to Do What You Want, Like Magic! All-Natural "Miracle" Cures Offer Relief from 120 Common Ailments—No More Dangerous, Expensive Drugs, Surgeries, or Medical Treatments! Shed 10 Years in 10 Days! Magic Words and Phrases Help YOU Project Power, Personality, and Style!

For two years, virtually every sentence I wrote ended in an exclamation point.

The Pendleton Press is owned and run by a big, cheerful faux cowboy named Jack Baron. Six-and-half-feet tall—seven feet in western hat and boots—he's a self-made multi-millionaire in the old style. Which is to say, by the sheer brute force of his carnivorous charm and dishonesty.

He pays his employees absurdly well, easily twenty-five percent above industry standards across the board, from editor-in-chief to custodian. In exchange, he insists on treating his employees like family. Like some other self-made, self-absorbed men, Baron seems to have no sense whatsoever for what might constitute socially acceptable behavior. He would belittle and berate grown men, industry-hardened veterans of the worst the publishing business had to offer, until they fled the building in tears. He was infamous for ass-slapping and tit-swiping female staffers. I once saw him dangle an acquisition editor's four-year-old child over a steep stairwell by her ankle, his idea of "giving the little nipper a ride." His employees were justifiably terrified of him. But they couldn't leave him. He paid too well.

Customers, on the other hand, love Jack Baron. Fearful old ladies who have lost their husbands, ill people living on disability checks, desperate people waiting for someone, anyone, to wave a magic wand over their lives and transform them into something endurable—they all love Jack Baron. They send Baron letters, lengthy laundry lists of the troubles they've seen. Baron sends them free books.

The books are filled with lies. Decades ago, the advertising copywriters wrote the books themselves, under fictitious names. They called themselves "medical researchers" and "acclaimed business entrepreneurs" and wrote books filled with "medical miracles" and "proven fortune-building strategies" that they made up at their typewriters. White hair turned to dark hair. Crippling palsy dispelled in minutes with a turnip. The road to riches, starting with no money down. That sort of thing. The copywriters would write the direct-mail ad materials to sell the book and then, if the response was sufficient, write a book to fit the ad.

Eventually, modern business ethics intruded—much to Baron's disgust—and the Pendleton Press was forced to grow more sophisticated in its practices, hiring actual shady health gurus and actual shady con artists and hustlers as authors. The lies never changed much, though. And Pendleton still sells plenty of books to new generations of desperate and stupid people.

I was brought to Pendleton by the creative director there, Archie Hodges. Archie was a rumpled and beleaguered ad guy who, like me, was down on his luck and on a downward trajectory through the ad business. I'd known him in better days, before he was undone by marriage woes and drink, and I was undone by . . . well, by the peculiar shortcomings that have undone my life.

I knew Archie was doomed the day I arrived in Pendleton's offices. Archie was what Jack Baron called a "Gloomy Gus," and Gloomy Gusses were avoided at all costs in Baron's fiefdom. Even as Archie was walking me through the corridors of

Pendleton on the day of my first and only interview, I could see that Archie's colleagues were regarding us with unconcealed pity.

Archie didn't lure me to Pendleton under false pretenses. He laid out the situation pretty honestly over the course of four scotch-and-sodas in his usual lunchtime haunt, the Happy Mandarin.

The Happy Mandarin, located directly across the street from Pendleton, was a dim and fusty haven for daytime drunks, very thinly disguised as a Chinese restaurant. Its front room contained a few formica-topped tables, some framed, yellowing pictures of menu selections, and an elderly cook, who always sat at one of the tables, chewing a toothpick and reading Chinese newspapers. Its back room contained a full-service bar, a row of cracked-leatherette stools, and a dusty glass display case filled with cigarettes and mysterious Chinese novelties.

The bar was tended by a neat, sharp-featured Chinese guy who conveyed his disdain for his customers by ignoring all but the most frantic drink-refill gestures. He would also bark the price of each drink as he slid it across the bar, no matter how many times he had made the same drink for the same customer in the past. The lunchtime clientele of the Happy Mandarin consisted of a revolving group of six or seven regulars, of which Archie was the only Pendleton employee.

Archie needed a direct mail writer who could produce reams of shabby, deceitful direct mail copy under short or already-elapsed deadlines, with little or no supervision. Archie would help with the workload for as long as he was still around. Which, he warned me, probably wouldn't be long. It was a crappy, dispiriting job, it paid well, and he advised me strongly not to take it.

I took the job. Archie shrugged dejectedly, drained his drink, and began grimly waving at the bartender for another one.

Why did I take it? For the same reason Archie offered it to me. Because I was the man for the job. Because I'd reached the end of the line and I knew it. Even my headhunter, my career search specialist, wouldn't talk to me anymore. I needed that job. I needed that money.

Archie was let go, finally. The HR people had him hustled out of the building by security guards just before the Christmas holidays. His replacement—a hard-faced ladder-climber and office-politicker with a lazy Florida drawl that lay in her sharp-toothed mouth like bait in a trap—set me straight on my future with Pendleton right away. She came from the marketing side; she had no ad-writing experience or talent and little patience with those who did.

She called me into her office, pretty much as Pendleton's front door was closing on Archie's ass. My problem, she said, was one of appearances. Appearances were important. My writing was all very fine and nice, she said, dismissing it, lingering over the i's in her languid southern way. But, frankly, any college kid could come in and approximate its quality for half my salary, with little drop-off in sales. What she needed was a big-picture guy. An enthusiastic go-getter, a guy who could sell ideas to the senior editors on the other side of the building, get excited over the product line, and turn that momentum into sales. She needed a self-starter. She needed someone presentable. And I just didn't have that look.

After six months, Pendleton eliminated the position of in-house copywriter entirely, outsourcing the work to freelancers. My new boss looked relieved to have the whole ridiculous, unsightly business of ad creation—her ostensible responsibility— put out of the building. She'd be sending me work, she assured me, with a look on her face that assured me she wouldn't. Or rather, would, until she could find someone more presentable to do it. Which took another six months, as it turned out.

So now I'm out of the advertising business. Of the things I'll miss about life, I'll miss advertising the least. The first few years were the best. Scurrying around the offices of first one New York ad agency, then another, getting coffee for flashy, domineering ad execs and creatives. Sitting, dazzled, at round-table brainstorming sessions, watching ad writers and artists toss silly ideas about with great flair and style. Beavering away into the night with those same ad writers and artists, up against deadline, finessing those silly ideas into silly ads. Happy-houring with the other junior staffers—proofreaders and administrative assistants and paste-up guys—bemoaning the execs' stupidity and envying them their charisma.

But that's the thing with advertising. It's a young person's game. The key is to hit the ground running and scoot through the ranks until you ascend to a position that has little to do with actually creating advertising. One of those walking-around-with-a-coffee-cup jobs. Because actually creating advertising—the lying, the pandering, the false-flattering, the market-nicheing, the small-printing, the focus-grouping, the lowest-common-denominatoring, the relentless call to the basest of instincts—is too stressful for all but the very young.

So I died. Professionally speaking. Oh, I lingered for a while, by virtue of a mildly persuasive writing style. But writing won't save you, in the ad-writing business. My last boss was right about that.

What's required, what's absolutely indispensable, is belief.

Belief in the product. Belief in the client. Belief in the sanctity of the marketplace. Belief in the very lies you're writing, as you're writing them.

My last boss had it. That belief. Jack Baron had it. Maybe you have it, Trent sympathizers and law enforcement folk.

Archie didn't have it. I didn't, either.

Belief is key. You've got to buy in. You've got to have the ability to believe. To suspend disbelief indefinitely.

You can get by for a little while, without belief. I did. But you won't get far. You can't keep nonbelieving a secret. It wails like a fire alarm in a church on Monday, wherever you go.

Nonbelieving offends believers. It raises questions, raises hackles. Sets you apart from the team. And then you're gone.

Belief can be difficult in any business. But it's especially hard in the advertising business. And in the ad business, it's hardest for writers.

Artists, ad execs, marketing people—they can hold the lies at arm's length. The artists don't use words at all; they're just moving the graphic elements. I knew artists who could put together entire ads without ever reading a word, with only a general sense of the product being sold. The ad execs and marketing people can hide behind the big picture—market share and brand recognition and whatnot.

It's the writer who has to make up the lie. Write it down. Look at it, staring back up at him from the paper. It's the writer who—more often than not—has to work alone. Get his hands dirty with the lies.

But I'm digressing again, aren't I?

Why am I telling you this?

Mostly, just to rant. To give you some idea of how I got to this point where killing your precious Trent has become the best use of my last days.

But also because I'm trying to say something about belief. And about truth.

Advertising destroyed my capacity for belief. It ruined me for belief the same way your beloved Trent ruined me for trust and optimism. Advertising lodged itself in my capacity for belief, like a computer virus in my belief drive, and disabled it. Crashed it.

A little disbelief, a little cynicism, can be a good thing. But you can take disbelief too far, until you're seeing through everything, looking past everything, around the corners of everything. Until not believing becomes your excuse for never entering into life at all, for holding yourself aloof, apart.

Until you can't even believe in the things that are real, that are quantifiable. Until disbelief becomes an open invitation to despair.

That's what happened to me, I think. I was undone by disbelief.

This journal is my attempt to collect a few truths about my life, about what I did and why I did it. Something I can believe in, before I die.

That's my purpose here. To tell the truth, as best as I can.

But first, I'm off to the FedEx box with my last packet of lies.

§

Hey! Betty's back.

Betty, I'm happy to report, is pleased as punch with my progress.

Right, Betty?

"My boy was the same way. He'd grump around the house for a week without even stretching a canvas. Then the inspiration would hit and he'd be off like a shot, paint flying day and night."

I haven't the faintest idea why anything I'm writing now would be any more useful than the crap on the other sides of these pages. But hey, it's good to be appreciated.

"You just write what you need to write and let the Big Guy sort it out. That's my advice."

Are you reading my mind, Betty?

"Of course I am. I waited tables for thirty-five years. It comes with the territory."

Oh. I'll keep it clean, then.

Betty rolls her eyes. "I worked seven of those years at a truckstop diner off Route 401 in Fayetteville, North Carolina. If I could read your mind, I wouldn't see anything in there I ain't seen and heard before."

Got any good stories?

"You ain't gonna go back to your bad habits, just because I'm back, are ya?"

Like?

"Like chewing my ear instead of doing your writing work."

No, Betty.

"Good." She smiles over her knitting needles. "I want to hear the scratching of pen on paper, then."

Where was I? Oh, right.

There's no shortage of lessons to be learned in a hostage situation. Here's one I learned right away: If a particular person hasn't been heeding anything you do or say all along, he—or she—isn't going to start, just because you're pointing a shotgun at them.

"Jesus Christ, Randy," Felicia was saying. "Is this the best you can do?"

I had just suggested to Randy that perhaps he didn't know me as well as he thought he did. That perhaps he didn't know me at all.

"I'm in fucking danger here, I could be shot by a deranged . . ." Felicia searched for a suitably dramatic word, ". . . maniac, with a gun. And you're making with the hurt feelings. Who gives a shit if this psycho is or was or was not your friend? He's pointing a gun at me."

Actually, I was still pointing the gun at Randy. Alice, after trying to edge inconspicuously toward the door, was now edging the other way, toward the counter and Randy.

"Let me handle this, okay?" Randy said.

"I'm trying to. But you're not doing shit. Do I have to do everything?"

"There's nothing to do," I said, "except what I tell you to do."

"And you." Felicia was talking to me now. "Asshole. Who are you, to talk to me like that? What are you supposed to be? Scary, now? Because you have a gun? You wouldn't be so brave without it, would you?"

"No," I had to admit. "I probably wouldn't."

"You can't keep us here. What are you going to do if we try to leave? Kill us?"

Ah ha! I was ready for that one. "I already intend to kill two of us," I said. "I'm one of the two." I swung the barrel of the gun from Randy to Felicia, so that it was pointing at her rather fine chest. "Do you want to be the other one?"

"Felicia," Randy said. "He's not mad at you. He's mad at me. Let's not figure out ways to get him mad at you. Okay?"

But Felicia was considering her options.

"You're not going to kill anyone," she said. "Guys like you, you're all the same. Cry, cry, cry for attention, and when you don't get it, you start pushing everybody around."

"Oh, great," Alice said, surprisingly. "It's the amateur psychology hour." She was behind the counter now, a few feet to Randy's right.

Felicia was moving away from the front of the counter, backing toward the front door. Everyone was doing entirely too much moving.

"So what do you think?" Felicia was saying. "Because you have a gun now, everybody's gonna respect you?" She edged around the front of a motor oil display, not even bothering to go around behind it and use it for cover. "You pathetic jerk."

"Felicia!" Randy said.

"Stop right there," I said. I pumped the shotgun, loading another shell into the chamber. I set the stock to my shoulder.

"Felicia!" Randy said again. "Nathan!"

"You're not going to shoot anyone. Go ahead, you son of a bitch! Shoot me!"

THE END IS NEAR

I could have stopped her, I guess. But it already looked like she was going to be more trouble than she was worth. And two hostages seemed like plenty for my purposes. I lowered the shotgun.

Felicia was reaching for the door. She grabbed the handle. The bell above the door tinkled. And then she stopped.

"Wait a minute. Oh, wait a fucking minute." Felicia was looking at Alice, who had covered the remaining ground between herself and Randy and was hiding behind his shoulder. "Hold the fucking phone."

"Nathan!" Trent said loudly. "Are you letting Felicia go?"

A bitter little sneer was creeping onto Felicia's face. "Oh, wouldn't you just love that? You and your little geisha girl. Your little fortune cookie. Alone. I bet you'd save her life, wouldn't you, you cheating fuck."

"Leave," I said to Felicia. "Before I change my mind." Fat chance. "Leave."

But her hand had slipped from the door handle. She took a step back into the room. "I'm not leaving unless that boyfriend-stealing, backdoor whore leaves, too."

"Hey!" Alice yelped. "That's enough from you!" Her hand, though, was now on Randy's elbow. Incriminatingly.

"Felicia!" Randy said. "If he's letting you go, go! Nathan! Are you letting Felicia go?"

We all looked at each other for a moment, until a booming, metallic scrawk ripped the little silence we had going.

"Nathan!"

I turned and looked out one of the two front display windows of the shop. A police cruiser was parked caddycorner across two parking spots in the front lot. A police officer was standing behind the opened drivers' side door of the cruiser, holding a radio handset. There was a loudspeaker bullhorn mounted on top of the car door.

"This is Officer William Mazzini of the Lake Lenni Lenape Police Department, Nathan. I can see you through the glass."

I nodded at this, stupidly.

"I want you to set that weapon on the floor, Nathan, and let those people come out."

I pointed the shotgun at Felicia. "Leave," I said.

"Fuck you," Felicia said.

"Hostage taking is serious business, Nathan," the voice boomed and crackled. "There's still time for you to avoid making a serious mistake."

"Leave," I said again. Though already there was something in my voice, an element of pleading, that didn't inspire obedience.

"Make me, asshole."

"Last chance, Nathan. Release those people."

§

June 25th, morning

Five days left. And I have so much to do.

Can I master the art of inflicting punishment on another person in so short a time? Is five days enough time to learn how to delight in fucking people up?

Probably not. Maybe I can't learn it at all. Maybe it has to come to you naturally, the way it came so naturally, so effortlessly, to Randy Trent.

poultrywarehouse.com

Day-old hatchlings.

What do you think? Those Ridgway New Hampshires are looking in fine fettle, aren't they? Let's go with, oh, three thousand chicks.

Would you like to establish a permanent account with us and receive special preferred-customer discounts?

No, no. My days of thinking in the long term are over, thank you.

Enter credit card information and click enter.

Hmmm. Clearly the company MasterCard is the way to go here.

Specify delivery address, if different from billing address.

Where to, where to, in Trent's old-timey address book? This time, let's try ... G.

Goatburg, Getty, Grafton.

Grafton. Arnold Grafton (Colleen's Div Lawyer).

So what are the chances that "Div Lawyer" is short for Divorce Lawyer, and Colleen is Randy's estranged wife? Pretty good, I think, though I Googled "Colleen Trent" and didn't come up with anything definitive. There are no listings for a Colleen in Randy's book here, either, though who lists their ex-wife in an address book, especially if that ex-wife still lives in your old house?

Divorce litigation being such a dreary business, Arnold could probably use a little pick-me-up. And what puts a smile on your face faster than three thousand little peepers?

Click here to confirm your order.

Delivery within 3-4 business days. Thank you for your order.

Oh, no. Thank you.

This library I'm in, the Lake Lenni Lenape Public Library, didn't exist thirty years ago. The town, smaller then, made do with the high school library, using it as a public library during weekday off-hours, nights and Saturdays.

It's been quite a while since I've been in a library. A lot has changed. The rows of card catalogs are gone, replaced by computer monitors. So is the system of taking a card from the back of a book and ker-chunking it into a machine that prints the return date on it. Everything's computer stripped and tagged and data-entered now. Gone, too, are the long rows of encyclopedias—each volume battered, scribbled in, and inevitably missing the page you were looking for, a page torn out by some previous, lazier researcher of penguins or the French Revolution. Libraries subscribe to online encyclopedia services now.

The rest of the books are still here, though no one, staff or patrons, pays much attention to them. Hardly anyone strays near the dusty, neglected stacks at all. Some kids are downloading end-of-the-school-year term papers off the Internet. Other kids are trying to circumvent the computer porn lockouts. An elderly gent, dressed in matching pastel polo shirt and shorts, is sleeping over a Boston Globe in the "Newspapers of the World" kiosk. And there's me. Using the library's Internet connection to engage in consumer fraud.

Libraries still smell the same. That hasn't changed. That acrid smell of paper acidifying, books dying. The silence is the same, that self-conscious hush that accompanies the reluctant absorption of information. When I was a boy, I was the kind of boy who spent a lot of time in libraries. I loved books. If I was missing for a longish period of time, my mother would call the library and the librarian would shoo me home. Really.

Later, after my family moved to Lake Lenni Lenape, I haunted the high school library during school hours. I still loved books, though I often had other, more pragmatic incentives for library attendance.

contractorsupplydepot.com

Paints—Solvents—Solutions.

Fluid Applied Waterproofing Products.

Rubberized asphalt.

5-gallon can, $29.95. 10-gallon tub, $49.95. 55-gallon drum, $199.95.

Can you ever have enough rubberized asphalt? Better go with the 55-gallon drum. Just to be safe. Let's say . . . four drums.

THE END IS NEAR

Please enter the three-digit Security Code on the back of your card.

When I was in my teens, I was the kind of teen who used the school library as a refuge. A refuge from sports for which I had no aptitude, like gymnastics or basketball. A refuge from schoolyard confrontations. From social situations. You know the story by now, right?

Deliveries can only be made to the billing address for your credit card. Please re-enter.

What, no gift options for rubberized asphalt? Oh. Very well, then. A&B Auto Parts, Lakeside Drive, Lake Lenni Lenape, NJ.

So I spent a lot of time in the library, reading books and crafting absurdly over-researched reports and term papers. Hiding, in other words.

Which isn't to say that all my classroom experiences were terrible. Far from it. I had my moments in the sun, like anyone else. My typing class experience, for instance. Spanish class, too.

Our little high school offered three foreign language choices—French, German, and Spanish. The honors crowd took either French or German. French for the aspiring artistes, German for the science and math geeks. Spanish, a language with no discernable career or social utility, was reserved for the lumpen proletariat.

I was happy in Spanish. The particular variety of Spanish we were taught—a stiff, formal, stilted dialect more suited to asking for the hand of a 17th-century courtesan in marriage than for asking directions in the Bronx—seemed beautiful to me. And there was something about speaking in a foreign tongue that helped me overcome my natural aversion to speaking up, to being in the spotlight. I felt the way shy actors must feel, liberated by playing a role. The words weren't mine, so the person standing up, speaking, garnering attention, wasn't me either.

Click here to confirm your order.

Randy Trent arrived in my sophomore Spanish class in mid-semester, late March or so. He'd been kicked out of another class. Or kicked out of a cafeteria study hall or shop class because he didn't have enough scheduled academic credits. I forget which.

I watched my fortunes sink as he walked in the door. I must have slumped at my desk while he looked away, the way a cat will look away, pretending disinterest or obliviousness, when the mouse is trapped and the game is over.

Please allow 72 hours for delivery. 4-6 days for special orders. Thank you for shopping at Contractor's Supply Depot.

Oh, my pleasure.

The only class I'd shared with Trent previous to this Spanish class was a ninth-grade metal shop. That class was run like a POW camp by Mr. Weinfogel, a short, furious despot in thick, horn-rimmed safety glasses, who wore a short-sleeved white dress shirt every day of his life. Idle chatter was forbidden in his classes; taunting unthinkable. Trent, prevented from verbally abusing me, had to settle for mangling my projects—first a birdhouse, then a flower planter, finally a toolbox—in a vise. He would simply snatch whatever I was working on from my hands, carefully place it between the jaws of the vise, and then slowly, silently turn the crank as I watched, looking me in the eye and daring me to protest as my handiwork crumpled.

Spanish class was a much more congenial environment for Trent's special variety of sadism. It took him a day or two to register my presence and to assert his dominance over the usual crowd of back-of-the-room stooges and lackeys. The unstudious element. And then it started.

Na-a-a-a-a-a-a-a-athan.

Just that. The simple, bland crooning of my name.

Na-a-a-a-a-a-a-a-athan.

Over and over. At first, Trent took up his singsong chant only when I was answering a question. So I stopped volunteering answers. When called upon, I was forced to resort to the dullard's response. The know-nothing's response.

No se. I don't know.

Although I sure as hell did know. Trent, not to be deterred, began launching his eerie, tuneless offensives at random moments.

The teacher, a shy, overmatched little mouse with wild, colorless hair and an unfortunate name—Miss Henridden—was completely useless as defense. She seemed as cowed by Trent as I was and tried, like me, to ignore him.

Na-a-a-a-a-a-a-a-athan.

Na-a-a-a-a-a-a-a-athan.

This sort of sinister taunting—the use of someone's very name against them, sing-songing it in a bland-yet-terrifying way—has since, I'm told, become a staple of ballparks and sports arenas, used to jeer opponents. At the time, though, it represented a huge advance in taunting and hazing technology. Even Trent seemed surprised at its power and effectiveness.

Soon, others, sensing the sudden glorious proximity of anarchy, took it up as well.

Na-a-a-a-a-a-a-a-athan.

Na-a-a-a-a-a-a-a-athan.

And I was dismayed. Shocked. Unnerved. Trent's attacks on me were to be expected. They were part of a regime of terror that I took for granted. But the willingness of others to attack me caught me completely off guard. These were people who, until Trent's arrival, had been content to treat me with common decency. Now they were just as content to attack me, with the same casual ease.

But that's the way it is with people. They're every bit as willing to respect you and be kind to you as they are to torture you and humiliate you. It's all the same to them. They're just waiting for direction.

Na-a-a-a-a-a-a-a-athan.

In the end, I was utterly defeated. The suspense of waiting for the chant to start, each day, was as bad as the actual name-crooning itself. I turned on a kid or two, telling them to shut the fuck up, but it was pointless. There's little you can do, once the scent of blood is in the air. The whole debacle occupied maybe a week's time. A week and a half.

I was carrying an A average in that class, an A I could have used to offset Bs in probability and calculus. But it wasn't to be. Miss Henridden expressed muted regret at my dropping Spanish, though she knew I had to go. She was losing control of the class, but still hoped to limp across the June finish line somehow, before total chaos broke out. She suggested German—thinking, perhaps, that I might thrive in a more ordered setting—though she knew it was too late for me to catch up in another language. I dropped the class and limped off, gutshot, mortally wounded, to the library.

SWAN.com

Sex Workers Activist Network.

SWAN offers support, advocacy, and special services to the noble artisans of the world's oldest profession.

Visit our Gift Shop!

Rubber, Leather & Latex! Novelties, Notions & Lotions!

The Deluxe Suspension Harness is just the thing for the more adventurous submissives on your client list! Handsome black leather, with stainless steel fittings. Fully adjustable and stress-tested to 500 lbs! $229.99 With gold-plated fittings and ball-gag extension, $299.99

Whew. Pricey, but Trent's friends are worth it.

Say It Loud, Say It Proud ... with a SWAN cropped tee!

All cropped tee's 100% pure cotton, in sizes XXS, XS, S, M, L, XL, XXL, XXXL.

I'm a whore ... hear me roar!

Available in black type on white. Also, black on hot pink. Back, SWAN logo. $26

Let's go with the hot pink.

The librarian is signaling that my allotted hour of reserved Internet time is almost elapsed. Which is just as well, since I want to get the DVDs into the mail before lunch.

Ah, the DVDs. I haven't shared the story of the DVDs yet.

As it happens, Boy Trent and Miz Trent, the select circle of Randy Trent's loved ones, those known to me, has grown by one. The newest member of your little group is a charming woman—sadly, still nameless—who has a winning way with a digital camcorder.

I can't say I was entirely surprised when I popped the first of Trent's blank DVDs into my mother's DVD player and was rewarded with a video love-letter from an ardent admirer. The X's and O's inked onto the disc, little kisses and hugs, were a dead giveaway.

The film's director and star is big in a buxom, leggy way, the kind of solid, big-boned, mid-thirtyish gal who's fighting middle-age weight-gain tooth-and-nail. And winning, for the most part. She has long curly black hair, almost to her waist, lovely eyes of a clear, no-color gray, and a tiny mouth that seals into an upward-pointing notch, like a bird's mouth. She has a distinctively raspy voice, a tough-chick voice. She's flashy, but not brassy. Not quite.

Even rendered a little shadowy and bluish by the iffy lighting and sub-par production values of home video, she's quite lovely. Striking, I think, is the word. As an actress, she makes up in energy and enthusiasm what she lacks in formal acting know-how. She seems to have set a camcorder up on a tripod and let fly, scriptless.

There's the inevitable kissy stuff, the sigh-laden celebrations of Trent's features, his romantic prowess. The husky-voiced confessions of lusty thoughts and solitary deeds, inspired by said features, said prowess. And then she artfully sheds her clothes, to the tinny accompaniment of what sounds like a best-of-the-'80s music sampler. Glenn Frey, George Michael, that sort of thing.

Nice boobs.

And that's it. She blows a kiss and scampers out of sight, behind the camera.

I don't know what Trent's reaction to this video mash note was, but I suspect it might have been lacking in ardor. In the second DVD, the one with hearts inked on it, we find a more determined, though no less enthusiastic and charming, entertainer.

Dispensing with the stripping interlude entirely, she greets us—well, Trent—already naked. "Here we go, honeybear," she says. A bravura performance follows, as our smitten auteur lays open her heart and soul—and some less strictly symbolic apertures—in a passionate effort to win Trent's affections.

I won't go into crass detail in this, a family-friendly suicide note. Though if sheer rapturous volume of sob and cry is any indicator of sincerity, this girl really puts her heart into her work. I especially loved the knees-up bit, our star mewling and grunting, her rather sizeable toy testing the limits of her anatomy.

That's love for ya.

Love, true love.

Trent will want his DVDs back, of course. If he's even noticed they're gone. So I figured I'd put them in the mail to the places where he spends most of his time. His workplace and his local watering hole, the Sail Inn.

You have ordered one (1) Deluxe Suspension Harness w/ Optional Extension (Item No. A236); one (1) SWAN Cotton Tee, I'm a Whore ..., Hot Pink, Size XS (Item No. A940).

If your order is a gift, please enter name and address of gift recipient in the space below.

Tucked into Trent's address book, under C, is a business card from one Alice Chang, pharmacist at one of the big-chain supermarkets nearby. On the back, there's a handwritten heart, a

Chinese symbol of some sort, and a loopily scrawled telephone number.

Now what are the chances that this Alice Chang, Pharmacist, is the pretty little Chinese-American girl who was at Trent's table the other night, making awestruck eyes at our hero?

Under normal circumstances, not great. But my luck's been so good these days, I can hardly stand it.

Please enter a brief message to accompany your gift.

Hmmmm.

§

I guess I should say that there's a person or two trying to gain access to me here in the Observation Ward. Given all the restrictions and inconveniences I have to put up with—first and foremost being the surveillance camera, which is now on again—you'd think that I'd at least be able to avoid visitors I don't want to see. But the sad truth is that the security here is a travesty. Feeble septuagenarians and workfare placements, mostly. It's so hard to get good minimum-wage help, these days.

I woke this afternoon to find Randy Trent standing at the foot of my bed, holding a small pink vase full of flowers.

"Jesus, Nate," Trent said. "You look like shit."

I woke as I sometimes do, with my notepad clasped to my chest. I opened it and wrote, *How did you get in here?*

"I walked in, what do you think?"

Past security?

"What security?"

The security desk at the entrance to the ward. Guys walking around with radios on their belts.

"Those guys? Be serious."

You wouldn't happen to be dead, would you?

"Dead?"

Never mind.

"I think you got me confused with yourself." He was looking around for a place to set the flowers. "You should've seen yourself, after you let fly with the buckshot. I wouldn't've thought a guy could lose that much blood. Or that much head." He set the flowers on top of the machine registering my EEG. They were inexpensive blooms: irises, daisies, some tulips. "You're lucky they had a medivac copter already dispatched. You were in the air in, like, three minutes, tops."

Lucky!

"Fuck, yeah. I figured you were dead for sure." He eased himself into the chair by the door. "They tell you how long you're gonna be in here?"

A while, probably.

"What's that mean?"

It takes time. Facial reconstruction. Some other physical complications. This suicide watch thing.

My conversations with others—especially the living—don't occur with nearly the fluid ease that they manifest here, reconstructed afterward on the page. There's a lot of awkward, empty silence as I scribble and my visitor reads. This is especially true with Trent, who takes an unseemly amount of time to read all but the shortest replies. A little peeved notch appears in his brow as he deciphers my messages.

"You still wanting to kill yourself?"

I have my less-than-optimistic moments.

"I guess we been through that." He folded his arms and looked unhappily at me. "I would've hoped airing out your head with shotgun pellets would've cleared your thinking a little."

We have, indeed, been through that, Trent and I. That part doesn't occur on the other sides of these pages. It'll occur on this side of these pages. I'm still getting there.

Even if the doctors let me out of here, I'm still under arrest, right?

"For what?" Trent made a face. "Ain't nobody gonna press charges. You didn't hurt nobody but yourself."

Cops take a dim view of hostage-taking and threats made at gunpoint.

"What cops? Woody? Don't worry about the cops. Official word is, you were batshit, anyway. Worst it'll be is psychiatric . . . what, evaluation, for a while. You ain't going to jail."

What about Felicia?

"Yeah, well." Trent looked away. "You stepped in shit, there, buddy. Pointing a gun at her. Felicia don't like to be fucked with. And then the whole DVD thing."

They say once something hits the Internet, it's there forever. I wonder if that's true.

Trent grinned a little, still looking away. "Makes me glad I did all my foolish shit in the years before an Internet."

When I mailed them, I didn't even know who Felicia was. I hadn't met her yet. I was just trying to freak you out.

"Yeah, well. I tell her all the chicks have a sex tape out there these days, but Felicia's got no sense of humor. At least she's not on it sucking dick, like what's her face, the one with the boobs. Pamela Hilton."

Pamela Anderson?

"Whatever. If it makes you feel any better, you ain't the only one Felicia's pissed off at. At least you get to hide in here." He shrugged to indicate the room, the ward.

A woman scorned.

"Story of my fucking life." Trent pulled an envelope from his back pocket and looked at it. "Why I don't just get my dick cut off, I don't know. It just gets me into trouble."

You ever sort out those credit card purchases? Those gifts I sent to people from you?

"Any credit card worth a shit is insured against fraud, anymore. So it didn't cost me anything." He was peeking into the envelope he was holding. There was a single word written on the front. Randy. "Hell, those baby chicks you sent to Colleen's lawyer were pretty funny. Wished I'd thought of that."

So what's this? You brought me flowers?

"What am I, some kind of faggot? They're for Colleen. I'm headed over there next and I saw the flower shop downstairs, figured what the hell. Can't hurt."

The ex is actually letting you enter the house? Or are you leaving them on the doorstep, mystery-admirer style?

"No, I'm allowed in. Though she'll probably spread newspapers for me to walk on. Like a dog. Keep her floors clean."

Why the change of heart? She's warming up to you?

"Fat chance. She has me keeping an eye on Tyler. I just been down to the Pit. Now I get to make my report to Colleen."

The Pit?

"To talk to Tyler." He handed me the envelope he'd been studying.

Kids still go there?

Trent shrugged. "If they wanna screw around on their bikes. There's still a couple of places you can open it up, if you know where to look."

So what'd Tyler have to say?

"Nothing. Him and his friends, they're not used to being jacklighted by a parent back there in the Pit. They forget I wasted ten years jerkin' off back there, tear-assing around on bikes and fucking around. Makes 'em sulky, being caught by surprise."

I opened the envelope. Inside was a greeting card, bearing a sepia-toned image of two chubby-cheeked, grinning toddlers, a boy in tiny top hat and tails and a girl in a wedding veil, a tiny bouquet tied to her wrist. Inside, in sturdy, no-nonsense script, was a message.

September's three weeks away and your boy still doesn't have one thought in his head about what he wants to do with his life. He's got that trailer-trash girlfriend of his, Courtney, filling his head full of moving-in-together ideas. You'd think he'd of learned all he needed to know about babies moving in together and making more babies from looking at me and you. But no, he just looks right threw me anyway. So I thought maybe you could give Tyler the news flash about what happens to bonehead children who think their in love. —C

I looked up at Randy.

This Courtney. Does she have long red hair? Own a motorcycle?

"No, no. That girl you saw up at the house is Deirdre. She's been a running buddy of Tyler's since, jeez, fifth grade, at least. She's a good kid."

That girl you saw up at the house.

I didn't know what to say. I would have blushed in embarrassment, if I'd had any face left to do it with. It hadn't occurred to me, until that moment, that Randy Trent might have read any of my journal. Not that it wasn't widely available as court evidence, as I've said. I guess I just hadn't pictured Randy Trent reading.

"This Courtney's a fake blonde with fake tits who hangs with Rodney Planter's crew, out at Big Chief Cycle Repair and the tattoo parlor next to it. Graven Image. She don't ride, herself. But she likes guys who do."

I was looking down, peeling back pages of this journal, which was lying beside me on the bed. Virtually any page I peeled back had something unflattering to say about someone, usually Randy, on its reverse side.

"Colleen don't like Courtney because she thinks Courtney's one of these chicks wasting time at community college, taking bullshit classes, waiting to catch a husband. Colleen would like her a lot less if she knew that Courtney's four years older than Tyler and is paying for college working as a stripper over at Lolly's, out on Route 10."

You've read my journal?

"Tyler ain't much smarter than I am, but he's smarter than Colleen gives him credit for. He's just having his little go-go girl thing."

Trent noticed that I'd written something and bent to look. This is the way it often is, when you're always writing your words. When you can't speak. The conversation's always running ahead of you. Trent straightened.

"Fuck, no. I ain't much of a reader. Felicia read it. She ran copies of some of the good parts and put 'em in the mail to me. With yellow ink on the important sentences."

I'd managed to make it pretty clear to Trent, during the hostage fiasco, what I'd thought of him. Still, I'd never pictured him reading my personal, private thoughts about him. I'd pictured everyone else reading my personal, private thoughts, of course. But Trent was supposed to have been dead. Like me.

"Some other people read it," Trent was saying. "They tell me, the shit I done to you, I oughta at least have caught an assful of buckshot."

I don't necessarily still believe a lot of the crap I wrote in that journal. I hope I made some of that clear, in the storeroom, at the end.

"Don't sweat it, chief. You had some legitimate beefs. I still don't remember half of that shit I did to you, but if somebody did it to me, I'd be looking to carve a hunk of meat out of them, too, believe me."

The past is gone, isn't it, Randy? Dead and gone.

"That's what I say. That's why I can't remember half of it. It's like that Foreigner song. Don't look back."

Boston, wasn't it? Don't look back.

"Whatever the fuck. I came up here, actually, for a reason."

I looked at him.

"How'd you like to do some drivin' for me? Parts delivery."

There was a silence while I looked at him, shocked.

"I mean, it's a shit job. It don't pay nothing. Not like the writing business." He thought about it. "Eleven bucks an hour. Twelve-fifty, if it turns out, you don't suck at it."

Driving? You'd hire me? To work for you?

"Well. Once your face gets fixed up. Garage mechanics got strong stomachs. But not that strong."

I'm really touched.

"Right. In the head. It ain't no secret. But I need a driver. School starts in a couple weeks and the two kids I got have already given notice. I'm gonna be delivering myself if I can't get somebody else to do it."

Why don't you hire Tyler?

"Colleen won't let me. She wants the kid in the parts business about as bad as she wants him dating strippers. Besides, the kid won't work for me, anyway. For someone who don't work much, he's doing okay for money."

Oh.

"Yeah, yeah, don't give me 'Oh.' I know what you're thinking. But I don't see how. There ain't shit going on in this town, I don't know about. And I ain't heard word one about Tyler dealing weed. Not word one."

That hadn't been what I was thinking. Truth be told, I know how Tyler is earning his money. A witch told me. We'll be getting to the witch later. We won't be getting to the source of Tyler's funds, though. You, Death, presumably already know about Tyler and his money. And no one else who might come into possession of this crudely scribbled account needs to know. This is my confessional, after all. Not Tyler's.

Parenthood's turned you into an anti-drug crusader, Trent? Didn't you do a little dealing, back in the day?

"Weed. Weed and some acid. Diet pills. But it was a different frigging world back then. There were head shops in the malls, for christ sake. Everybody blew a little weed. You couldn't get in trouble for it."

I didn't.

"Didn't what?"

Experiment with illicit drugs.

"Yeah, well. You didn't get out much. The point is, I don't mind the kid tokin' up some weed. You can't stop that. Every kid does it. 'Cept you, I guess. But dealing is out. Frigging cops land on you like a pallet of bricks." He shook his head, dismissing the idea. "He ain't, though. I'd know about it."

Sure. Then he's probably not.

Trent read this and rocked impatiently in his chair. "Don't give me shit."

I'm not. What?

"Don't give me shit. I run auto parts stores. I see half the crankheads, half the wall-eyed stoners in this county on a daily basis. Nobody's buying from Tyler. Anybody sells anything in this town, I know about it."

Sure. Absolutely.

Trent was looking at me, considering. Fortunately, I no longer have to make any effort to keep a straight face. The enamel and plastic tubing and medical bandaging do that for me.

"You don't know anything I don't know, do ya?"

Me? Who's gonna tell me anything?

"True." Trent looked away, out the window, still considering. "Kids have ways of making money. Off the books stuff. Construction. Repair. Tyler's pretty handy."

So you're going to report this wealth of information to Colleen.

"Yep."

Maybe wrangle some lovin'.

Trent smirked. "I'd settle for a cup of coffee." He set his hands on his thighs and rose from the chair. "But you gotta start somewhere."

Words of wisdom, from the purveyor of parts.

"It's true. You gotta start somewhere." He retrieved the vase of flowers from the EEG machine and started backing toward the door. "You keep my offer in mind."

I will. Tell Colleen I said she can do plenty better than you.

"Yeah, yeah. Fuck you."

He pushed open the door, almost hitting a startled Asian orderly.

"Are you signed in at the desk?" the orderly asked.

"Fuck, no. I'm an intruder. How do I get out of here?"

The door swung shut behind him.

§

June 26th, 4am

Forty-five years I lived, without ever guessing that my true genius, my calling, lay in deception. In conniving. Duplicity.

I needed an opening. And now, I believe, I'm in.

Oh yes, loved ones of Randy Trent. Young Tyler Trent and Miz Trent.

I'm in. I'm in Randy's circle.

That's right, Tyler. I have a name for you now. Nothing on you yet, Miz Trent. But I'm working on it.

I've just now returned from the Sail Inn, from a long night of chatting and drinking and having a good old time with my new buddy, Randy Trent. And with you too, Felicia, camcorder-wielding admirer of Trent. So let me welcome you to the target readership of my suicide journal, now that I have a name to attach to your lovely body and talents.

Welcome aboard, Felicia!

So. How did I get into Trent's good graces?

Well, to start with, I needed an accessory. A temporary partner in crime who would willingly play a key role in my deception of Trent, then conveniently disappear. In short, I needed a person as unsavory as myself.

But where, you might ask, does an isolated, unconnected person like myself find that kind of willing, convenient, and unsavory person, without attracting undue attention?

Why, an unsavory place of business, of course.

So I went to Moore's.

Moore's is one of the very few Lake Lenni Lenape establishments to survive intact from my own boyhood here. It's actually located outside the town limits, in what was once a remote section of low, scrub-covered hills below town, not far from the train station. Twenty-some years ago, if you were driving around out there, you were going to or from Moore's or the train station. There was nothing else. Now, however, you could be making a trip to any one of several big-box retailers that have sprung up in the vicinity. There's a huge Wal-Mart, a huge Costco, a Home Depot, a Target, a Lowe's, and a couple of chain restaurant franchises.

And Moore's. Moore's is still a low, flat-roofed, windowless, concrete bunker. It was once painted an exotic shade of day-go purple. Now it's painted white and unchanged otherwise but for the paving of its parking lot and the addition of a long sign that says Sophisticated Entertainment in glowing neon-green script. Moore's is a go-go bar and grill that, for some reason, was never called Secrets or Rumours or Scandals, like other operations of its kind. It's always been called Moore's, though, really, it could just as easily be called The Saddest Place In The World.

THE END IS NEAR

I arrived at about eleven am, before the arrival of the regular lunch crowd and just as the neon-green Sophisticated Entertainment sign was popping to life. You can get an egg sandwich from Moore's foul grill as early as 7am, but you can't order a beer until 9am. And there's no entertainment but TV until 11:30, when the first dancer goes on.

When I lived here in the early 1980s, the drinking age was eighteen, though Moore's ID policy rendered the law moot. I wasn't the kind of teen who frequented bars, but any student at Lake Lenni Lenape High knew that you could be carded at Moore's only under specific circumstances. That is, if the bartender didn't like you, you were being a pest, or there were cops in the bar who didn't like you. Otherwise, you were good to go. Moore's was also well-known for the entrepreneurial pursuits of some of its patrons, who sold drugs, and those of Moore's dancers, who sold services in order to buy drugs.

I can't say what the interior of Moore's looked like in its heyday. Today, though, it's a dump. You enter the bar through a little annex tacked onto the front of the bunker. The interior is echoey, by virtue of all the concrete, and dark as a mine shaft everywhere but up on stage. It's so dark you have to stand by the door for a full minute or so, your nostrils assailed by the odors of frying food and forty years' worth of spilled beer, until your eyes can distinguish empty barstools in the flickering TV light.

Who's here at this hour? Unemployed day laborers, mostly. They start queuing up outside the Home Depot and the Lowe's at 6am. The best and most reliable workers are snapped up early by licensed contractors and builders on their way to job sites. Laborers who don't make the first cut have to hope that an individual odd-jobs handyman will stop by, needing help on a complex project. After that, there's nothing to do but harass civilians, usually housewives, who are buying light fixtures, potting soil, and such. If that doesn't pan out, you're off to Moore's to await midday and, perhaps, a half-day gig with one of the teams of contractors that stop in for burgers and beers at lunch.

Oh, and they're all illegal immigrants. I should mention that, right? Columbians, Mexicans, a few Russians and Chinese. They are people accustomed to doing back-breaking manual work for undocumented cash payments. Once I could see my hand in front of my face, I looked around and saw Hispanics gathered around several tables away from the bar, a huddle of Chinese guys smoking furiously in the shelter of a propped-open emergency door at the back of the room, and some Russians sitting, each alone, at the bar. I only knew that the Russians were, in fact, Russians, because I ended up talking to one.

A bartender approached to take my order. She was an older woman. I'm making a point of not boring you, dear readers, with needless descriptions of peripheral players, though I will say that it's a unique woman who, though nearly bald, doesn't feel the need to wear any sort of cap or wig or scarf. She was wearing a rubber surgical glove, dark stains at the fingertips, on her right hand. "I ain't seen you before," she said.

"Hah, no," I said. "First time."

"Hope we pass the sniff test."

I ordered a beer and she went to get it. As she filled the glass from the tap, the silence around us was sledgehammered by a howling blast of '80s hair-metal music. This lasted for several moments until an invisible offstage hand modulated the volume. The bartender returned with my beer and lifted my twenty off the bar with gloved fingers.

"Maybe you can help me," I said.

She looked at me without expression.

"I need to hire someone to do some work."

"What kind of work?"

"A small job. Nothing big."

She sized me up. "Yardwork? Repair?"

"No, not like that. It's more like . . . something else."

The bartender sucked a tooth, audibly. "Whyn't you wait 'til one of the girls comes out, talk it over with her?"

"No, no, not like that, either. I mean . . . I need a guy. For an errand."

"Well ain't you mysterious." She went to the register, deposited the twenty and brought me back a stack of singles. While she was gone, the first lunch-crowd early birds, guys in bulky workboots and caps embossed with builder's supply brands, began to enter.

"It's nothing illegal," I said.

"I don't want to hear nothin' about it. It ain't my business. Guy need to speak English?"

"He needs to understand English," I replied, clarifying needlessly.

"I'll pass along the message."

She went off to take lunch orders, leaving me to my own thoughts for a while. At exactly 11:30 on the digital clock above the register, I watched as curtains parted in a doorway behind the bar and the first entertainer of the day appeared. Dancing is usually regarded as a young woman's game, but that's not the case here. At Moore's, the last and lowest station on the dancing-for-dollars circuit, youth and beauty are fanciful rumors from distant lands.

The woman clambering up onto the stage encircled by the bar looked like a middle-aged housekeeper. I don't say that to be snide or funny. These women are middle-aged housekeepers. I've had opportunity to talk to some of them, and they all work for maid services when they're not here. Some of them are hard to understand—their grasp of English is limited and their accents impenetrable—but they all have a tale of woe about mopping and scrubbing half the day and flashing their tired boobs the other half of the day.

They make very little money cleaning and even less here, at least during the daytime hours. The woman doing the first turn of the day, a Russian or Slavic woman with a preposterous jet black wig, a perfect round bob of fake hair, planted atop her head, was dancing for nobody. The Hispanics and Chinese, evidently penniless for the most part, stay away from the bar. The Russian guys sit at the bar, cough up a dollar on the first pass, and then wave the women away imperiously on subsequent visits. The lunching electricians and carpenters do the same thing, scarcely raising their faces from their burgers and fries. How much money are these women making, gyrating and disrobing onstage in the midday gloom? About four bucks a pass, I'd say.

When the Russian housekeeper reached my place at the bar, she dispensed with the dancing and leaned forward chummily, her elbow on the bar, her chin in her palm. "You are new here," she said.

"Yeah, that's right, new."

She grinned broadly, her teeth startlingly white between that black wig and the rough, chapped flesh of her hand. "You are a builder? Build things?"

"No."

"You like pretty girls?"

"Me? Sure." I retrieved a dollar from my stack of bills and slid it across the bar to her.

She looked at the dollar and then up at me, her eyebrow cocked in mock consternation. "No," she said. "Like this." She picked up the dollar and grasped it at opposite ends, snapping it wide and turning it front to back before my eyes, like a magician demonstrating the material integrity of a handkerchief before using it to make a pigeon disappear. Then she hooked a finger into the top of the sheer teddy she was wearing, pulled it forward to expose her breasts, and plunged the other hand, with the dollar, inside. She caressed her breast with the dollar, tweaked her nipple, and then withdrew her hand, leaving the dollar pressed between breast and lace. "See?"

"I see."

She lifted a dollar bill from my stack and held it out to me. "Now you do."

Which I did. Her breast had the heft, surface consistency, and softness of a ripe orange. Dense. Big pores.

"You like a private dance?"

"Me? Oh, no. I don't think so."

"Out here. Is no good. Back there," she tossed her head in the direction of the curtained area she had entered the room from, "is much better. We get down to business."

"Business?"

She slouched comfortably across the bar, her chin back in her hand, and made a show of appraising me. "You have a big dick, I think." Beeg deek. "I can always tell."

"Really?"

"Really. You will show it to me. Make me go—" Here, she raised her arm and rested an upturned wrist lightly across her forehead, in a pantomime of damsel's distress.

"Oh, " I said. "Um, how much is that?"

She lowered her arm, fluttered her made-up lashes and patted her breastbone daintily, still the damsel. "For you? Hardly nothing."

"Well, that's very flattering."

"Fuck off, sister."

I turned from the dancer to see we had been joined by the biggest and jowliest of the solitary Russians on the other side of the bar.

"Fuck off yourself," my new lady friend said. "I am working here."

"Fuck off," our forbidding visitor said again, without overt malice. He was looking at me. "I am Boris."

"Boris. Okay."

"You need some help." I hadn't seen the barmaid talk to this guy, and she hadn't brought him over, but he certainly looked like the kind of person you'd recommend for a mysterious errand. His accent, as I've said, was Russian or Eastern European, though he seemed darker complected than the typical emigrant from those latitudes. Perhaps he had some Middle Eastern blood. Or perhaps this is what you look like when your day typically involves low-shelf vodka shots and draft beers in disreputable go-go bars at eleven in the morning. He had a big, soft face, and tiny eyes placed wide in his head. He was wearing a big sweatshirt, size XXXL at least, with the name of a rap mogul's clothing line emblazoned across the front in foot-high letters.

"Maybe," I said.

"I will come back later," the Russian housekeeper said. She gave Boris a dirty look and toddled away on her lofty heels. She did, too. Come back. Several times. She would later tell me her name was Tanya, though both "Tanya" and "Boris" may have been putting me on, with the names.

"An errand. Mystery, like."

So he had talked to the barmaid. "No mystery. Just a simple job." I reached into the front pocket of my pants and withdrew a small stack of bills. Five hundreds folded once. I unpeeled one. "What I need is, a favor."

Boris matter-of-factly plucked the hundred out of my hand and pushed it into a front pocket of his jeans. "What kind of favor?"

"I need you to put on a show, like. Pretend to beat me up."

Boris reached around me and pulled a cocktail straw from a dispenser on the bar. He tucked it into the corner of his mouth. "I am not a showman."

"There's more money where that came from." I returned the money to my pocket, lest he simply snap the rest of the bills out of my hand. Then I added, "It's not illegal or anything."

"I do not care for legal or illegal. You are some kind of," and he said a word I didn't get, some kind of foreign term.

"What?"

He held up an open palm and punched it sharply with his fist. "A butt puncher."

"A what? Oh, jeez, no. You're getting the wrong idea. This is, like, an insurance thing." I looked around at the other patrons, but no one was paying any attention to us. And the music, now some kind of aggro, punk-metal thing, was loud enough to cover our voices, surely.

"Insurance."

"Insurance scam. One punch and you're done."

"Where does this happen?"

"Somewhere else. Not far from here. Later tonight."

He thought about this for a moment. "I do not think so." He started to turn away.

"Wait. Wait! One hundred now, two hundred when we get to where we're going."

He had stopped, but was facing away from me. "What, one punch." He was still gripping his fist in his other hand. "How long is this?"

"Just a half-hour car ride, a few minutes' wait, one punch, and a cab ride back to here."

"Two hundred now."

"Two hours, tops. One punch. A cab ride. To anywhere you want to go." I plucked another hundred from my pants pocket. "Four hundred dollars."

Boris took this bill, too. "You would not fuck with me."

"I'll pick you up here. Probably around eight or so. I'll need a cellphone number."

"Whack the head, cab out."

"In the eye." I pointed at my left eye. "Not the nose or mouth." A broken nose or jaw would mean a trip to the hospital, which I definitely didn't want. A black eye would merely serve as a pointed reminder to Trent of a debt he owed me.

Boris was rubbing the knuckles of his fist with his other hand. He seemed to be weighing his options, despite already being richer by two hundred dollars.

He looked at me. "Insurance. I know insurance jobs. Five hundred."

"Three hundred more later."

He nodded. I handed him a pen and he wrote a phone number on a napkin.

And we were off.

And so am I. I'm going to bed. The sun is coming up, I'm drunk, I'm tired, I can barely hold my head up. More of the story in the morning. Well, later in the morning.

I'm in. I'm inside.

§

Oh, Death. Now you've gone too far.

What could you possibly be thinking, sending me somebody I know? Is my situation not sufficiently humiliating? Sufficiently desperate? Do I now have to share it with people from my former life?

"Jesus, buddy," someone said. "Can't say much for your new look."

I jackknifed up in my bed to find Archie Hodges standing by the door, hands in his pockets, looking at me. Archie, my old creative director at Pendleton. Archie, who's on the other sides of these pages somewhere.

"On the bright side, you can throw away the shaving razor, huh?"

I snatched my pen and pad from the bedside table and wrote, *Archie! How did you find out I was here?*

"Same damn way everybody does." Archie looked as if he'd just stepped out of his old office at Pendleton. White dress shirt with toner-stained cuffs, baggy suit pants, threadbare tie at half mast, hangdog expression on his face, left eye bloodshot.

The newspapers? Somebody at Pendleton?

"No, ya dumb fuck. The Big Cheese sent me. Something about some copy you're dragging your heels on." He pointed at the transcript on the floor by the bed. "This is the job?"

Big Cheese? My God, Archie. You're dead?

"Dead? I don't know. I'm here, aren't I?"

Do you remember dying?

"Do I . . . " Archie had picked up the transcript and was thumbing through it. "Do I remember dying. No, actually. I just remember getting my marching orders from the Big Kahuna."

Maybe you're not dead, I wrote, not too optimistically.

"Maybe." Musingly, still thumbing. "But then what am I doing here, wasting valuable living moments visiting you?"

Good point. Maybe you're dead.

"Pretty anticlimactic, if I am." He grinned his characteristic slack, open-mouthed grin. "Guess I must have died quick, huh? Maybe Wile E. Coyote dropped an Acme safe on me."

If you're dead, I'm sorry to hear it. See it.

"Thanks. I'm sorry to be dead. If I am." He'd stalled in one section of the transcript and was reading. "Though now that I think of it, things were pretty much going downhill, anyway."

I had suspected this, of course.

Job problems? Health problems? After Pendleton?

"Job problems. Life problems. The usual shit." He raised an eyebrow at the transcript and then faced me, reading from it. "Archie was a rumpled and beleaguered ad guy. I'd known him in better days, before he was undone by marriage woes and drink." He looked up at me. "Thanks for the name check, buddy."

I reached out for the transcript, but Archie had flipped it over and was trying to puzzle out my handwriting on the backs of the pages.

Sorry, I wrote. I held my pad up.

"Forget it. So you're blocked up, huh."

By which he meant writer's blocked. In our Pendleton days, Archie had had little patience with the notion of writer's block. He had a little mental picture of the writing process that he would share with me whenever my page count flagged. Words are shit, he would say, and your talent's a shovel. In the writing game, the guy who shovels the fastest, wins.

It's kind of an unusual assignment.

"Yeah, yeah. They all are. The Customer, what does he want"

Truth, I guess.

"Huh." Archie handed the transcript to me. "No wonder you're blocked up. The truth from an ad writer. Like squeezing good Scotch from a turnip."

Did you have to pass some kind of test? To die?

"Test?"

Like this. Like I have to. Have you met any waitresses?

"Hang on there, sloopy. I'm not entirely sure I'm dead. I mean, just because you say so . . ."

True, maybe you're not dead. The doctors here would say that you're a hallucination.

"A hallucination?"

A figment of my imagination. Caused by the buckshot in my head. Or unmetabolized toxins going to my brain.

"Whoa, wait a minute." He snapped his fingers twice, thinking, then pointed a chubby finger at me. "Liver damage?"

A little dysfunction, maybe. It's the least of my problems, right now.

"Fuck. I had that. That toxin thing, too." He snapped his fingers again, trying to remember. "Hepatic ... encepholagraphy. Encephalopathy? Something like that?"

Sounds like it.

"Uncleared poisons go to your head."

I guess so.

"Really. Serious shit." Archie looked at me blankly. "It could be that."

I don't know. You seem very real.

"Uh-huh. I feel very real." He seemed to think about it. "On the other hand, I guess I can see the doctor's point, too."

You can?

"Well, either you're having delusions caused by a head full of buckshot and unjiggered poisons. Or I've been sent by Death to kickstart your wordsmithing." Archie shrugged. "Which seems more likely?"

I guess the first choice.

Which left us at an impasse.

I don't know what to think. I don't know what to do. If you're a hallucination, why can't I wake up from you?

"I don't know. And if I'm just your hallucination, why am I having thoughts inside my own head, right now? Why, for instance, am I having unflattering thoughts about you? Why am I thinking that I sure could use a drink, right about now?"

I don't know.

"Maybe I'm imagining you."

Oh. Great.

"Hey, just a suggestion. Another possible explanation. Either way, if there's nothing you can do about it, seems to me you might as well enjoy the ride, huh?"

You're not helping.

"And I'm here to help, right?" He grinned his loose grin. "And the sooner I help, the sooner I can get outta here and grab a drink somewhere."

I guess so.

"So whaddeya say we leave the heavy mental lifting to the folks in the offices with windows, huh? As I understand it, you've got a deadline here."

Don't you care if you're real or not?

"I'm gonna assume I am real, until someone proves me wrong, buddy. Besides, either way, I got a job to do. Not to mention my own agenda, which includes the aforementioned drink somewhere."

Okay.

Archie jammed his hands into his pockets and walked to the foot of the bed. "The Big D's got a truth jones, is my understanding. So throw in some truth schtick. How hard is that?"

Pretty hard.

"Oh, please." Archie looked aggrieved. "Finesse it. Picture your audience. The Big D's asking you to review your life, right? You're dying and he's like the Ghost of Christmas Past. Dickens? Bit of undigested beef? He wants to squeeze your balls until . . . what?" He looked at me, prompting.

I shook my head.

"Until you see the error of your ways, fuckhead. Whaddeya think? Don't you watch Christmas specials on TV?"

I shrugged. Everybody does.

"Epiphany. Lessons learned. Better person for it. Rebirth. Never too late. You know." He waved his hand in the air vaguely, as if dispelling an odor. "Redemption. God bless us, every one. Readers love that shit."

It's not as simple as all that.

Archie was watching the readout on my heart monitor. "Broad strokes, that's what's needed. A happy ending. The great default option for the American narrative. You'll think of something. You're just pressing, that's all."

You try it. See how easy it is.

"Me, no. I'm gonna get out of here and conduct a metaphysical experiment." He walked over to the door. "I'm gonna go find a bar. If I get served, I'll figure I'm real. When I get back, I expect to see some truth on those pages. Or something as close to the truth as a washed-up ad writer can manage, anyway."

I'll try. I am trying. The *am* underlined several times.

"Make the customer happy, Nathan."

Easy for you to say.

"Everything's easy for me to say. According to you, I'm either dead or imaginary. Not much at stake, right?"

And then he left. Like Betty, through the door. No poofs or magic acts.

So where is he, Death? Is he really coming back? Do you let your minions take happy-hour breaks? Is he back in the aether, the eternal twilight of death, awaiting another assignment? Or is he tucked back into one of the unhinged cabinets of my deranged subconscious?

Right, right. I know. Get back to work.

But before I get back to it, I just want to say this. No more surprises. Any more unwelcome surprises, and the deal's off. Okay?

Right. Back to work.

I wish I had an epiphany. A lesson learned. Instead, all I have is story. A story as pointless, as random, as unrewarding as everyone else's story turns out to be, in the end.

After Felicia wouldn't leave Randy's store, things got awkward.

"If you won't leave," I said, "then get behind the counter with the other two."

"Don't think you can order me around," she said. She clicked past me in her heels—fairly high heels, I think I've mentioned—and went behind the counter, forcibly inserting herself between Randy and Alice.

"Okay, Nathan. You want to do things the hard way, we can do 'em the hard way," the cop, Officer Mazzini, said through the bullhorn.

I looked through the front display window, to where another police cruiser was pulling in next to Mazzini's. The cop inside the cruiser lowered his passenger side window, talked to Mazzini, looked at me, talked some more. Then, apparently hearing what he needed to hear, he hit the flashers, blue and red beams sweeping and spinning in the late afternoon sunlight.

"So what now?" Randy said. "You got us here. You got me here. What are we gonna do?"

I turned to look at Randy, then Felicia, then Alice.

"What is this shit, I don't know who you are?" Randy said, trying again. "What are you trying to say to me, Nathan?"

"I know what we can do," Felicia said, to Randy.

We all looked at Felicia.

"We can listen while you tell us what your ex-wife was doing at your apartment at midnight last night." She folded her arms, high and tight. "If, as you say, you two aren't fucking."

"This isn't the time, Felicia."

"Au contraire, fucking Pierre. Now is exactly the time. What better way to pass the time with our gun-pointing friend here? I'm sure your new piece of ass would like to hear this story, too. Wouldn't you, honey?"

"You know what?" Alice said. "You are a very unpleasant person."

"So what were you and the ex up to?" Felicia continued, ignoring Alice. "Bridge game run late?"

Outside, two more police cruisers—most, if not all, of the Lake Lenni Lenape police force—had joined the first two. Four cops were huddled in earnest conversation about fifteen feet from the display window of the shop. They were making no effort to hide. If I had been the kind of hostage-taker bent on general mayhem, I could have retrieved the pistol from the bag and winged one of them with a shot, just to get things going. I had two hand grenades in the bag, as well, in case things got really interesting.

"Why are you wearing that dress?" Randy said.

Felicia's hand went to the steep neckline of the slinky scarlet wraparound number she was wearing. "I figured I'd give you an eyeful of what you'll be missing out on, once you boot away the best thing you ever had for . . ." she cut a baleful glance at Alice, "whatever."

People were starting to gather on the other side of Lakeside Drive, emerging from Salvatore's Pizza & Subs and Nan Pratt's Country Store. The beer signs were glowing in the windows of Holly's Tavern, and the late Monday afternoon crowd was just climbing off their barstools to join in the fun. I could see PJ on the front stoop of Nan Pratt's, his flattop haircut and jug ears bobbing above a tight circle of new admirers as he related, presumably, the tale of his narrow escape from the hostage situation.

"So are you gonna tell us or what?"

"There's nothing to tell, Felicia. She's worried about Tyler. That's all."

"Tyler."

"Yes. Tyler. Our son. Colleen's worried about," Randy looked at the ceiling, sounding like a man with a gun pointed at him, "about his future, I guess. Graduation's come and gone and the kid's, I don't know . . . got no direction."

"Tyler. How convenient."

Randy looked at Felicia, his brow furrowing. "How's that?"

"I'm just saying. It's all very convenient."

"Tyler's not a convenience. He's our son and he's got his head up his ass."

"Alright, people," Officer Mazzini bullhorn-squawked. "Go about your business. There's nothing to see here." The people— four or five older folks from Nan's, two kids in pizza aprons from

Salvatore's, some afternoon drunks from Holly's, and another group of kids excitedly bouncing around on freestyle bikes—had started to edge into the road.

Mazzini turned and looked at me, only a few feet away. "Whaddeya say we pull the plug on this before it gets out of hand, Nathan? Before we get a whole circus going?"

I just looked at him. There wasn't much to say. He was a thirtyish cop, tan and fit, barrel-chested, his upper arms stretching the short sleeves of his tunic. His mustache and eyebrows were so dark and square they looked fake. He wore mirrored shades, which he reached for and took off when he addressed me again.

"Any minute now, we're gonna have the whole dog-and-pony show out here and we're gonna have to start going by the book. Nobody wants to see that, Nathan. Not me, anyway. You come out now, it's you and me, we go back to the station, maybe it's all just a misunderstanding, you know? Something we can sort out man-to-man."

"So what's this?" Felicia was saying. "What am I, supposed to feel sorry for your ex-wife now?"

"What?" Randy said. "Felicia, what are you talking about?"

"At least Colleen has a kid to worry about. Do you ever think about my feelings? Do you ever think, oh, maybe, I don't know," Felicia lapsing into full petulant sulk, "maybe I might want a child?"

"What are you saying?" Randy seemed dazed, as if he were only just then realizing that he was having a conversation with Felicia. "You want a what?"

"I'm saying that I'm not getting any younger, you son of a bitch!" Felicia snatched up the air filter that Randy had set on the counter and bounced it off his head. It rolled away, back into the storeroom. "I'm saying I didn't have ten and a half months to waste on you, just so you could toss me over for some . . . some new fortune cookie!"

"Hey!" Alice barked. "Watch it, sister!"

"What's going on in there?" Mazzini bellowed through the horn.

"Ten months, practically eleven months, I've been out of circulation! Catering to your every fucking whim! And for what? For what? So you could choose this sneaky little bitch from Column B!"

"I have made an effort to be nice up to now," Alice continued, levelly, furiously, "but I'm not going to take any more shit from you. You watch your mouth."

Felicia spun on Alice and faced her down, her hands twitching at her sides. "Me! Me watch my mouth! Why don't you blow somebody else's boyfriend, you little backseat whore!"

That's when I fired my second shot. And everything started happening very fast.

§

June 26th, 3pm

Oh, good lord.

How do they do it? How do they hang out in that godforsaken Sail Inn, night after night after night, emptying pitchers and bottles and kegs, and not die?

I'm no stranger to strong drink, as should be obvious by now. But these people. These fucking Sail Inn regulars. My hat's off to 'em.

I spent most of last night raising glasses of beer with Randy and his bar friends. My new buddies.

Looking back at this morning's entry, I see I wandered afield somewhat in my description of the events at Moore's. The dancers and clientele and all. Sorry about the surfeit of information. On the other hand, given my condition at the time, I'm surprised that I don't have to translate it into English, from the original Martian.

I see I left off at Moore's. With Boris, my new conspirator in crime and deception. I see also that I was rather impressed with myself and my skill at plotting intrigues. The truth is, my elaborate plans could have unraveled at any moment. I just got lucky at a few critical junctures, that's all.

When I got to the Sail Inn, I was happy, though not particularly surprised, to see Randy Trent's Ford F-250 still in the lot. I'd been in the Sail Inn earlier, to make sure Trent was there. It had been seven thirty, then. It was eight thirty and the sun was setting when I returned with my new partner. Trent was still holding court at a long table full of his buddies, most of them wearing uniform tunics with the words A&B Auto Parts Softball printed on the back. There were a few girls, too. The pretty Asian-looking girl from the other night wasn't among them.

I had four tasks to complete, in rapid order.

First, I gave Boris another hundred, the third of five, and told him to wait in my car. He seemed incurious about the cover story I'd given him regarding an insurance scam of some sort. He also seemed, if not plainly inebriated, at least a little tight, like someone who might have spent his whole day at Moore's.

I went into the bar and called a cab, watching Trent carry on with his friends as I did so. The dinner they'd all been sharing was cleared away, but Trent wasn't looking like someone about to leave. The bar wasn't very crowded, but it was noisy, the way a bar will be when most everyone knows most everyone else.

I directed the cab service to send a cab to the Lakeside Drive boat docks. The Sail Inn, despite its name, is not a waterfront bar. You can't sail in to it. Its back lot is about two hundred yards or so above Lakeside Drive, on the other side of which are the boat docks and lake. The Sail Inn's connection to the sailing life—besides its cheesy nautical décor—is a long, weedy path from the back of its parking lot to the road and the docks. Thirsty sailors can tie up at the dock, but they have to cross the street and climb the steep hill to get to the Sail Inn. The cab, the dispatcher said, would arrive in fifteen minutes.

It arrived in five. I barely had time to get down the hill to meet it. My buddy, I explained to the driver, had gone for a beer. I would go get him, but it might take a little while. I gave the driver a twenty—generous enough to keep him there, not so generous as to arouse suspicion—and told him it might take as much as half an hour. The driver, a shaven-headed punk rock type accustomed to waiting outside bars, shrugged and slid a thick paperback off the dashboard. Ayn Rand. Ambitious cabbie.

I climbed the hill, already winded, and returned to the car. The spot next to Trent's truck was vacant and I backed my car in next to it and looked around. It was fully dark by this time. Boris and I were the only people in the lot. I reached into the back seat and grabbed a thick wool blanket. A rusty hammer— plucked from its hook in my father's workshop, where it must have hung undisturbed for thirty years—was tucked inside the blanket.

I got out of the car and pressed the blanket to the driver's side window of Trent's truck. Here again, my plans could have tripped up in their too-intricate traces. But the window blew out at a single blow of the hammer, with a dull, unsatisfying pop. No commotion, no witnesses. I removed the blanket and tapped out the remaining glass with the hammer, careful to keep the glass inside the truck. The darkness of the lot—it was lit only indirectly, by an orangey bug light over the bar entrance and the beer signs in the bar windows—provided plenty of cover.

I stowed the hammer and blanket in the trunk of my car, and went over the plan with Boris again. Punch, hill, cab.

"You should have nothing to worry about," I said. "The guys inside are like me, they're not going to chase after you." Paunchy, tired, middle-aged guys, I meant.

"Where's this cab?"

"Come on. I'll show you." We got out of the car and went to the back of the lot. The yellow roof light of the cab, the only light out there, was just visible through the trees. I showed him the path—overgrown but passable, even in the dark—and we returned to the car.

I ran through the details, one more time.

"When I call you, you'll have a minute or two before I leave the bar. When I come out, I'll walk right to the truck. You'll get out and meet me by the window of the truck. We'll wait, probably only a second or two. I'll turn to you and hand you these two bills," I held up two hundreds, folded around my index finger, "you'll take them, punch me, and hit the path. The driver's got twenty. Here's another fifty." I handed him another bill. "That's it."

"Yeah, yeah," Boris said. "Let's wrap this up. I have shit to do tonight."

"Remember," I said. "Left eye. Not the nose. Not the jaw."

He grunted noncommittally. I left him in the car and returned to the bar to watch Trent. Later, I had to go down the hill again and toss the cabbie another twenty. Trent didn't begin his back-slapping, wisecracking departure until almost ten o'clock.

I double-timed out of the bar, just ahead of Trent, and turned to watch the bar entrance. Boris got out of my car and met me at the truck. The door of the bar swung open and a leggy, tall woman appeared, followed by two people—a tall, gangly guy in one of the A&B softball shirts, and Trent. Trent seemed to be wrapping up some kind of joke.

I pushed the money on Boris, waited a beat, and called out "Hey!" Loudly.

And then I was flat on my back, looking up into the face of a beautiful woman, silhouetted against the star-strewn night sky. Even in the unflattering orange glow of the distant buglight, she seemed angelic, her eyes wide-set and remarkably clear, flecked and sparkly like little miniature night skies themselves, her soft dark curls dangling and tickling my face.

"Fucking A," she said in a gravelly, bar-chick voice. "You okay, sweetie?"

I was looking up, dreamily, content to breathe in her scent of fruity perfume, cigarettes, and beer. And then I remembered where I was, remembered that my plan was contingent on Boris's escape.

I lifted myself up onto my elbows and looked around. The acrid iron scorch of blood and shock was in my nose, but I couldn't tell if I was bleeding. It was just me and the woman there; the guys were gone.

"Where are they? Where's the kid?"

"The kid?"

"The kid who hit me." A bit of disinformation. "He was a black kid, I think." The shameless suburban lawbreaker's last refuge. Racial profiling.

The woman looked at me for a bit, then stood up and looked through the window into Trent's truck. She shook her head. "Fucking thieves," she said.

I sat up and raised my hand to my face. The left side of my face was numb and my hand came away wet. Alarm sirens and bells were shrieking in my head. My hand was slick, but not noticeably discolored. I seemed to be weeping tears like an opened faucet.

"Randy almost had him, but he got away." She looked off in the direction of the lake. "Don't worry, though. They'll catch him. PJ's fast as any nigger. They'll get your wallet back."

I reached for and felt my back pocket. Right. Empty.

"Fucking nigger," the girl said again.

"They chased the kid?"

If they chased Boris all the way down to Lakeside Drive, two hundred yards over difficult terrain, then there could only be a few possible outcomes, most of them very unfortunate indeed. They could catch Boris. Boris could give himself up. Boris could get in the cab, but the cabdriver could be too slow in pulling away. Boris could escape on foot, leaving the cabdriver, Randy, and this other guy, PJ, together at the bottom of the hill. Or Boris could get away in the cab.

The fact that Boris had stolen my wallet actually worked in my favor. It gave him added incentive to get away.

"Fucking thief punched Randy a good one, so he got a head start. I wouldn't bet against Randy, though. Or PJ." She squatted beside me again and reached out to tip my face into the meager light. "You're gonna have some shiner, there."

So we waited. It was dark and I was still groggy, but this woman seemed familiar. Even her voice seemed familiar. But I couldn't place her. Five minutes or so passed as the woman fretted over my contusion and I fretted over my increasingly vulnerable situation with regard to conspirator and cabbie and Trent.

And then I heard voices coming from the darkness.

"I'm telling you," somebody was saying, "I heard the car door slam. I saw the cab drive away. He must've got in it."

"What the fuck," someone else, Randy, said. "What kinda truck thief has a cab waiting?"

"Maybe he wasn't gonna steal the truck. Just stuff in it."

"Right. Wait right here, driver. I'll be back with a bunch of radios in a minute."

"I saw what I saw."

"Thieves don't commute by cab, PJ. It increases overhead."

"So where'd he go, then?"

"The way he was running? He's probably halfway back to Newark by now."

Two figures emerged from the darkness at the other end of the parking lot. Randy and the other guy, PJ. Lady Luck obviously has a thing for dead guys like me. When they approached the truck, I saw that PJ's uniform front was dirty and he was holding his arm out before him. He was inspecting a bleeding scrape on his forearm.

"He got away?" Felicia said.

"I would've had him," PJ said. "It's dark as fuck down there."

"PJ took a header." Trent looked at the woman, then at me. He cocked his head at an angle. "You. Didn't I see you . . .what? The other day?"

"It's dark as fuck down there," PJ said again, sullenly.

"Yeah, you did." Great. Now, Trent's memory kicks in. "At the bar."

Trent nodded. He touched the area around his right eye and then looked at his hand.

The woman, meanwhile, had leaped up from her crouch over me and had fitted herself to Trent, her arm around his waist, her trembling hand to his precious furrowed brow.

"Oh, honeybear," she said. "Are you alright?"

Honeybear. I looked at the woman in surprise. Oh. Right. Of course.

"Yeah, yeah, Felicia. I'm fine."

It was you, Felicia. You were, well, you. Felicia, the raspy-voiced woman from the tapes, the star of Randy's amateur porn videotape collection. A member of the small contingent of loved ones—joining young Tyler and lovely Miz—to whom this suicide missive is addressed. You were inspecting Trent's face for signs of damage.

"You're not fine!" you cried. "Your eye! You're gonna have a black eye."

"Won't be the first I had." Trent's attention was wandering to the window of his truck. He disengaged himself from you and peered inside, at what I knew was a mess of tiny safety-glass cubes scattered across the inside of the cab.

"Fucked up," he said. He looked back at me. "So what happened?"

I already had these lines rehearsed.

"I was coming out to my car, to leave, and I saw this guy leaning into the window of this truck, your truck, and he looked suspicious. Black guy, he was. I'm pretty sure."

Trent looked up at this. "Black guy?"

"I think, yeah. It was all very quick. He looked like he was trying to do something unusual. So I came up behind him and I said hey, and he must have decked me."

"Huh." Trent looked around the cab of the truck. "He left my laptop on the passenger seat. And my first baseman's mitt on the dashboard. That's worth three hundred, easy."

"Fucking nigger," Felicia said.

"Those bats behind the seat cost me five, six hundred apiece."

"At least he didn't get those," I said.

"Yeah. Good for me. I owe ya one. You saved my shit." Trent grinned suddenly. "Fucking guy popped me a good one, didn't he? He was pullin' on your wallet and I had him," he held his hands out before him, demonstrating, "right in my hands. And he got away."

"I can't believe someone tried to break into your truck," you said, Felicia. "Maybe you should get an alarm."

"Alarms don't do any good."

I looked dumbly at the truck. It hadn't even occurred to me to anticipate an alarm. I'd thought that kind of thing, car alarms, was an '80s thing, like The Club, that metal bar that used to attach to your steering wheel. Lady Luck, patron saint of the already dead, checking in again.

Trent popped the lock and pulled open the door of his truck. He reached inside. "What was your name?" he said over his shoulder.

"Nathan."

Trent emerged with his laptop and glove. He kicked the truck door shut. "Come on, Nathan. Lemme buy ya a beer. Least I can do." He gestured at my eye. "Brittany'll get you some ice for that."

And so my elaborate—elaborately half-assed—plan paid off. I was in.

You're probably thinking—Felicia, Tyler, Miz—that I went to entirely too much trouble, just to strike up a conversation with your Randy Trent.

Maybe. But I think not. Your Trent is a big fish in a small pond. Or, more accurately, a big mosquito on a small puddle. Businessman, eligible man about town, charming thug. He's got a lot going for him. He's got plenty of Rotary colleagues to gladhand, bar buddies to backslap, chicks to fuck. And no time for the unpromising likes of me.

And that's what I wanted. A little of his time. Time to talk to him, on an equal footing, before I killed him. Because there are things I want to know. Questions I want to ask. Questions to which I want honest answers. Not the kind of answers— dishonest, false-flattering, self-saving answers—you get when you're pointing a gun in someone's face. The kind of answers I'm sure I'll hear plenty of, when I am, in fact, pointing a gun in Trent's face.

I guess I could have tried to waylay him at the bar, spring some lame line of conversation on him. But your Trent is too busy, too popular, too self-absorbed, to offer much in response to such a low-fuss approach. And I, frankly, have no gift for small talk. I doubt I would have gotten much more from him than I got the first time I saw him, when he shocked me with his very existence.

And I wanted more. I needed to get into his good graces.

True, my plan did involve some risk of exposure. And I did have to submit—rather stoically, rather bravely, I thought—to minor head and eye trauma. But I also got to smash Trent's truck window. I got to see—and cause, indirectly—the blackening of Trent's eye. I got to look up, dazed, into your beautiful eyes, lovely Felicia. Almost certainly, my last intimate moment with a woman.

And, as I've said, I'm in.

We re-entered the bar and there was much predictable hubbub. Women cooed and clucked over Trent's injury, hung on every word of his drab, colorless account of what happened. Men charged outside, then charged back in, excitedly trying to imagine something, anything, that could be done. I wobbled, lightheaded, to the bar, where I was joined by Trent, by his friend PJ, and then by you, fair Felicia.

In the light of the bar, I could see that you weren't quite the angelic vision of loveliness that you'd seemed in my post-punch stupor. You were your video self—tall, busty, your mouth a little tiny, a little bird-like, your arms a little long, knobby at the elbows and wrists. Still holding middle age at bay, though. And not unattractively so.

Brittany, the barmaid from the other night, brought us beers.

Trent lifted his glass. I lifted mine.

"I gotta thank you again," he said. "That laptop has about three months of unbacked-up records and transaction files in it. From my shops. So I'd've been screwed. So thanks."

"You're welcome." I sipped my beer. "Are we going to call the police?"

"We can if you want. Won't do much good. Your wallet's already in the woods somewhere. You have anything important in it?"

"No, not really." Which was true. A driver's license, assorted other IDs, a little cash, a clutch of maxed-out credit cards. Nothing I'll ever need again. "What about your truck? The window?"

He grimaced. "I'll have a new window in it by lunch tomorrow. Every body shop in the county owes me a dozen favors." He reached into his jeans pocket, pulled out a business card, and handed it to me.

A&B Auto Parts, Randall Trent, Proprietor, it said. It listed three locations.

"You ever need body work, you show 'em that card," he said. "They'll give you a good deal."

So the police weren't called. They could have made trouble for me, though the chances of that happening would have been slim. They would have had to encounter the story of the cab and then take it seriously enough to track it back to the right cab company, dispatcher, and driver. A lot of footwork for a smashed window and lost wallet. Still, they were a nuisance I was happy to avoid.

PJ didn't hang around long enough to share any conspiracy theories involving midnight cabs. He was a tall, big-eared kid who, I was told by way of introduction, was employed at one of Trent's stores solely because of his prodigious softball skills. He wasn't legal to drink and, the postgame dinner being long over, was looking to go home. Which he did.

The rest of us had little compunction about drinking the clock around, however. Beer followed beer. Shots of liquor appeared, at the behest of overexcited bar patrons. The tale was told a second, a third, a fourth time, my own role in the event gradually accruing heroic luster. More shots appeared, disappeared.

What do these bucolic barflies do for livings, that they can hold down barstools and sponge up alcohol as Wednesday nights keel over into Thursday mornings? Got me. Fur trapping? Deerjacking? Coonwhacking? I don't know. Perhaps, like me, they're making an elaborate business of killing themselves.

Randy and I got acquainted. Or reacquainted, from my perspective. We talked.

Oh, we chatted. We familiarized. We became thick as thieves.

Brittany brought us matching icebags for our eyes. There was much hilarity, much witty joust and counterjoust, at the sight of us, mirror images, with our icebags pressed to our eyes, left and right respectively.

We talked about old times.

"So you live around here?" Trent asked. "How come I ain't seen you around before?"

"I used to live here. About twenty years ago. Little more. I came back to settle my mother's estate and sell her house. She passed away recently."

"Oh. Sorry to hear it."

"It's okay. We weren't close."

Trent raised an eyebrow at me. When I didn't say anything more, he said, "Twenty years ago, you say?"

"Roughly."

"I know I keep asking this, but bear with me. What's your name again?"

"Nathan," I said, "Nathan Fisk, Lenape Class of '86." '86 seemed safe. Not too recent, but not too long ago.

"Fisk." He shook his head. "After my time."

"Really. You never left this area, huh?"

"Nope, not me. Too stupid to leave. I got into the parts business when all the smart guys were gettin' out."

"Huh. Maybe you knew my older brother. Charlie."

"Charlie. Charlie . . . Fisk, you say?" He thought about it and shook his head. "Don't ring any bells. Not that I remember a whole lot from those years. Who'd he hang with?"

"Mike Clemens, Tiny Underwood, Georgie Hemple," I said, reeling off some names from our own graduating class.

Trent looked puzzled and shrugged. "My memory for names is shit. Faces and stuff that happened, that I can remember. But names . . ." He shook his head.

"Annie Baxter, the Sumlin twins, Reese Fitzgerald." I won't even bother to elaborate on the grim irony of my remembering all these names, while Trent remembered none of them. I paused and then added, offhandedly, "Nathan Huffnagle."

"Huffnagle." Trent mulled this one over. "I think I remember some twins, come to think of it. Girls?"

"Skinny kid. Smart. Honors program?" Even I, who knew me intimately, had few qualifiers to attach to my name. Good typist, hardly seemed relevant.

He made an effort, then gave up. "Not my crowd, I guess," he said.

"He used to go out with Terry Brentwood." Bumping myself up to boyfriend, what the hell.

"Who did? You?" Trent whacked the bar with his fist, hard, causing his drink and yours, Felicia, to jump. "There's one I know. Every kid in town went out with Loose Lips Terry. For about fifteen minutes."

"What? What's this?" you said, Felicia. You'd been listening to some furry, bullet-shaped guy in a softball tunic, clutching a beer mug to his chest and saying something about general lawlessness, the need for more right-thinking Americans to stand up, take a bite out of crime.

"Chick used to live here," Trent said. "Terry Brentwood. Sweet girl, she was. Generous to fellas in times of need."

"Yeah? A lot of girls you know are that way, I hear."

"Real trouper," Trent said fondly, remembering.

"No shortage of those troupers around. Then or now," you added, rather darkly.

"So I hear," Trent said, false benignly, smiling into his beer glass. "Me, I like to stay outta trouble."

"Funny what you hear, if you listen hard enough," you said. Pointedly. This, anyone could see, was an addendum to a larger, ongoing conversation. Even I, after all, knew of at least one girl Trent had on the side. "Sometimes I hardly know what to believe."

Trent looked at you blankly for a moment, Felicia, then turned back to me.

"So what about you?" he said. "You got outta town with the rest of the smart guys. Whaddeya do?"

"Marketing," I said. "Ad writing."

"Oh, yeah? Like, 'Have a Coke and a smile,' 'Get a piece of the Rock,' that kinda thing?"

"More like direct mail advertising. Products and services."

"Oh." Already losing interest. "We all gotta make a buck, I guess." He turned to you, Felicia, and said, "What the fuck. Don't be tryin' to score points off me, Fel. I'm injured here, right?"

And you, good sport that you undoubtedly are, gave him a squeeze and whispered something sweet in his ear.

"Don't get many old classmates up here, I guess," I said, looking to cut the lovey-dovey stuff off at the pass. This was my show, after all, Felicia. And I had my own agenda, as well as a pressing deadline.

Trent looked at me, while still grinning at whatever it was you had whispered. "Not so's they'd need their own float in the Homecoming parade, no. We had a few up, a couple years ago."

"A couple years ago?"

"Twenty-fifth reunion. Misty-eyed rah-rah types and an open bar, over at the Holiday Inn convention center, as I understood it."

"Really. You were there?"

"Me? Fuck, no. I ain't much for looking back. The kinda people would've gone to a reunion wouldn't've been my crowd, anyway."

"Oh."

"Besides, I was too stupid to get my sheepskin, back in the day. So, technically speaking, I'm Class of Nothin'. My boy's gonna graduate before I do."

"Your boy?"

"Tyler," Trent said. "Class of . . . whatever this year is. Class of now."

Your name, Tyler. Welcome aboard! Grab a seat in the back!

Just then Brittany appeared with more ice for our icebags. "Your boy's graduating?" she said. "Must take after his mother in the brains department."

"He does. Takes after her in the stubborn department, too," Trent said.

"Well, congratulations. Medical care is on the house." Brittany sealed a refilled ice bag and pressed it to Trent's darkened eye. "Ain't graduation tomorrow?"

"Friday. Tomorrow's Parents' Day."

And I, befogged by head trauma and alcohol, said, "Parents' Day?"

"Parents' Day," Trent said. "It's a school thing. The kids have graduation practice while the parents hang out and then there's some kind of parent-teacher-student dinner."

"I don't think I remember that. Parents' Day."

"Didn't used to have it. The school started it a few years ago so's the parents would have a chance to see their kids sometime during graduation. Because after graduation, every kid in town's off to the shore or some party somewhere."

"Huh." I hadn't attended my own graduation. But I was thinking that I might just attend this graduation, Tyler's graduation. "Graduation's late this year, isn't it?"

"Snow days. Kids had friggin' half of February off."

And then we talked some more.

And more, plenty more, all of it increasingly sketchy and gap-filled in my memory. I remember some things and not others. I remember a brief scare when someone burst into the bar and reported that they'd heard on the police scanner that the cops had caught the black kid in a drunk-driver trap on the River Styx Bridge.

Oh no, it's true, I thought. Crime doesn't pay. But then someone else pointed out that we hadn't even reported a crime, and I felt better.

I remember an increasingly testy war of words between you, Felicia, and Randy. Something about Tyler's graduation. You hadn't realized that Randy was going to be there with his ex-wife, and you weren't going to be there. You wanted to go. Randy preferred that you didn't, for what he felt were obvious reasons. You did not see the obviousness of his reasons. It got, if I remember correctly, a little unpleasant.

I remember baiting Randy, dangerously, about his thuggish past. I remember suggesting that he had once beaten up my fictitious brother, Charlie Fisk.

"No," he said, then, "Maybe." He thought about it. "I could have, but I don't remember it."

I remember suggesting to Randy that he'd been a kind of roving terror amongst the losers and dirtbags and faggots of LLLHS, whacking them when they got out of line, giving them what-for when they were asking for it.

"Yeah, well," Randy said, facetiously modest. "I guess. Probably. I had a lot of growin' up to do, truth be told."

And I remember one awkward exchange, very late in the evening. The beers, the shots, the libations had taken their toll. And I must have been, regrettably, trying to please. To impress. God only knows what combination of comments and retorts engendered the following.

"Fucking nigger," I said. "He'll get his, won't he?"

I remember the word feeling odd in my mouth. I must have been trying to pry one more outrageous comment from Trent's head. One more log for the fire of my hatred for him.

Trent looked at me soberly. "I don't like that shit," he said.

"What?"

"That word. Nigger."

"Nigger?" I was drunk, admittedly, but shocked, too. "But I heard you say . . ."

"Nigger? I don't think so."

"No." I concentrated, dimly. "Maybe it was somebody else."

"Felicia," Trent said. He looked chagrined. "She can be ignorant, sometimes. It ain't her pretty side." He thought about it. "That guy, he wasn't that dark. Arab, maybe. I don't know."

He let it go at that.

I must have said goodbye to everyone. I remember a flash of something, in the parking lot, some backslapping, hallooing farewell. I must have driven home, though I remember no part of it. I remember hunting and pecking, squinting, one-eyed, at the laptop. And then I woke up, crying, waylaid by hangover.

These fucking Sail Inn regulars. They'd be the death of me, if I weren't already the death of me.

§

In retrospect, firing that second shot was pretty stupid. The cops might have blown my head off—beating me to it by about eight hours—if they'd been more proactive and trigger happy.

Instead, luckily, the cops ducked behind the opened doors of their cruisers. Most of the onlookers ran back to the stores and the bar across the street.

"Do something, Bill!" somebody was yelling.

"He's gonna kill them!"

"He's executing people in there, and you're standing here with your thumb up your ass!"

"What the fuck am I supposed to do!" Mazzini was yelling back. "He's got people in there!"

"Not for long, it sounds like!"

We could hear all this pretty clearly in the shop because Mazzini's amplified bullhorn was still on and this argument was being blasted at us at teeth-rattling volume. I was standing with my shotgun pointed at the ceiling, another snowfall of plaster dust accumulating on my shoulders. Felicia and Alice were clutching the counter, looking stricken. And Randy was looking at me like he was calculating the odds of something.

It took me a moment to realize what it was he was thinking about. The shotgun.

"Don't even think about it," I said calmly. "This isn't some fucking bird gun. It's a military-issue Remington 870 close-quarters-combat shotgun. Five-round magazine capacity, plus one in the chamber. Four rounds left."

Trent still looked to be thinking, so I jacked another round into the chamber. That damned gun made a beautiful sound. No wonder our red-state brothers love them so much.

"Don't do it or I'll shoot you and one of them," meaning the girls, "right after you."

Which was utter bullshit, of course. But only I could be absolutely sure of that.

Trent and I looked at each other. We silently set aside the fiction that this was a situation that Trent was refusing to take seriously. Trent let out a breath and shrugged his shoulders. "Okay," he said.

Outside, onlookers were offering strategies to the cops.

"You need a sharpshooter. Pick him off."

"Tear gas. Lob a tear gas grenade in there. That'll get him out."

"Telescopic sight, bang. Get the bodybag."

"Guys," someone else was saying. "Guys."

"You offering your services, Tully?" Mazzini was saying. "Get the fuck back, why don't you?"

"I ain't leavin' cover. Nut'll shoot my ass."

"Concussion grenade's what you need. Stun grenade. Knock him on his ass."

"Guys. Bill?"

"Fuckin' idiot. He's got hostages in there. You can't throw a grenade in."

"Bill!"

"What!" Mazzini yelled.

"Your bullhorn is on." It was PJ talking. "Everybody inside half a mile can hear you guys talking."

"Shit!" There was an amplified clunk and the bullhorn was turned off.

I could see I needed a change of venue. I was still pointing the shotgun at Randy. I reached down with my free hand and picked up the cloth bag at my feet. Then I advanced on Trent and the girls.

"Move!" I said. "Into the back room!"

We all shuffled into the back room like we were prisoners on a chain gang. When we were far enough in, I kicked the door shut behind us with my foot.

"The theme of the next few hours," I said, this part rehearsed, too, "is this. Actions have consequences. Causes have effects. Every action has an equal and opposite reaction." I pointed the barrel of the shotgun very squarely at Trent's forehead, making a dramatic show of squinting and aiming. "Payback is a bitch."

"What's this shit you're talking, Nathan?" Trent said. "Nobody's gonna get hurt. Don't talk shit you don't mean."

"Let's start with your first question, Randy. I thought you wanted to know what I meant when I said that you don't even know who I am."

Trent tracked the permutations of this statement in his head. Then he said, "I know who you are. You're Nathan ..." He searched for it, for one of those names he was no good at, but it wasn't there. "Charlie's brother."

"There's no Charlie Fisk. No Nathan Fisk, either."

Trent grunted.

"Don't you even want to know who I am, Randy?"

"You're a fucking pain in my ass, is who you are. You got a beef with me, let's take it out in the alley, like men. And leave the girls out of it."

"Believe it or not, Randy, I didn't come in here, armed to the teeth, so that you could punch me silly one more time before I died."

"Too bad. Because you sure got it coming, the way you're carrying on in my store."

"I'm Nathan Huffnagle. You ruined my childhood. You ruined my life."

"Okay," Trent said, switching gears, processing. "You want to be a little more specific?"

"More specific? Why? How long is the list of people whose lives you've ruined? Do you have ruined people, hellbent on vengeance, coming in here every week? Should I take a fucking number? You ruined my life! You beat the living shit out of me on a weekly basis. You humiliated me for sport! You cost me an A in Spanish! You stunted my personality and made me emotionally incapable of forming meaningful long-term relationships with women."

"I . . . what?" Trent shook his head. "You mean, like, you can't get it up?"

"Emotionally incapable, you ignorant son of a bitch! Emotionally incapable!"

There was a brief silence. I was audibly panting, winded by recapping my life for an obtuse, oblivious thug.

"This is about a . . . a schoolboy grudge?" Alice said, disbelievingly.

"I told you," Felicia said. "He's some kind of nightmare misfit. The pariah from hell."

"This all happened a long time ago, right?" Trent said. "When we were kids. Is that what you're saying?"

"You know, I'd be getting a lot more satisfaction from killing you, if you'd extend me the simple courtesy of remembering who I am."

"You ain't saying I made you into some kind of faggot, are you?"

"Will you forget that last bit about women for a second? Okay? Can we focus on the big picture here? The senseless beatings and humiliations and tortures?"

"No, no, wait a minute," Alice was saying. "You mean you've been going around hating Randy Trent for . . . what? Twenty years?"

"Yes," I said. "Well, no. Not every day. Off and on. And it's been more than twenty years."

"Of hating Randy?" Alice was looking at me, wide-eyed. "Oh, Nathan. That's really sad."

"It's kind of a long story. But I've got it all written down. In my journal."

"Didn't . . . hasn't anything . . ." Alice didn't seem to know where to go with this, without being impolite. "Your journal?"

"He's the fucking kid nobody liked," Felicia snarled. "Jesus Christ, honey," meaning Alice, "every school has one."

"To be perfectly honest," I said, offended now, "I had already intended to kill myself before I ran across Trent here. That was a coincidence. I just happened to be in town." I shrugged. "So I figured, what the hell, kill two birds with one stone."

Nobody said anything.

"And hold on a fucking minute, anyway!" I yelled, dismayed suddenly at losing my forward momentum so easily. "Why do I have to explain myself? Why do I need a reason to kill this guy? Is there a statute of limitations for crimes of bullying and sadistic harassment?"

"Look, I ain't gonna swap ten-dollar words with you, Nathan," Trent said. "I'm getting the picture. I can see you're pissed off. As for whatever it is I've done—"

"Are Trent and I supposed to be even-steven now? Have bygones summarily been declared bygones? Is that what you guys are telling me? Because I beg to differ. I really do."

"—I ain't exactly proud of it. I was a little hell-raiser, I know it. I had a lot of growin' up to do."

"Not anymore, you don't." I was quivering now. I was a little beside myself, admittedly.

Trent started to say something else, then just put his hands on his hips.

"Actions have consequences, Trent. You can't make a horror of someone's life and just walk away. And not even remember that you did it. If that's possible, then all of life means nothing. Not just for me, but for everyone everywhere. By blowing your head off, I intend to restore reason and order to the lives of all people. It's a public service."

"You fucking fruitcake," Felicia hissed.

"That's a bit much, Nathan," Alice said.

True, it was all a little over the top. I knew it. But what the fuck? It was my show. And it wasn't like I was expecting to put on many more shows in my life. Why not indulge myself? Besides, I still believed, at that point, that there was a germ of truth in what I was saying. A germ of truth I'd been trying—and failing—to convey up until then.

"An eye for an eye, Randy," I said, trying again. "What goes around, comes around. Do unto others as you would have them do unto you. That's why we're here. Now. Sit down on the floor, please. All three of you."

They looked at me and then at each other. Randy moved to sit down first. Once he was sitting on the concrete floor, Alice set the shopping bag she was still clutching on the floor and sat, too.

Felicia looked at the two of them in disgust, then glared at me.

"If you think, for one moment, that I'm going to sit on this filthy floor, in this dress, then you're out of your mind, you fucking psycho." She put her hands on her hips. "This dress cost me three hundred dollars."

She was interrupted by a new sound, a dull pop and a tinkle. We all looked to the back of the room, to the back door. It was a mullioned, multipaned wood-and-glass thing, much abused. The little pane of glass nearest the doorknob was broken and a hand was reaching in, fumbling at the knob. The hand turned the little lock mechanism and withdrew. The knob rattled. Then the hand reached in again, turned the lock mechanism again, and withdrew once more. The knob turned this time and the door crept open.

I guess I should have been doing something. Shouting a command or firing at the door. Up until then, I guess I had been relying on an internal logic of hostage situations that I'd derived from TV. I would hold the hostages and talk to the people outside, and the people outside would stay outside and listen to me.

It hadn't occurred to me that the people outside might simply walk in.

§

June 26th, before midnight

The Mudhole is closed this year.

There's a stop sign bolted to the padlocked gate, and a square of plywood signage bolted to the fence beside the gate.

Beach closed. Trespassers will be prosecuted.

I'm the only trespasser risking prosecution tonight. Almost hanged myself on that fence, getting over it. Now I'm set up at one of the picnic tables by the shuttered snack bar, my laptop screen a homing beacon for every moth and mosquito and gnat within a five-acre radius. I'm already about halfway through the economy-size can of insect repellent I brought with me.

So. Why am I here?

To do some on-the-spot reporting, of course. To spice up this sometimes dreary suicide note with a bit of in-the-field journalism, straight from the scene of the crime. Albeit thirty years after the crime.

I've got all the tools a journalist needs. My laptop. Bug repellent. A six-pack of beer, rapidly warming inside a paper bag. A crowbar. A hammer. And a heavy-duty flashlight.

So let's get started.

There's no official notice posted, explaining why the beach is closed. If I had to guess, I'd say . . . high levels of bacteria caused by septic runoff from the houses on the surrounding hills. But it could be anything, really. Club membership decline. Legal travail. Budgetary shortfall.

This place isn't officially named the Mudhole, by the way. There's a big sign just inside the entrance that says Welcome to Lazy Cove, Property of the Lake Lenni Lenape Homeowners' Association. That sign was there thirty years ago, too. But nobody called this place Lazy Cove. They called it the Mudhole. Because that's what it was.

Every year, the Association would have sand trucked in. Then they'd watch it disappear, overtaken by the lake mud. That mud was always cool and slimy on your feet; it'd give you a November shiver in the middle of July. Every year, too, they'd spray herbicides in the early spring, hoping to check the explosive growth of the lake weeds. By August, those lake weeds, nourished by the aforementioned septic runoff, would retake the cove.

I've been down to the water line. The lake weeds have been left to do their own funky thing this year. The beach is ankle deep in decomposing plant life, and the water . . . well, it's like the Sargasso Sea out there. Stinks, too. Like nature at work.

The floating dock—once a safe offshore haven from eavesdropping parents—has been dragged ashore and left to rot, boardsprung and treacherous. The diving docks on the left side of the cove are rotting too, yawing this way and that on decrepit pilings.

THE END IS NEAR

Back here, behind the beach, the Yogi Bear monkey bars, the Huckleberry Hound teeter-totter, and the Magilla Gorilla merry-go-round have been ripped up and left to rust, piled against the perimeter fence. The sandbox has been overrun by the soft, humid turf, only two sides of it still peeking out of the soil. The swing supports are still here, a line of connected metal A-frames, but the swings themselves, the chains and seats, are gone. The Snagglepuss slide is still intact, surprisingly. Though I'm not tempted. Doesn't look like it would support my weight.

The snack bar is shuttered, as I've said. There's no way of knowing how long it's been since "Tainted Love" last boomed from its jukebox. Or "Safety Dance." Or "Young Turks." Thirty years ago, you could bring forty-five cents to the snack bar window and get a boiled hotdog on a damp bun. For sixty-five cents, you could wait at the window, grooving to "Tainted Love" for the seventh time that day, and watch as the proprietor tossed a frozen coin of beef on the grill for you. Fried onions, five cents extra.

In addition to the reporter's supplies catalogued above, I also brought an extra pair of shorts and a towel. I'd thought I might enjoy a little midnight dip, if I got this far. Until I saw the water, that is. And the beach.

Instead, memories will have to serve.

I can remember once, my Uncle Keith picking me up over his head, marching me from our family blanket to the lake, and throwing me into the water. Doing it over and over, knocking the breath out of me each time. I remember what an astonishing novelty it was, to be played with like that, roughhoused with. How it felt to hit the water, hard, each time. I can remember teasing Uncle Keith to get him to do it again. Again and again.

My Uncle Keith was my godfather. His visit, the only one I can remember, would have come during a rare break in the stormclouds of his debilitating clinical depression. Uncle Keith was one of those young men who went to Vietnam and came back forever changed. He joined the Marines to learn a job skill, something in the electrician's trade, and ended up in the jungle. When he returned, he holed up in his room in my grandparents' house, writing poems to his rifle and emptying beer cans for days on end. He did this for almost a year. He was not one of those guys who talked about the war. He never talked about anything, in my scant memories of him. He simply hunkered down and wrestled, grimly, silently, with demons he must have been no match for.

One afternoon in 1977—after the end of the war that snapped his twig—he got into his Ford Mustang and drove from New Jersey to Florida, draining beer cans and tossing them into the back seat all the way. Twenty-four hours later, he got out of the car, left the keys on the front seat, and jumped from the center span of the old Sunshine Skyway Bridge. My Uncle Keith—a better, wiser person than me—didn't leave a suicide note. He didn't have anything to say.

Now, readers. Don't make a face. Don't get exasperated.

I know it seems, by now, that every anecdote related to the Huffnagles ends with some pointless tragedy, some graceless sour note. You must be growing weary of it.

Well, I'm sorry. That's just the way it is with the Huffnagles. Our family history is like a killing field. Virtually anywhere you stick a spade in the earth, you're likely to find a skull, a broken toy, a torn dress, a bit of damning evidence. Something hastily buried and assiduously avoided.

We'll find more before we're through, I'm sure.

But enough wool-gathering. Off we go. Tonight's featured attraction involves a little breaking and entering. B&E, as you law enforcement types say. My second such infraction, for those keeping count.

I'm off to the bathhouse.

Whew.

Well. I'm back again.

THE END IS NEAR

And let me say that my second B&E was much more difficult than my first. This frigging decrepit, abandoned bathhouse that I'm crouched in, tapping away in, was fucking Fort Knox compared to Randy Trent's hearth and home. The men's and women's entrances to the bathhouse were padlocked and nailed shut. It took me a half-hour of muscle-straining, nail-squealing, wood-ripping work to get in here.

I hope you all appreciate the extracurricular effort I'm investing in this tale.

The bathhouse walls, benches, and ceilings—every interior wooden surface, just about—have been painted redwood-stain red. When the bathhouse first opened, everything was bare, handsome wood. Until it became graffiti-crammed chaos. Now it's red, wall-to-wall and floor-to-ceiling, though I'm not entirely sure that this lurid slaughterhouse effect is any improvement. Only the carvings remain, torn into the wood by determined youngsters with an especially urgent statement to make. Messages meant to stand the test of time. Steve n' Shelby. All fags die. Blow Me. Aerosmith Rocks.

The bathroom graffiti is gone, too, the metal stalls all painted a uniform dove gray. You never see bathroom stalls covered in writing anymore, the way you used to in the seventies. Another casualty of the Internet, like want-ads and record albums.

Kids today can't be bothered to do much, it seems. You never see them around anymore. I've been all over this town in the last few days. The ball fields, the basketball courts, the convenience stores—they're all empty. Where are the bands of kids, sitting on summer stoops, in summer heat, asking each other, Whaddeya wanna do? and answering each other, I dunno. Whatta you wanna do? Repeated ad infinitum as June wilts into July? They can't all be away at camp, right?

Whatever happened to Lake Lenni Lenape's youth gangs? Where do unruly, unsavory youths congregate? Where do they look for trouble?

A place like this—a fenced-in, padlocked, prohibited beach, late on a fine starry June night—should be a powerful magnet tugging at every immoral compass in town. It should be drawing "at-risk" youth like laptop light draws blood-thirsty mosquitoes. But there's nobody here. And it's not because of beefed-up police surveillance, either. I've been here almost three hours now—long enough to write some crap, to break, to enter, to write more crap, and to empty a huge can of bug repellent and three cans of beer—and I've seen one police car. That one cop passed through the parking lot, made one desultory sweep with his spotlight, and was gone.

You cops have got it easy. You're spoiled rotten. With kids like these—tame, unambitious kids, not especially dangerous to themselves or to others—you cops are really just meter maids with guns.

I've set my laptop up on a bench in the central showering/dressing area of the bathhouse. The showers and sinks in here are armored with grime and lightly coated with dust. The water is turned off, of course. As is the electricity. My flashlight is sitting on the floor, pointing up, throwing a cone of dust-moted light up onto the beams and boards and rafters of the high-vaulted ceiling. Dead bugs and birds and a few bats litter the floor. Nature will always find a way in.

There's a men's restroom on the right, ladies' on the left, flanking this center atrium which contains women's and men's shower and dressing facilities. These latter facilities were separated, in the seventies-modern way, by a wooden wall that rose to about eight feet high. Men on one side could hear, but not see, women on the other side. And vice versa.

Even in its heyday, this beach club had a reputation for seediness. It was the kind of down-at-heels place where harried commuter parents could drop off a station wagon full of neighborhood brats and then speed off, hoping that the little monsters would somehow stay out of serious trouble for three or four hours. And this bathhouse became the clubhouse for those little brats, a home base for monsters all too determined to find whatever trouble they could. Or make some of their own.

Usually, I'd avoid this place. I'd piss in the lake. I mean, why not? The way the town's waste removal was designed, septic systems draining inevitably downhill into the lake, the whole town was pissing in the lake every day. Occasionally, though, I'd have to take a crap. As kids sometimes do. And that meant a trip to the bathhouse. Such a trip might result in only casual, offhand hazing and abuse. Boilerplate, uninspired stuff. Hey, faggot. Go whack off somewhere else. Maybe a punch, in passing, to the stomach, the kidney. If there were enough adults in transit through the restroom—on a Saturday afternoon, say—I might even escape completely unscathed.

One day—it would have been the summer after my freshman year of high school—was different.

After the usual hour or so of suppressing my bowels, I'd reached the point of no return. I had to go. So I raced into the men's room, crapped as quickly as humanly possible, and headed for the door, bypassing the sinks. As it happened, I might as well have washed my hands. I wasn't going anywhere.

Randy Trent was waiting for me in the men's room doorway. As soon as I saw him I turned around and looked to the back of the men's room. There was a doorway there that led to the men's shower room. As a last-ditch, desperate means of escape, I could have fled through the men's shower room, clambered over the wall between the men's and women's shower areas, run through the women's shower room, the women's rest room, and out to safety. I'd done it before.

There were three people standing in the other doorway, the one behind me. A runty sometimes-sidekick to Randy Trent known to everyone as Muttley, a redheaded, freckled jock-turned-stoner named Tom Navely, and Steve Tolas.

When I saw Steve Tolas there, I knew I was doomed. Even more doomed than usual.

Steve Tolas was two, maybe three years older than the rest of us there in the bathhouse, and had already dropped out of school. He was one of those guys riding a completely different arc through life. He was the kind of guy who, when he dropped out of school, nobody tried to reach out to him, give him the guidance he sorely lacked. Instead, school administrators were relieved. They cleaned the illegal drug paraphernalia and dead pigeons and Nazi flags and kidnapped hitchhikers out of Steve's locker and thanked their lucky stars.

Years before this day in the bathhouse, Steve Tolas once climbed the rope in gym—one of those climbing ropes that all nonathletic boys fear like death itself—all the way to the top, past the finish point, high up into the gym rafters. And then he jumped, just to see what it would be like. I saw him do it. I remember him war-whooping and laughing, lying on a gym mat, his forearm broken, his shoulder completely dislocated.

Steve Tolas was the only guy in our high school known to have done heroin. Shot himself up in front of a wondering audience of queasy, timid suburban kids in the storage room of a 7-11 convenience store, during somebody's night shift. Then he threw up in the milk freezer. He possessed an astonishing collection of obscure pornography, at a time—the mid-seventies—when it was not widely available. Certainly not to kids. He delighted in tucking this stuff—peculiar British whipping and caning magazines, "barely legal" magazines, women-with-barnyard-animals photos—into teachers' lesson planners. He was, it was said, an inveterate and enthusiastic torturer of animals. He sometimes boasted—casually, offhandedly—of fucking his own sister.

He was, needless to say, crazy and off-putting and evil in an off-kilter way that made even the Randy Trents of the world a little awestruck, a little nervous. He's surely dead by now. Or in jail. Or dead and in jail, chained to a wall and decomposing in some third-world-country, suburban-basement torture chamber somewhere.

I turned back to Randy Trent.

"Hey, buddy," Trent said. "We're havin' a little party inside. Us and some girls. They say they want to meet ya." He said this in an easy, guileless manner. Not that there was any need for guile. Or the absence of guile. He had me exactly where he wanted me. How bad things got would depend on how bad he wished things to get.

"No," I said.

Trent grinned at this. "What's the matter, faggot? You don't like girls?"

"Faggots don't like girls," Muttley sang. He was close enough behind me to singsong this directly into my ear. Muttley was an obsequious stooge, born to play second banana to somebody, anybody. The more vicious and thuggish the first banana, the better. He was such an obsequious stooge that even Randy Trent couldn't stand him, most of the time.

Muttley was runty, as I've said, with big hands and big feet and bad teeth. He had a real name, though I can't remember it. I can't even look it up in our senior yearbook, because he isn't there. Two years after our bathhouse encounter, Muttley would enjoy the distinction of being the only member of our class to die before graduation.

Jackassing around on the lake one charmed June night at the end of junior year, three of Muttley's "friends" pushed him from the boat they were riding in. Going back to get him in the dark, they accidentally ran him over, chewing him up pretty good with the propeller. Muttley sank to the bottom and stayed there for three days before the lake mud gave up his bloated corpse. After he was killed, in deference to his killers—who didn't mean to kill him, after all, and who were, unlike Muttley, popular with their peers—Muttley and his untimely death were rarely mentioned.

Muttley's name appears nowhere in the next year's senior yearbook, not even as a cryptic aside in someone's "Memories" sidebar.

He was very alive on this summer day, though. But he was the least of my problems.

"Girls are gonna be awful disappointed," Steve Tolas said. He was at my other ear. Tolas seemed roughly twice my size. He had a goatee, an earring, plenty of ropy, sinewy muscle, and powerfully bad breath. Syrupy and sour and corrupt. Why such a person would enjoy torturing a slight, timid freshman, I don't know. Perhaps he viewed it as one step up from torturing squirrels and rabbits and cats.

"You're not afraid of girls, are ya, faggot?" Trent said.

"Come on, kid," Tolas said softly, insinuatingly, into my ear. "The girls are tired of giving us head. They wanna suck your little dick. Don't you want some?"

"No," I said.

"You know what?" Trent said to Tolas. "I heard you can cure faggots of being faggots with, like, shock treatment. You ever hear that?"

"I think I heard that." Tolas was still hovering dangerously by my ear. He grabbed me at the elbow and Muttley grabbed my other elbow. "You sure you don't want to help those hungry girls out?" Tolas continued. "Giv'em some of that dick they want so bad?"

"No," I said.

"Too bad."

And then Tolas did a frightening thing. He licked the side of my head.

I don't mean he gave me a peck or a quick lap or a smootch, either. I mean he licked the entire side of my head. His grip tightened painfully on my elbow and he grabbed my upper arm with his other hand. Then he licked my head, starting near my chin, moving up along my jaw, pausing to plunge his tongue into my ear, then continuing all the way up into my hairline. His tongue wasn't rough or dry like you'd hope, fervently, that it would be. It was wet and slimy and enthusiastic, especially when he crammed it into my ear. If I hadn't just taken a crap, I'm sure I would have crapped my pants right there. Steve Tolas was, as I've suggested, insane.

Trent grinned and shook his head, looking away.

Muttley, his cosmic life clock running down even as we stood there, giggled and yelped, "You like that, faggot, don't you?"

I shivered and shook my head.

"Am I making you nervous?" Tolas asked.

I gritted my teeth and said nothing.

"Because I don't mean to. I like to think that," and he paused here for effect, "I have a smile for everyone I meet."

This caught Trent by surprise and he laughed out loud.

"No, it's true. It's true." His grip tightened even more on my elbow. "See?"

Tolas was smiling. It was a different kind of smile, a terrible thing. I don't have words for that smile, and I'm glad I don't.

"Jesus," Trent said, still laughing. "C'mon, let's go meet the girls."

Tolas and Muttley turned me around and marched me to the back of the men's room, through the door, and into the men's bathhouse area.

There were two girls in the bathhouse. And a couple of guys. Tom Navely, who'd retreated to the bathhouse as soon as things got ugly, and another guy whom I'd never seen before. I remember this guy was smoking a cigarette and having nothing to say. That's all I remember about him.

"We found this kid outside," Tolas said, "but he don't want to fuck you both. We can't talk him into it."

"Which one ya want to fuck first, faggot? Sheila," Trent indicated Sheila, "or Candace?"

"Steve, you are so gross," Sheila said.

"Why don't you guys grow up already," Candace said.

"C'mon girls," Trent cajoled. "Little faggot's afraid of girls. Whyn't ya help him out a little? Give him an education."

What kind of girls frequented the bathhouse? Well, girls like Sheila and Candace. Candace, I knew—knew of, I should say, I didn't know any girls all that well—from school. Through the eighth grade, she'd been a wisecracking, high-spirited tomboy, a star of youth soccer and basketball teams. Upon entering high school, she'd suddenly given up sports, much like Tom Navely, and taken up a very specific ideal of femininity. In Candace's case, this meant trading high spirits for world-weary cynicism, taking up smoking, adding the word fuck to every other uttered statement, wearing entirely too much makeup, and wedging herself into comically tiny denim miniskirts and calf-high suede boots. She had flimsy blond hair, unsuccessfully feathered into that year's haircut, and a pink, heart-shaped face.

Sheila, I didn't know. She was high school age, and might have been a student at the county vocational-technical school. She had that vo-tech look—painter's pants, Converse sneakers, a grown-out pageboy haircut. She was birdy and big-eyed, like a newly hatched sparrow. She might have weighed ninety pounds.

She held out a flask of wine to me. In later years, I'd recognize that wine as a cheap, fortified wine that the kids called Mad Dog 20-20. On that day, though, I was still young enough to not know what it was exactly.

"Cheer up," she said. "Have a drink."

Trent reached out, swiped the flask from her hand, took a swig, and passed the bottle to Tolas. "You girls don't want to help us out, we're gonna have to go back to Plan A."

Tolas upended the bottle over his mouth and then passed it back to Trent, over Muttley's grasping hands. "What's Plan A?" he said.

"Shock treatment. Desperate situations call for desperate . . ." Trent was lost for a word.

"Measures," Candace supplied. "What the fuck is wrong with you jerks? Let the kid go."

The kid. Let the kid go. I was the same age as Candace. I'd once been an elf to her Mrs. Claus in a second-grade Christmas play.

"Shock tre-e-e-tment. Yez. I zeenk your diagnosis ees correct," Tolas said, hammily playing the demented Doctor Freud/Doctor Frankenstein. "For zee hopeless faggot. But vot to do?"

"The one cure that always works." Trent passed the flask to Candace.

"Ye-e-e-e-s?" Tolas was crouched forward, raising and lowering his eyebrows like an animal-torturing, sister-fucking Groucho Marx.

Trent was smirking at me. "The royal flush."

"The royal flush!" Tolas barked joyfully. "Not just the standard flush?"

"No, I think the royal flush is the way to go."

"Ah. Zen, I de-fair to your expert ope-e-enion."

"You fucking guys," Candace said. She sipped from the flask, winced, and handed it to Trent. "The kid's half your size. Why don't you just leave him alone?"

"Vee vill need some pe-e-e-s? Eh?"

"Or shit," Trent said. "Girls?"

"What?" Candace said.

"Follow us."

Tolas and Muttley manhandled me around and we double-timed it across the men's shower area and back into the men's rest room, Trent a step behind us. I'm not sure if Navely and the nameless guy came with us or not. They may have had something to say during all this, as I'm sure Muttley did, but I can't remember any of it. Things were happening very fast, by now.

"Ladies?" Tolas called out. They hadn't followed us. In fact, we could hear them clambering back over the changing room wall to the women's side of the bathhouse.

"Fuck."

And we were on the move again. Out the front door, across the little vestibule in front of the bathhouse, and into the women's bathroom.

I remember there was an older woman washing her hands at a sink, a little girl, most likely her granddaughter, standing behind her, waiting for her to finish. The woman looked at our merry band charging in and just shook her head. She would have heard the carrying on in the shower/dressing area and would have been accustomed to the shenanigans associated with the bathhouse.

"You kids shouldn't be in here," this woman, my only hope, said.

"Fuck off, grandma," Steve Tolas said. "We're busy here."

And the woman left, little girl in tow. I remember that little girl's face, receding, being tugged away. The wondering look in her eyes, the thumb planted in her mouth, the way she seemed to be processing information, information she'd need later in life, as she watched me being dragged toward the stalls. And then they were gone.

"Which one's your favorite, Sheila?" Tolas said. "Which one do you usually use?"

"What?"

Candace and Sheila had appeared at the back of the ladies' room.

"For blowjobs, sweetheart. This one?" Tolas kicked open a stall door.

"Fuck you," Sheila said.

"Alright. Use this one."

"What!" Sheila giggled explosively.

"Use it! Faggot here wants the full royal-flush treatment." Tolas abruptly palmed my chin in one huge hand and rocked my head around to face Sheila. "Look at this guy. Who could say no to this sweet face?"

"I'm not pissing in front of you guys!"

"You know," Candace said, "you guys are beneath contempt. I'm out of here."

"We'll close the door. Now get in there."

"No! Get somebody else! Candace!"

"Are you out of your fucking mind?" Candace said. "What do I look like?"

"Sheila," Trent said.

"What?" Warily.

"Do you want a ride home later? Or do you want to walk home again?"

"Guys!"

"In!" Trent yelled, like you'd issue an order to a recalcitrant puppy.

Sheila swiped the wine flask from Trent's hand, drank a big swallow, and pushed it back into his hands. Then she scampered into the stall and shut the door.

"You guys owe me one," she said. As if she were doing some simple, commonplace favor. And then, "You guys are not leaving me here again."

I had started to struggle by then. I popped free of Muttley's grip. Trent pushed Muttley out of the way and caught up my flailing arm. I yelled out and Tolas twisted my other arm. Then there was just the sound of my heavy breathing.

"What's going on out there!"

"Nothing! Piss already, will ya!"

"I can't piss, if you guys are out there listening! Say something!"

"Hey," Tolas said over my head to Trent, "why did the blonde have lipstick all over her steering wheel?"

"I don't know," Trent said. I was struggling mightily, but there wasn't a tremor in either voice. "Why?"

"She tried to blow the horn."

Sheila giggled and started to pee. We could hear it outside, a real cascade of urine for such a tiny girl. The wine, no doubt.

"You guys are pigs," Candace said. She hadn't made good on her promise to leave.

Tolas gave Sheila a decent interval of time, about seven seconds, and then kicked in the door. Sheila yelped, but kept peeing. As she peed, I remember, she looked off into the space above our heads, maintaining, I guess, some sense of decorum.

"Hurry up," Trent said. "We're on a medical mission of mercy here."

"Mental," Tolas said. "Faggotry is a mental condition."

"Whatever."

Sheila wiped and leaped up, tugging her pants up as she slipped past us. Someone chopped at one of my knees and I pitched forward, hitting my head on the toilet rim.

"Oops," Trent said. "Sorry, faggot."

There were hands in my hair and my head was wrenched back and then forward and I was drowning in piss and stale toilet water. The cartilage in my nose was grinding and cracking on the porcelain; my jaw was popping; one of my teeth felt chipped, broken. And there was no air. I was drowning.

Do you know, can you guess, what this feels like?

I hope I'm not upsetting you, dear readers. Miz and Tyler and Felicia. I certainly don't mean to offend any tender sensibilities with this graphic account. You cops in the audience, I'm sure you've all heard and seen worse.

But I'm curious. Do you know what this feels like?

Not drowning. I'm not talking about drowning. I would have gladly drowned at that point. I would have welcomed drowning with a glad and eager soul.

I'm talking about being utterly, grotesquely humiliated and beaten by a group of people. Tormented by a group of people united in their indifference to your very being.

Do you?

It feels like the world has turned against you. Like everything that you thought you knew has turned out to be something else entirely. Turned inside out, reversed, upended. Turned, not just into something else, but into something unrecognizable, something alien. And something united in its hatred of you.

You rack your brain, trying to determine what you could have done to be worthy of such hatred. What is it that's so wrong about you, so powerfully wrong, that it has inspired this savage act of brutality?

There's no useful response, no helpful rationalization that applies to being attacked like that.

Outrage and fear. The simple arithmetic of self-hatred. That's all there is.

I could go on about man's inhumanity to man. The psychology of the crowd. On and on. But why? It didn't help then and it doesn't help now. It doesn't mean shit anyway.

Eventually, they let me up. Trent and Tolas swung me out of the stall and pitched me, hard, against the wall. I remember sliding down the wall. Trent and Tolas and Muttley probably had some other things to say, but I don't remember what they were.

Candace was still there. She hadn't left. I remember her and Sheila, crouching over me, Candace asking, "Are you alright?"

No, I wasn't alright. If it's possible to pick a worst part of this whole experience, then perhaps the looks on their faces were the worst part. Looks of pity and revulsion and fascination. I didn't say anything. They left then, to rejoin their heroes, who were already yukking it up, back in the bathhouse.

"Don't let it get you down," Candace said, before she left. "They're just fucking jerks."

I never went to the beach club again. I never swam in the lake. I simply refused to go. As it happened, refusing to go wasn't all that difficult. The unraveling of Huffnagle family life was already progressing to the point where beach trips—like most other social outings—were falling to the wayside.

I've moved my laptop to the bathhouse entrance. It's after five o'clock now and the sky above the hilltops is leaking indigo and the edges of things are emerging, firming up in that predawn half-light like the stunned un-light after a flashbulb flash.

Time for this ghost, this last ghost from the past—a past abandoned, nailed-up, redwood-stained, forgotten—to retreat from the light of the new day, to evaporate like the morning damp.

§

"Who the hell are you?"

"Danika."

"Who?" There was a young girl—sixteen, seventeen, at most—standing in the back doorway of the shop. She was a slight girl, olive-complected, with large, solemn eyes and waist-length black hair. She wore a huge pair of mid-calf-length, many-pocketed shorts, tied at her tiny waist with a long strip of brightly colored cloth, big chunky black shoes, a somber-hued paisley vest, and a frayed, black T-shirt. Her eyes were heavily mascaraed; her lips and nails were painted a matching glossy silver.

"Danika. It's my witch name. It means Morning Star."

"This is a bad time," Trent said. "The store's closed."

"No kidding. So's the whole street."

"What are you doing here?" I said.

"Helping you, Clyde. You know you didn't even have this door locked?"

"He doesn't need any damned help, you little ... witch!" Felicia sputtered.

"You have to leave." I pointed the shotgun at Danika. Well, in her general direction. "Get out."

"Why?"

"Because it's dangerous in here."

"Oh, please." Danika turned and closed the door behind her, locking it. Her black hair had a long, white streak in it, crown to waist, evidently dyed. "I'm the most dangerous thing in here, believe me." She looked around, her eye stalling on Felicia. "Is she helping you? Or is she a hostage?"

"She's a hostage."

"Then why is she standing up?"

"Well, she's . . ." I shrugged. "It's a new dress."

"Uh huh." Danika was looking around some more, sizing things up. "PJ's outside saying you have a shotgun, a pistol, and some kind of suicide bomb. That true about the bomb?"

"No. I have two grenades, but they're kind of old. Like, collector's pieces. They might not work."

"Too bad. Doesn't hurt, them thinking you're wired to blow, though." Danika took a few steps forward and peeked into the cloth bag that I had dropped to the ground. Then, before I could properly register what she was doing, she reached into the bag and lifted out the pistol.

"Hey!" I yelled. I raised the shotgun.

"Chill out, Clyde." She expertly released the revolver's cylinder, inspected the chambers, and shut the weapon. "Is that shotgun army issue? You been buying militia hardware?"

"Hey," I said again, more softly, wounded. "I don't even know who you are. I could have shot you just now, you know."

"Not likely."

"How do you know?"

"I'm a witch. Maybe I read your mind." She was peering into the bag again. "You're such a desperado, you packed yourself a snack." Now she was pawing through the bag's contents. "What's this other stuff you got in there?"

"Nothing."

"You brought reading material to a shootout?"

"It's not reading material," I said defensively. "It's ... a journal."

Danika was looking pointedly over my shoulder. "Heads up, Clyde," she said.

I turned to find Trent in a half crouch.

"Sit down," I said. I pointed the shotgun at him.

Trent didn't move.

"Sit down," Danika said. She raised the revolver.

Trent sat back down.

"Give me that gun," I said.

"It was a good idea, letting PJ go. It can't hurt to have someone on the outside, telling the cops what a dangerous character you are." Danika handed me the gun. "Especially a dumb fuck like PJ, who's easily impressed."

"How old are you?"

She looked at me calculatingly. "Nineteen."

"Oh, come on."

"You mind if I ask you a question?"

"Yes. Yes, I do."

"Did you lock the front door?"

"Did I—" Lock the front door. Of course not. "Does it matter?" Already, I was asking for advice.

Danika made a face and walked past me, through the door into the front of the shop. I heard the front lock ka-chunk into place. Then she was back.

Almost immediately, phones all over the shop began to ring. One of them was located on the wall by the door to the front area. I tucked the pistol into the waist of my shorts at the back, being careful not to shoot myself. Then I went to the phone and picked it up.

"Hello?"

"Nelson?"

"No," I said.

"Who am I speaking to?"

"Nathan," I said. "Nathan Huffnagle."

"Oh. Right. Sorry." There was a raspy sound, like a hand placed over the receiver, then, "Sorry, Nathan. This is Sheriff Albert Woods of the Lake Lenni Lenape Sheriff's Department. Everything okay in there?"

"Sure."

"There was a shot fired earlier. No one's injured? Everyone's okay?"

I looked over at my hostages. Trent was sitting with his back to a metal pole, scowling up at Danika. Alice was sitting cross-legged on the floor, clutching her shopping bag. Felicia was taking one of her heels off and glaring at me.

"Yeah. Everyone's okay."

"Good. That's good. We want to keep the shots fired to a minimum, huh?"

"Sure. I guess."

"Right. Can I ask you now . . . there seems to be some discrepancy about exactly who all's in there. With you."

"Okay."

"My information is . . . Randy Trent. A Ms. Felicia Fowler. And Alice . . ." More rasp. "No last name."

"Alice," I said. "What's your last name?"

"Chang," she said.

"Chang," I said.

"Thirty or so? Short black hair?"

"Yes."

"Okay. Trent, Fowler, Chang. They're in the back of the shop. With you. And uninjured. Am I right?"

"Yes."

"Okay. Now. Is there a fourth person in there with you, Nelson? Sorry. Nathan."

"Not exactly."

There was a pause, then, "You want to clarify that, Nathan?"

"Not an official person, no."

Albert let a reproving silence gather around that last reply. Then he said, "I'm just asking for information that will help us both. Right?"

"I guess."

"So who's the girl?"

I lowered the phone from my ear and looked at Danika. "Who are you?"

"I told you. Danika. It means Morning Star."

I raised the phone. "Can I get back to you?"

"Do you have a . . . a partner, in there, Nathan?"

"Can I get back to you, Albert?"

"There's nothing else you want to say?"

"No. Not at this time."

"Okay, then. Sure. Sure thing. Nathan?"

"Yeah?"

"You can call me Woody. Everybody does."

"Woody. Okay." I hung up the phone.

"He wants information," I said to Danika.

"They're waiting to hear your demands," Danika said. She had hoisted herself up onto a stool by the door, her blocky black boots swinging a foot off the ground. "They want to know what you want. Why you're doing this."

"I don't have any demands."

"You need to make some up, then."

"Why?"

"Because there are two kinds of hostage takers, Clyde. People who want something, and thrill-killing nutzoids."

"My name's not Clyde."

"If you're the second kind, that makes everybody outside very nervous. That makes everybody start thinking they better get in here sooner instead of later."

"Sooner." I turned and looked stupidly at the door to the front of the store. "Very soon?"

"Woody and Bill are just jumped-up park rangers. But the pros will be here any minute. Woody surely already has a call out to the state police."

"Oh." I thought about it. I turned back to Danika. "What should I want?"

§

June 27th, 11am

I've made an unsettling discovery.

I'm going off-topic here, loved ones of Randy Trent and Lake Lenni Lenape police, so feel free to skip to the next entry.

This morning I was clearing out the dining room junk heap when I came upon my sister Sherilyn's old toybox. Inside it, I found hundreds of old family photos, still tucked in the return envelopes provided by the photo developer, plus dozens of decaying 8mm home-movie reels, holiday cards, academic progress reports going back to elementary school, high school yearbooks, sports and scouting badges, and much more. I had no idea any of this stuff still existed.

I also found a sheaf of letters, rubberbanded in a neat stack, written by my sister to my mother, going back thirteen years, starting about six years after Sherilyn dropped off the map with Caleb the Jesus groupie. Two letters a year, pretty regularly, up to the last one, dated four months ago. There's also a writing tablet containing an unfinished letter from my mother to my sister, presumably my mother's last letter.

The letters are . . . disconcerting, to say the least. My sister is no longer married to Caleb the Jesus groupie. She escaped the Montana religious commune they had moved to—a commune where certain unorthodox living arrangements and conjugal practices were encouraged, if I read my sister's veiled descriptions correctly—and moved to a town in another western state. Once there, she was forced to obtain a restraining order against both Caleb and the commune. The People's Sect for the True Interpretation of God's Word. This would have been my sister's second restraining order against a significant other.

My sister had a baby boy, Isaiah. Not, evidently, Caleb's. Caleb—or some other member of the Sect, or the Sect itself—tried to make a legal claim on the boy, but that was resolved somehow. In my sister's favor.

She has another boy, Carson, by a man she lives with now. He's a well-driller of some sort, named, improbably, Rambo. They've lived together for seven years. They have a house somewhere. Sherilyn seems to have climbed through the ranks of some big telemarketing company out there, into a middle-management position.

And she seems happy. Happy in the bluff, no-nonsense way that my brother Thomas was master of, when he was alive. Happy in a way that I can't connect at all to the bruised, broken-winged, lost soul who disappeared from here, all these years ago.

It's difficult to properly express my surprise, my consternation, my happiness, at the details in these letters. She has two boys she loves, a companion she loves. A life. A sturdy, useful, good-humored view of the world, of life, of her place in it.

Sherilyn.

The thing is . . . everything worked out. It turned out okay.

And there's more. Sherilyn has been in contact with my brother's widow and children. So had my mother. Two years ago, Sherilyn and Rambo and Sally, my brother's widow, and Sally's second husband Matt and all the kids vacationed in Disney World. There are pictures of them there, cavorting amidst the pre-packaged, prefab Disney fun. I didn't know there was a Matt. At least one of these kids—Cody? Trevor?—is new to me.

They're being a family. A big, extended family. Go figure.

It never even occurred to me to contact my brother's widow to tell them Mom was dead. Thomas died twenty-three years ago. I'd figured—quite naturally, I'd supposed—that everyone had moved on. I'm astonished to discover that they were still staying in contact. That the gossamer, tenuous strands of family life were unbroken. It never occurred to me that anyone would give a shit.

As for my sister, she obviously doesn't know Mom's dead. After Mom died on the floor of the FoodKing, the authorities came to me. The oldest son. The only living relative they had an address for. My mother left no will, so the lawyers never knew my sister was still in the picture. They just started doing what lawyers do. Carving up my mother's meager estate into taxes and lawyer's fees.

There's more here, in these letters. Things I can't even put into words on the laptop screen. Not yet. Things about me. About our family. About the past. About what happened and what they've made of it. I don't even know where to start.

And this probably isn't the place for it, anyway.

§

"Don't you want anything?"

"No," I said. "Nothing from them." Meaning the cops outside.

"Oh," Danika said. "So you are a thrill-killing nutzoid."

"No, I'm not," I said, offended. "I'm here to kill him." I indicated Trent with the barrel of the shotgun. "It's not a nutzoid thing. I have legitimate grievances."

"What kind of grievances?"

"Personal stuff. You missed that part. And I really don't want to go back over it again."

"But if it's a personal thing, why do it here? You could've ambushed him in his house and had a good chance of getting away. Here, you're boxed in."

"Because he needs an audience, that's why," Felicia said, fuming. "Because his mother took his binky away when he was a baby."

"That's not true," I said. "The truth is—" I turned back to Danika. "The truth is, I don't have any plans to escape. This is it. I'm going to kill myself."

"Well, don't let us hold you up." Felicia again. "Go for it, loser."

"Cops get wind of that, they'll be in here like old ladies at a bake sale." Danika went to the door to the front room. She cracked it open and peeked outside. "You need to start thinking of some demands. Something to make the cops think you can be reasoned with."

When I'd pictured this climactic final confrontation in my mind, I'd imagined myself striding the room purposefully, shotgun in hand, presenting my case against Randy Trent like a seasoned trial lawyer, making cogent point after cogent point. Any hostages or bystanders present—perhaps even Randy Trent himself—would be forced to recognize the validity of my arguments.

If my spoken words, imperfectly remembered and laboriously longhanded here, should start sounding canned or stilted or preachy, it's probably because I'm reciting some stray tag-end of pre-prepared rhetoric. Something from those overheated daydreams.

Anyway, the reality is, hostage situations keep you hopping. They're just one crisis after another. There's little room for eloquence or dramatics. Cops and onlookers and hostages aren't the meek sheep you'd hope they'd be. They're a real piece of work, let me tell you.

"Showtime," Danika said. "Here come the state boys."

"Damn it! Already?"

There was a commotion outside, a hubbub of police radio chatter, slamming doors, and shouted orders and requests.

"I told you, it wouldn't take long. There's a state trooper barracks out on I-80, about fifteen minutes from here." Danika moved away from the cracked-open door. "Take a look."

I hesitated, looking at my hostages and then at the door. Danika came back to me and held her hands out.

"Okay," I said. "But you have to give it back."

"Sure. It's your show, Clyde."

"I wish you'd stop calling me that."

I handed her the shotgun and she went to a spot at the side of the room, about ten feet from Trent and Alice and Felicia. She stood there with the gun pointing at the floor.

I went to the cracked-open door. Outside, there were two vans with New Jersey state trooper markings and the words Emergency Response Unit on their sides, plus two new patrol cars, both state trooper issue. A lot of state troopers were milling about, holstering and unholstering weapons and taking their big round-brimmed hats off and tugging them back on.

There were a lot more civilians out there, too. Maybe seventy or eighty, by now. They'd all been herded back across the road. People were standing on the bumpers and hoods of parked vehicles, on newspaper vending machines and overturned garbage pails, and on the low brick wall in front of Nan Pratt's store. A kid had climbed onto the roof of Salvatore's Pizza and was helping other kids up. A lot of these people were speaking into cellphones and peering intently into the front of A&B Auto Parts, reporting on the nothing-much that was happening in here.

One of the parked vehicles was a van with a dish antenna and a little stage on its roof. A technician was up there, wrestling lights and a boom mike into place. A young woman climbed a ladder on the back of the van and joined the technician. She was joined by a pony-tailed guy who started fussing with the woman's hair and tweaking her suit. A spotlight popped on behind the woman, a ghostly blue-white dazzle in the late-afternoon sun. WNNJ News8 was lettered on the side of the van. First with the Facts.

"I can't believe it," I said. "There's already a TV crew here."

As I said this, the crowd across the street parted and another van appeared. CNN.

Behind me, the phone rang.

"Maybe that's the TV guys, now."

"Not likely," Danika said. "You'll be talking to cops from here on out, unless you demand media access. Speaking of which," the phone was on its fourth or fifth ring, "you think of something you want yet?"

We watched the phone ring for a while. It rang an eighth time, a ninth, a tenth, then fell silent.

"Yeah," I said. "I have."

§

June 27th, 3:15pm

Here's something that Randy Trent and I have in common. Neither of us attended our high school graduation ceremony.

Randy never graduated at all. He dropped out of high school in the early spring of senior year. And I, well . . . I had a lot on my mind, that spring. My father had self-destructed and my mother had been bedroom-slippering around the house in a silent daze for months by the time June rolled around. My younger brother had effectively moved out and my sister was doing whatever it was eleven-year-olds from broken homes do, to cope with things.

I could have gone to graduation anyway, of course. I could have skulked across that platform to polite, distracted applause, collected my sheepskin, orbited a few glad circles of celebrating families and friends, turned in my gown, and then walked the long walk home to the haunted house I lived in.

I could have, but I didn't. A lot had changed, that spring. And I'm not referring solely to the family implosion cited above, either. I had changed. Over the course of one very long night in March I had stopped being the person I had been and had become a person very much like the person I am today.

Oh, don't worry. I'll be getting to that story, too. In time.

So the high school graduation I attended today was my first. I can't say for sure that it was Randy's first. But I suspect it was.

How about you, Felicia? Not your first graduation exercise, right? I'm assuming you're a high school graduate.

Imagine my surprise to discover that you and I, Felicia, also have something in common. Not only are we both stalkers, but we're both stalking the same person. Different motivations, obviously. Yours amorous, mine homicidal. But still, quite a coincidence.

I'm sorry if my presence made you uncomfortable today. We must have made a comical sight, desperately avoiding eye contact with each other and ducking simultaneously every time Randy or the ex-Miz Trent turned to look up at the back rows of the bleachers, where we were hiding in our opposite corners.

I liked your disguise. The scarlet and gold LLLHS tee-shirt and matching cap, pulled low, were inspired touches. You blended right in with the crowd, while I, in my ridiculous camouflage jacket and geeky sunglasses, stood out like a sore thumb. Stood out like a homicidal stalker at a graduation ceremony.

And you, Miz Trent! You looked like quite the proud mama. Politely applauding each new graduate, then standing up and frantically clapping for your own boy. Snapping cellphone pictures and zipping them off to loved ones. At the same time, I thought you looked a little stiff and unhappy in such close proximity to your former hubby. You two barely spoke and there was very little of that just-friends vibe that divorced couples sometimes share. I'm just guessing based on body language, though. I know so little about you. Not even your first name. I'm still working on that.

Tyler, you looked very nice, very dignified, in your scarlet and gold gown and cap. Your dad could tell you that the scarlet and gold of the Lake Lenni Lenape Scarlet Storm used to be the scarlet and gold of the Lake Lenni Lenape Braves. They're the Scarlet Storm now, in deference, I imagine, to the sensibilities of Native Americans.

There are no Lenni Lenape sensibilities to offend anymore, it should be said. The Lenni Lenapes were musketed, bludgeoned, smallpox-blanketed, evicted, and exterminated with such cunning efficiency by emigrant Europeans that there are none left today. It's said—probably inaccurately, but what the fuck, if you want unimpeachable historical veracity, read somebody else's suicide note—that the last Lenape, one Indian Hannah, died in Pennsylvania's Chester County poor house in 1802 or so. There's a big old marker there, a boulder bearing a metal plate, attesting to the sad fate of the Lenni Lenape. I know, I've seen it myself.

But I digress.

THE END IS NEAR

The school colors are still the same, an autumnal scarlet and gold once meant to evoke red-skinned warriors in their buckskin loincloths and moccasins. Now meant to evoke, I don't know, luridly unsettled weather. And though I'm no expert, this being my first graduation, I suspect that the other things I saw today on the LLLHS football field haven't changed much either, over the years. The loyal sons and daughters of Lake Lenni Lenape still cheer lustily as the valedictorian's speech winds down and the band kicks into Pomp and Circumstance. Everybody still tosses their tasseled mortarboards into the air and hugs everybody else. Everybody still poses for pictures taken by and with proud papas and mamas. And everybody still has a little nostalgic tear in their eye.

Even me.

I'm sitting here in my car now, at the back of the student parking lot, alternately pecking away and sniffling, like a fool. Over what, I don't know. Myself, most likely. Most pathetically. My wasted life. My ignominious end.

When I left this town twenty-seven years ago, I was determined to never again let anyone destroy my spirit. The way Randy Trent had. The way my father had, with his interchangeable silences and rages. Those two architects of my despair—Randy Trent and my father—slipped out of town months before I did. When I left, when I went off to college that September, I swore no one would ever again have that kind of power over me.

That worked for a while, as a life philosophy. But I guess I must have needed something more, something for the long term that I never figured out.

There are still some stragglers here in the parking lot, parents hanging on to their kids for one more word, one more hug, one more photo, before they slip away, gone, into the future. You're long departed, Tyler. Escaped with your friends, impatient to raise postgraduate hell in some lake cabin or Jersey shore beach house. Your mom and dad are gone, departed their separate ways under the watchful eye of you, Felicia. And now, Felicia, you're gone, too. Only I remain, remembering.

In my father's absence, events of senior year came and went, things didn't get done. At home, bills didn't get paid, services were discontinued and shut off, graduation preparations were never made, and the silence was disturbed only by the muttering of my mother's TV.

But this isn't the story of my father and mother, is it? It's supposed to be the story of Randy Trent. That's why you're here, isn't it, Tyler and Miz and Felicia?

So on we go.

Randy Trent's departure was like the end of an enemy occupation of my life's territory. One day in April, the enemy just packed up its half-tracks and troop carriers and tanks and jeeps and left town. And the townspeople—that is, me— emerged, creeping from our war-ravaged houses, blinking and squinting in the light of day, listening with rapt fascination to the eerie silence of post-occupation.

Those days were marked, not by jubilation and partying in the streets, not by the ringing of church bells and the random flashbulbed smooching of GIs and liberated local girls, but by a bone-deep stillness. A profound and otherworldly absence of effect.

Randy Trent had waited until April of senior year to drop out. He rode the high school ride right through to the last event for which the old rites—the social order, letter jackets, lunch table cliques, a date for Saturday night, the respect afforded those with a reputation for easy violence and thuggery—would apply. The senior class trip in March. And then he got off. When he dropped out, he did so with great finality. He didn't linger around. He disappeared. I never saw him again, until a few days ago. By the time he left, everyone was looking the other way, to college and a future unconstricted by the boundaries of Lake Lenni Lenape.

For Randy, the future evidently meant auto parts. Perhaps he knew, even then, that he'd be out-earning almost all of us—smug future insurance adjusters and human resources managers and ad writers—in the short term and over the long haul, too.

But that winter and spring of our senior year, it must not have felt that way to Trent. It must have felt like all of life had become, overnight, preparation for a big party to which he wasn't invited.

Or maybe not. Maybe only I think that way. Maybe I'm projecting my own grim, sterile self-absorption onto obtuse Randy Trent.

I don't know.

I meant to say something here and I see it's gotten away from me. It was important, whatever it was, and I see it's not here, in these words on the screen.

Let me start over.

I remember this.

Listen up.

I remember hitting two home runs in a softball game in gym class, in the second week of June of that year. I would have been one of only a handful of seniors on the field that day, the other seniors taking full advantage of a school tradition that allowed them to cut classes at will, to wander the hallways, saying goodbye to teachers and classmates, exchanging yearbooks and droll, inked yearbook witticisms.

And I remember thinking—I remember this distinctly—thinking no, let's not go, let's stay, let's start over, let's do this thing right. Knowing, even as I thought this, that many of my peers had already done this thing right, or done it as right as they cared to, and were glad at the chance, finally, to move on. And it felt like it was only me, alone, rounding those bases, heading for home among bored, impatient underclassmen, that wanted to stop the clock, to start again.

I brought my high school yearbook with me today. It was packed along with the faded photos, crumbling film stock, and yellowing report cards in Sherilyn's toybox. I don't believe I'd ever laid eyes on this book before this morning. It might have been mailed to my mother's house after I left for college.

It took an effort of will just to lift its scarlet leatherette cover, embossed with the since-discarded Brave logo. There isn't a handwritten word in its pages, of course. Otherwise, it's packed with all of the stuff that packs everyone's yearbook. Team photos and highlights, blurbs about theater productions and academic clubs, threadbare jests about study halls and cafeteria food and scholarly misadventures. Cutest Couple. Class Cut-Up. Girl Mostly Likely To. Arty overexposed portraits of empty playing fields, snogging teen lovers in the distance, holiday dances and such, all meant to convey the fleeting nature of high school life, of life in general.

And there's a picture of me. I can't for the life of me remember this picture, this posed senior photo, being taken. But there I am, staring vacantly into the top right corner of the page, in jacket and tie, underneath a bad haircut, a crumpled smile on my face. The way the pages of senior photos were laid out, the pictures are distributed ten to a page, the pictures around the border and the senior bios and farewells all grouped together in the center. Page after page, ten photos and ten bios.

The page my photo occupies looks like all the others. You'd have to be counting the bios or looking for me specifically to see the difference. Nine bios, nine senior farewells, fill the middle of the page. I never submitted one. My name isn't on the page either. Just my photo.

The effect is an odd one. It's like one of those doctored photos offered as proof of the existence of ghosts. The family Christmas photo with the half-transparent image of the recently deceased child, standing and smiling enigmatically by the tree. The family barbecue picture with the reflected image in the glass patio door of someone who couldn't, shouldn't be there, surely not long-departed Grandmother Rose.

That's me. The ghost in the frame. There, but not there.

§

"Okay," I said. "We've got a lot to do and very little time to do it." I pointed the shotgun at Felicia. "You need to sit down."

"And you need to go fuck yourself."

I nodded at this, unsurprised, and looked around. I went to a coat rack in the corner and lifted a heavy gray rain slicker from it. I tossed this at Felicia's feet.

"Sit," I said.

"Eat shit," she said.

"You know, Felicia," I said, "I'm surprised we're getting along so poorly. I thought we had a lot in common."

"In your dreams, you little shitheel weasel."

Danika was looking from me to Felicia and back to me. She sighed a world-weary teenager's sigh. Then she went off to the racks of stockpiled parts, tall metal racks that filled the left side of the room. She was gone for a moment and then reappeared with two quarts of motor oil and a plastic bucket. She set the pan on the floor, removed the caps from the containers, and poured the oil into the bucket. She set the containers aside and lifted the bucket.

"Sit down," she said.

Felicia's mouth curled into a sneer. "You wouldn't dare."

"Really?" Danika tilted her head, curious. "Why wouldn't I?"

They looked at each other until Danika said, quietly, "Three."

"Randy!" Felicia said.

"Two." Danika hefted the bucket, the oil slopping back and forth.

"Sit down, Felicia," Randy said.

"One."

"Fuck!" Felicia kicked off one heel, then the other. She peeled her slinky dress a little higher on her hips and, using Randy as a brace, lowered herself into an awkward sitting position, the dress bulging dangerously. When she was down, she balled up her fist and struck Randy in the shoulder.

"You useless son of a bitch! Why won't you do something!"

"I am doing something. I'm sitting down."

"If shitheel here can't manage to shoot me later, maybe he can ask you to do it. You're so fucking obliging."

"Stand up, Randy."

Randy looked at me. "Why?"

"Just get up."

He got up.

"Fucking A," Felicia said, "now it's musical chairs."

"Get out of those clothes."

"What?" Randy said, incredulously. "Why?"

"Because I said so."

"See? I told you," Felicia said, disgusted. "He's got some weird shit planned."

"What's going on?" Randy said.

"It's not enough he's got us in this filthy storeroom at gunpoint," Felicia was ranting. "Now he thinks he's gonna play weird sex games with us. Make up for a lifetime of never getting laid."

"Get undressed. Now."

"I don't think that's a good idea, Nathan," Randy said. "We got a mixed crowd here. This girl here is what . . . fifteen?"

"Eighteen," Danika said, lopping a year off her previous assertion. "And I've seen plenty of things more sexy than your flabby old body, believe me."

"Again, Randy, I'm struck by your concern for the welfare of others. Your concern that tender sensibilities might be offended."

"Here we go again," Felicia muttered. "Another speech."

"I just can't help but wish that you'd've been half as concerned with appearances when you were tying me to a flagpole naked."

"When I what?"

"Tied me bare-ass naked to a flagpole and left me to hang there all night."

"Shit," Randy said, sadly. "This is something else I did, right." He shook his head and looked at the ceiling. "Jesus fuck."

"You tied Nathan to a flagpole naked?" Alice said.

"It was Randy's little way of celebrating our senior class trip," I said to Alice. "He and some of his goon friends dragged me out of the crappy hotel we were staying at and hogtied me naked to a flagpole. Nice crisp night in March. Maybe forty-some, fifty degrees. Left me there all night." I turned to Trent. "Don't remember that either, do you, Trent?"

"No."

"You tied Nathan to a flagpole naked?" Alice said in the exact same tone and cadence.

"No. Well. Maybe." Trent cleared his throat. "It could've happened. I don't remember it exactly." He shrugged. "I mean, I don't remember Nathan exactly, but that flagpole thing . . . I can remember a time." He cleared his throat again. "A time or two, maybe." He made a wry face. "It seemed funnier then than maybe it does today."

"Sicko weasel probably had it coming to him," Felicia grumbled.

I went over to the cloth bag that I'd brought with me, reached inside it, and pulled out a sheaf of paper. It was my journal, the original manuscript that this transcript I'm writing on was transcribed from. I'd printed out the journal earlier that morning. I set that aside and pulled out a thick square of neatly folded nylon material. Unfolded, it was maybe three feet by five feet.

I tossed this to Randy. It was a flag bearing the five-ring Olympic symbol on a white background. Beneath the symbol was an inscription, Lake Placid NY, Home of the 1980 Winter Olympic Games.

"Do you remember now?" I said.

Randy shook his head, puzzled. "No," he said.

Whoops. Hold the phone.

I have to interrupt myself here. Actually, I knocked off writing about twenty minutes ago and I'm just picking it up again now. I had to stop to receive a visitor.

I know it can be confusing, this going back and forth. But I'm just one guy with a pen, writing shit down. Shit happens, I write it down. I'm doing the best I can.

My visitor was Alice. She poked her head into my hospital room and then tiptoed in, bearing a little bouquet of flowers from the gift shop downstairs.

"Hi," she said. "I'm sorry I took so long to come by, but they've been saying at the nurse's desk that you're not receiving any visitors."

I'm not, I wrote.

"I know. But I figured if Randy could get in, anyone could do it. I can go, if right now's a bad time."

No, please stay. I'm glad to see you, Alice.

"Okay. In that case, you get to keep the flowers." She was wearing a simple, sporty little dress, sleeveless, black with big white polka dots. She looked terrific.

Thanks.

"And I won't tell you that you look great."

Thanks again. Who told you Randy was here? Randy?

"No. News just gets around. I haven't talked to Randy in three weeks or so."

Oh. Sorry.

"About what?"

You and Randy. Not working out.

"Oh, please. Don't be. There wasn't a whole lot there to work or not work. I knew he had issues. He leveled with me from the start." She set the little vase of flowers on one of my new machines, some kind of blood toxicity monitor. "It was a fun fling, for a few weeks. A summer thing."

And summer is over. It's what? Late August, now?

Issues, like Felicia being his girlfriend?

"No. Issues, like not giving up on his ex-wife. And his son."

You knew about Felicia?

"Of course I knew about Felicia. Felicia was nothing."

He's at that difficult age, isn't he?

"He loves his ex-wife and his son." Alice sobered a little, putting on a straight face. "You probably don't know that Felicia is suing Tyler."

Tyler? I wrote. *Why?* Although there could only be one reason why.

"It's just Felicia being vindictive. It's not even clear that Tyler has any financial stake in that porn site his stripper girlfriend runs. She just wants to get back at Randy any way she can."

WhoreznHeat.com. In the one brief moment that I got to see it, it appeared that Courtney and Tyler were the site's chief attractions.

How much could something like that even be worth?

"You'd be surprised. They were already up and running a teaser clip of Felicia with the sex toys when we were still inside the auto parts store. Apparently all you need is something like that, some huge escalation in search rate results, to get the revenue ball rolling. Once you're on the porn site map, new content and traffic come pouring in. Tyler explained some of it to me, but I didn't get it all. I don't think he understands it either, really."

That's amazing.

"I'd be surprised if Tyler's involvement goes much beyond being a stunt cock for Courtney. Courtney's the brains of the outfit. She knows a bunch of, like, black-hat programmer guys."

Randy never mentioned anything about this, when he was here.

"No, of course not. He's probably the last guy in this town who doesn't know."

He thinks Tyler is freelancing at construction sites.

"Good for him. Let him keep thinking that."

It's all my fault, isn't it?

"It's porn site money, Nathan. Don't worry your little head about it. Felicia and Courtney are two sides of the same coin. These Trent boys should be more careful with their dicks."

What with all this colorful language, I was grateful I had too little face left with which to blush.

You really like him, don't you? Randy.

"He's a sweet guy." Alice was grinning now. "He's not like most guys you meet. He hasn't given up trying to be a little better, as a person. You know? He still gives a shit."

Does he? I wanted to know. Or rather, I knew, but I wanted to hear it.

"Some guys are jerks and some aren't. Randy's not a jerk, but he suspects he is. And he tries to do something about it. You know?"

I nodded. Sure.

"A lot of guys you meet are the opposite. They're convinced they're nice guys, when they're really jerks."

I hope that's not me.

Alice raised her thin eyebrows, and then said, "No, you're not a jerk." But she didn't elaborate.

Are you seeing someone else now?

"Oh, there's a guy." She was grinning at me the way a pretty girl grins at a hapless buffoon, unsophisticated in the ways of love. "There's always guys."

For pretty girls like you.

"Are we flirting now?"

Step right up! Marvel as the Amazing Man With Half a Face flirts with a pretty girl!

"I think you need to polish your act on the nurses a little, before you have any hope of getting somewhere with me."

I never learned to flirt and now it's too late.

Alice had moved to the foot of the bed. "You know, they never did find that girl," she said, changing the subject. "Danika."

I heard that.

I heard it from the cops, actually. They came around to interview me once it became clear that I was going to be staying awake and alive, for the time being. They came in with high hopes that I knew something about Danika. That I might have some idea where she is now. Not an unreasonable assumption, given her fortuitous arrival, just as I was starting to look a bit overwhelmed by the logistics of hostage-taking. As it happened, though, I learned a lot more from the cops than they did from me.

Danika's real name—her earthbound, nonmystical name—is Susan Winfield. She moved to Lake Lenni Lenape with her parents in 2002 and disappeared, in the company of her father, last year. Her father had endured a disastrous 2006, losing his job, his marriage, his home, and a custody battle for Susan all in rapid succession. In June of 2006, he appeared at a birthday picnic outing Susan was attending, escorted her to his car, and drove off. Two hours later, the police, responding to an anonymous phone call, entered the Winfield house, where they found Mrs. Winfield duct-taped to a Nautilus machine in the furnace room. The police have been looking for Mr. Winfield and Susan ever since.

I, of course, couldn't help them with that.

"You know what the kids in town say," Alice said.

I shrugged.

"That Danika is dead, has been dead for a while, and it was her ghost that spent the day and night with us."

Wow, that's a seductive combination. Witch and ghost.

"She seemed pretty real to me."

Maybe. You never know, though. This last written by a man whose assumptions about ghosts and death and the afterlife have been revised a bit, in light of recent events.

"It's so weird, though. The way she appeared like that. The way she disappeared. They say a mouse couldn't have slipped out of there unnoticed, through the police barricade, the way she did."

Maybe the cops are giving themselves too much credit.

I hope that Danika isn't a ghost. I hope she isn't dead. I hope she's being seductively witchlike and ghostlike and very much alive and laughing at us all, right now. Somewhere. I hope that somewhere she's providing timely advice to some other clueless dipshit like me, in his hour of need.

We talked for a little longer, Alice and me. Then the nurses came and shooed her away. So they could do more tests on me.

Alice had to go anyway, she said. A date. Her new paramour.

Lucky guy.

"Maybe." Mischievously. "We'll see."

I hope I didn't freak you out too badly, blowing my head off.

"I'm sorry I fell asleep," she said. "I thought Randy and I were pretty close to talking you out of it. Blowing your head off."

There's nothing to be sorry about.

"I felt like we'd done it. That you were seeing reason. I never should have laid down. Those packing peanuts were a mistake. One minute we were talking and the next, bang."

Don't sweat it. I just hope it wasn't too gruesome.

"No," she said, backing away as she was being led by the elbow to the door by a nurse. "I've seen worse. I did two years of med school before I switched to pharmacology."

You were my favorite hostage, Alice.

"Thanks." She waved. "I'll try to come back."

I wrote *Great!* on my pad and held it up.

And it was great. It is great. Sometimes I forget that I'm supposed to be trying to die here, that these very words on the back sides of these transcript pages are devoted, entirely, to earning my death from you, Death.

I forget entirely.

And then I go back to work. Death's dutiful scribe.

I see I left off with the flags.

Randy was holding one of them up and looking puzzled.

Alice was taking one look at the flag and then looking at me.

"Oh, Nathan," she said, reproachfully.

"What?"

"Please tell me that you didn't . . ."

I waited a moment and then said, "Didn't what?"

"What's up?" Danika had come over and was lifting another flag out of the bag. "What are these things, anyway?"

"Didn't save them, after you were tied—"

"No!" I said. "That would be ridiculous. I bought them on the Internet. From Sammy's House of Sports Nostalgia."

"Oh," Alice said. But she looked skeptical. Sadly skeptical. "They don't look new. They look old."

"Of course they're old. They're genuine collectibles."

"Randy tied you up with Winter Olympics flags?" Danika said. "Years ago?"

"That's all they could find."

"They?" Alice said.

"Randy and two other guys. And a girl, but she was just there. She didn't help."

"Oh," Alice said. Again. Her voice was taking on that wary tone you use when speaking to someone you've just realized is even crazier than you thought. Which, in my case, would be an astonishing level of craziness. "So you didn't keep the flags they tied you up in. All these years."

"Of course not." I looked at her in disbelief. "Who would do such a thing?"

Alice looked up at me, at my shotgun, and shrugged.

Danika cleared her throat, a teen's approximation of droll humor, and walked toward the front of the room.

"It's to make a point," I said. "I bought them to make a point."

"Is there a TV around here?" Danika said.

"I don't have to explain myself to you people!" I yelled. "You don't know the whole story. You don't know the half of it."

"There's a little 13-inch in the breakroom," Randy said. "Over there." He gestured toward a dark doorway away from the shelving units.

It was happening again. I was losing steam, losing my way. All this talking, talking, talking. I whirled to face Randy.

"You!" I said to him. "Why aren't you standing there naked?"

"Let's leave off with the naked stuff," Randy said. "We got girls here and a kid. Not to mention whoever's outside by now."

"I'm tired of talking." I raised the shotgun and pointed it at Randy's head. "Get the fuck out of those clothes."

"Maybe this isn't necessary," Alice said. "We're all your friends here, Nathan."

"Speak for yourself," Felicia said. "You're the especially friendly one. Maybe if you fuck him, he'll let the rest of us go."

"I don't have time for friends." I was studying Randy's forehead hovering above and beyond the barrel of the shotgun. "I'm at the end of things. Forming new attachments may not be the best use of my time right now."

Randy's hands were at the hem of his auto-parts polo shirt.

"I can end this whole thing right here," I said. "I don't have to do the flagpole charade. It's not going over with this audience anyway."

Randy pulled his shirt up over his head.

"It wasn't enough, you're some kind of psycho loner head case," Felicia sneered. "Oh, no. You gotta have a thing for guys' dicks, too."

"Stay out of this, Felicia."

"Fairy," Felicia said, ignoring Randy.

We watched in silence as Randy removed his pants, shoes, and socks. He was still in reasonable shape for a guy on the wrong side of forty. The inevitable Sail Inn beer belly and a little unfortunate furriness. But not bad, overall. No wonder he was getting all the chicks.

"Underwear stays on," he said.

"Okay," I said. "Deal."

"Thanks."

"Go stand in front of that pole there." I indicated a support beam roughly in the center of the room.

Randy went to the pole and stood facing it.

"No. Face away from the pole."

He turned around.

"You want me to immobilize him?"

"What?" I looked at Danika. "Immobilize him?"

"Cast a spell to render him motionless."

"No. No spells." I picked up one of the flags and stood before Randy. "Danika, this is serious stuff. You're not supposed to be helping. The cops could say you were an accessory."

"I know, I know," she said dismissively. "I could get in big trouble."

I shook out one of the flags. "Put your hands behind your back," I said to Randy.

He clasped his hands behind his back.

"No," I said. "Straight back. Out and straight back." I went around behind Randy and tossed the flag away. "Further back."

Randy's hands moved further back at each side of the beam. I set the shotgun on the floor and tugged a pair of handcuffs from my left back pocket. I popped open the locks, being careful to keep the chain from jingling, and watched Randy's hands move into place.

"Closer together," I said.

I eased the cuffs up to his hands and shut them simultaneously around his wrists. The metal teeth on the cuffs made a nice, secure clicking noise as the locking mechanisms engaged. I'd never owned a pair of handcuffs before.

Randy wrenched his hands forward and sawed the handcuff chain back and forth against the pole. His head dropped forward. "Shit," he said.

"What?" Felicia said. "What happened?"

Randy took a deep breath, let it out. He raised his head. "Nothing."

I went around in front of Randy and we looked at each other. For the first time that afternoon, he looked worried. I grabbed the sides of his briefs, and swooped them down over his legs. He fought me for a bit and then let me unwind them from his feet.

Danika let loose with a surprisingly lascivious wolf whistle.

"Nice hammer," she said.

"You said the underwear could stay on," Randy said.

"True," I said. "I did."

I fitted the underwear around his head like a hat. Then I tugged it down over his face. I stepped back to examine my work.

"Humbling, eh?" I asked.

Randy looked at me through the leg hole of his underwear.

"Yeah," he said. "I guess."

I bound his ankles to the beam with a flag.

THE END IS NEAR

§

June 27th, 8pm

I'm feeling much better now, thank you. Calm, clear-eyed, steady of nerve and will.

Got a little weepy, a little maudlin, earlier this afternoon. All that pomp and circumstance, you know. Please accept my apologies. You'll find me much sturdier of temperament tonight, I promise. Your reliable reporter, back on the job.

Tonight, I'm reporting from the Pit.

I don't know if anyone still calls this place—a low-lying, five-or six-square-mile area of undeveloped woods and scrub west of town—the Pit. Maybe nobody calls it anything at all anymore. Plans to develop the Pit were abandoned in the late '60s, after developers discovered that every exploratory hole they dug rapidly with water.

Just as well, as it turned out. Because it's hard to imagine who would have moved into the houses intended to line the phantom streets of the remote Pit. Today, half the houses in the center of town have weathered For Sale signs forked into the lawn, half the storefronts are empty, and the lake is still suffocating in a stew of excrement, engine fuel, and weed bloom. Hell, things are so bad, even some of the bars are closing. But that's the story of this town. Becoming, then declining, without ever, somehow, being.

Thirty years ago, the bulldozed access roads into the Pit were already being retaken by scrub. They were still clear enough to allow passage to kids on foot, on bicycle, and on motorcycle, but overgrown enough to make it difficult for parents to get around. Not that many parents would have cared to, anyway.

Those dirt roads and cleared expanses are all long gone today. Thin saplings have become trees thirty and forty feet high.

The creeping ground cover has exploded into impenetrable briar patches and dense thickets of blackberry, poison ivy, and coarse juniper. I knew the way into the Pit by heart and it still took me a full half-hour of staggering, sweating, swearing travail to get a half mile in, as the daylight was fading. And I'm a bloody mess for my efforts, too, thank you.

So where am I? I'm at what was once a major intersection in ghost-town Pitville, where the main access road branched off into two smaller roads. The right fork headed off toward the lake and the left fork arrowed deeper into the Pit. That's all gone, as I've said. I wouldn't have found this place at all, if it weren't for the steep, rubbly hill of boulders and rocky outcroppings that rose above that old fork in the road.

Thirty years ago, on a Friday night in June like this one, there would have been fifteen or twenty kids down here. Motorcycling punks, a slumming jock or two, and a few girls. Enough beer and weed to set the stars reeling. A fire going, somebody's transistor radio chugging out a Foghat song, and the usual empty banter about nothing at all hanging in the humid night air.

There's nothing like that here tonight, though. There's just me.

The ripped-out car seats and discarded mattress box springs, the fire-blackened rocks and ten years' worth of rusting Schlitz cans are all still here, though you'd have to dig a little to find them now. Ground ivy and treacherous drifts of dead leaves have obscured the graffiti that covered much of this hill of rocks. I was up there before, uncovering some of those urgent messages from another time. Blow Me. Jesse Rules. Take It Sleazy! Amber Was Here, 5-12-71.

So here I am, with my own sixpack of beer, my laptop, a flashlight, and an indispensable can of bug spray. A little late for the party, as usual.

When did the kids stop coming down here? At least fifteen years ago, I'm guessing. The kids don't hang out in the malls and ball fields and convenience store parking lots anymore. So why should they be out here in the wilderness?

Oh, don't worry. I won't bore you with my inability to fathom today's kids. I've already bored you with that. I have plenty of other things to bore you with, as always. So let's get to it, before the beer runs out.

It all started with a mood. The kind of mood that inevitably leaves the door propped open for trouble.

In the fall of my senior year, I was just starting to save for the car I hoped to take to college. I was working nights—six nights a week, five hours a night—at the Groceria, a high-priced and unpopular supermarket in the Lakeport area of Lake Lenni Lenape. The walk to the Groceria from school wasn't so bad, about three miles by way of back roads and a shortcut across an abandoned golf course. But the walk from the Groceria to home was six miles, in the dark, more than a mile of it through the Pit. Each night at ten o'clock—after a five-hour shift of stocking shelves, retrieving shopping carts, and bagging groceries—I would take off my work smock and corduroys and put on a sweatshirt and sweatpants. Then I would run the first four miles home. I got so I could do those four miles in under thirty minutes. After that, I'd walk the rest. The Pit was far too dark and treacherous to run through at night. On a good night, without incident, I'd be home by eleven or so, get six hours of sleep, and do the whole school-work-run-walk thing again the next day.

Anyway, this one night, I was in some kind of mood. Some unhelpful, unproductive mood. It would have been a Friday night, near the end of another long week. I might have worked overtime, I can't remember. Often, my co-workers would come to me and ask me to cover extra Friday and Saturday hours for them. When I agreed, they would thank me effusively, as if the fact that I had nothing else to do wasn't perfectly obvious.

That night, I would have been depressed by my finances. At five dollars per hour, I was making a hundred and fifty dollars a week. Subtracting taxes, union dues, and fees for useless benefits left me with one hundred dollars to deposit in my passbook savings account. I was a long way away from affording a car that might actually run, never mind the extra costs of insurance and maintenance.

So I was in a mood, as I started down the access road into the Pit, that night in October. As soon as I descended into the darkness I could hear the sounds of kids having a good time. Music, shouting, laughter.

Usually, I was too smart, too cautious, too timid, to bumble into such a potentially harmful situation. I'd duck off the path and pick my way carefully through the undergrowth below the clearing where the kids would be gathered. That detour would add another ten minutes to my trip home, but it was usually worth the effort. The alternative had proven sufficiently humbling on a couple of prior occasions.

But that night, I just didn't feel like trekking through the brambles. I didn't feel like adding ten minutes to my trip. I was in a mood.

I marched down the access road, crossed the rocky runoff gully below the dirt road intersection, and started across the clearing.

"Hey, look who it is."

"What you doing out at night, you scum-sucking bag of shit?"

"Your mama send you out for more rubbers, Nathan?"

"Nathan, man. You bring any weed?"

"Nathan, you here to give us all blowjobs again?"

All the usual shit, from the usual crew of dirtbags. I recognized the voice of Randy Trent. Of Tommy Flanagan, a former football hero, graduated by then, who, I hadn't forgotten, had once made knowing reference to the assfucking talents of my typing-class love interest, Terry. Of Albie D'Onofrio, a lanky, happy-go-lucky clown and stoner, and Barbara Sutter, a brassy, red-haired, shapely senior, whose sudden month-long vacation that previous spring was widely known to have been for birth-abortive purposes.

"Hey, hey, Nathan. Where ya going?"

"Nathan, party with us, dude."

This is the way it sometimes went, when I was waylaid in the Pit. Assorted assholes, weed-lazy and beer-bleary, taunting me, while I crossed the clearing meekly, my head down and my little feet eating up the ground. But this time, because I was in a mood, I stopped.

"I'm going home," I said. "That's where I'm going." I saw that they had a fire going and they were grouped around it, sitting on logs and rocks. "I worked all fucking day and all I want is to be left alone by you assholes."

"Who-o-o-o-oa." A chorus of unfeigned surprise.

"Who you think you're talking to, douchebag?" This last from Trent. He rose from a log and took a step toward me.

I stood my ground. "Nobody," I said. "I'm not talking to anybody. I'm just passing through, minding my own business." And then, in an unprecedented act of bravery, I added, "Why don't you do the same, for once?"

"You just earned yourself a punch upside your pointy head." Trent took two more steps toward me and one sideways. He was trying to pop the top of a beer can.

What was I doing? My long day was going to be a lot longer, if it ended with a black eye. The fact that Trent was drunk made me even more nervous than I would have been already. My only real experience with drunk people at that point had been with my father. No happy outcomes to report from that quarter.

"Trent, man, sit the fuck down."

Trent seemed not to hear this, but I looked in surprise at the group sitting around the fire.

"Give the little dweeb a break. He worked all day, we don't have to give him shit."

Who was my new ally? It was Tom Navely, the jock-turned-stoner who'd ducked out of my bathhouse humiliation when it turned ugly, just over two years before. Tom's descent down the ladder of high school prestige was just about complete by then. In senior year, he was known for being stoned just about all the time. Like Trent, he would never make it to the graduation finish line.

"Yeah, leave the kid alone," Barbara Sutter said. "He's just going home."

Trent, who had finally managed to pry his can open, was moving toward me, a hamlike right fist clenched at his side. "Little shit'll be eating my fucking boot," he was saying.

"Fuck you, Trent," I said, though I was backing away. It was dawning on me that I might, for once, be able to outrun him.

"O-o-o-oh, you got it coming, dickbag."

But I didn't. And I didn't have to outrun him, either. Tommy Flanagan appeared behind Trent and slapped a big paw on his shoulder. Trent's feet twisted under him and he sprawled forward onto his hands and knees. His full beer can rolled, foaming, to my feet and stopped.

"Shit," Trent said. "My fucking beer."

"You, my friend, are shitfaced," Tommy said. "Go back to your log and reflect on your wasted youth."

"Fuck," Trent said. He groped around for his beer for a moment, and then gave up. He lifted up onto his knees and looked up at Tommy, blinking owlishly. "What's this shit you're talking to me?"

"Same shit as always, only more so. Go back to your log, you drunken hog."

Trent nodded at this, chagrined. He started trying to get up. Tommy Flanagan was one of maybe four guys Trent had gone to school with who could beat him in a fair fight. Flanagan owned an entire page of rushing and pass-catching records in the Lake Lenni Lenape Braves' record book. He was also precisely the kind of brutal goon who would normally have been delighted to watch Trent pound me into the turf. This night, though, he seemed to be experiencing one of those odd moments of false enlightenment that drinking and pot-smoking sometimes spark in brutal goons. The self-flattering urge to appear benevolent.

"Little geek," he said to me, "lemme buy ya a beer."

I looked guardedly at Trent. I looked at the kids around the fire. I looked at Tommy Flanagan. And, because Trent looked so utterly flummoxed by interior weather, and because I was in a mood, I said, "Sure. Why not?"

Tommy nodded regally. "Go geek go."

"If anybody put something in my beer," Trent was mumbling, "I'm gonna box some fucking heads."

Tommy ushered me over to the fire and presented me to the group. "Geek, group. Group, geek," he said, by way of introduction. "Geek wants a beer."

Albie scrambled up and started rooting around in a bag. He pried out a beer, a Schlitz, and offered it to me.

I popped the top and took a sip. It was warm and sour and explosively foamy. "Thanks," I said, once I'd gotten a mouthful of it down.

"Don't mention it," Tommy said. He was affecting a kingly air, as if to say: Look what I can do, raise the lowliest geek to almost human stature.

"Nathan, seriously, man. You're right." Albie, pie-eyed and earnest, was gesturing at me with a joint. "When you're right, you're right. And you are, like, seriously right. Why don't you have a fucking beer, man," he concluded, as if he hadn't just handed me one. "Kick back. Take a load off."

Trent had managed to shamble back to his log. Someone I didn't recognize handed him a beer. Trent took it and turned away, fumbling at it like a learning-disabled ape trying to get to a banana in a sealed jar.

"So who are you, Nathan?" a girl said. She had a very long, pretty face, big brown eyes, and straight brown hair, parted in the center, wrapped behind her ears, and pulled forward over her shoulders so that it hung into her lap. I didn't recognize her from school. She was sharing a log with Tom Navely.

Who was I? I tried to imagine a suitable answer. I took another pull from my beer. "I don't know," I said. "I'm Nathan."

"I'm Jessica," the girl said. She stood up, bent over to reach into a paper bag, but then stumbled sideways, almost falling headlong into the fire.

"Grab some log," Tommy Flanagan said to me.

I took a seat beside Albie.

"It's fucking black magic," Albie was saying to another kid I didn't know—a kid with a big head and a greasy shock of bright red hair, grease-blackened hands wrapped around a beer can. "Those pentagrams on ZOSO are a prayer to the devil. Page sold his soul to the devil. He lives in some black magician's old castle, for fuck's sake."

"Page fucking rocks out, man," the red-haired kid said.

"He is so beautiful," Jessica said. "He is so dark and beautiful."

"He's a fucking god," Barbara agreed.

"Jimmy Page is in league with Satan!" Albie looked from person to person around the fire, ending with me. "That is so fucking cool, man."

"Yeah," I said.

I took another sip from my beer. I'd had beer before, a few mouthfuls taken on the sly in the weeks just prior to that night. My father had just started bringing beer into the house. Which is to say, he'd just started brazening out the awkward pretense that he was just a normal drinker who could casually bring beer into the house without completely annihilating himself and all of us with it.

Beer had tasted bitter and vile on those occasions. But on that night, under the stars, in the company of that Pit crew, it tasted like heaven. Each mouthful was a corrupt little burst of bubbly nirvana. It tasted like something magical, like something skimmed from a magic lake and offered to me in a magic cup by a mermaid. By Jimmy Page in his black magic castle.

"In Through the Out Door was a buncha crap," Tom Navely said. "Pop shit. It's just as well it's over."

"Robert Plant's a faggot," Tommy Flanagan said. "I heard Jimmy Page is in France, recording a secret album with Jim Morrison and John Bonham."

"Oh my God!" Barbara shrieked. "Where did you hear that!"

"That is so cool," Albie said, grinning widely.

"That would be so beautiful," Jessica said. "So dark and beautiful."

Could it be this easy, I wondered? I looked at Trent. He was slumped and listing rightward on his log. I looked at the fire. I looked at the big yellow autumn moon hanging in the trees, the trees all shaking dead leaves onto our heads. The woods dark and impenetrable in every direction.

I cleared my throat. "I heard there's going to be a tour," I said. "Later this fall. With a new drummer."

"Wouldn't be any fucking good. You babies missed 'em when they were good," Tommy said world-wearily. "Whole Lotta Love, Moby Dick. It'll never be like that again." He started beating on a log in some mad John Bonham imitation.

We all nodded grimly at this. We lived in a fallen age.

"In . . . league . . . with . . . Satan." Albie seemed to like the sound of this.

And then an odd thing happened.

"Hey, mister. How come everybody calls you names?"

I turned around to find a young girl moving toward me, into the circle of firelight. Her brown hair was cut in straight, childlike bangs and she was dressed in overalls and sneakers. She might have been eight or nine years old.

"Who are you?" I said. I hadn't noticed her before.

"Dana!" Jessica said. "I told you, stay in your sleeping bag or I won't bring you out here anymore."

Oh, right. I looked at Dana's long face and hair. Jessica's little sister, evidently.

"How come everybody was calling you names?"

Dana had Jessica's deep bewitching brown eyes. They were a little unsettling on an eight-year-old.

I looked around and shrugged nonchalantly, as if to say: Ha ha. Kids.

"How come your clothes are so crappy?"

I looked at Dana. I knew I should nip this Q&A thing in the bud, but I didn't know what to say. I wished I knew how to nip things in the bud.

"Are you poor?"

Someone, I didn't see who, snickered.

"They're . . . they're not crappy. They're running clothes. I run in them."

"Are you a faggot?"

"Uh-oh," someone said. "Outta the mouths of babes."

"No," I said, stung.

"How come everybody says you're a faggot, then?"

"Go get him, Dana." This came from Trent. He was surfacing from his coma.

"Are you talking to me?" I said. I looked around as if there could be someone else to whom she might be talking.

"Yes, you, faggot." This earned Dana a round of happy hoots and hollers. The Pit crew was warming up to her act. She all but levitated off the ground, so happy was she to be the center of attention. "I'm talking to you."

So what do you do when an eight-year-old girl attacks you? Clearly, this girl was a tough chick in training, playing to the crowd. But that didn't make it any less disorienting, any less dismaying. What do you do? I didn't know then, and I don't know now.

"How come you have so many zits?"

"Hey," I said, trying to be reasonable, "that's not very nice."

"Now hold on, Nathan," Tom Navely said, mock-authoritatively, like a debate moderator. "I think it's a valid question. Why do you have so many zits?"

So much for my new ally. Had they planned this? All of them, set the girl like a snare? It didn't seem so. They seemed as surprised as I was. Only they were enjoying the hell out of themselves.

"How come you're so sad?"

This question was almost more shocking, for resembling a sincere question. Stupidly, I started to answer it. "Because I . . . well, I'm not sad so much as tired, I'm pretty much on my feet all day, and then you—"

"How come you do it with boys?"

"—you're kind of freaking me . . . what?" I stood up suddenly.

"How come you do it with boys in the ass?"

"I don't." My mostly full beer can was trembling in my hand.

Barbara Sutter, behind me, burst out laughing.

"Everyone says you do."

"Everyone . . . everyone who?"

Tom Navely, unable to resist, put on his moderator's voice again. "Yes, Nathan. Why do you do it with boys in the ass?"

Barbara was still laughing, helplessly now.

"How come your clothes are so crappy?"

"Yeah, faggot," Trent hollered. He was laughing, too, and had fallen off his log. "How come?"

"You already asked that." Unable to control the shaking of my hand, I set the beer can down on the ground. I took a step away from the fire.

"How come you don't have any friends?"

"That's enough, little girl," I said, trying for something like lofty authority and failing.

"Ooooooh," Jessica said. "Tough guy. Whaddeya gonna do? Spank her?"

I was taking a second, a third step away from the fire.

"How come you smell so bad?"

Someone more socially adept than I might have been able to deflect this little girl's attack, play it for laughs. Use it even, to some advantage. But not me. I was too clumsy, too lacking in even rudimentary social graces, haunted by too many ghosts, to defend myself.

"How come everybody hates you?"

By then I was in full retreat, Dana right behind me.

Something—a pebble, an acorn, a beer cap—bounced off my head. I had a good two hundred yards or so to go to the main road, and I didn't want to run. I wanted at least that. Not to flee in terror from an eight-year-old girl.

"How come you're such a scaredy cat?"

A rock—a pretty good-sized rock—clipped me in the head. I started walking faster, long strides eating up the dirt road.

"How come you're running away?"

And I was. Whether the words created the reality or I'd already been running, I can't remember. But I was, indeed, running away, trying to put this nightmare, like all the other nightmares, behind me. When I got to the paved road, I could still hear Dana calling out to me from the Pit.

That girl, if she was eight then, would be thirty-five tonight. She probably doesn't remember a thing about that night. But I do. I remember she seemed like a glowing-eyed spirit child sent from hell to wreak vengeance on me. Sent from Jimmy Page's black-magic castle to cast me out from where I didn't belong. A winged harpie in the shape of a child, ripping at my heart with beak and claw. I didn't sleep at all that night.

The road I escaped on was evenly graded dirt, two lanes wide. The intersection at the foot of this jumble of rocks was wide enough to allow a fairly lengthy game of football toss. Wide enough for high-speed motorcycle spinouts and wheelies and whatever other shit you do on a motorcycle. And it's all gone now. It's just trees and brambles and heavy treading. Sitting here on this hill, you'd never know any of it was even here.

Sometimes, in rare moments of clarity, I feel like I'm frozen in time, stuck, a stopped clock that's not right even once a day.

Twenty years further on from now, twenty years after I'm gone, on some gorgeous June night like this one, the boxsprings and carseats and garbage will have mouldered right into the turf. The graffiti will be ivied away, hidden under decades of dead leaves turning to dirt.

Perhaps, by then, these woods will be marching on to other conquests, trees pushing up through the foundation of the Huffnagle house and peeking out through the windows of the Trent house at 16 Reese Trail. The townfolk, perhaps, will have retreated to a few houses and a church and one last tavern at the edge of the dying lake. The town itself become just a memory, just another star-crossed developer's dream, like the Pit.

Before that happens, though, I have something to add to the scene. I have my own mark to make. I'd better do it now, while I have battery power enough in this flashlight to do it. I'll be right back.

There. I'm back. It took a while to find an unmarked rock and to clear the underbrush from it. Then the painting was time-consuming, too. All those letters, carefully blocked in black model paint with a ½" inch brush.

Nathan was Here. Fuck you All.

§

When Danika finally figured out how to tune in WNNJ Channel 8 on the little shop TV—it was channel 8 on cable TV, which we didn't have, and UHF channel 39 on free, through-the-airwaves TV—it turned out we hadn't missed a thing. There was a chubby chef on the air, setting fire to different kinds of flaming desserts. Less than two minutes later, though, he was preempted by a WNNJ News8 Special Report.

An old-style talking-head anchorman, rugged and white-maned, stared us down, explaining that the chubby chef had been yanked so that WNNJ could bring us a breaking news exclusive. He sent us live to the scene, where the pretty young woman on top of the truck, now properly fluffed and tweaked, was gripping a microphone and peering at us urgently.

"This is Samantha Jourgensen, WNNJ News8 correspondent, with a WNNJ News8 first-on-the-scene news exclusive." She paused dramatically. "WNNJ News8, First . . . with the Facts."

The camera rotated abruptly to show the store behind Samantha. "You see behind me the front of A&B Auto Parts in Lake Lenni Lenape, New Jersey. Inside, one desperate man, armed with a shotgun, a pistol, and a cache of explosives, has taken four innocent people hostage."

"Damn it!" Danika protested. "I am not a hostage!"

"What do we know about this man?" Samantha's earnest face filled the screen. "Very little. His name is Nelson Huffnagle. He appears to have some sort of grievance or grudge against one or more of the hostages inside. He is armed. He is dangerous." Samantha gripped her microphone in a white-knuckle grip. "Extremely dangerous."

"Hey, Nathan," Danika said. She clapped me on the back. "Great press."

"They got my name wrong," I said. "Why is Nathan so hard to remember?"

"In a moment, we're going to speak with the ranking New Jersey State Police officer on the scene. But first, we have a WNNJ News8 exclusive interview with . . . Peter Jones."

PJ's huge, lop-eared, freckled head suddenly filled the screen.

"Peter, you were inside the store when Huffnagle entered, were you not?"

"Yes, I was," PJ said. "I was in the store. I work there." He said this in the same curt, tight-lipped way Samantha was speaking.

"What exactly did Huffnagle say?"

"He said . . . well . . ." This question seemed to throw PJ off somewhat. "He said, this is a hostage situation."

"I see." Samantha pursed her lips, absorbing this fact. "Did he say why he was taking this extraordinary action. The taking of hostages."

"He . . . well, I think he's got it in for Randy."

"A vendetta of some sort. Randall Trent, a respected local businessman and the owner of the shop. Huffnagle told you this."

"He . . . not exactly. But there's been shit——" PJ's eyes went round. "This is live, right?"

"Yes it is, Mr. Jones. Please continue."

"There's been stuff going around. This Nathan guy, he's kind of a loose wing nut, right? I mean, I didn't put it together myself at first, but stuff's been happening, and all of a sudden Nathan's in the shop with firepower, and I kind of put two and two together, you know?"

"Nelson. I believe it's Nelson."

"First there was the tapes, then the——" PJ shifted gears. "Nelson. Right. Okay."

"What kind of firepower, Peter?"

"You mean, what was he packing?"

"Yes, Peter. What kind of firepower?"

"Well, he had a shotgun, a pistol, and a bag full of something. Looked like some kind of bomb, you know?"

Samantha addressed the camera. "A one-man army, equipped with high-powered weaponry and explosives. Right now, police on the scene are keeping their distance, hoping for a peaceful resolution to this dire confrontation." She turned back to PJ. "Peter, you were in there with Huffnagle. Is he a man who can be reasoned with?"

"Is he . . .?" PJ looked pained. He cleared his throat. "He's packing plenty of heat, I can tell you that."

"Thank you, Peter Jones." Samantha looked off-camera, then back. "We're about to go to a WNNJ News8 exclusive interview with Andrew Mitchell, commander of the New Jersey State Police Emergency Response Unit—" She blinked at some new communication from the periphery. "No. Okay." She looked up. "We're not going to get that right now." She addressed Peter again. "One more question, Peter. Can you tell us how you managed to escape?"

"Oh, sure," PJ said brightly. "I have a green belt in tae kwon do."

Samantha raised an eyebrow at PJ. "Are you saying, Mr. Jones, that you managed to subdue Huffnagle?"

"Oh, well, no," PJ harumphed, backtracking. "It didn't get to that. I think that he instinctively knew not to mess with me."

"Is it too late to kill PJ?" Danika said. "Maybe we could get off a shot from the front room."

"I see. Thank you, Mr. Jones," Samantha was saying. Then she sent us back to the dour talking head in the studio.

"Hey, how about that, Trent?" I said.

In addition to the handcuffs, Randy was bound to the pole at the ankles, knees, and chest by Olympic flags. I'd told him if he didn't behave, I'd use the fourth flag as a gag.

"What?" he said.

"Randall Trent, respected local businessman. You've really come up in the world, haven't you?"

He looked at me through the leghole of his underwear. "Pay your taxes on time, they call you anything you want."

The phone rang and we all looked at it again. I walked over to it and picked up the receiver. I was ready for them this time. "Hello?"

"Nathan?"

"Yes." Here, at least, was a guy who actually knew my name.

"Nathan, this is Sergeant Joe Nedney of the New Jersey State Police. How's it going in there?"

"Good."

"Good. Nathan, maybe you can help us out, out here. We're all a little puzzled by the young woman who locked the front door a few minutes ago."

"I have a demand," I said.

There was a short silence, and then, "Okay."

"In exchange for which, I'll surrender one hostage."

"Oh. Okay." Sergeant Joe Nedney seemed surprised. "Great."

"I'll give you Felicia Fowler," I said, like a kid putting a prized baseball card on the trading block.

"Alright. Ms. Fowler. Great. What do you want?"

"A pizza."

Danika opened her mouth to say something and then settled for a wry, open-mouthed smile. She shook her head and looked away, no doubt lowering her estimation of my criminal capacities yet again.

"And not just any pizza. I want toppings, too."

"Toppings." There was static on the phone line and then Joe came back. "Okay."

"I want the pie delivered to the front door. I don't want anybody anywhere near the back door."

"Okay."

"You're trading me for a pizza?" Felicia said, affronted. "You fucking idiot."

"What are they saying?" Danika wanted to know.

"They say they'll deliver it to the front door."

"Who will deliver it."

"Who will deliver it?" I said to Joe.

"A trooper."

"A trooper," I relayed.

"No way," Danika said. "They'll have some guy in here pulling some kind of special forces shit." She thought for a second. "Have Woody deliver it."

"Have Woody—" I placed my hand over the receiver. "Why does it have to be a cop?" I said to Danika. "If we can pick, we should have it delivered by somebody less dangerous. A pizza boy or somebody."

"You'll end up with a special forces guy dressed as a pizza boy. Woody, we know. And nobody's less dangerous than Woody."

"Send Woody with it," I said into the phone.

"Sheriff Woods?"

"Yeah."

"Okay. What do you want on it?'"

"On what?"

"The pizza."

"Oh." I looked at Danika. "What do we want on the pizza."

"No meat on my half. Eggplant and peppers. And not just green peppers, either. Red and yellow, too. Like they do at Carnivale's in Ledgewood."

I turned to Alice and Felicia, sitting on the floor. "Girls?"

"Fuck you," Felicia said.

"Mushrooms," Alice said. "And extra cheese."

"Eggplant and peppers, red, yellow, and green, on one side. Mushrooms and extra cheese on the other."

"Okay."

There was another silence. "What?" I said.

"Is there something you want to say about the third young woman in there with you?"

"Any comments?" I said to Danika. "Anything you want to say?"

"No," she said.

"Not at this time," I relayed.

"We'll call back in fifteen minutes," Sergeant Nedney said.

"Okay." I hung up the phone.

"What did they say?" Danika said.

"They said no way on the eggplant. Kill the Fowler girl if you have to."

"Fuck you," Felicia said.

§

June 28th, 10am

I'm in a stalker holding pattern.

An earlier-arriving stalker beat me to Trent's crappy apartment, leaving me out here in my car, tapping this out on my laptop.

Right. It's you, Felicia. Again.

I practically met you at Trent's door. If you hadn't grabbed the last parking spot in front of Trent's place, forcing me to park farther away, we would've been breaking in together. As it was, I was ten yards away from the front walk when I realized you were fighting the door, doing the plastic-card-in-the-door-jamb trick. Trent's really got to start deadbolting his door.

I hotfooted it back to my car, amazed you hadn't seen me.

Though maybe you did, eh, Felicia? Do we have a kind of understanding going, me and you? You won't acknowledge my shameful hobby if I don't acknowledge yours? Hmmm?

Anyway, you're still inside. You could be in there doing a little girlfriendly housekeeping, mopping the floors and dusting the knickknacks, though somehow I doubt it. You're looking for evidence, aren't you? Telltale traces of the little Asian girl or some other back-door honey. Aren't you?

Well, good luck, Fel. Trent's not exactly a big hoarder of mementos of love. Trent's not exactly a big hoarder of anything.

Since I have some time to kill here, I might as well share my thoughts with you, Tyler and Miz and Felicia. And don't worry, law enforcement types, I haven't forgotten you. As soon as I can get inside Trent's place, I'll have something for you as well. A minor misdemeanor or two, maybe even some real property damage. Be patient.

So. How do I say this?

The thing is, I've been having odd thoughts lately.

Odd thoughts about, well . . . living. Living, as in not dying. Not killing myself.

Irresponsible of me, I know. From your point of view, a craven bait-and-switch. And caused entirely by all the fun I've been having these last few days. I recognize this, and still, I catch myself what-if-ing.

What if I didn't have to die? What if I could live, now that I'm finally learning to enjoy myself like a normal human being?

What if I could live?

Fortunately, I don't have the wherewithal to entertain these delusions for long. I'm just about out of money, for instance. My prospects of acquiring more money without, say, knocking over convenience stores, are pretty slim. The roof over my head is essentially a day-to-day proposition. The day my mother's house sells is the day I'm out on the street. There are also issues of staggering debt, pervading isolation, and general end-of-the-roadness.

Plus, too, my health isn't all it could be. I think I'm suffering from the early onset of arthritis. Some mornings I can barely get out of bed, my joints are so swollen and achey. It feels like ground glass in there. My digestion is shot; all but the blandest, microwaved treacle casts my insides into an uproar. Excuse me for saying so, but just about every crap I take is an adventure, these days. Even my looks are shot. Not that I was any big deal in the looks department to begin with, but lately, that guy looking back at me in the mirror has been one blemished, hollow-eyed, yellow-skinned motherfucker. Are people supposed to look this bad at forty-five?

If I had ever intended to see age forty-six, I certainly wouldn't be getting by on my good looks. It's only now occurring to me that our twenties and thirties are a good time for building a nest egg, a life framework, that would make our forties, fifties, and sixties livable. Savings, family, friends, outside interests. That sort of shit.

And I really missed the boat there.

I think I've covered some of these bases already, elsewhere. I'm not blind to the mistakes I've made. Yet, unaccountably, I'm still experiencing this strange temptation to live.

I have to be vigilant in the face of this weakness of will.

I have to remind myself that the living is easy precisely because I have nothing to lose. Because I'm already dead. The moment I elect to go on living indefinitely, all the constraints of my old life return with a vengeance. I go back to living the way I was before, only worse. The hole I'm in is much, much deeper now.

I have to remind myself that I haven't, in fact, figured out how to live better. I've only proven extraordinarily talented at dying.

I have two and a half days left, each day—Saturday, Sunday, a little of Monday—more precious for being one of the last I'll ever see. There's no way back. That's the way it is.

It's been fun, but I don't want to overstay my welcome.

Felicia, you left Trent's a few minutes ago. There isn't, as we both know, a whole lot to see in Trent's place. You didn't look like someone who found what she was looking for, I have to say.

Now I'd better get a move on, myself. I don't think Trent works a full day on Saturday, and I wouldn't want to meet him in his kitchen. I'll be right back.

Okay. I'm back. Mission accomplished.

Law enforcement officers, here's a couple more crimes and misdemeanors for the Huffnagle file. First, another B&E. And second . . . what would you call stopping up someone's kitchen sink drain and leaving the water running? Malicious mischief? Vandalism? Destruction of private property?

Whatever it is, I'll take one of those, too.

§

I woke up the other day and I wasn't here. I was somewhere else.

It was you, Death. Fucking around again.

I thought we had a deal. No more fucking around.

Of all the places to send me. Of all the people to send me to.

Are you out of your mind?

At first, I didn't understand why you would do such a thing to me. I mean, I'm working as hard as I can here.

And then I flipped this manuscript over and checked. I knew I had included a flash-card synopsis of my family history somewhere in there. I looked at what I had written and what I had left out.

THE END IS NEAR

Oh, Death. You son of a bitch.

I woke up in a mid-morning barroom, in Fort Lee, New Jersey in the spring of my eighteenth year. I woke up in Pete's Peek-In.

My father was slumped over the bar, just the way he had been on that freakishly warm March morning. He looked up at me and grinned a ghoulish grin. His gone-round-the-bend, been-drinking-since-I-don't-know-when grin.

"Hey, look who's here," he said. "Not such hot shit now, are ya?"

I was looking around. Daylight fell into the room through several small transom windows near the ceiling, cranked open at this hour, well before noon. Outside, I knew, it was a beautiful spring day, the first warm, comfortable day of the year. A few days later, the daytime temperature would top seventy in the Catskills, a record for that date in late March. I reached out very slowly and touched the rail of the bar.

"What are you looking at, punk? You don't hear me when I'm talking to you?"

My father, I might or might not have explained before, had three distinct personalities. He had his normal, sober personality, characterized by a sort of self-effacing silence. In his sober state, he was there but not there; he wandered around quietly, looking like someone who wished he was somewhere else.

"Twenty, thirty years ago, I told you your whole life story. Right here in this bar. And did you believe me? Did you, you little holier-than-thou shit? Huh? Fuck, no. Not you."

He also had his onset-of-drinking personality, which expressed itself as an ominous, backslapping, flinty-eyed joviality. In this phase, he would suddenly be all over you, taking sudden interest in your doings and offering over-enthusiastic praise of your many qualities and accomplishments, most of them utterly imaginary. This was his All-of-Parenthood-in-a-Day phase. This phase might last as long as several hours.

"You fucking prick. Not so holy now, huh? I offered to buy you a drink. You remember what you said to me? Huh?"

And then there was this personality. His in-the-midst-of-the-binge personality, a snarling, sneering meanness that would have seemed over-the-top on a cartoon villain tying a damsel to the train tracks.

"You told me you didn't drink."

If this was a dream, why wasn't I accepting my outlandish circumstances in that odd passive way of dreams? Why was I wondering what the fuck I was doing back in Pete's Peek-In with my father? I was still feeling the bar. It felt very real, right down to the tacky, sticky circles left by last night's drinks.

"And I said to you, I said, oh yes you do!" He cackled at this.

I looked from the surface of the bar to my father. He was sitting very erect on his barstool now, in the drunkard's half-assed approximation of sobriety. He had the same nasty-looking gash that I remembered from thirty years before, a messily scabbed-over cut about three inches long over his right eyebrow. The flesh of his face had a morbid fish-belly cast, out of which his batshit eyes glittered triumphantly, twitching and rolling like flashing beacons in a very gray, storm-tossed sea.

"I'm talking to you, punk."

"Why are you here?" I whispered. "Why am I here?"

"Why are you here?" My father grinned in happy contempt. "You're here because you're a dumbfuck pansy quitter. A quitter so pathetic, he can't even quit right, blowing the wrong half of his head off."

He pursed his lips and considered the shot glass on the bar before him. He reached out slowly and lifted the glass daintily between thumb and forefinger, pinky extended, the way a certain kind of drunk does. The kind of drunk who likes to pretend that there are elaborate and necessary rituals attendant to drinking. He brought the glass to his lips and tossed the shot back. Then he set the glass back on the bar with exaggerated care.

"I'm here," he said, and cleared his throat, "because the Big Guy sent me."

"The Big Guy?" I said, alarmed. "Death? Death sent you here?"

"He sent me to give you a message."

I looked at my father, aghast. "A message?"

"Get your shit together. You don't have as much time as you think."

My father was gesturing at the bartender, who was studiously ignoring my father, the only patron in the bar at that early hour.

"Death says this? About time running out?"

"What? Am I not speaking English now?" My father raised the empty shotglass and brought it down sharply on the bar. "Hey, Anton, you fucking kraut!"

"I'm running out of time? What is that supposed to mean?"

"I don't know. That's all there is. You're running out of time."

"Out of time for what? For not dying?"

That's the only thing at stake here, right? It would seem to me, I'd have all the time in the world for not dying.

"You got some kind of job to do, is my understanding. And you're fucking it up. No big surprise there, I could've told him. You fucked up every job you ever had." My father was plucking angrily at several day's worth of beard on his face, a tired fuzz all patchy red and gray. "Anton, you fucking Nazi! Get your head out of your ass!"

"Nobody said anything about a time limit. He must have meant something else. Did he say anything else? Anything at all?"

"Look." My father's hand was in the air, stalled in mid-beckon. "I already said more than I intended to say for that motherfucker. Me and the B.G. don't see eye-to-eye. He said deliver the message, I delivered it. Now you both can go to hell."

"But there must—" I stopped, puzzled. My father wasn't the kind of guy who got along with many people. But going toe-to-toe, mano a mano, with Death seemed a little ambitious. "What do you mean you don't see eye-to-eye?"

"I mean I don't like the way that motherfucker does business."

Anton had finally given up and was approaching my father's place at the bar. "What now?" he said.

"Set me up again," my father said. "And bring me a draft, too."

Anton sighed. He was wiping out a plastic ashtray with a rag and looking at a spot about two feet above my father's head. "I do you a favor and you're right back, all over my ass."

"Fuck you. Come on." My father pulled a clutch of filthy bills from his shirt pocket and extracted a five. He threw it on the bar.

"I told you we're closed. We don't open 'til eleven. That one shot was a courtesy. I said you could have one shot, if you promised to leave. Now you leave."

"You're open at nine am! You don't ever close!"

"Management's discretion. I say we're closed, we're closed."

"Fuck you!"

Anton's attention had drifted to me. "Who are you?"

"I'm his son."

Anton made a sour face. "Sorry to hear it."

"What do you mean you don't see eye-to-eye?" I said.

My father cocked one viper's eye at me. "Just what I said. He don't like me and I don't like him."

I shook my head. "Why not?"

"Why the fuck you think, you little bitch? Because of Thomas!"

Thomas. The normal Huffnagle. Mowed down one rainy night by a drunken driver.

"That kid would've been something. He had the smarts," my father tapped his temple, "and he knew how to use 'em. He had the skills and the brains both." He turned back to Anton. "I ain't leaving 'til you bring me a shot and a beer."

"You were four years in a hole when Thomas died. What do you know about it?"

"Motherfucker took my boy. And for what? For nothin'. He couldn't take pissy-pants, too good to get his hands dirty. Oh, no. He had to take Thomas."

Pissy-pants being me, of course.

"Motherfucker does what he wants though, don't he? Run Thomas over on a mission of mercy, directing traffic. And for what?" My father was no longer talking to me; he was talking to Anton. "So pissy-pants here can throw away thirty more years on nothing."

"How do you know what happened?" I said.

"Boy would've been something. Would've made his dad proud." My father pivoted on his barstool and goggled at me, newly infuriated. "I got eyes in my head, don't I?"

"You were dead. Dead and forgotten."

"Yeah, well." Sullen, now. "Maybe life ain't the straight line you'd like to believe." He turned to Anton. "You bring me a shot and a beer, I'll leave."

"That's what you said last time," Anton said.

"This time for true. For real."

Anton set the well-scrubbed ashtray on the bar. "A can of beer," he said. "I bring you a can of beer, you take it with you. You don't even open it in here."

"What do I need a can of beer from you?" my father barked incredulously. "I can get a can of beer from Lucky's, for half what you charge. Less."

"Then go to Lucky's," Anton said.

"I ain't giving that fucking chink my money anymore."

"Uh huh." Anton picked up another ashtray. "And he ain't taking it no more, is what I hear."

"Fucking chink." My father drummed the bar rail with his fingers, considering his options. "Bring me the can of beer," he said.

I heard a noise behind me and I saw that there was someone else in the bar. It was the kid I remembered from all those years ago, the Hispanic kid who had been about my age. He was still about that age, still loading packs of cigarettes into the vending machines.

Anton placed a can of Pabst Blue Ribbon on the bar. "Now leave."

My father reached out and gripped the can. Then he grinned evilly and pulled the pulltab off the can. It was the old-style can, with the sharp, wedge-shaped pulltab that came off. He threw the tab behind the bar. "Let's hear some jukebox," he said.

Anton nodded, smiling a small smile. "I ain't going to call the cops this time," he said.

My father took a drink of his beer and set the can down on the bar with a flourish. "Mighty white of ya, barkeep."

"Are you listening to me?" Anton spread his arms and gripped the bar rail on his side of the bar. He looked closely at my father. "It ain't going to be the cops this time. You got five minutes."

"Five minutes or what?" my father said, like someone who already knew the or-what.

"Five minutes and it's Ted and Frenchy. They come down here and we close the door. Door'll be closed before you even know what happened. And then you can discuss it with Ted and Frenchy."

The smile was gone from my father's face. "Fuck you. You wouldn't."

"Five minutes." Anton released the bar rail, straightened, and walked away.

THE END IS NEAR

My father lifted his can of beer, sipped from it, and set it down. "Same everywhere you go, some Big Cheese knocking the little guy down."

The décor—like the beer can, like my father's familiar rants—was unmistakably Reagan-era '80s. First term. The shaggy felt sports pennants, the old-fashioned metal behemoth of a cash register with the price signs that leaped up like tombstones behind the glass, the jukebox filled with 45s, the Berzerk video game lethargically bleeping and blooping behind me.

"Fucking Big Guy, taking my boy away from me."

I looked at my father, knowing, then, what I hadn't known the first time I'd been to Pete's Peek-In. That he'd be dead in six months. Robbed of some little clutch of filthy bills, bludgeoned, drowning in his own vomit.

"That boy was the light of my life."

Dying alone, in a tenement courtyard, people drawing the window shades on his last gurgling breaths.

"If you loved Thomas so much," I said, "maybe you shouldn't have deserted him. Deserted all of us. Deserted us and killed yourself." Not that any of us missed you much, I could have added, but didn't.

"Look who's talking about killing himself. Mr. Fucking Half-a-Face." He looked at me smugly. "I was right, last time, wasn't I?"

It occurred to me, then, that I was talking. That I wasn't writing things down. I reached up and felt the cold enamel of my jaw prosthetic. How was I speaking?

My father grinned widely, revealing a front space where a tooth had been, until fairly recently. "You gonna tell me you don't remember our little talk in here? Our last talk? A father's last words to his son?"

"I remember it." I could hear my voice in my ears. My father could hear it. But I had no jaw, no tongue, to speak of. "You can hear me?"

"Oh, you should've seen yourself. You thought you were hot shit, didn't ya?" His evil grin crept wider. "Oh yes you did."

I peered up at the corroded, rotting tin ceiling of the bar, orange and black in the morning light. "Okay, Death," I called out. "I'm ready to go now."

"Oh yeah, I told ya." He lifted his beer can decorously, took another sip, set it down. "You're the same as me."

If we were all here, me and my father and the bartender and even the Hispanic kid, did that mean that my mother was outside with the Fort Lee cops? I turned away from my father and moved slowly to the door. The door was propped open, allowing more daylight in.

"The same as me. The same devil inside ya," he called after me, "I watched you pop out of your ma and I saw it. Right then. In your baby face. We're the same."

I stepped into the doorway and looked out. Everything outside was brightly lit, unnaturally bright. And empty. No cars, no people. Just the broad, empty street and nothing moving anywhere. Utter silence.

"Only you have none of my redeeming qualities. You're weak. And spineless. A pissy-pants crybaby. You got your dad's demons and nothing to fight 'em with. You gotta be strong. Strong of mind and body. And you ain't got none of that."

"Okay, okay!" I clutched the doorframe and yelled the words from my frozen, artificial jaw. "I'm ready to go!"

"Your ma ain't out there, pissypants," my father said. "She's long gone. It's just me and you, this time."

I turned away from the door. My father was reaching into his shirt pocket. He tugged out the greasy wad of bills again.

"What do you say we try it again?" he said. "Anton! Bring a drink for the kid. Some decent scotch. None of that house-label shit."

"No, thanks," I said. Though I wondered, would it be possible to drink it, the way it was possible to talk? I'd thought my drinking days were all over.

"You got two minutes," Anton said.

"Fuck you." My father peeled a bill off and threw it on the bar. "Let's see some of that good stuff."

Anton looked blankly at my father. "It's your funeral," he said. He turned around and lifted a bottle from the back row of bottles. He set a glass on the bar.

"The good stuff!" my father said, approvingly. "That's it."

Anton splashed some scotch into the glass and slid it away from my father, toward me. "On the house," he said. "Any son of that sorry sack of shit has one coming."

My father cackled. "Bet you ain't too good for it now, are ya, pissypants? Bet you don't mind sharing a drink with your dear old dad now, do ya?"

I approached and looked at the shot glass on the bar. I looked at my father. The muscles in my throat clenched and I shuddered like a rabid dog.

"I'm really ready to go," I said. "I really am."

"You sure?" someone said.

It was the Hispanic kid who had spoken. He was still standing by the cigarette machines, holding an empty cardboard box. He was very slight, with a wispy mustache and a Superman logo tattooed on his arm.

"Things back at the hospital might not be much better than they are here."

"You're him? You're Death?" I said, doubtfully. This kid didn't look like the Big Guy.

"Ain't worried about turning out like me now, are ya, Mister Fucking Half-a-Face?" My father upended his beer can over his mouth and then slammed it on the bar. "You wish you could be half the man I am now! Don't ya? At least I got a fucking face!"

"No," the kid said. "I just work here."

"At least I'm not a fucking pansy quitter! Drink your fucking drink, ya goddamn pansy!"

Two men had entered the bar. The second to enter turned and quietly closed the door behind him.

"Drink it or I'll take my fucking belt to ya, like the old days. Tan your fucking ass for ya!"

The first man was looking sadly at Anton. "We got trouble here?" he said.

"I'm ready to go," I said to the kid. "Nowhere could be worse than here."

"Whoa, hey, Frenchy!" my father was protesting, too late. "I'm leaving! I'm leaving!"

"Okay," the kid said. He grinned. "That's the way you want it. Hang on."

And I was flat on my back and the ceiling was whirling crazily above my head. There were high rails on either side of my bed and people I didn't know were grasping the rails and running in place. No, not in place. The ceiling was whirling because I was moving. Very swiftly. Plastic bags of solutions—two clear, two blood-red—were rocking above my head, strung from metal poles.

The foot of my bed crashed through a pair of swinging doors and I was wheeled into a brightly lit room.

"He's awake," somebody said.

"Good timing," someone else said.

A pair of eyes appeared above me. They belonged to a man in green hospital mask and surgical cap.

And then, finally, embarrassingly, I was thinking this: I don't want to die.

"What?" the guy in the mask barked.

For the first time since my arrival here at the hospital, at this Long-Term Care and Rehabilitation Unit, I was thankful I didn't have a mouth. I was thankful I wasn't able to whisper, cravenly, I don't want to die.

Although my eyes probably told the story.

"Put this guy out," the guy, the doctor, growled. "Come on. Move it, sister."

A black mask appeared over my face.

And then I was here. That was two days ago. This is the first time they've let me sit up. Dr. Croate's been here and gone several times. She says I suffered some kind of radical internal hemorrhage. Blood backed up into my spleen, causing an artery or two in my spleen to rupture. That spleen's mostly gone now. Expect me to be less splenetic, from here on out.

But all of that is another story.

I just want to say one thing here.

I didn't have that coming, Death. That scene with my dad.

I'm carrying my end. I didn't deserve that.

And you know it, too, you son of a bitch.

§

June 28th, early afternoon

I know I suggested I might try again. That I might tackle these letters from Sherilyn to Mom, the one from Mom to Sherilyn. But I don't think I will.

I'm out of time, for one thing. I've got less than forty-eight hours left.

And you probably don't want to hear it, anyway.

You probably think I've wasted enough of your time already.

Suffice to say, my sister is alive and well. She has her own life, a happy, fulfilled life. My mother knew where she was, for years. They corresponded back and forth, sometimes about me. Surprisingly often, about me. They worried about me.

I know where my sister lives. Her return address is on each of these envelopes. Though I won't be contacting her. My sister's happy life will be happier for not overlapping any part of the festivities to come, two days from now.

Here's one of my sister's letters to my mother. Picked at random, it's no more insulting and wrongheaded than any of the others. I'll staple it below, if I remember to do it, when this journal comes out of my printer on Monday morning.

[Attach Sherilyn's letter here.]

> Dear Mom—
>
> No, my feelings aren't hurt. I could have predicted that he'd sneak away before I got there. And don't blame yourself, either. It's not your job to watch him every minute.
>
> Believe me, I'm used to Nathan's ways by now. I know he cares about me (and you too!) even if he is incapable of expressing it. That boy's got some growing up to do!
>
> Maybe next time, we'll have the big brother-sister reunion. We'll see.
>
> I can see your point about cleaning the vomit off the stoop and moving his car from the front lawn to the driveway. Yes, you do have the neighbors to think about. But why couldn't you wake Nathan up and have him do it?
>
> What kills me about Nathan is the way he can harbor these life-and-death grudges against dad on the one hand and then act exactly like dad sometimes, on

the other. Maybe its like you say. They're too much alike.

You indulge him too much, ma. I mean, I worry about him, too, but you have to draw the line. If you clean up after him, what reason does he have to change? If you act like nothing's wrong, why should he do a reality check and do something about it?

Jeez, ma, look at him. Living in a drab little city apartment with no woman, no real life, no nothing, so there's nothing to get in the way of his drinking and his depression and those terrible gloomy ads he writes. Just like dad though he refuses to see it. For an intelligent guy, he sure can be a blockhead when it suits him!

Some day he's going to wake up and realize all he's missed out on in this life. I just hope its soon enough that he can do something about it.

Oh, but listen to me! I'm getting to be a tough old broad in my old age. 39 this month. That's the age where you stop counting! Rambo took me to Las Vegas for the weekend (my first time!). We stayed at the New York, New York Hotel and Casino. It was just like NYC, but without the dirt and crime and beggars. It even had a little Grenwich Village!

It was so nice to see you again! It's so hard to believe that seventeen years have gone by! All the bad stuff (dad and Caleb and poor Thomas and the fights we had, ma) seem like another lifetime, don't they? It's true what they say, time heals all wounds.

Carson's STILL talking about the llama that sneezed on Isaiah and blew llama snot all over him at the Turtle Back Zoo. And the door on the side of the house. (Ma, you really have to do something about that porch. Someday someone's going to walk out that door and sue you. You know?)

Believe it or not, we got Carson to give up his Pokemon blanket. We helped him leave it out for the Pokemon Blanket Fairy. The Pokemon Blanket Fairy takes the blanket and gives it to another littler boy who needs a Pokemon blanket. And leaves a new Sony Playstation for Carson, I might add. I told Rambo, here we go, out of the frying pan and into the fire. He said, No sweat, in five years we'll call the Sony Playstation Fairy. I said, Sure we will. In the meantime Rambo plays the Playstation as much as Carson, and he's 46 this summer.

Oh my, what else? Isaiah wants a summer job, this summer. I told him you have your whole life to have jobs. But what can you tell a boy? They already know everything. He says that kids his age work at Great Adventure, the amusement park. Their parents just have to fill out a permission form or something. I said, we'll see.

THE END IS NEAR

I got another promotion. Remember
when I said how weird it was, telling
people what to do? Now that's all I do.
That and do performance reviews. I
haven't worked the phones in months.

And that's about it. Rambo sends his
love. He says next time he's coming for
sure! (Don't worry! It won't take me
another seventeen years to come East.
Maybe next year! We'll see.)

Love—S

I could take apart these letters, debunk their content lie by lie,
restore the record, put the sharp needle of grim reality to each of
these perversely cheery speech balloons.

But you know what? I'm not going to.

Instead, I'm going to say something about family, here.

I said a little before, providing a fun-facts, short-form history
of the Huffnagles. And now I'll say a little more. And then I'll be
done with it.

We never put a foot on the ladder of respectability, and it
wasn't for lack of money. My parents worked at decent-paying,
union-protected jobs—commercial printing and clerical work,
respectively. Rather, it was because my parents spent most of
their time and effort and money trying to escape our house and
our lives. Drinking and hiding and fleeing. It was because they
didn't give a shit. Or enough of a shit.

This is an old story, told many times by many people, and it
must be wearying to read. It's wearying to write. But I'm almost
done, I promise.

In her later years, my mother conceived a detailed fantasy
history of our family. In it, we had all endured hard times as a
family, with stoic grace. We didn't have the luxuries that some
had, but we struggled through it together, grew to be better
people for it. Those of us who lived, anyway. Times were hard,

but we could be proud of ourselves. This elaborate fantasy past was a gift that my mother gave to herself.

Some people say, you can believe what you want to believe, but that won't change the facts. But it's not true. What you believe is the facts. Becomes the facts. My mother forgot the realities of our long-ago lives the way Randy Trent, evidently, has forgotten that I ever existed. These beliefs become, for them, the facts. Their memories are benevolent to them in this way.

When you're young, you need your parents. You need them desperately. To feed you, to encourage you, to clothe you, to provide a home that you can bring friends to, to teach you something about life, to pick you up when you're down, to be proud of, to provide a simple, stable base from which you can grow up. You need them.

And then, a few short years later, you don't need your parents anymore. You can love them, trust them, dote on them, admire them, use them as babysitters, go to Disney Land with them, be grateful to them, cherish their memory when they're gone.

But you'll never need them again. Not in that terrible, primal way you do when you're young. Parents get that one chance, and then it's over. In the wink of an eye.

We—my brother, my sister, and I—learned very early in life that our parents couldn't be trusted. That we couldn't count on them. That's an enormous weight to bear when your parents are all you have.

Years later, during my infrequent visits, my mother would sometimes entertain herself with her fantasies of our tough-but-noble family history. The tragedies we overcame. The strength we drew from hardship. Like my sister, I didn't disabuse her of these lies. I didn't even mind, so much. I liked my mother, after a fashion.

By then, I could afford to. I didn't need her anymore.

THE END IS NEAR

§

I don't see why I should continue with this.

"No?"

He went too far this time. Your boss. With this Dad thing.

"He's not my boss. Or, at least, he's no more my boss than he's anyone's."

Today's emissary from Death is, cleverly enough, a nun. Not your newfangled nun in pastel pantsuit and sensible Thom McAn flats, either. I'm talking flowing black habit, wimple, curled-up black booties like witch shoes, the full nun effect.

If he won't play by the rules, why should I?

"As I understand it, Mr. Huffnagle, he makes the rules."

And changes them when it suits him. Does he treat you like this?

"His methods and motivations may be inscrutable to us."

Well, you may be used to that sort of relationship with authority figures. But I'm not.

She tucked up her lower lip and left it at that.

I looked at her with curiosity. She's a big woman, with a wide, friendly face and lively blue eyes inevitably accentuated by her head gear. She sits by my bed with her hands folded in her lap, an expression of good-humored severity on her face. She has a slight accent, mildly sing-songy. Scandinavian-American, maybe. From one of those cheese-producing northern U.S. states.

Do nuns still do the whole conservative dress thing?

"They did in my day. And we weren't lacking for novices, either. Draw your own conclusions."

When was your day, ma'am?

"Not so long ago. When was yours?"

I don't think I ever had a day, ma'am. In the heyday sense.

"I've been warned that you have a talent for chatter, Mr. Huffnagle. And you may call me Sister Rafaella."

Have you been talking to Betty?

"No, I haven't had the pleasure."

Really. I looked at my visitor some more, my pen poised above my communication tablet, then I wrote, *Were you surprised at how the afterlife turned out, Sister Rafaella?*

"Surprised? No. I'm sure I simply hoped for an opportunity to serve. And hoped to be worthy of the task when the time came. Sentiments you might profitably reflect upon, Mr. Huffnagle."

No heavenly choirs of angels, though. Right? No Saint Peter at the gate?

Sister Rafaella gave me one of those satisfied, Mona Lisa smiles peculiar to spiritual types. "Who knows where the journey ends, Mr. Huffnagle? I like to believe that there might still be heavenly choirs, at the end of the day."

Maybe. I hope so, Sister R.

"I foresee only more bedrest at the end of your day, however."

I know, I know. I'm just tired of Death playing fast and loose with the rules, that's all.

"It's his game, isn't it, Mr. Huffnagle?"

So it appears.

"Get back to work, now."

I looked at the transcript on the bed beside me. I thumbed through some pages of densely handwritten scrawl. Just looking at the thing gives me hand cramp.

"When you're done, perhaps all your questions will be answered."

Is that true?

"You're doing fine. Don't stop now."

I saw that I had left off just before the arrival of the pizza.

Alright, I wrote to Sister Rafaella. *Here we go.*

"Alright," I said to Alice and Felicia and Danika and Randy. "Here we go."

THE END IS NEAR

I had just hung up the phone. Woody was outside with our pizza. I had ordered it about fifteen minutes before.

"That's pretty good service," Danika said. "Remind me to take hostages next time I order a pizza."

"Maybe they're afraid I'll change my mind."

Felicia had stood up and was smoothing the wrinkles in her red satin dress. "Why don't you just kill yourself now and save everybody a lot of trouble?" she said. "You're going to kill yourself anyway. Why wait 'til the last minute?"

There was a sharp rapping at the outside front door.

"Hello?" someone called.

I went to the inside door and pulled it open an inch. A jowly, middleaged guy in a tan uniform was standing before the door, holding a pizza box. He had deep-set, basset-hound eyes, a paunch that sloped heavily over his belt, and a thin bathtub ring of gray hair at the sides and back of his head. His holster was conspicuously empty. He looked like a character actor, like the kind of guy who plays the small-town sheriff in a Burt Reynolds movie.

I raised my shotgun and edged into the front room.

"You're Woody?" I called.

"Yep."

"Nathan Huffnagle."

I went to the door and unlocked it. Then I looked out the display windows. The state police were trying to keep things orderly, using a long line of sawhorse barricades to keep the growing crowd well behind the police vehicles. There were a couple more news vans—WNBC News4, Eyewitness News—on the scene and I could see a couple of different crowd interviews in progress, each interview surrounded by a dense knot of people standing on tiptoe to get a better look. Or to be seen on TV.

People were passing six-packs of beer up to other people on the roofs of Holly's Tavern and Salvatore's Pizza. A camera on one of the news trucks dollied around, doing a sweep of the roof crowd, and everyone on the roof stood and cheered, some raising beers and waving, like a crowd doing the wave at an '80s sporting event. Some kids started frantically snapping a bedsheet. They spread it out and held it up to the camera. Someone had painted a message on it.

KICK HIS ASS, RANDY!

"This box is kinda hot," Woody said.

I moved away from the door. "Come on in."

"We had to send a trooper over to FoodKing for the yellow and red peppers," Woody said. "They might be a little underdone."

"That's fine. Take it in back, there. Through that door."

Woody walked past me into the back room. I followed him and shut the door behind me.

"Into the center of the room," I said.

Woody walked a few steps forward. "Hey, Felicia," he said.

"Oh look, it's Woody," Felicia said bitterly. "We're saved."

Woody looked at Randy, flag-tied and handcuffed to the beam, naked but for the underwear on his head. "How's it goin', Randy?"

Randy shrugged. "Could be better."

Woody nodded at this. He looked at Alice, sitting cross-legged on the floor next to her shopping bag. "Miss Chang?"

"Alice," Alice said. "Hi, Woody."

"How you holdin' up?"

"I'm good. I think everything's going to be okay here."

"Uh huh. I think so, too." Woody shifted the pizza from hand to hand again. "I don't think we met before."

"I work in the pharmacy in the Pathmark out on Route 10."

"Okay," Woody said. "Sure, I know that one." He turned last to Danika. "I don't think we've met, either."

"We haven't." Danika had returned to the stool by the back door and was perched on it, swinging her big black shoes about. "You should've brought some soda. Or some bottled water."

"True," Woody said. "I should've thought of that."

"How do you want to do this?" I said to Woody.

"Nothin' much to do. Felicia, if you'll just leave through the front door, we'll be all set."

Felicia folded her arms, an aggrieved expression on her face. She looked at Randy, at Alice, then at Randy again. "Sorry fucking ending, this is," she said.

Woody looked at her and, when no one else said anything, said, "How's that, Felicia?"

"It's nothing that concerns you, Woody." Felicia was still standing in place, one leg cocked forward in her sheath dress, looking disgusted and making no move to go anywhere. "It's just the same shit again, my ridiculous life playing itself over and over, like a broken record."

"Maybe we could talk about it outside," Woody said, like someone who was sensing a new complication that he didn't want to address right then.

"You know what?" Felicia said, more heatedly. "I don't remember saying I was willing to go anywhere. I don't remember agreeing to be traded for a fucking pizza by this low-class, outcast weasel. You," she said, pointing at me, "don't have the right to trade me for anything. I do what I want to do."

"I don't think that's the point here," Woody said.

"You better pray you die." Felicia was still pointing at me. "That Woody shoots you, if you don't have sense enough to shoot yourself. Because I'm gonna make sure you regret the day you crawled out of your hole."

"Felicia, come on," Randy said, through his underwear. "Go. We'll hash the rest of this out later."

"Oh no we won't," Felicia hissed, whirling on Randy. "Because I don't want to hear it. You can have your little slanty fortune cookie whore. See if she does for you what I do. Did. Did for you. God, I must've been out of my mind."

"I told you before—" Alice started.

"And you!" Felicia yelped at Alice. "You win, honey. He's all yours. And wait'll you find out what a fucking prize he is, too. What a fucking prize they all are. Every single goddamned one of them. You think you're hot shit now, with your tight ass and your new tit job. Wait ten years, when the same guys you're stealing now are fucking girls half your age behind your back, taking them to the same damned places you go, flaunting them, making a fool of you at every turn, in front of your own fucking friends."

"Why don't we just . . ." Woody was looking for someone to hand the pizza to, but no one was making any move to take it.

"I'm standing here, trying to figure out which one of these good-for-nothing weasels is worse. The one making a fool of me or the one pointing a gun at me. And you know what?" Felicia took two steps toward Alice, so that she was standing over her. "They're all the same. Either they think the world owes them a favor because their mommies spanked them. Or they use people up like toilet paper. Woody here was probably the same, back when he could get it up.

"Bullies. All of them. You can have 'em, honey. Fuck both of 'em. All of 'em. This one," meaning me, "will be glad to die without his virginity. And this one . . ." Felicia walked over to Randy and stood before him. "This one . . ." She swung her open hand back behind her head and cracked Randy hard across the face, rocking his head sideways. "Fuck you, shithead! Some day, you'll realize what you threw away!

"I am through with men." Felicia marched to the door to the front room, yanked it open, and marched through it. "I am going to move to Florida and get myself a goddamn dog." The bell above the outside door tinkled and she was gone. A surprisingly loud cheer erupted from outside.

We all looked at the empty doorway.

"Jesus," Danika said. "What a bitch."

I shrugged. I didn't know what to say.

"New tit job?" Randy said.

"Untrue," Alice said. "That woman's a snake."

We all looked at the doorway some more.

You know what, Sister R? I'm not even sure I know why I'm doing this, anymore.

I was holding my communication pad up for Sister Rafaella to see. She had been leafing through one of the magazines the hospital orderlies sometimes drop off here. Entertainment Weekly, it looked like.

She lifted her eyes and read my pad. "You're doing it for yourself," she said. "For you."

What if I'm not sure I want what I want? What if I want something else?

"Oh. I see." Sister Rafaella seemed to consider this. "Then I guess you could take that up with him, too. When the time comes."

And when will that be?

"Soon." She smiled pleasantly at me.

How soon?

"Very soon." She leaned over and tapped the transcript with a big pale finger. "Work." She went back to her magazine.

So.

We were all looking at the door that Felicia had just exited through.

"You're Stacy's boy, aren't you?" Woody said to me, after a while.

I looked at Woody, surprised. "Yeah," I said.

"I was sorry to hear about your ma."

I shrugged, looked away.

"She was a tough-minded woman, Stacy. She didn't take nothing from nobody. We had ourselves a conversation or two, over the years."

I didn't doubt it. In the course of serving summonses, most likely. Unpaid bills, unpaid traffic tickets.

"You know, Nathan. You still got plenty of options." Woody was talking quietly and slowly, still holding our pizza. "Maybe now's as good a time as any to think about some of 'em."

I looked at Alice. "Could you take that pizza?"

Woody handed the pizza box to Alice. "I wish I knew how to say this better. I wish you could see this situation from my side of it."

"You do? Why?"

"If you could see it from my side, you'd know what I know. You'd've seen enough people do stuff that could've been easily avoided. Stuff they wish they hadn't done."

"Thanks for your time, Sheriff."

Woody looked at me for a long moment. Then he started moving toward the door.

"Enjoy your pizza," he said. "Salvatore's makes a good pie. It ain't Carnivale's, but what is?" He turned to Alice. "Is there someone we can contact for you, Miss Chang?"

"Have someone tell my parents I'm fine. That I'm going to be okay."

"Sure thing." Woody glanced at me, then looked at Alice and nodded. "I'll tell them that."

He turned to Danika. "How about you, Miss? Is there someone we can contact for you?"

"No."

"You sure? There must be somebody, wants to know you're okay."

Danika lifted her big shoes and studied them for a moment. "No. I'm good."

"You mind if I ask, how it is you happened to be here? You look a little young to be needing auto parts."

Danika eyed Woody coolly. "Fate."

"Uh huh. I figured." Woody was looking closely at Danika. "You from around here?"

"Not anymore."

"But you were, though. We met before?"

"Maybe," she said. "Do you walk the paths of the spirit realm? Are you an acolyte in the Church of Wicca?"

"No," he said. "I ain't."

§

June 28th, early evening

It's official. I'm packing heat.

I am keeping and bearing arms, though not in a legal, registered sense. A shotgun and a pistol, specifically. Courtesy of Ziggy.

Or someone I'm going to call Ziggy, anyway. I can't do all your work for you, law enforcement representatives.

I just got back from the local VFW. The bartender there was a big sixtyish, heavy guy without, it seemed, a hair on his body. Not just bald, but eyebrowless, armhairless, everything. Imagine a big pink Mr. Clean, without the shaggy eyebrows.

"Are you a veteran of one of our nation's foreign conflicts, honorably discharged from a branch of our armed services?" he asked.

"No," I said.

"Good for you. Wisht I'd been as smart." He mopped the space on the bar before me. "I'm John. People call me John."

"Nathan." We shook hands.

"What'll ya have?"

"What's on tap?"

"Got Rheingold on tap," he indicated three Rheingold taps, "Bud and Bud Light in bottles."

"Rheingold, I guess."

"Good choice." He set a glass beneath the tap. "So what brings you to our thriving establishment?"

"I'm here to meet Ziggy."

"Uh huh." He didn't seem particularly surprised. He set the beer before me and slid one of my dollars off the counter. "Gotta charge ya civilian prices, my friend."

He made change from a cash box beneath the bar and put a quarter before me. "Happy hour ends in twenty minutes," he said.

"Thanks." I looked around.

The bar was a gloomy, oak-paneled room that occupied most of the basement of the VFW hall. I'd entered upstairs, into a hushed, high-ceilinged hall with a stage, a dozen slowly turning ceiling fans, and acres of sprung, gapped, and splotched oak floorboards. Down here in the basement, hundreds of framed photos—fading, yellowing black-and-whites mostly, some pastel-hued '70s Polaroids—hung on the walls. Members hoisting brews, posing with dead deer, dangling fish from fishing lines, hoisting more brews, being men together. There were about ten tables, all with chairs piled on them, and two pool tables covered with big vinyl mats. A big TV behind the bar was showing a baseball game with the sound turned off. And there was John. I was the only happy-hour customer.

"Slow for a Saturday, huh?"

John shrugged. "Early yet. Probably get a few guys in here after dinner."

"You know Ziggy?"

"Zig? Sure, I know Zig."

Which about did it for conversation, until Ziggy arrived. I was into my fourth beer and my third dollar when a fire door at the front of the room shrieked open on arthritic hinges and a little guy in big boots vaulted into the room.

"You Nathan?"

"Yeah."

He swayed across the room and held out a hand. He was about five-foot-two and grinning up at me like a chimpanzee. "Ziggy," he said.

"Hey," I said.

Ziggy was the kind of guy who, seventy years ago, ran a still in the woods outside of town and sold hootch to the locals. Fifty years before that, he trapped muskrats and squirrels and raccoons, and came into town four times a year to sell pelts and stock up on butter and bacon and flour. He was that kind of guy. Born out of time. Born too late.

In this modern incarnation, he wore baggy green pants and a greasy flannel shirt with the sleeves cut off. His huge boots were mended with gray duct tape and he had a John Deere cap pulled forward on his head so that the bill all but touched his nose. He had apple cheeks, red-rimmed eyes, and a gray-stubble beard. He could have been any age at all, from thirty to sixty-five.

"Whyntcha buy me a beer," Ziggy said.

"Sure thing. Rheingold okay?"

"Don't pull that stuff on me," he said. He climbed up onto a barstool and perched there expectantly. "That guy with the outboards come by, lookin' for me?"

"Nope," John said. He set a beer before Ziggy.

"Yah." Ziggy looked around. "Where the hell is everybody?"

"They're hiding in the can, waitin' for you to go. We barely got all the hookers and trained seals in there, before you showed up."

"Yah. I figured." Ziggy lifted his beer and drained half of it. "If I need to take a leak," he belched, "I'll just piss in the sink behind ya, then."

"Make yourself at home, Zig."

Ziggy turned to me. "It ain't what it used to be, here," he said. "Used to be, on a Saturday, you'd have guys three deep at the bar, yellin' and carryin' on."

"Really," I said.

He looked at me over the rim of his mug. "You a vet?"

"No," I said.

He shrugged. "'S okay." He took a more leisurely swallow of his beer and set the mug on the bar. "Did two tours in Vietnam in the sixties, before it went into the shitter. Sixty-six and sixty-eight inta nine." Vietnam to rhyme with ma'am, not with bomb. The way crafty little ferrets with guns probably said it in the sixties. "People say that war was for nothin', but it weren't."

"No?"

"No, sir. Showed the Commies we was as batshit as they was." He grinned like someone happy to have a new audience for an old joke. "Back when it mattered."

"We lost that war, though," I said.

"We sure did." He finished his beer and slid the mug down the bar to get John's attention. He pointed at my money. "Now we're all wearin' the same chains, Gooks and Joes, both."

I looked at Ziggy. "Chains?"

"The Federal Reserve. The international bankin' cartels. Don't you read the news?"

"Oh."

"Hard rain's a gonna fall."

I nodded sagely at this. "So," I said. "You have some guns for sale."

John slid another beer in front of Ziggy.

"Yep, I do." Ziggy looked at the new beer benignly, hands spread wide on the brass bar rail. "Used to be, Saturdays, they couldn't fill the pitchers fast enough. We used to have a guy, Fast Jimmy Stanton, used to stand up on the bar and let fly with the oldies. I Got a Crush on You. Angel Eyes. That shit. Beautiful voice." He shook his head. "John!" he yelped suddenly, like a terrier. "Remember Fast Jimmy?"

John was leaning against the bar sink, waiting for one of us to need a refill. "Sure," he said.

"Yep." Ziggy was still admiring his new beer. "Fast Jimmy had a way with the ladies. That's why they called him Fast Jimmy."

"Fast Jimmy had a way of skipping out on his bar tabs." John folded his arms and studied the silent baseball game. "That's why they called him Fast Jimmy."

"Yeah, that too." Ziggy sipped his beer. "Stroke got him. Spent two years in the VA meat locker, blinking once fer yes, twice fer no. Good man, Fast Jimmy."

"'Nother dead soldier," John agreed.

"Ya see?" Ziggy was talking to me again. "Ain't nobody here no more. These new guys fightin' for Big Oil and Citibank," Ziggy made a face, "you don't see 'em in here. Buncha fuckin' button pushers anyways."

John grinned at this. "Least they won a few. Kicked some sand nigger booty."

"Soon it'll be us against them. We'll see how those button jockeys make out then." Ziggy was fondling his mug, not to be detoured. "Three deep at the bar. Them days is gone, gone, gone."

I looked around. They sure were.

"I, umm, I'm kind of pressed for time," I said. "Can we take a look at what you got?"

"Yah, yah." Ziggy tipped his beer mug up and placed it, empty, on the bar. "Gimme five minutes," he said to John. "Don't go shuttin' up shop while I'm in the lot."

"Sure thing, Zig. On your way out, tell the bouncers to let a couple more customers past the velvet rope, why don'tcha?"

"Yah, yah." Ziggy slid off his stool, landed on the ground, and started ambling toward the door in his side-to-side shamble. "Three deep at the bar," he said, as I followed.

Ziggy's car was a Chrysler Monte Carlo. I'm no good at years of cars, but this one looked like a late-eighties model, dusty gold with a front quarter panel of dove gray primer. The back bumper was bound to the frame with four lengths of rusty chain and bore two bumper stickers. One said *Gun Control Means Using Two Hands.* The other said *Wife and Dog Missing. Reward for Dog.*

"You were lookin' for what? Shotgun, right?"

"Yeah," I said. I pulled an index card from my pocket, one of the ones I'd taken from the sporting goods store's bulletin board, and read the mysterious phrase on it aloud. "Woodside 12 Gauge 28"."

"The Woody," Ziggy said. "Nice piece." There was a rusty hole where the Monte Carlo's trunk lock had once been. A chain ran through the hole to a padlock that dangled beneath the bumper. Ziggy pulled out a ring thick with keys and undid the lock. "I got some other stuff, you're interested."

"I don't know," I said. "Maybe."

Ziggy lifted the trunk to reveal a small arsenal of weaponry. Rifles and shotguns—some in carrying bags, some not—boxes of ammunition, and several sinister-looking plastic carry cases. Ziggy lifted out a long gun and handed it to me, casually. I looked around the lot, but we were the only people around.

"Ain't new, but it's been cared for."

"Great." I quickly handed it back to him. "I'll take it. Does it come with . . . instructions?"

Ziggy looked at me.

"I'm thinking of taking up hunting," I said.

He cracked the gun open. "Open it, load it, shut it," he whacked it shut, "point it at something. It ain't rocket science."

"No, I guess not." I figured I could always look up the finer points in some website somewhere. *How to Shoot People with Guns.* I reached into my pants pocket and pulled out a handful of bills. "I'll take that and whatever bullets go with it."

Ziggy eyed the roll of bills, mostly hundreds.

"I got some other shit you might be interested in." He propped the shotgun up against the side of the car and pulled one of the plastic cases from the trunk. He popped it open to reveal a darkly gleaming pistol with a long barrel. "Smith & Wesson .44. Big ol' ox clocker."

"I, ummm, I'm not sure I brought my ID with me. My federal ID."

Ziggy grinned like a happy ape at this. He had bright white teeth, the most false-looking false teeth I've ever seen. "Me neither. Look at us, two galoots without IDs. You want the pistol?"

What the fuck, I thought. "Yeah, I'll take that too. And some bullets."

"Real peace of mind, there. In tryin' times." Ziggy closed the case and set it aside with the shotgun. Then he lifted the Woody and pointed it off into the distance, sighting down its barrel. "You know," he said, "if you was less of a hunter and more of a, say, a guy concerned over home protection, I might have a piece or two, might interest ya."

"Oh?"

"Sure." He put his knee on the bumper and dove headfirst into the trunk. "Man's gotta protect his hearth and home." He reappeared with a long vinyl bag, holding it up by its carry strap. Special Ops Combat Shotgun. You got the New World Order knocking at your door, this is your new best friend." He leaped out of the trunk and presented it to me. "Ain't cheap, though."

"Well," I said, "I've got money." I took the bag. It was surprisingly heavy.

Ziggy was already back in the trunk.

"You know," he called out to me, his feet swinging before my eyes, "I got some collector stuff you might wanna see." He leaped out of the trunk, holding two boxes of ammunition and something wrapped in a greasy towel.

"I think I'm good to go," I said. "What do I owe you?"

Ziggy put the ammunition aside and straightened. He reached into the towel and produced a very long knife, like a small sword. He held it up to my face.

"Oh, no," I said. "No, I don't think so."

"See that?" Ziggy was pointing to a tiny embossed symbol at the hilt. "Wehrmacht bayonet. Ever seen one of these before?"

"No," I said.

"Eighty-five bucks," Ziggy said.

"Huh. Well, thanks, but no. I don't think so."

Ziggy shrugged. "I got some shit ain't easy to find." He looked around the empty lot of the VFW, as if his next words were going to be more incriminating than the stockpile of apparently unlicensed, unregistered weaponry sitting beside the car. "Stuff I can't drive around with."

"Okay. I'll keep that in mind," I said. "I've got your number." I waved the little index card at him.

"You let me know. Anyway, I got a few grenades in here somewhere," he said. And he was back in the trunk.

§

As soon as the door closed behind Woody, Alice handed the pizza to Danika and turned to me.

"You're the one who mailed that DVD to the Sail Inn, aren't you?"

I looked at Alice in surprise. "How do you know about that?"

"It's been on the bar DVD player since Friday night."

"It has? They're playing that disc? In the bar?"

"After hours. It's very popular."

I looked at Randy, then back to Alice. "I addressed that disc to Randy. Care of the Sail Inn. They opened it?"

"You thought they wouldn't?"

I was trying to remember which DVD I'd mailed to the bar. The stripping one or the masturbation one.

"You guys have a soda machine around here?" Danika said to Randy.

"There's a little fridge in the breakroom," Randy said to her, looking at me. "What disc? What's this about a DVD?"

"Don't you open your mail?" I said.

"My mail? Where? At home?"

"Here. I sent the other disc here, to the store."

"What other disc? You know how much mail I get here?"

"So it's probably here somewhere." I looked around. "Where do you keep the mail?"

"I don't know. PJ opens the store mail."

"So I guess I don't have to ask who sent me this." Alice was tugging a box from the shopping bag she had with her. She threw the bag aside, set the box on the floor, and reached into the box's open end. She pulled out a dense jumble of black leather straps and gold fittings.

"What's that?" Danika said.

"It's a Deluxe Suspension Harness with Gold-Plated Ball-Gag Extension." Alice held it up before herself. "It comes with a hundred-and-twenty-eight-page book of instructions. Not the kind of thing I often receive at work."

"You sent it to her job?" Danika said to me.

"All I had was her business card."

"It looks like a day's work just climbing into this thing." Alice dropped the harness to the floor and reached into the box again. She pulled out a hot pink t-shirt, shook it open, and draped it over her shoulder.

I'm a whore, hear me roar. The shirt I'd ordered, an XS cropped tee, was little larger than a handkerchief. Good thing I didn't go with the XXS.

"Cool," Danika said. "Lemme see that."

Alice tossed the shirt to Danika and reached into the box again, pulling out a single sheet of paper.

"Dear Alice," she read, "I'm gonna squeeze some hot mustard onto your egg roll. Love, The Rand-Man." She looked at me. "Is that the best you could do?"

"I was pressed for time," I said. "My hour of Internet rental time was almost over."

Danika had walked down one of the aisles, admiring the T-shirt. In a moment, she reappeared with a sixpack of Coke. "Napkins?" she said.

"Paper towels," Randy said. "In the bathroom. Is someone gonna tell me what the fuck is going on?"

I looked at Alice.

"O-o-o-h, no," she said. "It's your party."

I turned to Randy. The naked video or the sex-toy video? Could've been either one. "Apparently, there's a disc in the Sail Inn's DVD player that . . . ah, features Felicia's considerable improvisational talents."

Randy cocked his head. His expression was hard to read with the underwear on his head.

"With and without clothes," I clarified.

The light went on inside the underwear. "You," Randy said. "You're the one who flooded my apartment."

"Yeah," I said. "That was me, too."

Randy shook his head. "I thought it was Felicia. What the hell made you grab those DVDs? They weren't labeled or anything."

"A happy accident. I also have your copy of The French Connection. And The Last Emperor."

"You mailed that DVD to the Sail Inn?"

"One there, one here. I marked them both, Attention, Randy Trent. It's a damned shame, the lack of respect people have for our federal institutions. The sanctity of the US Mail."

I could see Trent grinning through the leghole of his underwear. "So Felicia's gettin' herself off with a rubber dick on the Sail Inn TV? Oh, she's gonna like that."

"With a what?" Alice exclaimed. "My god, no. She does a little . . . like, striptease dance. Which she has no business doing, by the way, with that fat ass of hers."

"Jesus," Trent said, still grinning, "the boys would've been in for a treat if they'd got the other one. Felicia's got this big old rubber—"

"No!" Alice cut him off. "I don't want to hear a disgusting word about it."

Trent had his head turned and was looking at the door to the front room. "She's probably finding out about that DVD right now, with half a dozen news trucks for company. She'll probably be back in here any minute, packing heat herself."

"How bad was the flooding at your place?" I said, to change the subject.

"The flooding?"

"At your place."

"Flooding? Not too bad. Floors are so off-kilter in that rat trap, most of it ran right out the back door."

"Not too much damage?"

He shrugged. "What's to damage? I been divorced twice. I don't own anything."

"Are we going to eat or what?" Danika said. "I'm starving here."

So we ate. Danika handed out slices on paper towels to me and Alice. She offered to help Trent eat, but he said he wasn't hungry.

"What's this with the strappy thing?" Trent said, as he watched us eat.

"The suspension harness," I said. "That was your gift to Alice."

"My gift?"

"Yeah, I took a company credit card from your apartment and I—"

"No, no. No, no, no." Trent was shaking his head back and forth. "Don't tell me. I don't want to know. Forget I asked."

I shrugged. The pizza was pretty good.

So then we ate in silence for a little while, until Danika broke the silence.

"You mind if I ask a question?" she said, as we each started in on a second slice.

"Maybe," I said.

"Why didn't you just short-sheet Randy's bed thirty years ago and get on with your life? I mean, thirty years is a long time to be pissed at somebody."

"I told everybody before. Before you got here. Trent's part in this was an accident. A happy accident, like the discs. He just happened to be in the wrong place at the wrong time." I turned to Trent. "Two Sundays ago, I was just about to go home and kill myself when I ran into you. At the Sail Inn."

"Felicia's probably on the roof right now," Trent said. "In army-issue camo, with an M16 and a knife in her teeth."

"Still, though," Danika said. "A little sugar in the gas tank. Paint bomb. Locker fire. You could have gotten it off your chest, then."

"I had a lot on my plate that year. Okay?"

"Let me guess. You don't want to talk about it."

"Not really," I said.

We all chewed for awhile.

"These peppers aren't cooked at all," Danika said. "They're just slapped on here."

"The eggplant's pretty good," Alice said.

"Look. The thing is, I've already covered all of this. In great detail. I've already dealt with motivation. It's all in my journal. In this bag." I pointed at the rough cotton twill carryall. "It makes everything pretty clear. You should read it after I'm gone."

No one had anything to say to this last.

We ate some more. I was surprisingly hungry. I had packed a light snack—an apple, some yogurt—but I hadn't really anticipated being very hungry in the last moments of my life. The truth, however, was that I was ravenous. I understood, for the first time, why prisoners on death row order prodigious last meals. Danika popped open a second can of Coke.

"What's it like being a witch?" I said.

"You know," she said, "I used to have self-esteem issues, too."

I looked away, exasperated. "Is that what I asked? And what do you mean, 'too'? I don't have self-esteem issues."

"Right. You're just talking about killing yourself."

"I am not talking about killing myself. I *am* killing myself. There's a difference. And I know exactly what I'm doing. It's the most natural, most justifiable action in the world. Any rational person in my situation would do the same thing, believe me."

"Okay, okay. You don't have to bite my head off."

"I'm making a point here. A very important point. The point is, I am not indulging in self-pity. This is not a cry for help. It's my time to go and I'm perfectly happy to go. So let's put away the pop psychology."

"Right. Gotcha."

"It's like when the Indian braves would go to war, they would say," I adopted the stilted, sprung-syllable English of movie Indians, "It is a good day to die."

"Cool."

I opened another Coke.

"So what's it like being a witch?" I said.

"Better than it was before I was a witch." Danika shrugged. "I had self-esteem issues."

"Again, with the self-esteem issues." I was getting angry, then.

"Well, you asked. That's part of the answer."

I didn't really want to get into this. Every moment I wasted on idle conversation was another moment the police outside had to brainstorm some kind of high-tech, special-forces commando intervention. But I couldn't help myself.

"You know, I find that very hard to believe."

"What?"

"That you suffered from low self-esteem. Is that what you're saying to me?"

"Why?" Danika said. She seemed genuinely curious. "Why is that hard to believe?"

"Because you just walked right into the middle of a hostage situation and practically took over. Because . . ." I thought about it. "Because you're very self-possessed. For a kid."

"I'm not a kid."

"What are you, sixteen, seventeen?"

Danika let that go, causing me to hope that she wasn't even younger.

"I wasn't always like this. I used to be afraid of people. I wouldn't say boo to anyone. I used to think I was shit because my parents were shit. Because they treated each other like shit. And me like shit. I didn't know any better."

"And then you became a witch," I said, "so you could say boo to everyone."

"I used to do a lot of speed," Danika was saying. "And I used to have a drinking problem. We'd have whole cranked-out weekends that would end on, like, Tuesday. Booze and crystal and more booze. I had a really bad drinking problem."

"Wow, Danika," Alice said. "That's rough."

"It was. I went through hell and came out the other side."

"Wait a minute. Wait a minute," I said. "Danika, what the hell are you talking about? What are you, really? Sixteen? I don't think I'm ready to hear old war stories from a junior high school kid."

"I'm not a junior high school kid. And why not?"

"Because there isn't enough time for someone your age to have a drinking problem and hit bottom and recover and offer wise counsel, okay? I know you kids live fast. I watch MTV, too. But that's too short a time frame."

"I had my stomach pumped three times before I was fourteen. Twice in the emergency room and once in a basement by some guy, some biker guy who almost killed me. I had an abortion at fifteen. How I even conceived a child, in the physical shape I was in, I don't know. I'd be so cranked-out, I'd go four, five days without eating. When I hit bottom, I opened my heart and I found the Path. Witchcraft saved my shit."

"I'm not prepared to listen to the wisdom of the ages from a kid. Shouldn't you be in school?"

"It isn't wisdom. It's experience, that's all."

"Witchcraft," Trent said, from his beam. "I guess I should've figured that."

Danika turned to look up at him. "Why?"

"Because witchcraft and bad luck are running buddies, in my book. And because that's the way my luck's running these days. Bad. That's why."

"What do you think you know about witchcraft?"

"Enough to keep an eye on my wallet, whenever it shows up."

"Your wallet?" Alice said.

"Never mind. It's a long story. Ancient history."

"Witchcraft isn't what you think it is," Danika said to Trent. "It's not Halloween and goth music videos and stuff. It's an empowering lifestyle. It's a life devoted to achieving perfect balance with all worlds. Physical, mental, psychological, spiritual, astral," she said, ticking them off on the five fingers of one hand. "Living in harmony with all things."

"Yeah, yeah. I've heard the whole line of crap before, thanks. From my second wife. You kids have too much free time on your hands, is what I think. My boy's the same way. A few years from now, you kids are gonna wish you did something useful with these years your shitting away."

Danika looked impassively at Trent. "How nice for you, that your life is so perfect you can afford to throw stones at other people."

"Where the hell are your parents?"

"They're divorced. Like you are," Danika said. "They generate a lot of negative psychic energy. Also like you."

"Like me." Trent adopted an expression of bitter amusement behind his underwear. "Good thing I'm not pointing a gun at anybody."

"Don't start in on Clyde. Clyde's aura is deeply confused, self-conflicted," Danika said to Trent. "He radiates a very non-violent, non-aggressive aura, for someone holding a shotgun. It doesn't take a witch to see that."

There was a sudden roar of applause and cheering from outside. I was tempted to go and see what was going on.

"I guess it doesn't," Trent said in a different tone of voice, after the noise had died down. "Take a witch to see that. I'd be in a better frigging mood if I wasn't tied up, is all. I got kid issues of my own. Witch issues, too, actually." He flexed his bonds.

"I wish you'd stop calling me Clyde," I said.

"We could certainly use some of that perfect balance and harmony around here," Alice said to Danika. "I noticed you're not shy about pointing guns at people."

"Witchcraft isn't all sweetness and light," Danika said. "And violence isn't incompatible with harmony and balance. Violence is part of the cycle. It can be spiritually cleansing. Especially for someone with Clyde's aura."

"Thanks for the heads up," Trent muttered.

The phone rang, then. It was Woody.

"I just wanted to say, Nathan, that we're feeling a lot better out here."

"Who is it?" Danika said.

"It's Woody."

"They're probably encouraged. He was probably wearing a wire."

"Thanks, Woody," I said into the phone. "We aim to please."

"You told us what you were going to do and you kept your word. That's a good sign. We're all gonna be okay, Nathan."

"Could be."

"So where do we go from here?"

"I have a second demand."

"I got a pen right here, Nathan. Let's hear it."

"I want a cake."

"A cake."

"Nathan!" Danika protested. "I'm not letting you answer the phone anymore!"

"Right," I said. "A birthday cake."

"Okay. Birthday cake for who?"

"For me, Woody. It's my birthday."

"It is?"

"It is. You can look it up."

"Okay. Well, happy birthday, then. What do you want on it?"

"I want the cake to say, Happy Birthday, Nathan."

"Happy Birthday, Nathan. You got it."

"Thanks."

"Ummm," Woody cleared his throat and the phone crackled. "Is this a . . . ah, trade? Or just a straight request?"

I put my hand over the receiver. "Alice, do you want to go, in exchange for the cake?"

"It's your birthday?" she said. "Really?"

"Yes. It is."

"How old are you?"

"Forty-five years old today."

"Forty-five." Musing. "Are you going to shoot me? If I stay?"

"No, I'm not going to shoot you," I said, embarrassed.

Alice turned to Danika. "Are you going to shoot me?"

"Not if Clyde doesn't want me to."

"Danika, you are not shooting anyone. I do all the shooting here." I looked at Alice. "I won't shoot you, I promise."

"No," Trent said. "No way. Alice, you're leaving."

Alice sized me up for a little bit. "Then I'll stay. Until after the cake."

"No, Alice." Trent was jingling his handcuffs and pulling at the flags. The flags, decrepit polyester material from another era, were already falling apart. "You have to go."

Alice looked at Randy. "I'll be okay. He's not going to shoot me."

"Maybe not. Probably not. But you don't know what could happen. It could be something no one's expecting. The cops could burst in here and you could get shot by a cop. Caught in a crossfire. Go now. Let us figure this thing out ourselves, me and him."

"I think less will happen if I stay. I want to stay." She sat back down on the floor and folded her legs in front of her. "Until after the cake."

"Fuck," Trent said. He looked at me. "You don't have a knack for releasing hostages, do ya?"

I shrugged.

"You don't need the girls anymore. I'm not going anywhere. Tell Alice to go and we'll move this thing along."

"I am moving this thing along," I said. "As fast as I can." I took my hand off the receiver. "I've still got a point or two to make."

"If anyone gets hurt in here, besides me and you, I hope you can live with yourself."

I resisted the obvious rejoinder. I lifted the phone to my mouth. "This one's a straight request," I said into it.

Woody said something, but I couldn't hear it amid the noise from outside. Another spontaneous roar of shouting and applause.

THE END IS NEAR

§

I got to the Sail Inn last night and as soon as I grabbed a stool, someone was hallooing me from across the room.

"Hey, Nate! Nate!"

I looked around and it was Trent, sitting behind a beer at the other end of the bar.

"How ya doin', Rand."

This is how we are now, Trent and I. We're greeting each other like old buddies, mates at the Sail. Rand and Nate.

"I saw you the other day, at the graduation."

"Yeah? Didn't see ya." So Randy had seen me after all. So much for my undercover spy skills. I lifted my beer in a toast. "Congrats on your boy."

"Thanks." Trent lifted his glass of beer to me, sipped, and then carried it over to where I was sitting. He took the empty stool next to me.

I should stop here, I believe, and do some introductions. First, a re-introduction. I no longer have to refer to you with a generic salutation, Miz Trent. I can now address you by your given name. Colleen. I guessed correctly, the other day, based on the evidence in Randy's address book. Hello, Colleen.

Also, I have a new introduction to make. We have a late arrival to the party. A young woman by the name of Alice. Why Alice, you ask, so very late in the program? Because Alice, too, has a stake in Trent's sharply declining fortunes. She's the little Chinese-American honey Trent's been keeping on the side. She's the Alice of the pharmacist's business card tucked into Trent's address book. So make room, make room, everybody. Pull up a chair for Alice.

Alice, I hope you haven't spent a frantic few hours wondering what's become of your sweet Prince Charming. Fretting over whether Randy has drunkenly wrapped his truck around a tree or been apprehended by the police and thrown into the drunk tank. Or fallen into the clutches of some evil—and as yet unsuspected, undetected—arch-nemesis. Rest assured that nothing of the kind has happened. Trent's merely asleep, in my driveway.

As you know, Alice, he was kind enough to drive me home this morning. After I went in, he might have closed his eyes for a second, preparing for the drive to your place. But now his truck's been running for more than two hours and its headlights are fading to a frosty sparkle in the first light of dawn. His big disheveled head is pressed to the glass of the side window and the lids are drawn over his iceberg eyes. Trent works hard and plays hard, so we'll leave him to his well-earned slumber on this Sunday morning, a day of rest.

"What brought you out to graduation?" Trent wanted to know.

"Some death-benefit paperwork for my mom. She worked in the cafeteria at the high school for the last few years or so."

"Oh."

I was taking a chance, but what the fuck. We were almost at the finish line now, Trent and I.

"So I saw the festivities going on down the hill, figured I'd take a peek. I'm surprised I didn't see you there. You were there with . . . umm—"

"Colleen. My ex-wife. My first ex-wife."

"Right. Colleen. Must've been nice, the whole family together again."

"Oh yeah," Trent said, a little glumly. "Just like old times."

I noticed, then, that Trent had brought a card over, a greeting card, along with his beer. He had set it down on the bar before him. There was a Model-T-type jalopy on the front of the card, packed with circus clowns. Rendered faux-artily, mostly black-and-white, with touches of pastels peeking through here and there.

"Did it feel strange, being back at the old school?" I asked him.

"Hmmm?" He seemed to have been thinking about something else. "At the high school? No, I'm there all the time. Tyler gets in trouble almost as much as I used to."

"Hell raiser, huh?"

"Not so much anymore, really." Trent raised his beer mug and looked into it. "I don't know what the hell he does anymore, to tell you the truth." He drained the mug and slid it toward the bartender working the taps. "Two more," he said.

"He's at that tricky age," I suggested.

"Tyler's tricky age started at six months old and continued out to now." The bartender placed new beers in front of us. "Colleen wants me to talk to the kid, but talking to Tyler . . ." he shook his head, "doesn't always work out."

"You didn't get to talk to him at graduation?"

"Oh, sure I did. You know how it goes. Hi and goodbye." I didn't know, but I nodded anyway. "The kids all got parties to hit, girls to fuck, liquor cabinets to empty, rental cabins to destroy." Someone entered the bar and Trent looked up, like he was expecting someone. Then he looked at me. "I told him not to drive and to enjoy himself. Last free-and-clear night of his life, he should remember it."

I was surprised to hear this. "Last free-and-clear night? How's that?"

Trent shrugged. "Before adulthood comes knocking."

"You sound like the voice of experience. I thought you didn't graduate."

"I didn't." He grinned. "That don't mean I didn't hit the parties, fuck the girls, empty the liquor cabinets, and destroy the rentals."

"I bet you did." I did a very unNathanlike thing, then. It was completely premeditated. I reached out and clapped Trent on the shoulder. A guys-being-guys swat on the shoulder. Ha-ha-swat.

I'm not the kind of guy who goes around swatting guys. I'm usually the opposite of that kind of guy. I'm the kind of guy who needs—who jealously preserves—a big circle of unviolated personal space. I'm not a glad-hander. A back-slapper. Hell, even with women, I need a lot of personal space. I'm not a public-display-of-affection kind of guy.

I swatted Trent, though. I did it on purpose, because I wanted to touch him before I killed him.

What did he feel like? He felt solid, like a guy who's done a lot of warehouse work. Lifting and carrying. He felt more real to me, then. Like a real person. And I wanted to know that. That I was killing a real person.

"Fucking almost killed myself," Trent was saying, "getting shitfaced on Wild Turkey and wheelying a motorcycle off the end of a dock into Lake Mohawk."

"Whoa. Why'd ya do that?"

"Tommy Flanagan was at the end of the dock, pissing me off. The idea was to go into a slide and get him to jump off, into the lake. But the dock was wet and I hit the brake and went right off the end without even slowing down."

"Wow. How'd you get the bike out of the lake?"

"I didn't. It was hard enough getting me out, I was so fucked up. The bike's probably still in there. It wasn't my good bike. It was a crappy little Yamaha I had for fucking around." He grinned again, remembering. "Got Flanagan to jump, though."

"Good deal. Whatever happened to him? Tommy Flanagan."

Trent looked perplexed. "Fuck if I know. He musta left town ... eighty-five? Eighty-six?" He leaned back on his stool and folded his arms, thinking. "It's like everybody else, you know?

THE END IS NEAR

You see 'em around all the time and then, two years later, you realize you ain't seen 'em in two years."

"He helped me out of a tight spot once. Flanagan. Saved me an ass-kicking."

"Flanagan?" Trent looked surprised. "Flanagan gave out a lot more ass-kickin's than he ever saved anybody. I know, I was on the receiving end of a couple of 'em."

"What about Steve Tolas? Whatever happened to him?"

"Steve . . ." Trent burst out laughing. "We did this the other day, didn't we? Me and you. You throwing out names. You sure got a head for names nobody remembers anymore." He looked at me closely, reassessing. "I'm starting to think there's something funny about you. Like maybe I should be remembering you from somewhere."

"Me?" I said. "Maybe. Like I said, I was only a couple of years behind you."

"Nathan." He was shaking his head. "Nah, I don't know. I've got no head for names and dates and shit. What was it? Fish?"

"Fisk," I said.

"Fisk." He laughed again. "Fuck, no. Nothing there. You gotta catch me some time when I ain't drinking."

We both looked down into our beers, grinning like fools at the treachery of time, of memory. At the way it all gets away.

"Steve Tolas," I said, after a while.

"Steve Tolas. I ain't heard that name in . . . I guess, twenty years."

"He was some crazy motherfucker," I said. "Where'd he go?"

"Steve Tolas." Trent scratched his head. "Steve Tolas wasn't a motherfucker. He was a sisterfucker. There's a difference. That guy . . ." He winced at some memory. "He was the craziest guy I ever knew, I think. And I work in the parts business, where there's a crazy fucker under every rock, just about."

"He's probably dead," I opined.

"He probably is, that's for sure. That guy started out completely batshit and then he started making speed. Made him worse. He was the first guy anybody knew about, up here, brewing bathtub methedrine. Probably honked up more'n he sold. I saw him pull some shit . . ." He waved a hand, dismissing the subject.

"Like what?"

"No," Trent made a face, "it don't bear going into. Tolas was the kind of speed freak, liked to get into people's heads. He liked to fuck people up. He was a speed freak. He started out crazy and went off the deep end."

"Not like you," I said.

Trent looked at me. "Not like me, what?"

"You liked to fuck people up, too. But Steve was peculiar about it."

"Peculiar." Trent was actively sizing me up, now. "You knew Tolas?"

"I knew of him. My memory was, he used to hang with you."

Trent thought about this and started nodding. "Yeah, that's true. Sometimes. I ain't proud of it. I used to buy speed off him. He practically gave the shit away. And I used to trade the speed for pot and blotter acid and sell that. I used to turn a big-ass profit, that way."

"Fucked a few people up, too. You and Tolas."

I was really pressing, and I knew it. But I wanted to hear him say it. Trent was still grinning, but in a different, warier way, now.

"We had this conversation, too, the other day," he said. "People I beat up, back in the day. You don't have a hatchet to grind here, do ya, Nate?"

"No," I said, "I'm just trying to remember the way it was, back then. Being out at graduation has me feeling a little . . . nostalgic, I guess."

"Nostalgic. I never get that, myself." He drained his beer mug again and slid it across the bar. "Two more," he barked at the bartender. He turned back to me.

"I busted some heads in my day." He smirked humorlessly. "Maybe even yours, if that's what you're getting at. I don't know. But I ain't that way, anymore. I learned a lot of things the hard way, and one of 'em is, you can't go around busting people's heads. There's a—" He stalled. "There's a, like a . . ."

"Price to be paid?" I suggested.

"No. More like a karma thing, that builds up, you know?"

"Karma thing? I didn't take you for a new age mystic, Randy."

"I ain't. I picked that up, karma, from a girl I knew once. But the point is, you go through life creating misery, it hangs over you like a . . . like a cloud. You can't live like that."

"No," I said. "You probably can't."

"It's not just self-interest, either. I may be a stupid fuck, but eventually even I figured out, there's a better way to live. You know? It took me a long time, longer than I care to think about, to figure out how to live like a normal person. To give people a fucking break. To grow up. You know?"

"Sorry I'm late," someone said.

I turned to find the lovely Chinese-American girl Trent had been with the other night. She was looking up at Trent with big mischievous eyes, her mouth pursed up tight and small as a cranberry. When Trent turned to look, her mouth sprang wide in delight, like a bouquet of roses produced from the white glove of a magician. It was you, Alice. You were wearing a little floral-print sundress and strappy shoes. You were looking like the kind of girl who knows she looks great and is just pleased as punch about it. Looking—if I might say, Felicia—like a formidable adversary.

Welcome to the party, Alice.

"Sam had to leave early," you said. You gave your hair—shoulder-length, ruler-straight, lustrous and black—a toss and set your tiny handbag on the bar. "So I had to lock up and make the bank deposit myself."

"What, nobody from the grocery department can make a frigging bank deposit?" Trent said. He looked relieved to have you there. "They have to send a ninety-pound chick out into the night with a bag of money?"

"A hundred and three pounds, and very fast on my feet."

"If I was in the grocery department," I said, "I'd carry your money bag." The new, charming Nathan, freed up at last by the proximity of death.

"I bet you would." You gave me that sleight-of-hand smile. "The mysterious Nathan, crusader against crime."

"Yeah. How did you know?" I grinned. "Who I am, that is. My name."

You looked at me, amused. "Your eye. Randy told me you got decked saving his stuff."

Right. My eye. When you spend as much time as I do alone—or among indifferent strangers—you stop thinking of yourself in terms of what you look like. The island castaway effect. I realized then that Trent's eye had mostly healed, while my eye was still, I was sure, an eyesore.

"I'd've been in deep shit, without that laptop," Trent said. "I'd've missed the other stuff, too."

"So tell me, tell me," Alice said. "What happened?"

"What? I told you. Some kid was breaking into my—"

"No, no. The graduation."

"Oh. Tyler got his diploma. We took a lot of pictures."

"Yes, yes, I know that. And Colleen? She give it up for you, or what?"

"Oh, jeez." Trent looked embarrassed. "Nah. She didn't have much to say."

"Did you try what I said?"

"Nah, I didn't try that. I just tried to talk to her. She's ... I don't know."

I wondered what Trent could possibly want you to give up, Colleen. Disputed alimony, I thought. Some valuable bauble secured in the divorce settlement, perhaps. Something he could give to you, Alice. I wouldn't find out the truth until much later that evening. This morning.

"She gave me another card," Trent said.

You looked at the card on the bar, Alice. "Uh-oh," you said.

"Yeah, well."

"About Tyler again?"

"Sure." Trent flagged the bartender down on his way past. He ordered three beers and three shots—here we were, off to hell in a handbasket again—of some evil crap called Goldschlager. "I don't know what she's thinking. Thinking the kid's gonna listen to me."

You picked the card up from the bar, glanced at the front, and opened it. You read the contents, then looked at the front again, before placing it back on the bar. "She's got a sharp way with a card, doesn't she?"

"Oh, yeah, she's a scream."

"Well, don't get gloomy about it. You're wearing her down. Next time, you'll get somewhere." Where, I wondered. You looped Randy's arm in your own. "In the meantime, you're stuck with me for the night."

"She wants Tyler to enroll up at the community college. But the kid's got other ideas, I guess." Trent seemed oblivious to your arm-in-arm embrace, in a way I couldn't imagine being, in his place. "She wants me to talk him into it, but what am I supposed to say? The kid's already got further along than I did. He's got his high-school diploma."

"What are Tyler's other ideas?"

"I don't even know. Maybe he doesn't have any."

"Colleen didn't say?"

"She don't say much. To me, anyway."

"Ex-wives are tough cookies. Women scorned." You turned to me. "How about you, Nathan?" you said. "Not married?"

"Nope. Not me."

"Never been? No kids?"

"Nope."

"How old are you?"

"Forty, well, forty-three." I'd almost forgotten to subtract a couple of years.

Trent laughed aloud. "Jesus. Here's a guy, knows how to stay out of trouble. Forty-three years old and never married. How the hell do you manage that?"

"Got me."

Actually I know exactly how I've managed that. Here's how. By staying up all night, drinking beer and listening to Joy Division records. Worrying. Ordering takeout Chinese food. Sabotaging potentially supportive relationships. Reading eight-pound, free-associative, postmodernist novels about nothing. Cursing the fates. Becoming increasingly unemployable. Getting fat. Renting movies. Waiting for my life to start.

That about covers it. Forty-five years—well, twenty-five years—of never getting married. Mystery solved. Let's move on.

"I just never met the right woman, I guess."

"Uh huh." Trent considered this. "I heard that story before." He turned to you, Alice. "See? That's my whole problem. I gotta stop meeting the right woman."

"Or cut down to two or three of the right women per month, anyway." You pulled a stool over between Randy and me and picked up your shot. "To the right women," you said. "And the wrong men who love them."

We lifted our little shot glasses and drank.

And then we talked.

What did we talk about, Alice? Everything, I guess. Everything and nothing. The stuff people talk about in bars.

THE END IS NEAR

People came over and chatted us up. Guys in cowboy boots and NASCAR caps, guys in ridiculous pointy shoes and leather vests, pretty girls on the prowl in microshorts and tiny halter tops, less fortunate girls in more sensible clothes. We talked to everybody. I had a great time.

Here's an odd thing I've noticed lately.

Now that I'm dead, I find I'm more likeable than ever. And, perversely, I like people more. Where I used to sit and seethe over real or imagined slights, or suffer full-blown crises of self-doubt over something as simple as saying hello to a stranger, subjecting every remark, every casual action, to the most rigorous psychological analysis, now I just sit back and indulge in not giving a fuck. I enjoy the hell out of myself.

Why should I care? Now that I'm dead, I have no stake in so-and-so's ignorant political views. In so-and-so's refusal, despite two full hours of hocking and snorting and sniffling, to simply blow his nose. In that ridiculous ogre's insistence on telling his wife to shut up every time she opens her mouth to say something.

That guy over there? The one with the Whip 'Em Out Wednesday cap with the two big tits protruding from it? More power to ya, fella. That pretty girl's utterly laughable taste in men? No skin off my ass. Live and let live, I say. Except in my own personal case, of course.

The thing is, I've never been happier or more at ease in social situations. I know I've said this before, but I'm going to say it again because it's still true. I should've killed myself years ago. I'm having the time of my life, now that I'm dead.

If there's one thing about my previous life that I regret, it's this: I should have stopped giving a fuck years ago.

We were having so much fun, it took me a while to get a moment alone at the bar. After a few hours or so of bar frivolity, Trent wandered off to the men's room and you, Alice, went to put some money into the jukebox. That's when I slid the jalopy-and-clown greeting card toward myself and opened it.

The handwriting on the inside of the card—your handwriting, sweet Colleen—was blunt, without flourishes, not girly at all.

> Time for your yearly parental contribution. Talk to your boy about what he thinks he's going to do with his life, now that school's over with. Tell him that there's still time to avoid ending up being the town laughingstock, like you.
> —C

Whew. Harsh words, Colleen.

I thought, then, that my impression at the graduation, my sense that there was still some lingering animosity between the two of you, was correct. I wondered how much you would miss Randy when he was gone, Colleen. I wished, then, that I could meet you. Though I knew I never would. I was already out of time.

Of course, the reality of your relationship with Randy was more complicated than I knew then, standing at the bar. I'd find that out very soon.

Trent returned from the men's room, his hands undoubtedly unwashed. And you, Alice, returned from the jukebox. We returned our attentions to the matters at hand. Drinking far too much and talking the clock around. Talking the clocks right off the walls. Talking until the room lights came up and the traffic lights behind the bar went from green to yellow.

"Last call! Last call!"

My last "Last call!," I suspect. I let Trent buy the last round.

Trent raised his mug. "To new friends," he tapped my mug, "and good-lookin' chicks." He tapped yours, Alice.

I raised my own mug. "To karma," I said.

Trent grinned agreeably at this, while you, Alice, looked at me oddly. The traffic lights behind the bar went from yellow to red.

"Okay," Trent said. "To karma, then." He raised his glass again. "What goes around, comes around."

We emptied our glasses and beamed at each other, happy as clams.

"C'mon, c'mon," the bartender cried. "Go the fuck home! Do something with your pitiful lives, why don'tcha?"

We spilled out of the Sail Inn into the gorgeous June night—you embracing Trent, me embracing one of my last hours in this vale of tears. I looked up at the night, the stars, feeling exalted and brave and martyred. I tripped over one of the railroad ties on the margin of the parking lot and pitched into a shrub.

"C'mon, dipshit." Trent helped me up. "You can barely walk. I'll drive ya home."

"Oh? And you're ready to dance the lead in Swan Lake, right?" Though already I was thinking I wouldn't mind a ride home, mano a mano with Trent.

"Fuck, yeah. You think I can't dance?" Trent was walking you to your car, Alice. "Secret of my success with women. Dancing."

"I'll be okay. I can drive." I was following Trent to your car.

"Yeah, you can drive. Right into one of the drunk-driver traps on the River Styx Bridge and Abel's Crossway. Do you even have a driver's license? Or did you lose it with your wallet, the other day?"

"I lost it, I guess." Not that I cared. "I don't want to see you get into any trouble on my account."

"Me? For what? Driving?" Trent opened your car door and closed it after you got in. You, Alice, had sensibly switched to coffee two hours before. "Ain't a cop in town don't owe me a favor," he called over his shoulder. "You got any favors to call in from the local cops?"

"Me? No."

"Then you're comin' with me." Your driver's side window came down. Trent said something quietly to you and turned back to me. "Where do you live?"

"In the Hills. Off Sutton Terrace."

"No shit. I grew up out there."

"Really."

"Yeah." He said something else to you, Alice, then started walking to his truck. "C'mon."

"Nice to meet you, Nathan," you called out sweetly after us. "See you again soon."

Not likely, I thought. But I was delighted to meet you, Alice.

And then we were off, Randy and I.

The inside of Trent's truck was as big as the bedroom of the last apartment I lived in, the apartment I was evicted from less than a month ago for nonpayment of rent. The dashboard and center console were filled with arcane, high-tech doodads bristling with knobs and digital displays and switches. I had to move his laptop and softball equipment from the passenger seat. The window I had smashed days before had been replaced.

"Hand me a beer outta that cooler behind you."

I turned and saw a red cooler in the space between the seats. I got a beer for Trent and one for me.

"You grew up out there in the Hills, you say, twenty years ago?"

"Hudson Trail."

"No shit. You must've not got out much."

The truck bounced out of the rutted parking lot and leaped onto the blacktop of Lakeside Boulevard. Its powerful engine pinned me into the leather seat as we accelerated away.

"Nope. I was a real homebody. Where'd you live?"

"Reese Trail. Off of Rollins."

"No kidding. That's close."

"Yeah, it is. Colleen still lives there, in the house I grew up in."

"Really. That's weird."

"Is it? It's paid for, I guess. She didn't want to take Tyler out of school, and couldn't see moving somewhere else in town, just to move."

"Makes sense."

"Uh huh." There was indeed a police trap on Abel's Crossway. Trent drained his beer in a gulp, rolled down his window, and pitched the can at the cops waiting in ambush. A couple of cops gave us the finger. "So you never been married. That's a long haul, twenty years of no one telling you what to do."

"You think that's weird."

"Weird? Nah. Not necessarily. Nobody gets married anymore. Kids Tyler's age think it's all bullshit. Getting married, having kids. They wanna hang out, do shit, have some test-tube baby when they're fifty. I don't know. Maybe that's the way to do it."

I finished my beer and looked for somewhere to put the empty can. Trent took it from me and pitched it into the roadside scrub. I had to remind myself that I no longer cared about littering and nuclear winter and the evils of political campaign financing.

"It's not like I gave the kid much to look forward to, marriagewise. Getting divorced twice." He raised the window. "Hand me another beer."

I fetched him another beer. And one for myself.

"We married too young, maybe. Me and Colleen. I was working eighteen, twenty hours some days, gettin' the shops established. Colleen was knocking around the house," he popped the beer open, "that house she hated, waiting for me to get home all the time."

"She hated the house?"

"She did, back then. My mother died in it, the year before me and Colleen got married, and Colleen said the place was haunted. That my mother was haunting her dreams, telling her to get out. Colleen hated the house anyway, the look of it. The smell of it. Didn't think much of my mother, either, actually. She wanted to live in a new house, near other young people."

"And she ended up there."

"Funny, the way things work out." Trent yawned and set his beer in a cup holder. "Fortunes of divorce. Charity was luckier."

"Charity?"

"My second wife."

"Oh."

"See all the fun you're missing?"

"I guess so."

"Me and Charity lasted only two years and she got the Spartan Hills place. I built that house new on an acre and a half, four bedrooms, porch around three sides of the house, a pool. Nice spread. What they used to call a starter mansion. A McMansion. Before property values went into the shitter."

"That's what she got, huh? Not bad, for two years' work."

"She was a smart cookie, Charity. I met her when I was in some kinda . . . stage, I guess. One of those life-is-passing-me-by stages. You gotta watch out for those."

Randy turned off Lakeside Boulevard and onto Sutton Terrace. Sutton Terrace skirts around the edge of the Mudhole and then climbs off into the Hills section of Lake Lenni Lenape. I watched the Mudhole and the bathhouse go by on my side and then looked at Trent. His eyes were on the road, his mind on the story he was telling.

"We met and got married within a year," he was saying. "She was, like . . . a hippy-dippy chick, you know? Astrology and karma and witchcraft. She was always lighting candles and walking around barefoot and talking about crystal energy and my, like, aura."

"New Age mysticism."

"Yeah, like that. When I met her, she seemed . . ." Trent eyes narrowed as he tried to recall his long-ago reasoning. "She saw things a way I never seen things before. Peace and harmony and stuff. She caught me right at the time I was starting to look around myself, wondering about the way I'd lived up 'til then. Wondering why I felt like shit all the time. I knew something was wrong, but I couldn't put my finger on it. And then Charity showed up and I guess I jumped on that."

"Oh, right. Karma," I said. "This is when you decided to turn over a new leaf, like you were saying in the Sail. When you decided to become the new, peaceful, pacifist version of you."

"Yeah, well. It was the mood I was in at the time. It didn't hurt that Charity was twenty-four and pretty hot in the sack, and I was what, thirty-three, and starting to have this . . ." He was lost for a word.

"Early middle-age crisis," I offered. "Charity didn't work out, though."

"Nah, she didn't work out." The truck was climbing high into the hills; the road was getting narrower, the mailboxes further and further apart. "In the beginning, we had the house construction and decorating to distract us. And the fucking. But after that, it was a joke. It lasted two years only because I was in the shops all the time. I was expanding from two shops to five, that year."

"Too much airy-fairy New Age stuff?"

"You know, I could've lived with the witchcraft and crystals and stuff. It was the other stuff, there was no getting past. My idea of a good time is a steak dinner and a movie. Her idea of a good time was going into Dover or Morristown, getting pie-eyed on Ecstasy, and dancing all night at one of those all-night disco dances, those . . ."

"Raves?"

"Raves. I thought she was a little old for that shit, never mind myself. So it's not like I could have joined her, even if I wanted to. Which I didn't. And there was other shit, too. I never caught her screwing behind my back, but it was pretty plain she was. That all-night rave crowd, they were all fucking like bunnies. In the end, we both agreed to pull the plug. She had this whole spiritual, I-don't-care-about-material-things attitude going, so we agreed to do a no-fault, no-lawyer separation deal."

We'd reached the end of Sutton Terrace, where it intersects with Rollins Trail, and he made a right, instead of the left that would have taken us to my mother's house.

"And then at the eleventh hour," he grinned wolfishly, "she bushwhacked me with some New York hotshot lawyer. Mental cruelty, infidelity. Me and my doofus Lake Lenni Lenape lawyer never knew what hit us. Charity got two of the shops outright and a slice of the profits from the remaining three. Plus the house, the Grand Cherokee, the boat. I had to buy the boat back from her. She turned around and sold the two shops to my top competitor."

"That's rough."

"I guess. I probably had it coming, stupid as I was. She's probably up there tonight, in that McMansion full of empty rooms, skinny dipping and burning candles and chewing some young stud's ear about the evils of material things."

"Sounds like she took you for a ride."

"Uh huh. That's what Colleen says. What can I say, I say to her. It's only money, right?"

"I guess so."

"I give Colleen cash, extra, off the books, where I can. Which ain't often, anymore. The auto parts business is shit, these days, with the discount chains everywhere." He rubbed the stubble under his chin and his eyes grew distant. "You know what?"

"What?"

"I'll tell ya this. Colleen was the best thing that ever happened to me. Problem is, it took me eighteen years to figure it out. And our marriage lasted eight."

"So go back to her."

"Spoken like a guy who never married." Trent made a right off Rollins, onto Reese Trail. "You sure you ain't queer? You sure don't know much about chicks."

I waited, remembering a time when being called a queer by Randy Trent had been a soul-annihilating experience.

"I'm not even allowed in the house. Her house. I haven't been in that house since Christmas," Trent tried to count back, "seven years ago, maybe."

"Long time."

"Yeah. Anyway, Colleen's set in her ways. She says I ruined her for men. She wants more help with Tyler, but she ain't having none of me. She's. . ." He thought about it for a while, trying to puzzle it out, before giving up. "set in her ways. That's all."

"Pissed about Charity," I offered.

"Pissed about Charity. Pissed about the chicks I was doing on the side, when we were still married."

Trent turned off the truck's headlights and we rolled to a stop a little ways off from 16 Reese Trail, the pale, tiptoed home of three generations of Trents. At this early hour, 3:10am by the digital clock in the dash, the house was dark but for a yellow insect-repelling light beside the front door.

"I ain't proud of it. The chicks on the side. But I was a kid, I didn't know any better. These little nowhere towns, there's nothing else to do. You're in a business like mine, working with the public all day." He puffed out his cheeks and blew, chagrined. "You meet a lot of public."

It seemed like then or never, if I was going to raise the issue I wanted to raise.

"It must've seemed weird, about Tyler. Another Trent boy in that house. Raised by another single mom."

"Divorced mom. Not single mom. Divorced mom. There's a difference. Tyler knows who is damned dad is, even if his dad ain't around much." Randy was looking at me, raising an eyebrow, trying to decide whether I'd gone too far or not. He barely knew me, after all. Then his mental scales tipped and he looked back out the window.

"It wasn't entirely my idea. Leaving. Colleen threw me out of the house." He twitched his head, irritably. "Not that I didn't give her plenty of reasons."

I finished my beer. I lowered the window and, holding my breath and shutting my eyes tightly, whipped the can out the window. It was, as far as I can recall, the first time I'd ever willfully littered.

"I can say that I regret it. That we were kids. I was a kid. That I didn't know any better. That this town is full of bored chicks that'll climb into your pants before you even noticed they walked into the room. But who wants to hear it? Not Colleen. Hell, not me."

"So going back is out of the question." I was panting, winded from the act of littering. And helping Randy plumb his soul.

"Probably. She'd go frigging batshit, if she knew I was even out here." Trent put the car in reverse and turned to look out the rear window of the truck. He didn't release the brake, though. After a moment, he put the truck back into park.

"You ever get a ... a general sense, like, that something's wrong, and you don't even know what to do about it?" Trent wasn't looking at me. He lifted his beer can out of the cup holder, took a sip, and put it back. He was still gripping the shift lever.

"Are we talking karma again?" I said.

He shook his head, presumably taking my comment for flip drollery.

"Lately, I just get this sense . . ." He stopped, started again. "I'm sure I'm not the only guy, thinks this way, but there's things—" He squinted, trying to press his thoughts into coherent form. "Something needs fixing, you know?" He was shaking his head, prepared to give up. "I don't know."

"Something's been lost," I suggested.

"Lost." He tried it out, puzzling at it. "I guess so. Or . . . got away. There's so much that it's too late to fix. You know? I know that. But it feels to me, lately, that there's things that can still be fixed. That are getting away, right now. That there's time to fix some of this shit, and if I don't do it, I'm gonna be sitting here in this truck, ten years from now, probably with some other three-am drunken fool for company, regretting what I wasn't doing today." His hand tightened on the shift lever. "Whatever it is I should be doing."

"Something with Colleen. And Tyler."

"Tyler, I'm already doing every goddamn thing I can do. The kid's full of himself. Like I was. He's at that age, you can't tell him nothing." He put the truck back into reverse. "I'm thinking of Colleen. Then Tyler." This time, he took his foot off the brake and the truck started to roll backwards, tires crunching on the gravel.

I was watching the Trent house recede and wondering, again, what you would make of the events to come, Colleen.

The truck was accelerating, backwards, down the middle of the gloomy road. Trent popped the lights on. "Anyways, to make a long story longer, I've been thinking I'm willing to give it a shot. Me and Colleen."

"Good for you." I lifted my beer in a mock toast. "Go for it."

"It won't be easy, but fuck it, you know? It'll be worth it, to get back where we were, me and Colleen."

"Save you some alimony."

"It won't be easy," Trent said, not to be put off by drollery. He did a backwards K-turn in a wide section of road, tires tearing up gravel, headlights raking the trees, and then we were moving forward, to my mother's house. "But I can fix this thing. We're not going anywhere. Me and Colleen. We got time. I got nothing but time."

"Sure," I said. I looked at my watch.

I figured Trent had about thirty hours left. We both did.

§

I'm running out of ways to say that I was wrong. That everyone else was right. That my life was a fool's errand.

I'm sure there's something else you must want from me, Death. Something I'm not getting at. But I can't imagine, for the life of me, what it could be.

Anyway, since I'm growing tired of inventing new ways of saying how wrong I was about everything, I'm going to let someone else take over for a while. My sister. She brings plenty of fresh enthusiasm to the job.

Right. My sister was here this morning. My room, with its ban on visitors, gets more visitor traffic than the hospital gift shop.

"You haven't changed one bit," she said. "You son of a bitch."

My sister sure has. I hadn't seen her in almost two decades. Since she disappeared with Caleb the Jesus groupie. I was surprised to see how much she's come to resemble my mother.

I'll assume you're referring to my personality and not my appearance.

"I was referring to your behavior. As for appearance, you actually look much better." She had an expression on her face that was new to me. An expression I wouldn't have associated with my little sister before this. A kind of Plains Stater's good-humored forbearance. "You should have seen yourself six weeks ago, in the emergency ward. You were pretty fatootsed."

Fatootsed?

"Fatootsed. I think it's Jewish for fucked up. But maybe not, I don't know. Carson brought the word home one day and now we're all using it. Speaking of which, when you get out of here, you're coming home with me."

Home? I wrote, startled. *To Oklahoma?*

"That's where home is, yes."

I can't go to Oklahoma.

"Yes, you can. You will. There's nothing keeping you here."

I've mentioned before, I know, somewhere on the other sides of these pages, my sister's astonishing six-month transformation from hefty bleater and whiner to breathy-voiced beauty. While I was away at college. And now here she was, transformed again. Transformed into my mother. Or someone very much like my mother, anyway.

She has my mother's mouth, tucked down on both sides in a prim not-quite-frown. My mother's pallid flesh, easily freckled, easily blotched, too fragile for the light of day. The same shape of face, long and narrow and flat, like a shield. Sherilyn is a lot thinner than my mother, of course. But you can see already how she will fill out like my mother. Not fat, but sturdy. Big in the knees and elbows and ankles.

Sherilyn has, too, my mother's way of looking out at the world. Her head tipped down and her eyes tipped up, wide and mock-serious, as if everything in the world were too droll, too silly, to be looked at directly. And she has my mother's way of sitting in a chair—hunched forward, arms crossed before her, legs crossed—as if she were gathering herself up, folding herself up into a package small enough to disappear entirely.

"It was lucky for you, you were in a coma," my sister was saying. "Six weeks ago, I was more likely to kick your ass than take you home. I'm a lot calmer, now."

Home, into your house? Does Rambo know about this?

"If I hadn't suggested it, he would have. He's all for it. Family is important to Rambo."

I've never even met the man.

"Family is family. You'll stay in the guest bedroom until you get your feet under you again."

No. Thank you, but no. Tell Rambo to put the surrey with the fringe on top back in the garage. I won't be needing it. I can't move to Oklahoma.

"And why not?"

Too flat. Too dusty. Too tumbleweedy. And I haven't punched a cow since my blind-dating days.

"Look, we're not going to fight about it. Not today, anyway. How are you feeling?"

I don't know if the doctors told you or not, but I've got health issues. I might be here for a while.

"When you can go, you'll go with me. You're family. Stop being a jackass."

Can we talk about something else?

"Okay. Sure thing." She raised her head, stuck her chin out, and said, in a different, icier, tone of voice, "Let's talk about how I found out Mom was dead from the TV. On the news reports of you and your . . . thing."

Hostage situation. I got picked up on the OK news?

"CNN. How could Mom die and you don't even tell anyone?"

Who was there to tell? I didn't know where to contact you.

It was odd being in the same room with my sister. We had the most elemental of connections—we were brother and sister—and yet we had very little shared history. She was twelve when I went away to college and stayed away, eighteen when she married, twenty when she disappeared.

"You said I was dead."

I did?

"In that journal of yours."

Oh. That.

"Yeah, that. A real piece of work, that thing."

I didn't say you were dead, exactly. More like, missing and perhaps dead.

"Thanks. You knew that was a lie."

Dramatic license. I hate it when people read journals like they're the autobiographical truth. Besides, I corrected myself later. I stapled one of your letters into it.

"You knew I was alive all along and you knew where I was. There was a return address on every letter I sent you."

Letter?

"Every letter. You know. The letters I've been sending you off and on for years. The letters you never answer."

Well. Off and on. I move a lot.

"Sure you do. So you never got even one of them. And Mom wasn't on your case, trying to get you to be civil to your own sister."

We didn't talk much, me and Mom. The truth is, I suspected you were around somewhere.

"You suspected. Terrific. Nathan Huffnagle, junior detective."

Knew. I knew you were around somewhere. But what was I supposed to do? Bring you in from OK and then kill myself? Suicide is not a group activity.

"And your sister-in-law Sally? And your nephew, Cody? You forgot they were alive, too, right? You didn't think Cody might want to know that his grandmother had died?"

Thomas died so many years ago. I guess I figured they had moved on, by now.

"You figured they'd stopped being family, somehow." Sherilyn was doing a lot of good-humored Plains-States-style forbearing. "You know, believe it or not, not everyone's like you. Not everyone refuses to give a shit about anyone. Not everyone refuses to believe that anyone gives a shit about them. That anyone gives a shit about anything."

I mentioned you guys in my last will & testament. That whole two-for-the-price-of-one thing. I was saving you guys a bundle on airfare, lodging, and funeral costs.

"Right. That will in your crappy journal. I read that, too. I hope when I die, nobody treats it as an inconvenience. As a cost-savings opportunity."

See, I'm not picky. Just dump me anywhere. Put me in a trash bag, by the curb. I won't mind.

"You're coming home with me to Oklahoma. You'll meet Rambo. You'll meet your nephews, Isaiah and Carson. We're going to teach you common decency. We're going to teach you to eat with a knife and fork, and wear shoes, and have respect for the dead."

I've been the very model of civility and politeness with the dead. Ask any of them.

"We're going to take you home and civilize you, like they do with boys who have been raised in the woods by wolves."

Wolves? I should have been so lucky.

"And you can get off your high horse about Mom and Dad, too. Finally. You're forty-five years old, for chrissake. Grow up, already."

What's up with this whole pro-family thing? It's all over your letters to mom. You get it from Rambo?

"Some of it. Mostly I got it from having a family of my own. You should try it sometime."

And what's up with that name, anyway? Rambo. Did he give himself that name? Is he a veteran of some East Asian conflict? Is he the gruff, silent type? Is he a walking arsenal of weaponry?

"He was born with it. In Louisiana. He's named after some Confederate war hero on his mother's side."

Nice.

"And don't even start on my letters to mom. I can't believe your gall. Attaching one of my private letters to that piece of shit journal of yours. Not to mention, you called me," Sherilyn stopped to get it right in her head, and then recited, 'loud and insolent, round with baby fat, and quick to cry at insults both real and imagined.'"

The frigging journal again. Take my advice, Death. Don't leave a journal lying around unless you are one hundred percent certain you're actually dead or going to be dead very soon.

When you were twelve. I'm sorry.

"And then you called my wedding a grueling, lockstep, extended-service affair."

I don't think I said lockstep.

"You called something lockstep."

Maybe. That sounds like me.

"You know what I thought, when I read that journal?"

Oh, boy. Please. Spare me.

"I thought, my god, nothing's changed." My sister feigned astonishment, which looked like Plains States forbearance, but with wider eyes and the corner of her mouth more tightly, more sardonically, tucked. "It's thirty years later and he's still that same teenager, storing up grievances."

Those things you said about me in those letters of yours were just as outrageous as anything I said. I'm the one who should be complaining.

"I thought, this must be what it means to be crazy. The world keeps going on and you just stay stuck in the same place, obsessing about the same ancient crap."

You said that Dad and I were the same.

"First of all," my sister held her hand, palm out, at me, "reading a journal intended for everybody to read, like your piece of crap, is very different from reading someone's private letters."

You said that Dad and

"I heard you the first time. Read you, whatever."

Yeah? And?

"Not the same. I didn't say you were the same. And I was answering something Mom wrote."

You certainly didn't disagree.

"Mom said that you took after Dad. In some ways. I had to agree."

Exactly. Thank you. That's very flattering.

"Will you look at yourself? That shitty journal of yours shouts it from every page."

It's not enough that you let Mom off the hook for every atrocity of our childhoods. And Dad, too.

"Tell me you're not killing yourself the exact same way Dad did."

Now I have to BE Dad.

"With loneliness. And drinking. And fucking up job after job after job. And isolating yourself. And more drinking. And finally with a fucking shotgun. For what? What are you paying for?" Sherilyn spread her arms wide to indicate my unfortunate condition. "Why are you doing this to yourself?"

Now everything is the same as everything else. I'm the same as Dad. And Dad's the same as me. And nothing means anything. And I'M supposed to be the crazy person.

"Why can't you just let people in? People are trying to get in and you just bar the doors and windows. My God, even this Randy Trent person you tried to kill. Even he's trying to get in."

What do you know about Trent?

"More than you, evidently. Enough to know that he's a decent man who's looking out for your welfare, out there in the world. Whether you know it or not."

I AM NOT DAD.

"Oh no, no. You're not Dad. You're arrogant and pigheaded and antisocial and self-destructive. But you're not Dad."

We glared at each other for a moment.

"You're too smart to believe in anything. Or try anything. Or learn anything. Or be anything."

THE END IS NEAR

My journal again. This is what happens when you write a suicide journal and live to tell about it. It's like giving everybody a box full of tools to take you apart with.

"Look at yourself, refusing to have a life. Turning away from life, so you'll never have to risk making a mistake, or owe anyone anything, or forgive anyone, or depend on anyone, or learn anything, or change your mind about anything."

Hey, I'm not the one who hid away in some crackpot religious commune for years. Doing god knows what with god knows whom. Making pipe bombs in the basement and freely interpreting God's Word.

Sherilyn made a sour little smile at this. "I've made some mistakes," she said evenly, after a moment. "But at least I learned from them. At least I haven't shut myself away from the world."

At least killing myself was my own idea. Not something I got sweet-talked into by some power-tripping Jesus freak in a panel van.

After that, we sat in silence for a while. A pretty long while. Well, I always sit in silence. But Sherilyn was quiet, too. So quiet that I reached behind myself, after a few minutes, and turned up the volume on my heart monitor, just for the ambient noise.

Thank you for coming, I wrote, after a while.

"Can't they at least give you a laptop or something to write on?"

I'm on Medicaid or some shit. I'm lucky they give me these cheap-ass disposable pens.

"I'll bring you one of the kids' old ones."

It might not even be allowed. I could use it to beat myself to death.

"I'll ask downstairs. I'm sure it will be fine."

How are the kids?

"Oh, they're fine. They send their love."

What are they up to? What are they like?

"You'll see for yourself, soon enough." She seemed determined to leave it at that, but then didn't. Couldn't, like any parent. "Isaiah is sixteen now. He's an amazing diver."

Diver?

"Diver. He works at the Six Flags park near us. He's a featured attraction in the swim show. He dives ninety feet into a pool. It scares me so badly, I still haven't watched him do it. In person. I've only seen it on tape. He's won medals doing it. Platform freestyle, or some such thing."

That's amazing.

"Rambo officially adopted him years ago. And Carson's eight and enrolled in the accelerated learning program at his school. They're such great kids."

That's great. That's really great.

Isaiah was now four years older than Sherilyn was when I left Lake Lenni Lenape. I waited for Sherilyn to say something more. I, after all, had little to offer in the what's-new category. Little that wasn't common knowledge, anyway. Little that wasn't part of a police report. After a while, I started again.

How come you and Rambo never married?

"Oh, Rambo wants to. He formally proposes, the whole hearts and flowers deal, every year on my birthday. I've been putting him off. The way I see it, we've both been married once each, and look what it got us. I'm just taking it slow. We've got a good thing, I tell him. We'll get it done. Maybe when Isaiah is out of high school. Rambo says he'll have Isaiah as best man."

Rambo. What a sweetheart.

"We think so."

How's your job? Does telemarketing pay? Are people rude to you?

Sherilyn took a deep breath. "It's not so bad as you'd think. You get some hang-ups, some four-letter words, but mostly, people are pretty decent."

It's true, they are. Decent.

"It's more of a problem sometimes, getting off the line, because you've got quotas to meet, than it is people being rude or hanging up on you. It's surprising how many people just want to talk."

I've come to believe that more than I used to. To see that. People are mostly decent.

"I don't do much calling anymore. I got into supervision, then list management. I miss it sometimes, though. Calling."

Are you staying at the house?

"No. I'm staying at a motel in Ledgewood. The sheriff's department locked the house up."

First time in thirty years anyone's bothered to lock the house up.

"True." Sherilyn permitted herself a little smile. "And there's still nothing in it anybody wants."

They let you in?

"Tuesday. The sheriff sent an officer up with the key."

Sheriff Woods. He was nicer to me than he needed to be. Was it weird being back in the house, after all these years?

"I was there last year, when I was up to visit. I wouldn't call it weird. Sad, more than anything. I look back, now, and I try to remember the good things. The happy things. It wasn't all terrible."

There was plenty of terrible, though. You were too young to recognize a lot of the early stuff.

"Right. And you were too packed-up-and-gone to recognize the late stuff."

True. I've sometimes felt like I left you in a tight spot, in that house.

"What else were you going to do? I would've done the same thing. Hell, I got out of there when I was eighteen, too."

At least you didn't have Dad to deal with.

"No, I didn't. It was an empty house with empty cabinets and empty closets and empty rooms and nobody paying the bills. Mom eating and living and sleeping in the living room. Coming home from work and watching TV until she fell asleep in the recliner. Every night for years."

I was so happy to be out of that house.

"The phone turned off. Oil deliveries stopped. In the winter, we had one kerosene heater for the whole house. The pipes burst three, four times. The septic system backed up and stayed that way for weeks at a time. The electricity was off half the time. We were very popular with the neighbors in those years."

I bet.

"When I left, I thought I'd never waste another word on her."

But you changed your mind. You wrote her.

"Yeah, I did. Six, seven years later. I was in Oklahoma, by then."

We looked at each other. Finally, I wrote, *Why?*

"You want to know why? You really want to know? Why I forgave her? And even Dad?"

That seemed like more information than I'd really asked for. But I shrugged.

"I went out into the world and I found out that shit happens. That's what happened. I went out into the world and took some chances and made some bad decisions and I saw the shit that can happen without your ever meaning it to happen."

You grew as a person.

"Don't you get fucking glib with me, Nathan. You haven't earned it."

I reached over and turned up the volume on my heart—thub, thub, thub—and we listened to that for a bit.

"There's a lot of ways to let someone down, mister. And you don't have to go too far out of your way to find 'em. When Isaiah was two, he and I were living in a SRO welfare motel on Cheyenne reservation land in Montana. Do you even know what SRO means?"

Standing room only?

"Single room occupancy. One room, no bathroom, no cooking, no nothing. A bed and a dresser. We were wearing whatever I could wash in the sink in the bathroom at the end of the hall. We were eating out of vending machines. Did I plan any of that? Is that what I wanted for my child? Did I do it out of laziness? Or vindictiveness? Or not giving a shit? No. And it happened anyway."

After you left the religious nuts.

"After I got away from the Sect, yeah. I got a ride out of the Sect compound on a delivery truck. When I got to the nearest town, I had Isaiah, a paper grocery bag full of clothes, forty-two dollars that I stole from the lord high whoever's desk, and a busted cheek I got from the delivery truck driver. He'd heard about us Sect girls, everybody up there had heard something about us, and he wanted some for himself. That's how I got out of the Sect. It took me ten months of two shifts a day, at a box factory and a diner, to get out of Montana. And I had to get us out of Montana, because the Sect harassed us the whole time."

There was nothing to write to any of that. I studied my floppy, suicide-proof pen, while Sherilyn looked at me.

"Nice life for a two-year-old boy, right? And that's just hitting the high points, Nathan. Not the daily shit and humiliation that a woman on her own, with a baby boy, in a fleabag motel, in a fleabag life, has to put up with just to get by. So why don't you open up your precious journal and write some truth about me? I'd deserve it, right?"

It's not the same thing.

"Yeah, well, it never is." She straightened in her chair and put her hands on her knees. "Not me, everyone says. I'm different."

You at least wanted something better for your child.

"You think Mom and Dad didn't?"

You made a mistake and then you fixed it. It's not the same thing.

"Try raising a family of your own someday, and you'll see how easy it is to make mistakes. How easy it is to let someone down."

I didn't know what to say to this. It was odd, not having the last say on a point of Huffnagle history. I looked at my sister, gone for so many years and now returned. Returned as a sassy, commonsensical Plains Stater with a good heart, overachieving kids, hard-won wisdom, and little patience for simple fools like me.

"Did you ever hear the story of how Mom and Dad met?"

I looked at my sister, alarmed.

"Yeah. How they met. It's an interesting story. I only heard it myself last year. Mom told it to me, after all these years."

I don't think we need

"Dad was seventeen years old and waiting for his eighteenth birthday, so he could enlist in the army. He was working as a mover. A furniture mover for a moving company. His mother, our grandmother, took him out of school when he was sixteen, when his father, our grandfather, died. His mother sent him out to work, to bring money home. This is before grandma remarried."

to go into ancient history here.

"No?" Sherilyn said, looking at what I'd written. "I thought you liked stories. So anyway, that's what people did, back then. First generation Dutch-American, right off the boat, in some cold-water walk-up in Manhattan up above Harlem somewhere. If the family was in trouble, you pitched in. School was secondary.

"So Dad met Mom moving furniture. One day, he was packing up an apartment full of furniture that was going back to Ireland. Mom's dad, our grandfather on that side, was going back to Ireland. His health was bad—he was dying, actually— and he was going back to Ireland. His wife, our grandmother, had died that same year. Mom, our mom, was going to live with her sister, who'd just married. Mom was sixteen that year."

I never heard any of that.

"And that's how they got to talking. Mom and Dad. Mom had lost her own mom and was losing her dad, and Dad had just lost his dad. They had that in common. When Dad went off to the army, mom wrote him and he wrote back. Month after month, until dad's three-year hitch was over. And then they got married."

Mom told you this?

"Yeah. She seemed almost embarrassed to tell it. It was something she must not have known how to talk about, until recently, I think. Her mom died terribly, of cancer. And her dad just left. And then he died, too."

My God.

"It must have been rough. But everybody's got a story, you know?"

You're making a point here, right?

"Who, me? No, you're the big point-maker in the family. You're the only one who can afford to be. You're the one who hasn't made any mistakes."

I didn't reply to this. There was nothing to say.

"I was in a police car," my sister said, after a while, "leaving Newark Airport, sirens and the whole deal, when you . . . you know."

Removed most of my head with a shotgun.

"I was probably half an hour away. Not that my speaking to you would have changed a thing. Not that anyone's speaking to you would ever change a thing."

What do you want me to do? Forgive? And forget? Fine. I'm doing that all the time now. Everyone, I forgive you. Boy, I feel so much better.

"You might start by forgiving yourself. Work up to the more difficult forgiving."

Words. It's all just words. Words, words, words. Take it from an ad writer. Words don't mean a thing.

"Then you should stop writing shitty ads and journals and start having a life. A real life."

In Oklahoma. I could be okay in OK. I could start drilling for oil, like Rambo.

"Nobody drills for oil in Oklahoma anymore. Rambo drills for water. And don't make fun of Rambo. He saved my life when no one gave a shit. He raised Isaiah as his own, when he didn't have to, when the Sect was after him."

He's a good man.

"Man enough to care about something. You oughta try it sometime."

Like Trent. Trent and Rambo. It's hard to take anybody named Rambo seriously.

"It's hard for you to take anyone seriously."

I shrugged and turned away. I turned up the volume on the heart machine another notch. Thub-thub-thub-thub-thub-thub.

There was another long, silent stretch between us.

Sherilyn broke it, finally, by saying, "You're coming home with me. To Oklahoma."

No. I'm sorry. I'm not. I can't.

"You are. I won't even bother to point out the realities of your situation. I'll just say this. I'm your family. We're your family. We love you."

The little pen felt large and unwieldy in my hands, then. This last bit, the casual use of the L-word, would have been something else she'd picked up in the Plains States, like common sense and forbearance. It wasn't a Huffnagle thing, surely. Huffnagles weren't users of the L-word. We couldn't afford that kind of emotional largesse.

"I shouldn't have let so many years go by without coming out here. I shouldn't have let you ignore me. I should have come out and treed you like a squirrel."

You tried to keep in touch. That's more than I did.

"Now I'm here and Mom's gone and you're . . ." Sherilyn watched the heart monitor.

Fatootsed.

"I certainly didn't come all the way out here to fight with you. I don't know what I expected. I guess I hoped, after all these years, we could at least talk. Finally."

I never was much for jawing. Even when I had a jaw.

"No. Not you," Sherilyn said. "That's your whole story. You never needed anybody. You don't need anybody."

Besides. I like to think that we have been talking, over the years.

"You do, huh?"

I never signed up with that don't-call registry. I receive a lot of telemarketing calls.

"Oh, fuck you, Nathan. "Just . . ." She was shaking her head. Maybe she was grinning. A ghost of a grin. ". . . fuck you."

§

June 29th, noon

Hoo boy.

I guess if I had it to do over again, I wouldn't be spending the next-to-last day of my life, my last day for quiet reflection, enduring another wretched hangover.

But then, too, if I were living some other, worthier life, I wouldn't be back here at Moore's with the lunch-time crowd.

I'm enough of a regular now that I can prop my laptop open on the bar and write without anyone giving me the leery eye. The bartender lady with the rubber glove—Rosie, as it happens—even lets me run a cord over the bar and plug into an outlet. I'm told that I'll have to unplug if someone orders a blender drink, but that hasn't happened in three days. I have to take the laptop with me every time I go to the men's room, of course.

Tanya has already been by with one of her cheerfully obscene and specific business proposals. Boris is here, too, hunched over the bar by the opposite register, drinking shots of vodka and ignoring me as if he were someone who hadn't stolen my wallet a few nights ago.

You arrive at a certain station in life and a place like Moore's just makes sense, I realize. The scope of my life has narrowed to the point where there just aren't that many places left where I can hang around without attracting attention. And the lunch special here isn't all that bad, surprisingly. Better than the crap I was microwaving at Mom's house.

I've been drunk in better places.

Several years ago, I remember, I encountered an old drinking buddy in a men's room at the St. Regis Hotel in Manhattan. We were both attending company Christmas parties, mine thrown by the ad agency I worked for then, his thrown by some laboratory equipment sales outfit he worked for. I was somewhat the worse for wear at that point in the evening, already hoisting my third sheet to the wind. He looked just fine. He'd stopped drinking a few years before, something old drinking buddies sometimes do.

So we talked a bit in the lobby, exchanged requisite pleasantries carefully calculated to enable us to be free of each other as swiftly as possible, without feeling we'd slighted each other. As we were winding it up, I asked him, "So, are you happy?"

And he said to me, "I don't chase happiness any more."

I remember I was annoyed, because I hadn't intended the question in any deep philosophical sense. I'd merely been asking him if selling lab equipment was preferable to selling office connectivity solutions, his previous gig. And the guy bushwhacks me with some bumper-sticker wisdom about the futility of seeking happiness in a bottle.

I was young enough then to distrust sobriety in all its forms, as well as the Zen-like koans often associated with that way of life. But I knew what he was talking about. That first twenty minutes or so, when you come home from a hard day at work, or stop in your favorite bar, and drink that first beer, and it feels just like happiness. The way that that sense of well-being recedes with each subsequent drink.

But here's the thing I could tell that guy now that I didn't know then. You can get to a stage in life where happiness has nothing to do with it anymore. Happiness is so far out of reach, it's stopped even crossing your mind.

Nobody in Moore's is drinking to attain a temporary state of happiness. There's no "happy hour" at all in Moore's, by the way. The shot prices for various liquors are written right on the labels of the bottles in thick-markered scrawl. They stay the same, regardless of the hour or your circumstances.

Oh, and your circumstances? They're always bad, here at Moore's.

The people in Moore's might drink less if they had other options. But they don't and there aren't that many damned ways to get through a day. I know, I lived that way for a while, until my life entered its unique and fascinating final stretch.

So what do they do—what do *we* do—here at Moore's? We try to cut a deal with the length and expanse of the day. We live on reduced terms. We give up on the illusion of happiness. We try to feel the emptiness less. We board up the windows and the doors of our existence and we hunker down and we live.

But now here comes Tanya again and I've got to go. I've got a date.

§

Damn it. I'm running out of room on the back sides of these pages. Just when things were starting to get good, too. Just when you finally showed your face, Death.

It was bound to happen. My big, loopy, awkward scrawl has been getting bigger and loopier by the day. So I hope you don't mind if I continue on the fronts of these journal transcript pages,

Death. There's plenty of room in the margins and I have no intention of stopping now.

So. I woke up this morning to this.

"Wake up, Nathan."

I opened my eyes to find an elderly black woman walking past the foot of my bed. Her face was age-spotted and dewlapped, deeply lined. She was pushing a bucket on wheels. There was a mop sticking out of the bucket, which she propped against the wall. Her hands were all tendon and muscle and bone, age-spotted like her face.

I retrieved my writing pad and pen.

"Time to talk, my friend." Her white hair was covered by a hair net and she was wearing the blue institutional smock that all the hospital cleaning people wear. She was fat, too. Heavy-bosomed and stout enough to stretch the seams of her big smock tightly.

Who are you?

"You've been calling me the Angel of Death."

It was you, Death. In the flesh, at last. Plenty of it, too.

I thought about this before writing, *Not sent*, double underline, *by the Angel of Death?*

"No."

You're the Big Guy?

You sighed. "I'm different things to different people, I guess." You were looking around yourself. "People see in me what they want to see."

I want to see a heavyset, elderly black woman in a custodial smock?

"I guess so," you said tiredly. You had found what you were looking for, a chair in the corner, by another of my newer life-support monitors, and you were sliding it over to my bedside. "You mind if I take a load off?"

The Angel of Death? I was writing. *Like in God and his heavenly angels?*

THE END IS NEAR

Hey, I thought, maybe Sister Rafaella was right. She'll be delighted. I held up the pad.

"Don't fuss with the pad," you said, waving it off. "I can hear you."

Like heavenly angels? I thought.

"And don't get all religious on me." You lowered yourself slowly into the chair and breathed a sigh of relief. "I'm tired and I've got a lot to do."

What about Betty and Sister Rafaella and Archie? Are they angels, too?

"Forget the angel part, okay? I'm sorry I mentioned it."

Archie, an angel. Jeepers. That's hard to believe.

"We have to talk, Nathan."

Were they real? Betty and Sister R. and Archie? Or were they ghosts you made up and put in my head?

"Of course they're real. They're real to you, aren't they? What else matters?"

Oh, no. Oh no, you don't. You're reading my own thoughts back to me. If you can't come up with some original material, I'm going to write you off as a delusion. I'll start believing the doctors.

"Maybe your thoughts are getting closer to the truth. Maybe you're actually getting somewhere."

And what's this shit with my father? I ought to kick your angel ass for that one.

I have to say, it felt so damned good to be communicating to someone without scribbling. I felt almost like a real person again.

"Your father had a message for you. You might have heard it, if you knew how to listen."

Oh, I heard it alright. Fucking loud and clear. Maybe you don't know me as well as you think you do.

"It's not my job to know you. It's yours. And you can save all the swearing for your journal. Who do you think wants to hear all that bad-word stuff? It just slows everything down."

Oh, excuse me. Excuse my heavy-handedness. And look who's talking. You send me a knitting waitress and a nun? Who's next? The hooker with the heart of gold?

You smiled a sad little crimpled smile at me. You put your hands on your knees and moved to the edge of your seat. "I'm not here to argue with you," you said. "I'm here to tell you that your time is growing short. You'll need an answer soon."

Well you might as well hit the timer, Angel. I don't know what you want. Except the obvious.

"I know you're frustrated. But you're very close to the truth. Closer than you think."

The truth, again. Believe it or not, Angel, I'm getting a little tired of all this Jonathan Livingston Seagull shit, you know?

"Maybe you're just trying too hard. The truth might be staring you in the face."

The truth is staring everybody in the face! I was wrong! I admitted it! I wrote that, the first time around. Everyone else was right, everything that happened in my life was my own fault. Everyone I ever knew grew up and changed for the better, while I stayed the same. I poisoned my life with resentment and envy and self-loathing and hatred and fear. How many different ways do you want me to say it?

"Just one way. The right way."

Yeah, right. Easy for you to say.

"Go back and read your own pages." You had shifted forward enough to attempt rising from the chair. You started up, very slowly, using the mop in the bucket for leverage. "The truth's right there. You're writing it more and more often as you go."

I am?

You paused for breath, halfway up.

"Sure you are."

I find that very hard to believe.

"I'm sure you do. If you were a product, that statement would be your . . ." You were standing, more or less. Hunched a little forward. Turning for the door. "What do you copywriters call it? Tag line?"

Trademark. Angel?

"Yes?"

All these people who are dying. Is everyone writing the story of their lives? At the end?

"Of course not. You happen to be writing. Because it's your way. If you were someone else, you might be digging a ditch. Or making amends for a betrayal. Or cleaning out the attic."

Oh, wow. That's depressing.

"The point is, the writing itself is meaningless. It's the understanding that matters. The accounting. Everyone accounts for their life in their own way."

I'm trying, Angel.

"I know you are." You were wheeling your mop and bucket toward the door. "You're doing good. You are. Don't be discouraged."

It doesn't feel like I'm doing good.

You were in the doorway, your back to me. "The next time we speak, which will be very soon, you'll have an answer for me."

Angel. Wait. Wait. Wait a minute.

Your bucket clattered against the door and the water in it sloshed. You said "Excuse me," to someone in the hall. And then you were gone, the door easing shut behind you.

§

June 29th, 3pm

There are two Huffnagles buried in Lake Lenni Lenape.

They're buried in Locust Knoll Cemetery, in the low hills west of the lake valley, close enough to Moore's that I can see the big box stores off in the distance. Both graves have a weedy, dusty, neglected aspect. Thomas's family is long gone, these days. In Texas, somewhere. And I can't imagine that Mom came up here much.

Thomas's stone is a short square marker of tan marble, with a cross on top. Thomas Huffnagle, Loving Husband and Father. I tried to interest Tanya in it, but she's not much for other peoples' reminiscences.

I gave Tanya the last two hundreds in my diminished money roll and she walked out of Moore's to my car with a lime-green acrylic cardigan thrown over her shoulders and sweatpants pulled up over her micro-miniskirt. We drove up here and fucked in my car at the end of the access road to Quadrant B. She was as cheerful and matter-of-fact in the act as she was in her no-nonsense propositions.

Now she's content to sit on a stone a few graves over from my father's, looking off into the distance, sipping from a pint of Jim Beam and watching clouds pile up in the west. It was sunny this morning, but a thin gray overcast is overtaking us, lending everything a flat, lusterless, two-dimensional feel. When I'm done here, I'll have to take Tanya back to work.

My father's tombstone is a low gray stone, about two feet high and three across, with HUFFNAGLE across the top center and room for two names, left and right, below. Nathan Huffnagle, 1940—1985, is etched on the left. The space on the right is blank, Mom having escaped to that sisterly grave in Tuxedo Junction, New York.

I don't believe I've mentioned that Dad and I share more than self-destructive proclivities and a fondness for spirits. We share a name, too. He's Nathan Robert, though. And I'm

Nathan James. Strangely enough, I see, we also share a roughly equivalent life span. Forty-five years. Go figure.

Tanya and I have Quadrant B pretty much to ourselves on this dim June afternoon, which is probably just as well, since I don't think it's customary to pay one's respects by sitting on the dear departed's tombstone, tapping on a laptop and drinking a beer.

Rest assured, Trent kith and kin, that I'm not about to prattle on again about my family. I'm surprised they figured as prominently as they did in this journal. I hadn't intended to mention them at all, and they just started popping up here and there, at mostly inopportune times. But we're all done with them, now.

I'm here, instead, to absorb the finality of death. The realness of death.

There's a powerful temptation, when you're about to kill yourself, to fantasize about how sorry everyone will be when you're dead. To imagine that your passing will cast a shadow over the lives of the living.

But if you go down that road, you're really fantasizing about "living on" in the memories of others. Which is to say, fantasizing about living. That's when your stoic and noble suicide becomes the embarrassing "cry for help."

Fortunately, I have little incentive to indulge myself in that manner. There's really no one left who gives a crap whether I'm alive or dead. Not even blunt, hard-faced Tanya, despite her gratifyingly enthusiastic performance thirty minutes ago. So I'm in an excellent position to appreciate the utter finality of death.

If, however, that was not the case, if I was hoodwinked by the illusion of "living on" in the memories of the living, this cemetery would be offering a harsh corrective.

I mean, just look around. Look at these people. They're all dead. And they're on their own.

Look at Abrams here. Cyril G. Born 1910. Died 1973. Last visited . . . oh, I'm gonna say 1975. All he's got on this plot are a few weeds. His stone has a ten-degree forward tilt. He doesn't even have a cheap plastic flower holder on his grave, much less flowers.

Bradford's going it alone, too. Allan J. Born 1938. Died 1980. Dead at forty-two, before he could even polish his golf game sufficiently. You think his buddies from the sales office ever get out here? Fuck, no. They're all in retirement colonies in Boca Raton, cheating at cards and fucking each others' bored wives.

And Neill, here. Ben Neill. Born 1913. Died 1981. There's a big old divot out of his tombstone, probably sliced out by one of the earthmovers the gravediggers are tear-assing around in. You think his wife and kids have noticed that divot? Be real. It's been fifteen years since one of them even pulled the musty old photo albums from the attic to look at the yellowed pictures, much less came out here to set a gladiola at Ben's defiled stone.

Nathan Robert Huffnagle here has it pretty good, by comparison. He's living large, in the land of the dead. He's got an actual visitor, two if you count the Russian stripper with the fake boobs and big ass. That first actual visitor is about to join him in the largest and least prestigious club there is. The club of the dead, the club of complete and utter insignificance.

These people are dead.

They're non-factors.

And so am I.

See ya in hell, Dad.

§

"You know, if I was a guy," Danika was saying, "and I was tied naked to a beam with chicks around, I'd be concentrating so hard on not getting a hard-on, I'd probably get a hard-on. Reverse psychology."

Danika was switching on a gooseneck desk lamp that she had set in the middle of the floor. Night had crept up on us, in our storeroom stronghold. She twisted the flexible neck back so that the light pointed straight up.

"Danika, please," I said. "Let's not be talking about . . . you know."

"Hard-ons. Right. I could get in trouble. Like it was my idea to tie him up naked." Danika made a sour face and looked at Alice. "Guys are so ridiculous."

"I'm forty-five years old," Randy said. I had removed the underwear from his head. I'd gotten tired of looking at him through the leghole. "I can't afford to waste a hard-on here. I only get one or two a week, if I'm lucky."

"Au contraire, fucking Pierre," Alice said, her voice a hard, raspy parody of Felicia.

We all had a good laugh at that one.

"How about you?" Danika asked, meaning me. "You were just, what, eighteen? You pop a chubby, when you were tied to that flagpole?"

"I was seventeen." I remembered my time lashed to the mast of that empty night. I remembered my three visitors, one after another, in the dark of that night. "No, I didn't. I was too cold. Too scared."

"Oh," she said, sobering. "Right. March."

There was another great burst of cheering and whistling and clapping from outside.

"What the fuck?" I said. I got up this time and went to the door to see what was going on.

"They've probably got this place bugged by now," Danika said. "They can probably hear every word we're saying."

I opened the door a crack and peeked outside. The sun had set about an hour before, but it looked like midday out there, what with all the police and TV lights. Several spotlights were trained on the windows of the store, and the fronts of the bar and pizzeria across the street were bathed in the same gaudy white glow. Roof lights—the red and blue of cop cars, the yellow and white of rescue vehicles—were spinning everywhere.

People were really packing in behind the sawhorse barricades across the street. A couple of beach balls were being batted around in the crowd. One buxom young woman in front was waving a big hand-drawn sign. *We luv U Randy!* There was a big arrow-pierced heart on the sign. The roofs of the buildings opposite were now filled to capacity. I watched another bedsheet banner spring open, revealing its message. LLL Scarlet Storm Football #1!!!

There was no big organized cheering section, though. In fact, the cheering had died down almost entirely. The people I could see were just standing around, talking to each other.

"I don't know what they're cheering about," I said. "Random excitement, I guess."

"Maybe some chick's flashing her boobs for the crowd," Danika said.

I shut the door. I walked over to Randy.

"It was an unusually warm day for March," I said. "The day you tied me to the flagpole. I think it was a record for that day of the year. It got cold at night, though."

"I think I remember that," Randy said. "At that senior trip. It was warm, wasn't it?"

"But colder at night." I looked closely at Randy. I wasn't carrying the shotgun anymore. Randy couldn't leave; Alice and Danika didn't want to. For most of the remainder of the evening, the cops could have burst in at any time and put an end to the thing without a shot being fired. "So you do remember."

"I never said I didn't remember tying someone to a flagpole." Randy shrugged. "I just couldn't have said who it was. Exactly."

THE END IS NEAR

"I promised my readers I would ask you why you did what you did. Why you cast a shadow over my life that exists to this day. Those were my exact words."

"Your readers?"

"Of my journal." I hiked a thumb at the untidy sheaf of paper lying ignored beside my cloth shopping bag and the empty pizza box.

"Okay. What was the question?"

"Why did you ruin my life?"

Randy looked at me. To his credit, he didn't look intimidated or even particularly self-conscious, considering the position he was in. Tied and handcuffed naked to a beam. Not that he looked great. Not that he looked like Clark Gable in a pirate movie. He just looked like a guy making the best of a bad situation.

"Nah," he said. "No." He was shaking his head. "I didn't ruin your life. I made it hard on you, for a while. I ran you ragged, I guess. Because I was an asshole and I didn't know any better. But I didn't ruin your whole life."

"How do you know?" I demanded. "You hardly even fucking remember any of your part in it."

"No one can ruin someone else's life for them. You can only do that for yourself."

"That," I said, getting right in Randy's face, "sounds suspiciously like New Age bullshit to me. Is that something you got from Charity?"

"It's just something I know."

And then the phone rang. I would've ignored it, but I didn't get the chance. Danika leaped up and scampered over to it, presumably to keep me from getting to it first and using up my third demand on a paper clip. Or a kind word.

"Hello?" she said. She listened for a second. "It's Glinda, the Good Witch of the North. Who's this?" She listened again, then put her hand over the receiver. "It's Woody," she said to me. "Your cake's ready."

I looked at Danika, then at Randy. I pointed a finger in his face.

"I'm going to get a better answer from you," I said. "At the very least, I'm going to get that." I turned my back on him. "Send in the cake."

"Bring in the cake, Woody," Danika said into the phone. "Right. You. Oh, and some soda. Diet cola."

"And some seltzer," Alice said. "And napkins."

"And a six-pack of beer," I said. What the hell, I was going to be dead in a few hours.

The cake was a round chocolate cake with vanilla frosting. Store bought, but tasty. It occurred to me, too late, that I could have had the cops bake me one. The cake had pink and blue frosting flowers on it, and the words Happy Birthday, Nathan written in neat blue frosting script across its top. There were two big candles, in the shape of a number four and a number five, planted in the center of it.

"How's it going, in here?" Woody wanted to know.

"Pretty good. Nobody's dead yet." I'd had to retrieve the shotgun. "Put the cake on the counter there. Next to the TV."

"That's what we like to hear." Woody set the cake by the TV, which was turned on with the volume turned all the way down. He'd also brought a paper shopping bag, from which he pulled two six-packs of soda, the beer, cups, plates, plastic utensils, and napkins.

He arranged all this on the counter and turned to me. "Happy birthday," he said.

"Thanks, Woody." I looked at the cake. "Hey, forty-five."

"Forty-five's a big one. I remember forty-five. I remember thinkin', here it is, middle age. There ain't no turnin' back now."

"It's true. It's a big one."

"Hey, Randy," Woody said. "Ain't you forty-five, too?"

"Yep," Randy said.

"Forty-five." Woody grabbed his belt buckle with both hands, the way fat, jolly, despicable sheriffs do in Burt Reynolds movies. "Thirty-five, you ain't a kid anymore. Forty-five, you ain't young anymore. Fifty-five, you're old."

"I guess so," I said. I could see that Woody, though fat, was neither jolly nor despicable. He was, like Trent, a sensible man trying to make the best of a bad situation. "Sheriff?"

"Yeah. Is there anything else we can do for you, Nathan?"

"Yes, there is, Woody. First, you can light those candles."

"Sure thing." He looked around. "Anyone got a match?"

"Top drawer, under the counter," Trent said. He was bound to the post facing the other way, so he had to turn his head and peer over his shoulder.

"Thanks. Quit smokin' myself. Almost ten years ago." Woody found the matches and struck one. He lit the candles. "Except for a celebration cigar, now and again, when the occasion calls for it."

"Okay," I said. "Pick up the cake."

"Uh huh." Woody picked it up.

"Both hands, underneath. Hold it a little higher." The candles were burning brightly in the half-light of the storeroom. "Okay. Bring it here."

Woody approached, the cake held aloft. He stopped before me. "Here ya go."

"Okay. Now sing Happy Birthday."

"Ah," he said. "You're sportin' with me now."

"I'm afraid so," I had to admit. "But I want to hear it anyway."

"You do, huh?" Woody looked at me disapprovingly.

"Yeah. I do."

"I ain't much of a singer."

I shrugged. "Give it a shot."

"Uh huh." He cleared his throat. And then he started to sing. He sang like a man unaccustomed to singing, forsaking shifts in tone and pitch entirely. He sang like a guy who just mouths the hymns in church.

"Happy birthday to you. Happy birthday to yo-o-ou."

On the second phrase, Danika joined in, adding a much-needed vocal flourish on the second "you." Alice jumped in at the beginning of the third line, and Trent surprised me by joining in at the end of the third line, supplying a hefty bass note for my name.

"Happy bi-i-irthday, dear Na-a-aathan."

And then everybody sang the last line, "Happy birthday to yo-o-o-ou." The candles flickered before my eyes.

"Make a wish," Danika said.

I pretended to think about it for a moment, though there was nothing left to want and all my wishing was behind me. Or so I believed, then. I guess if I had it to do over again, I would have wished for better aim with that shotgun.

I blew the candle out. Danika and Alice applauded.

We sent Woody on his way after that, with a big piece of cake on a paper plate. Danika made him promise not to turn the slice over to the special forces guys to be bagged as evidence.

"Nobody gets the cake off my plate, young lady," he said. He looked at me. "There's a bottle opener here on the counter. Those beers ain't twist-offs."

"Oh," I said. "Thanks. I didn't think of that."

"I ain't going home, so if you need anything, I'll be out there."

"Okay." I couldn't foresee any reason I'd see him again. I was all out of requests. "Thanks for everything."

"Sure thing." Woody was still standing in the doorway. "You mind if I ask you a question?"

"No. Go ahead."

"You still ain't said why you're doing this."

"Is that the question?"

"The question is, I guess, why are you doing this?"

"You see that bunch of paper over there?" I pointed the shotgun at the journal on the floor.

"Yeah."

"It's all in there."

Woody was looking at the journal. "I ain't much of a reader," he said. "I'm hoping you'll tell me yourself, when this thing is over."

"Take it easy, Woody."

"You too, Nathan. Remember what I said about regret, huh?"

"I will."

Woody was eating his cake on his way out.

And we ate ours. It was getting late and Randy was hungrier now, so Alice fed him some cake. I put the soda and beer in the fridge, opened a beer for myself.

"So what's this with you and Colleen?" Alice was asking, between putting forkfuls of cake into Randy. "You haven't said, what she was doing at your place, all night."

"Not all night. Just late." Randy ate another bite. "We did what we always do. Talked about Tyler."

"At midnight?"

"She was freaked out. She's been waiting on Tyler for two days. She had to get out of the house, so she drove to my place."

Alice forked more cake into Randy's mouth. "Where's Tyler?"

"We don't know. He still hasn't come back from graduation. He called on Saturday morning, left a message, but that's been it. Colleen's pissed and worried, both."

"I'm sure he's okay, if he called. Kids get to be eighteen . . ." She wiped Randy's mouth with a napkin. "they get harder to keep track of. How about you and the ex? Any Sunday night hanky panky?"

"With Colleen? Nah. It ain't like that. She just wanted to blow off steam about Tyler."

"She turned you down, huh?"

Randy rolled his eyes at the ceiling.

"Hey, hey, hold on." Danika got up and went to the TV on the counter. She turned up the volume. "It's coming on again."

I looked at my watch. It was ten o'clock, the beginning of the local TV news hour. I had entered Randy's store more than six hours ago. Time just flies on by, when you're holding hostages.

The evening news anchor was a black guy with graying temples and mustache. There was a large graphic superimposed beside his head. It was a handgun with a little red star at its muzzle, meant to signify gunfire, against a background of an outline of New Jersey. Arranged to the right of this logo were three words, Standoff in Sussex.

"—drama unfolding in the small Sussex County community of Lake Lenni Lenape," the anchor was saying. "At approximately four o'clock this afternoon, an armed man entered an auto parts store there and took four hostages. Since then, the man, one Nathan Huffnagle, has made two unusual requests and released one hostage. Three hostages remain. For more on this breaking story, let's go to Samantha Jourgensen, live at the scene."

As soon as Samantha appeared, atop the WNNJ truck with the crowd behind her, there was another startling roar of applause from outside. On the screen, people in camera range were yelling and waving their hands. A couple of them had handmade signs. The four of us in the storeroom looked at each other. That's what the random applause was. The crowd had been cheering its own appearance on various TV news programs.

"We are entering hour seven of the Standoff in Sussex," Samantha was saying. Another of the Standoff in Sussex logos occupied the bottom right corner of the screen. "Police here at the scene refuse to comment for the record, but it is our understanding that they are growing increasingly worried." Samantha wrinkled her brow in empathy. "Nathan Huffnagle's erratic behavior, his odd requests for a pizza and a birthday cake, combined with disturbing information unearthed by police and news sources about Huffnagle's past ..." Samantha gave the mike a white-knuckle squeeze, "is adding intensity to an already tense situation."

"Who's the chick with the ribbon sign?" Danika said.

Prominent behind Samantha was a young woman, a freckled redhead in a skimpy tank top. She was holding a sign with a big hand-drawn yellow ribbon on it and a message. *Come Home Safe Randy!!!*

"I don't know," Randy said.

"Right now, we can tell you that the man holding those three hostages—"

"I am not a hostage!" Danika said, peevishly.

"—is one Nathan Huffnagle. But who ..." new shot of Samantha, from the other direction, framed by the store, "is Nathan Huffnagle? At this hour," pause to glower at the camera, "that is something of a mystery."

"Here's what we know." There was a shot of my mother's house, strategically shot from the side with the missing porch and the door hanging in space. "Nathan Huffnagle was born forty-five years ago in this house in Lake Lenni Lenape."

"Untrue," I said.

"What's up with that weird door?" Alice said.

"Oh, cool," Danika said.

"Huffnagle lived here for the first eighteen years of his life. And yet ... little evidence remains of the life he lived here. In fact, WNNJ News8 has been unable to find anybody," Samantha raised an eyebrow, "who remembers him at all."

"Well, it was almost thirty years ago," I said.

Samantha disappeared, replaced by a photo-studio shot of a pallid, dorky kid wearing a dress shirt tight at the neck and a necktie as wide as a lobster bib. It was my high school yearbook picture.

"Oh, my," Alice said, sympathetically.

"Huffnagle, shown here in this senior class yearbook photo, appears to have drifted through the Lake Lenni Lenape school system without leaving a mark. Records suggest a student not gifted in academics or sports, a loner with few friends or outside interests."

"What? Records suggest that I was a loner? What kind of record is that?"

"And then the story grows more intriguing," Samantha was saying. She paused for emphasis. "Turn a few pages in that same Lake Lenni Lenape high school yearbook, and you'll find this photo."

A toothily grinning, high-cheeked boy with arresting gray eyes peered out of the TV at us. He was wearing a shirt with a discreet front ruffle and a high collar. A gold chain glittered at the shirt's open neck. It was Randy Trent's yearbook photo.

"Whoo-oooo!" Alice sang in a chirpy falsetto. "Night fev-er, Night fe-e-e-e-ver!"

"Fucking A," Randy said.

"This is Randall Trent, hostage and owner of the auto parts store where today's drama is unfolding. It has been rumored, though not verified, that Huffnagle harbors some grievance regarding Trent. Perhaps a grievance that goes back . . ." long pause, "almost thirty years. But that, I repeat, is not corroborated at this hour.

"After receiving a degree in literature from the state university, Huffnagle embarked on an unremarkable career at the fringes of the advertising field." Trent's yearbook photo was replaced by a picture of the Pendleton Press corporate office. "That career came to an end six months ago, when he was fired by the Pendleton Press, a small publisher of, ironically, self-help books."

There was a shot of the back of my former boss's head, as she half-jogged to her car in the Pendleton parking lot. "Pendleton executives declined to comment on Huffnagle or his employment history, except to say that he had been terminated."

Samantha appeared again, with the crowd behind her. The crowd cheered again.

"Huffnagle dropped out of sight about a month ago. WNNJ News8 tracked Huffnagle to his last place of residence. For more on that, WNNJ News8 correspondent, Fuller McIntosh. Fuller?"

Fuller was a meek-looking, balding guy, maybe five feet four, wearing a blazer and bowtie. He was standing in front of my old apartment building.

"Samantha, Huffnagle's last known place of residence was this apartment building in Hoboken, New Jersey. We spoke to Sergey Lokmanov, the landlord of the building."

Sergey was filling the doorway of my old apartment building, looking trapped and grouchy, his eyebrows wriggling in a single furry line across his forehead. Sergey was a slab-muscled Russian emigrant with a stern face and imperious eyes. He looked to be roughly twice the size of Fuller.

"Mr. Lokmanov, can you tell us something about Nathan Huffnagle?"

"Huffnagle?" Sergey said, crossly. "He don't live here no more."

"Yes, Mr. Lokmanov. But what kind of person was he?"

"What kind of—" Sergey looked perplexed. "He was a tenant. Tenants move in and they move out. I don't know nothing about them."

Sergey didn't live in the building, a four-floor building of putty-yellow brick with two apartments on each floor, but he was often in it. Years before, he had installed a mistress in one of the third-floor apartments. Then, last year, he had installed another mistress in a first-floor apartment. There were Lokmanovs, newly arrived from Russia and possessing little English, on the second and fourth floors.

"He was the kind of tenant who kept to himself," Fuller suggested. "A loner."

"He didn't pay his rent," Sergey said. "I hadda kick him out."

"Did you notice any other peculiarities? Irregularities?"

Sergey squinted down at Fuller.

"Odd things," Fuller said.

"Yeah. He didn't pay his rent. Played his music too loud. The other tenants complained."

"He was a problem tenant," Fuller summed up.

"I had worse," Sergey said, grouchily.

Which was true. The third-floor mistress liked to express her disdain for the first-floor mistress by leaving her garbage—greasy paper bags containing smelly cat food tins and used kitty litter, mostly—at the first-floor mistress's door. The first-floor mistress would respond by stealing the third-floor mistress's mail and throwing it out. Sergey was a pretty good landlord, as landlords go. He only evicted me because he had to. Because I never paid the rent.

"So there you have it. A classic case." The little Fuller guy pivoted on the stoop and glared at a second camera. "Nathan Huffnagle. A loner. With financial difficulties. Fuller McIntosh, WNNJ News8. First . . . with the Facts."

Samantha appeared again, pressing a headphone into her ear.

"We're about to go live to an on-the-scene news conference featuring the first hostage to be released. Felicia Fowler is—" Samantha was blinking, listening. "No. No, I'm sorry. We're not going to get that."

"You dodged a bullet there, chief," Randy said to me. "You think you got problems with cops, I'm tellin' you, Felicia's your real problem. You better turn yourself in to the cops now, ask for asylum. Witness protection or something."

"Shut up, Randy," I said.

Somehow, I hadn't anticipated the media deconstruction of my life. Or no, worse. Not deconstruction. That wouldn't have hurt so much. I hadn't anticipated something much more damaging. The accurate portrayal of my life.

"Hey, I'm just thankful you took the heat off me, gave Felicia something else to go on the warpath about. I owe you one, buddy."

"Have we forgotten, has everybody forgotten," I looked around for my shotgun, "that I'm supposed to be killing you? Just before I kill me?"

Alice and Danika looked away uncomfortably.

"That I'm a paranoid lunatic out for blood? For vengeance?"

Randy was behind me. I didn't look at him.

"Who is Nathan Huffnagle?" Samantha was saying. "What does he want? All we have right now are questions. And those questions are making authorities at the scene very, very nervous. Samantha Jourgensen, WNNJ News8. First . . . with the Facts."

Danika was up, turning the sound down. Then she sat crosslegged on the floor again. "Anyone want more cake?"

Nobody did. After a while I stood up and looked around the room. I had left the shotgun by the refrigerator. I retrieved it and got myself another beer.

"Okay," I said, when I returned. "I think I'm starting to overstay my welcome here."

"Don't let the media piranhas get you down, Clyde," Danika said.

"They do it to everybody," Alice said.

There was another wave of shouting and carrying on from outside. Another live report on another station.

"It's time for us to talk, Randy." I opened my beer. "We're just about at the end now."

I turned to the girls. "You girls had better——" I stopped. "What are you doing, Danika?"

Danika was still sitting crosslegged. She was opening some of the many pockets on her huge, baggy shorts. Before her on the floor she placed a small tube of model glue, a plastic shaker that said SALT on it, and four stubby red candles. She produced a piece of string and, finally, a shiny steel disc, about three inches wide. She looked up at me.

"Do you have a picture of yourself?"

"A picture?"

"You know, like a wallet photo or something."

"No. I don't carry pictures. What are you doing?"

Danika had turned and was looking at Trent. "Do you have Internet access?"

Randy looked puzzled. "Yeah. We take orders online. Everybody does."

"Where? In front?"

"Front counter."

"Danika," I said. "We've had fun up 'til now, but I have to ask you——"

She walked by me and let herself through the door into the front of the store. Within five seconds of Danika shutting the door behind her, the phone started to ring. I went to the door and peeked out. Danika was booting up the computer.

"Danika!" I hissed. "Get back in here."

"Be right there," she said, her back to me.

There were about twenty police officers on the other side of the store's display windows, watching us.

"You know, you're going to have a lot of explaining to do, when this is all over," I said. "And I won't be there to bail you out."

"Let me handle that end," she said. She was searching for something on the Internet. The phone was still ringing. "Hey, do you want to see something?"

"What? What are you doing?"

She typed some more, then backed away from the keyboard, so I could see the screen. "See this?"

I looked at the screen, at the website she'd called up, and then looked quickly away. "Jesus, Danika. I hardly think this is the time or the place for that sort of thing."

"You know who that is?"

"Who? The girl?"

"No. The guy."

I looked again. "No. How would I know who that is?"

Danika told me who it was. "Oh," I said. He looked different on video. But I guess everyone looks different without clothes on.

The phone stopped ringing.

"Go back inside." Danika had gone back to the keyboard and was typing something else in. "You've probably got two or three snipers reading the wrinkles on your forehead through night-vision gunsights, right now."

"What are you doing now?"

"What I came out here to do. Go inside. I'll be with you in thirty seconds." If the forty pairs of law enforcement eyes watching her every move were making her self-conscious, she didn't show it. The printer beside the computer monitor hummed to life and queued up a piece of paper.

"Go," Danika said.

"Okay, okay." I shut the door.

Inside, Trent was wrestling with his flags again.

"Hey, Nate," he said, "you mind if I ask you a favor?"

"No, go ahead."

"Can we untie these flags at my feet and knees? The circulation in my legs ain't what it used to be."

"It's not?" I looked at his legs. They were starting to look a little pale and unhealthy.

"Not to mention, I ain't exactly used to standing for this long."

"Do you know how long I was tied to the flagpole at Mount Lookout Lodge?"

"It ain't like I'm going—" Randy stopped. "No. How long?"

"Almost eight hours. From ten pm to a little before six the next morning. Long enough to lose the feeling in my hands and feet. When I was released, I had to crawl up the hill to the hotel on all fours."

"Oh."

"Right. Oh." I took a sip of my beer and set it on the floor. "I don't remember you stopping by to see if I was okay. Or offering to make me comfortable."

"No," Randy said. "I guess I didn't."

"Your memory being what it is, you probably forgot me entirely by midnight of that same night."

Randy didn't have anything to say to that.

There was a box razor on one of the shelves by the time clock. I sliced the flags at the point where they wrapped around the beam. They came apart easily.

Randy slid down the beam so that his ass was on the floor and then straightened his legs before himself. "Man, that feels good," he said. "Thanks."

"Don't mention it." I was holding up one of the Lake Placid flags, feeling the rotted material, looking at the faded interlocking Olympic circles, remembering.

Danika returned then, with some sheets of paper. "Hey, is that a razor? Let me see that."

I gave her the razor and she sat on the floor, setting first one piece of paper, then another over the three-inch steel disk. Each of the sheets of paper had a picture on it. They were pictures of me, downloaded from the Internet, each a different size. My yearbook photo again.

When she found a picture she liked, one the same size as the disk, she cut the picture out, using the razor to trim around the circumference of the disk. The disk, I saw, had a small hole near the edge.

"Danika?" I said. "What's up? What are you doing?"

Alice got up and went to a switch by the door. Rows of florescent lights sputtered on above us, freeze-framing everything in a grim, garish luminescence.

"No," Danika said. "No lights. Turn them off."

"Don't you want to see what you're doing?"

"I can see." She pulled the goosenecked lamp closer to her and started gluing the picture of me to the disk. Then she cut a small hole in the paper where the hole on the disk was, and ran the string through it. She tied the ends of the string together.

Alice turned the overhead lights off. There were small, high windows along the side walls of the storeroom, and two big windows in back, plus the little windows in the back door. Light from the circus out front was leaking through most of them.

"Bring me those matches on the counter," Danika said to Alice.

Alice handed Danika the matches and she used them to light the four candles. She looked around. She set one candle at the front of the room, saying, "West," then set the other three down, saying, "East," "North," and "South." Then she unscrewed the top from the salt shaker and drew a circle with the salt at the center of the candles, about a foot in diameter. When she was done, she looked at me.

"Ready?" she said.

"Ready for what? This is some kind of witch thing?"

"It usually works best at noon on the day of the new moon, but we'll have to improvise."

"Improvise what?"

"This spell. Here. Hold this." She handed me the disc with my picture on it and grabbed my elbow. She tugged me over into the center of the circle of salt. "It's a spell for personal protection."

"Oh, Danika. I don't know. I'm not much for witch stuff."

"I know you're not. If you were, you wouldn't allow yourself to be so unhappy. Not to mention, you'd be embarrassed to be seen in public with that feeble aura of yours."

"It's bad, huh?"

"Weak stuff. Are you going to trust me or what?"

Where would I have been, without Danika's help? In jail, almost certainly. Already dead, if I had been really lucky.

"Okay," I said. "You're not going to draw blood or make me eat a live newt or something, right?"

"No," she said. "Face south." She indicated the southern candle. "Hold the amulet and repeat after me."

I clasped the disc before me. "Okay."

"All-father above, all-mother below, I place me in your care."

"All-father above, all-mother below, I place myself in—"

"Don't correct for grammar, Nathan. This is magic, not an English quiz."

"Uh huh." I repeated it verbatim.

"Now. Repeat it two more times south, then three times west and three times north."

"Will this work, if I'm not necessarily a firm believer in witchcraft?"

"It will work a lot better if you open your mind and heart to the spiritual world around you. If you try to live in harmony with the powers and spirits that surround you. Lacking that, it won't hurt that I'm here, giving you a little psychic boost. Stop interrupting. Aspire to harmony."

When I finished all the chanting and turning, Danika said, "Okay, face the east."

I turned and she said, "At each dawning, spirits of the east, recharge my amulet."

I looked at the disc with my goofy high school yearbook photo glued to it. I would be wearing this thing when the cops found my body. I supposed it would give Woody something to wonder about. I repeated after Danika.

"You're really supposed to offer this concluding prayer in the nude, each dawn, for the next fifteen days," Danika said. "But we're going to have to make do with what we've got. Ready?"

"Yep."

"Put the amulet on, around your neck, and repeat after me." And I did.

"Lady queen, lady queen, lady queen. Shining maiden, strong woman, wise crone. To you I offer reverence and gratitude, from you I learn wisdom and compassion. Yours are dominion, power, glory. Yours are grace, nurturing, justice. Thus it is. Thus let it ever be."

§

June 29th, 5pm

I'm running out of time. The time required to do things and then write about doing them. One of the two has to go.

You've probably noticed already that these entries are growing increasingly brief and terse. Well, you'll have to excuse me, dear reader. I plead time constraints.

This afternoon, the next-to-last afternoon of my life, I'm burning the trash. Trash burning is illegal in this neighborhood, so, officers of the law, you may want to add another citation to my file.

First to go into the flames are some odds and ends from around the house. Recipes, ancient school records, financial statements, two rolls of twenty-dollar bills that I found stashed in a coffee can in the furnace room. Either they were Dad's or

Mom forgot about them. They flaked apart in my hands as I removed the rubber bands from them.

Next into the fire is my own embarrassing stuff. Samples of my ad writing, mostly junk from the disreputable later years of my career. Sales letters, brochures, other crap I used to send out to potential freelance clients. Ugly stuff, mostly. All gone. Computer discs, too, packed with endless 1's and 0's that I corrupted, tortured, into unembraceable shapes—warping, melting, dripping. Everything. Gone. Transmuted into a higher form. Carbon and some poisonous, plastic resins.

Last into the fire are the family photos and letters I found in Sherilyn's toy box. I'll spare one and attach it where I said I would, earlier in this journal. And I think I'll spare one more, the last unfinished letter from Mom to Sherilyn, attached for your perusal:

> Dear S—
>
> It hurts me to hear you be so critical of your brother. He's done a lot with his life, too, S. A writer! And living in the City the way he does. That takes plenty of get-up-and-go, doesn't it? (Oh, I never liked the City, myself. I always think of your father's terrible little apartment. And the bugs!)
>
> Yes, Nathan marches to his own drummer. But so did his sister for a while too or have you forgotten? Should I have drawn the line on you too?
>
> I drew the line on your father, and what good did it do anyone?
>
> I'll not make that mistake again.
>
> Some things you have to leave up to the grace of God. There are times I

despaired for both of you, God knows. But God gives no one a burden they can't bear.

That's what I told Nathan when he came home that morning, out of sorts, the morning you were on your way here. (I had to push his little car onto the driveway because I couldn't drive it! I never could get the hang of those stickshift cars, with their little clutch pedal and order of letting things out and finding gears. Your father tried to teach me once and we ended in an awful row. But your old ma can still get behind the plow and push!)

Nathan's a ranter and raver, like your father was, when the devil gets into him. It's all for nothing! Nothing means anything! Just like your poor father, gone so many years now. After I cleaned N. up (and the stoop, too! But you know that story) I told him.

I told him, God has a purpose for each of us and its revealed in time. Open your heart and you'll see.

But he's like you. Stubborn. Like me, when I drew the line on your father, God rest his tormented soul.

When you're in the middle of it, everything can look confused and tragic and senseless, but in time it all makes sense. I look back now and I see how beautiful it all is, like a pattern! God's pattern. I see you with your two beautiful,

talented boys and Nathan with his writer
life and I say My God, Did I do that? But
I didn't of course. It's all God's plan. All
along.
    Even Thomas, up in heaven. And your
father. Everything has a purpose. And it's
revealed to us in

That's all there is. She must have set down her pen, put the
letter away, and went off to the supermarket to pass another bad
check. Then went to meet her God, launched from the floor of
the FoodKing.

I know I said I wasn't going to say anything more about the
letters, about my family. But I've been thinking about all of it.
There's something about these letters that gets to the very heart
of everything I'm trying to say here, in this journal.

My sister did what I did, in the end. She let my mother
construct her elaborate fantasies about our hard-but-noble family
history. Let her take shelter in the empty musings about God's
mysterious ways that come so easily to those whose all-too-
unmysterious weaknesses and failings have made the lives of
others miserable.

What else could we do, right? What's done is done. Any
reasonable person learns to forgive and forget. To move on.

Right?

But make no mistake about it. That's what they want. The
strong, the cruel, the arrogant, the self-serving, the negligent, the
careless. It isn't enough that they should beat us and bludgeon
us, starve us for love and affection, strip us of our basic human
dignity. Oh, no. We should be complicit in our own destruction,
too.

They count on us to succumb to our better natures. To help
them distort and conceal and rewrite the truth. To forgive. To
forget.

Why?

Because if we can simply forgive and forget, let it go, let others reconstruct events in ways they can live with, then the truth is lost, and everything—kindness and neglect and love and indifference and valor and cruelty—is the same.

And if everything is the same, then nothing matters. The strong and the brutal and the criminally irresponsible are free to trample the rest of us underfoot. And it doesn't matter. Nothing matters at all.

Truth. And vigilance. That's all we have. We the weak, the victimized, the abused. It's all we have. The obligation to never forget, never forgive, to never just . . . let it go.

§

Trent's been by again.

He came galumphing into my room, in the midst of one of Sister Rafaella's reminiscences about her missionary work in sub-Saharan Africa in the '30s. Stealing water from rich landowner's wells in the Congo. Sister Rafaella barely had time to vacate the chair by my bed before Trent was sitting in it, looking at me.

"You knew about Tyler," he was saying. "Tell me you didn't know, you son of a bitch. And you didn't tell me."

Tyler?

"Tyler and that stripper and the website. Colleen's in shitfit heaven."

I waved after Sister Rafaella, who was sailing out the door, her long black habit in full flutter, her witch booties silent on the tiles.

Maybe you better start

"I've been hearing for weeks that Felicia is suing some jackoff website, thinking, well, good for her. And now it turns out she's suing Tyler."

at the beginning.

"Don't even bother. I know you know about it. Couldn't give me a heads-up, huh?"

Who's going to tell me anything?

"Whores In Heat. Dot com. I hear Tyler's all over it, boning that dumb bunny. At least he's gettin' paid for it, which is more than Felicia can say."

And even if somebody did,

"And you don't know anything about this, right?"

it wouldn't be my place to say anything.

"No? It wouldn't, huh?" He was about to say something else, then he changed his mind. "She's suing him for some stupid amount of money, like eight million dollars."

I'm sure this Courtney has her liability buttoned up. All these porn sites are LLCs, right?

"Oh yeah. Courtney. She's a real self-starter, that one. Fake tits and a genuine head for business. I don't know how much she cut Tyler in for."

I kind of regret the Felicia video thing. I should've anticipated that those videos would fall into the wrong hands.

"That damned kid of mine. I don't know what to make of it. Half of me says the kid's on the road to ruin, the other half says the kid's smarter than I am. I don't know. Probably it's both." He shook his head. "Fucking his girlfriend on the Internet. They're, like, some kind of Internet celebrities or some such. They're piling up credit card billings." He made a rueful face. "Man, some days I feel pretty old, you know?"

Tyler tell you all this?

"Tyler?" He laughed humorlessly. "The last couple of days, when he was missing? He wasn't at the shore. He was in Vegas, at some adult video convention. Colleen found him on Google News."

Is he still out there?

"He got home this morning. I ain't ever seen Colleen so mad in my life. She took a soup spoon to him. Hit him, right over the head with a soup spoon. A ladle. In the kitchen. Eighteen years, she never hit that boy before. Hell, she ain't even hit me before."

Who deserved it more than you?

"She took him by the ear and dragged him to the county college admissions office. Got Tyler registered for fifteen credits." He was still grinning, mostly in wonderment now. "Mostly computer science and website design, I hear."

Good news.

"I guess so. There's more, too."

I appended a question mark to my last two written words.

"Yeah. Good news. I'm back in. I'm moving back in with Colleen. Just on the couch, but what the fuck, it's a start."

Congrats.

"The deal is, it's only for as long as Tyler still lives at home. Colleen wants another eyeball on the kid. A father's influence, like. But who knows? It's a foot in the door, anyway."

That's terrific. Good for you.

"I got my stuff in the truck. Two boxes and a suitcase." Randy was just starting to look around. He was checking out some of the imposing new machinery they'd moved into my room. "How you doing in here?"

Okay. I'm starting to have hyperrealistic dreams about sausage and pepper sandwiches, but I'm okay.

"I heard you had a little adventure, the other day."

And those big cups of salty fries, like you get on the boardwalk. You know?

"Something about your liver? Or your spleen?"

And cold foamy beer in a paper cup.

"They get that fixed up or what?"

That soft ice cream, used to come out of the machine, vanilla and orange swirl. In a wafer cone.

"Any news on when they're gonna stick a face on you?"

No. Not yet.

"Uh huh."

Randy's initial flustered animation was starting to subside. He looked around himself some more. The machine measuring my blood glucose bleeped at him.

"Christ, it's like NASA Mission Control in here."

Hey, I have something I want to say. As long as you're here.

"Okay. Shoot."

It's something I should have said that night in the storeroom. That I should have said last time you were here.

Now he was looking at me warily. "What's that?"

The stuff you did to me, all those years ago, that's not why I tried to kill myself. Okay? It wasn't your fault.

"I know that," he said.

You do?

"Yeah."

Because I could see how you might think it was your fault, after all I said, that day.

"No. I knew. You made your point. And I made mine. I mean, I treated you like shit, I know. But that was thirty years ago."

He seemed to be waiting for me to write something, but I didn't.

"I didn't help, running you ragged back then, but anyone could see you've had other shit on your mind lately, that had nothing to do with me. That . . ." he was grasping for words, trying to express himself accurately, "that you had a bunch of ideas that weren't helping you in the getting-on-with-life department."

Last week, you were just in the wrong place at the wrong time.

"If it was all about me, you could've killed yourself a long time ago, saved Woody a lot of time and effort."

So I can rest easy. You're not tearing yourself up.

"Fuck, no. I got other things to worry about."

The stuff I was talking about that day, it all happened a long time ago. It doesn't mean shit. I wanted to make sure you knew that.

"I was sorry you tried to blow your head off, but I didn't take it personal." He grinned at me. "Don't look back, right?"

Don't look back. Boston. You know, I can't remember a single other word from that song, except 'don't look back.' What was that song about?

"It was about . . . don't look back. Like . . . look forward."

I always liked the first record better. The second was all filler and out-takes and stuff.

Am I the only one for whom the central truths of life come so hard-earned, at such great price? Sometimes it seems that way. Lately, I'm beginning to sense that everyone else is just skating around on the thin ice of life, gracefully plucking up these essential truths, which are just lying around on the ice, waiting to be picked up. And everybody's doing graceful double lutzes and figure-eights while they're doing it. And I'm flailing about on the ice, skateless, half-dressed, freezing, cracking my head and limbs, leaving blood spatters on the ice, plunging through holes into the frigid water below, clambering out, and plunging in again. Picking up absolutely nothing, for all my clumsy, graceless travail.

"The fuck, you talking? That second album was classic. It was the third one, the one they did all those years later, that was shit."

Were you ever tempted to just grab the shotgun from me? You might have stood a pretty good chance of getting it.

Trent raised his eyebrows. "Easy for you to say. Try saying it from the business end of the shotgun, instead of the butt end."

You must have been tempted, though.

"You weren't exactly combat ready. That witch kid had more on the ball than you did."

I don't know if I wouldn't have just stood there and let you take it. The shotgun.

"You know what? I didn't think you really wanted to shoot anyone, to tell you the truth. And I didn't want to force you to. I thought, the longer we talked, the longer everybody talked, the less likely it was you'd shoot anyone."

Except me.

"Except you. And we almost got past that, too. Another half hour of talk, of anything, just sitting around, and I don't think you would've done it. I shouldn't have fallen asleep. I can't believe I fell asleep in a hostage situation."

That's what Alice said, too.

"Yeah? I heard she was up here. How's she doing?"

Great.

"She mention me?"

Nope. She forgot all about you, once I entered the picture. She has a thing for guys who eat intravenously.

"Fucking ladies man, huh?"

Damn straight.

"Good. So you won't be tying up guys and stealing their underwear anymore."

You know, I think I could have killed you, if I'd done it right away. Before I knew you.

Trent read this and grinned. "Maybe."

That first night in the Sail Inn, I could have picked up a steak knife and plunged it into your chest. Then I could have made a run for it.

"Sure," Trent said. "It's true. That was your best shot."

§

THE END IS NEAR

June 29th, 7pm

Just hours left, now. Time to take care of business.

This seems as good a place as any to set my Last Will and Testament.

First of all, don't bury me in the damned ground. And under absolutely NO circumstances am I to be buried in the empty hole in the ground next to my dad. Cremate my body and then just toss my ashes anywhere. I'm not picky. Give my ashes to my sister Sherilyn. I left an envelope bearing her address on the refrigerator at my mother's house. She'll know what to do.

Secondly, my personal belongings could fit in a shoebox. Sherilyn can have those, too. Throw the damned crap out.

Thirdly, the house is no gift to anybody. It could be that Sherilyn can afford to pay the taxes and not sell the house. But why would she want to? Getting rid of the house is a job I leave to Sherilyn. Sorry, Sis.

Sherilyn, you'll probably want to contact Thomas's widow Sally and his son Cody. If any of the family makes the trip up here, you might want to have a dual funeral for me and Mom. Some cookie-cutter, two-for-the-price-of-one thing will be fine. You should be able to save some money there.

And, well, that's about it. I'm not sure if any of this is legally binding without a notary public's seal, but then, I'm not asking for much, either.

§

"I want to talk about what I'm here to talk about."

Randy looked up at me from his sitting position on the floor of the storeroom. "I guess we've been through this."

"Not to my satisfaction, we haven't."

I was wearing the amulet around my neck. The little glued-on picture of my geeky high school self was very likely undermining my authority at this critical juncture. But I couldn't take it off. I didn't want to offend Danika.

"You want to know why I ruined your life."

"Let's try an easier one first. Why did you repeatedly pound the shit out of me, physically and psychologically, when we were kids?"

"For the same reason I beat everyone else to shit, I guess." Randy shrugged. "I was an asshole when I was a kid. I said as much before. I ain't proud of it."

"But why? That's what I want to know. If there were a reason, a simple understandable reason, I could blow our heads off now and be done with it."

"I just did it. It doesn't get any simpler than that."

"Were you an evil person? Did you feel evil? Did you delight in the pain of others? Do you think you had some kind of mental illness? Psychological damage? Sociopathy? Was it your upbringing? Nature or nurture, Trent? Which?"

Randy looked away. "I don't know."

"You pounded the shit out of me and humiliated me at every turn because . . . you were an asshole. Is that it? Is that all there is?"

Alice was sitting beside Randy, keeping her comments to herself. Danika was trying to tune in one of the major networks on the TV. Outside, the crowd was starting to surrender to boredom and the late hour. I could hear catcalls and horn bleats from some of those departing. There were still hundreds of people out there, though.

"Seems like there ought to be more to it than that, but there ain't." Randy thought about it. "I grew up hard. That's all I wanna say. I ain't one for excuses."

"No. I grew up hard. You were living the life of the carefree, brutal, stupid, happy-go-lucky thug. There's a difference, Trent."

"I had a thin skin. A quick temper. You weren't the only one, got beat down by me."

"And that's supposed to make me feel better? A thin skin? About what? What did I ever do to you?"

"Look, I ain't saying there's any excuse for what I did. Because there ain't. But there's other sides to every story. Okay? I had my own shit to carry around, believe me."

I shook my head. "Like what?"

"Jesus, Nate. You know what I'm talkin' about." There was a look on Randy's face that took me a moment to identify. He was pissed off.

"What."

"Nothing." He either couldn't say it or refused to say it.

"What?"

"Nathan," Alice said. "Don't be obtuse."

"What? Say it."

"I had problems in the father department," Trent said stonily.

"Your father. You didn't have a father." I thought about this. "Shit," I said, "There are worse things. You could've had mine."

"I'd've taken him. There was a time, I'da taken anybody's."

"Well, surely your mother—" I stopped, started again. ""Did she ever—"

"The word you're looking for," Trent said evenly, "is bastard."

"So you were embarrassed."

"Embarrassed? No, I wasn't embarrassed. I did what I had to do. When you got a bright sign blinking over your head that says Bastard, you do what you have to do. You beat the living shit out of anybody that even looks at it. And then you beat the shit out of the next guy, too, just to provide an example."

"I don't remember ever giving you a hard time about that. This father thing."

"Then maybe you were just the next guy." He smirked grimly. "Look, all this shit is ancient history. It took me a while, but I got it all corrected in my mind, now."

"So the reason you—"

"The reason I beat the shit out of you, if I did, was because I wanted to. Because it made me happy. You don't need to read any more into it than that."

I started to say something and then realized I had nothing to say.

"And while we're on the fucking subject, I think we've all heard plenty about how crappy your life was. I don't know what you're thinking about everyone else's life. Everyone else's life isn't some fucking party cruise, you know."

"Well, mine is," Alice said.

Randy shot her a dirty look.

"Sorry," Alice said. "Just trying to lighten things up."

"Look," Randy said. "I said all I got to say. I said more than I got to say. If you still need to kill me, then I guess you got to do what you got to do. But I advise against it."

"You do." The shotgun felt even heavier in my hands than it normally did. I realized I hadn't seen the pistol in at least a couple of hours. I wondered where I'd left it.

"I do. Same way I advise against you blowing your own head off."

"You advise against it. Why?"

"Because I got a few good years left. We both do."

"You, maybe. Not me."

"And because . . ." He was thinking about it. "Because there's things that can happen, that can't be fixed. I found that out later in life than I ought to of."

"That's your reason."

"That's my reason."

THE END IS NEAR

That was it, then. I hefted the shotgun in my hands. All the talking was over now. There was nothing left to do but start shooting.

Maybe, if Randy Trent had been someone other than who he was. Maybe then I could have killed him. Maybe, if he had been the leering obtuse teenage thug of thirty years before. That guy, I could have dropped like a target duck in a shooting gallery. Maybe.

Maybe if he wasn't the flawed but essentially decent man he'd become. If he hadn't grown up. Maybe then I could have killed him.

But probably not.

I knew then that I was going to die the same way I'd lived.

§

June 29th, 8:45pm

I promised, early on, to give you my reasons for killing Randy Trent. Not to defend them, just to express them.

Have I? Somewhere in these pages? I don't know. Maybe not.

I promised, at the very least, that my reasons for killing Randy Trent would be no worse, no less justified, than his reasons for torturing me, all those years ago. Maybe that's all I've accomplished here.

Not much.

I don't know what I expected. The further along I got, the more I lost my way.

Tomorrow, I'm going to Randy's store to finish this thing. Today, while I have time, I'll share what I've discovered.

Randy Trent's become a better man than I would have thought possible. He's no saint or anything. I wouldn't lend him money or tell him a compromising secret. He's just a decent, ordinary guy. He's grown up. Like many people do, evidently.

And me? Well, I guess we've already heard plenty about me. Suffice to say, I'm even less of a man than I previously suspected.

I'd like to say that we deserve each other, Randy and I.

It comforts me to say that.

In the end, we each lived up to the worst in the other. Only his worst was so very long ago, and my worst is today.

§

"You're not going to kill anyone, are you, Clyde."

"No, Danika. I don't think so."

"You're not even going to hold out for goodies, make a break for it. Are you?"

I let that one go. It was pretty obvious by now, that none of that stuff was going to happen.

Across the room, Alice was upending a big box over Randy's head, showering him with styrofoam packing peanuts.

"Hey. What are you doing?" he said.

"What does it look like?" She picked up another box and upended that one. "I'm making a bed. If we're going to be here all night, I'm going to lie down. My ass is killing me from sitting on the bare floor all day."

"What? You're gonna lie here?" Randy was batting away pellets. "I don't have any clothes on."

"No, you don't." Alice was emptying a third box. "And don't get any ideas, either."

"Don't give me any ideas. You need to get out of here."

"Alright, Clyde." Danika turned the TV off and started buttoning and zipping up the many pockets of her shorts. "I've gotta go."

"You'll be missed, Danika."

"Maybe our paths will cross again."

I let that one go, too. "Are you going to be okay out there? They might give you a hard time."

"Don't worry, Clyde." She reached out and grabbed me by the elbows. "They won't see me."

"They won't?"

"I've got a spell for just this situation. I'll walk among them invisible."

"Ah. The invisibility spell. Good choice."

Danika was turning me around, steering me by the elbows. Once we were reversed, so that my back was to the back door, she started pushing me backwards. "Where are we going?" I said.

"Right here." We stopped when I was right up against the door. "Feel that?"

"What, the door?"

"No. The moonlight."

"Oh." I looked out through the top panes of glass in the door and up into the sky. It was a little before midnight. The moon was very high and small in the sky.

"The moon is a powerful agent of change and rebirth," Danika said. "If we do not like what we see in the light of the moon, we can call on the Goddess of the moon to help us change the future for ourselves. Feel the light of the moon."

"Goddess of the moon, huh? Are you going to make me invisible?"

"Pay attention," she said. "We're going to ask for the Moon Goddess's blessing. We're going to ask her to watch over you. To help you make changes for the better. Quiet your mind. Feel the light of the moon."

"I'm not one of those people who sees much in the night sky, Danika. I'm kind of a cold, hard realist about the stars and moon and night and stuff, you know?"

"Shhhhhh."

Danika released my elbows. She backed away from me, crossing the room toward the first rank of shelves.

"You're leaving, Danika?" Alice said.

"Yeah. It's time. You two keep an eye on my man Clyde, here."

"We will," Alice said. "Don't worry."

"Make sure he's okay. Make sure he stays that way. He's got a long journey to travel. I can feel it."

"We got it covered," Randy said. "Don't sweat it."

Danika climbed the shelf unit lightly and nimbly and pushed out a little ceiling panel that I hadn't noticed before, a trap door that entered into some kind of attic crawlspace.

"You get hassled out there," I said, "you make sure they know you were a hostage. You were an innocent victim."

"I've been a lot of things," Danika said, "but I don't think I've ever been an innocent victim. Are you concentrating on the peaceful light of the moon?"

"I am." And, strangely, I was. Now that everything was done, everything decided, all the variables no longer variable, I felt very calm. Relaxed. At peace. It was all over. And the moonlight, maybe, was part of that.

"Don't worry about me," Danika was saying. "I'm going to be the Mysterious Spirit of the Standoff in Sussex. Some day, people will speak of me in whispers, when they dare speak of me at all."

"I don't doubt it."

"Okay, now be quiet. Be quiet and just be. Feel the moon."

I felt the moon.

"Now repeat after me. Ready?"

I lifted the medallion with my picture on it from my chest and looked at it. My hapless younger self looked back up at me, a reproach. I released it and closed my eyes.

THE END IS NEAR

"Thank you Beautiful Goddess of the Night, for all You have shown us here."

"Thank you Beautiful Goddess of the Night, for all You have shown us here."

"I will keep some of your light, Beautiful Goddess, that it may illuminate my path and make my future serene and secure."

I repeated that, too. Who was I to say there wasn't a Moon Goddess? I'd been wrong about enough things in forty-five years.

"I am surrounded by the pure white light of the moon. Nothing but good shall come to me; nothing but good shall go from me. I give thanks. So let it be."

Once I'd repeated that, I said, "So. Am I invisible?"

"No, you're not invisible. You won't be needing invisibility, where you're going."

"So what am I?"

"Wiser, I hope. That is a spell for acceptance of the future."

"Acceptance of the future," I said, chastened. "That's a good one. I wish you'd caught me earlier with that one. When I was sixteen, maybe."

"See ya on the other side, Clyde."

"I hope so, Danika."

She leaped up through the trapdoor then and was gone. I heard a light scrabbling in the attic, like squirrels running across the roof, then a thump, and then nothing. Seconds passed and then whole minutes and there wasn't a shout or a whoop or a siren or a bullhorn crackle. Nothing at all.

§

June 29th, 10:15pm

Here we are, folks. Back at the beginning. The Sail Inn.

Seven days ago, I was about to raise a last glass to the end of my life.

Now here it is again. That last glass of beer. And a jigger of good scotch, too. Sitting on the bar before me.

Whoa, hey, hang on.

I was gone for a time, but here I am, back again.

Felicia, it's always a pleasure. I was actually happy to see you, one last time. Despite your adversarial posturing.

You walked into the bar and it was apparent right away you were looking for someone. No mystery as to whom, either. You made a point of ignoring me for a while, as I was tapping out the few lines above. You stopped at a couple of tables, talked to a few friends, refused a few drinks and proffered seats, not tarrying long. On your way back to the front door, you stopped and sized me up.

"What are you writing?" you said.

"Hi, Felicia." The laptop was sitting open on the bar. "Good to see you."

"What's that?"

"Nothing yet. I've got some work to catch up on. I'm a writer, you know."

"No, I didn't know. What kind of writer?"

"An ad writer."

"Yeah? What kind of ads?"

"Nothing you would have seen, I think."

"Right." You looked at yourself in the mirror behind the bar, tucked a stray curl away.

"Have a seat?" I said. I indicated the empty seat next to me.

"No thanks. You haven't seen Randy around, have you?"

"Randy?"

"Yeah. Randy."

"Nope. Not tonight."

You lifted your handbag off your shoulder and set it on the bar. "How about last night?"

THE END IS NEAR

"Last night?"

"Yeah. The night before this night."

"Right, yeah, I talked to him for a bit. Last night."

Brittany, the barmaid came by. "You sure you don't want anything, Fel?"

You ordered a seltzer with cranberry and fixed me with a steely eye. A clear, gray-flecked eye that I once compared favorably to the star-strewn night sky. "Was he with anyone?"

"With anyone? Well, no. Everyone was just kind of . . . with everyone else. Hanging out."

"No one came here to meet him."

Ah, I realized. Rhetorical questions. "Meet him?"

"Meet him."

"Ummm, no. Not that I noticed."

Now you may be wondering, Felicia, why I would cover for Trent. I'd just spent the last week making Trent's life as difficult as I could, after all. Why not get him into hot water with one of his girlfriends, too? Right? It's a good question.

Maybe I thought to spare you the pain and humiliation that the news of Trent's amorous shenanigans would inevitably cause. Why should you lose a night's sleep over someone who'd be dead the next day? Right? Or maybe I thought to protect the other woman. You, Alice. Lovely Alice whom, I must say, I took an immediate shine to, the night before.

Maybe, perversely, I was protecting Trent. Maybe I didn't want you to kill him, Felicia, before I'd had the chance. Or maybe, even more perversely, I was enjoying a brief stint in league, in conspiracy, with Trent. Two liars, deceivers, causing more trouble than they were worth. I don't know. It was utterly unpremeditated. I surprised myself.

I knew it would all come out eventually. These things always do. Perhaps the two of you, Felicia and Alice, will have a good cry about it together, at Trent's funeral. Perhaps you already have, and the two of you are thick as thieves, as you read these words.

But you were hardly done with your cross-examination of me, Felicia. Brittany brought you your drink and you looked me over again.

"There's something weird about you, isn't there?" you said.

"Weird? I don't know. Is there?"

You pulled a pack of cigarettes and a lighter from your handbag. You took your time about lighting a cigarette. "I keep seeing you in places you have no reason to be," you said, finally.

"You do?" This is what I was reduced to. Answers like random parrot squawks. "Like where?"

"In places I am. Places where, I know why I'm there, but I can't figure out why you're there."

"Why are you there? In these places?"

"Because I'm protecting my interests. Why are you in them?"

I didn't know what to say to this. "Isn't it against the law, smoking in bars?" I said.

"Yes. It is." You looked away to blow a cloud of cigarette smoke behind the bar. "I figure, either you're queer for Trent or you got something in the works nobody knows about. Which is it?"

"Oh. Neither. I just . . ." I shrugged. Again, I didn't know what to say.

"Mmmm," you said, looking displeased. You plucked a shred of tobacco from your tongue. "You just have a way of showing up where you don't belong."

"I guess so."

You returned your cigarette pack to your handbag. "You know, the other night I saw something a little strange. Not oh-my-god strange. But still, strange. I didn't think much of it at first."

"Oh? What was that?"

THE END IS NEAR

You took a sip of your seltzer. "When me and PJ and Randy left the bar the other night, there were two people standing by Randy's truck. You and some guy nobody's seen around here before. Randy was telling some stupid joke he's told a thousand times and PJ was laughing at it for the thousandth time and I was watching you guys. You reached out to the guy and it looked almost like you handed him something. And then you yelled 'Hey.' Really loud. With what happened next, I figured I must have seen it wrong."

"That's strange, alright."

"Yeah. It is." You took another drag from your cigarette and then dropped it to the floor. You crushed it out with the toe of one of your shoes. "You know, I've been coming to this shithole bar for more years than I care to remember. You know how many cars have been broken into here, in all that time?"

I shook my head.

"One." You lifted your handbag from the bar and slung it over your shoulder. "When you were lying on the ground and I was waiting with you, you didn't look like a guy who was happy to find out that two guys were out chasing the guy who'd just slugged you and stole your wallet. You know?"

"I didn't?"

"No. You looked worried." You weren't looking at me anymore, Felicia. You were looking at yourself in the mirror behind the bar again, as if it pained you to look at me. "How much longer you gonna be in town?"

"Not much longer."

You nodded at this. "Good idea."

Then you turned on your heel and left.

Farewell, Felicia. You were a smarter cookie than most of the yobs in this town.

So here I am again, right back where I started. In the Sail Inn with a last glass of beer. And a jigger of decent scotch. No reprieves this time. The bar's mostly empty on this Sunday night, so the chances of my encountering a bank officer who once refused me a loan or a reckless driver who once cut me off in traffic are slim. So my killing rampage will end with one killing. Well, two.

So now I'm counting the money in my wallet. Forty-seven dollars. I'm adding it to the fourteen and change on the bar in front of me. Sixty-one dollars and change. The sum of my net worth. Actually, the sum of my liquid reserves. My net worth would be some preposterous amount of indebtedness out of all proportion to my earning potential. If, in fact, I still had any earning potential.

I'm looking around the bar. I'm figuring that sixty-one dollars should cover it. I'm calling Brittany the barmaid over.

"A round for everybody," I say, in my big-spender voice, even as I'm typing this. "Tell them it's a toast."

Brittany looks at me, at this laptop I'm tapping on, and says, "Okey dokey."

Brittany goes from person to person along the bar, taking their drink orders. It doesn't take long. Brittany probably knows everybody's regular drink and their more expensive, hey-look-somebody-else-is-buying drink by heart. Besides me, there are ten people at the bar, all people I've seen in here at least once, if not every time I've been here. Twelve people now, counting the two kids, who, recognizing the situation—some maudlin and lonely drunk buying a round, indiscriminately—have just scurried to the bar.

There are two moderately pretty girls sitting a few seats down from me. Twentyish, pale, and conspicuously bored, they have the look of barmaids on their night off.

"What's the special occasion?" one of them, the one with the longer, more ornate earrings, says to me.

"I'm killing myself."

"Really." She watches as her drink, something muddy in a rocks glass, arrives. "Join the club."

"Hey, buddy!"

Some guy across the bar is hailing me. He's wearing a Harley Davidson t-shirt and a Harley Davidson cap. He doesn't look like a biker, though. He looks like the kind of guy who would wear a matching Harley Davidson tee and cap.

"If we drink these, it don't mean we have to be your friend or nothin', do it?" He replays the question in his head. "Does it?" he corrects.

"No," I say. "It don't."

"Good." He picks up his gratis shot and drinks it, not waiting for my toast.

I finish typing the words above and lift my own glass.

"To Nathan Huffnagle," I say, loudly enough to be heard across the bar. "He came, he saw, he learned nothing of value, he left." I drain my jigger and set it on the bar.

"Here, here," the two kids, the ones who'd hurried to the bar so as not to miss out on the free drinks, say.

Harley Davidson across the bar raises his beer bottle. "Here's to gettin' laid ... and gettin' paid."

"Here, here," the kids say again.

Now I am looking upon the final neon beer sign. I am hearing the last 'last call.' I bequeath a small tip to the barmaid.

Oh, don't worry, dear readers. I'm not leaving you yet. I have one last story to tell.

Meet you back at the house.

§

"She's asleep?"

"Yeah."

Alice was burrowed into the hill of styrofoam packing peanuts she'd made, her head resting on Randy's bare leg.

"That's my life's story with women," I said. "I never could hold their attention for long. Not even at gunpoint."

Trent grinned at this. "She works pretty hard. She works fulltime at the pharmacy and goes to school at night, too."

"That's hard work," I said. "I put myself through college that way. School during the day, loading trucks through the night."

"Yeah? What you study?"

"English literature."

Randy grinned some more and then he laughed. Alice stirred in his lap.

"You humped freight all night so some guy could tell you what poems mean?"

"Five and a half years." I laughed, too. "Believe it or not, it didn't seem like a dumbfuck idea at the time."

"Yeah." Randy slid further down the beam, into the nest of pellets. He was still grinning, but he looked tired. "That's what I say about my second wife."

I was tired, too. It had been a long, stressful day. None of us were young any more.

I got up then and went to the door. I opened it a crack and peeked out. It was after midnight now and the scene outside had the look of an encampment. The casual onlookers, the people with short attention spans and jobs to go to the next morning, had departed, leaving the vigil to those with fewer claims on their time. It being June—July 1st, now—that meant kids, mostly. Teens.

For a week and a half, I'd looked in vain for the kids of this town, wondering where they kept themselves. And now here they were. Little groups of them were sharing blankets on the roofs of the buildings opposite, gossiping and laughing and making out. The crowd behind the barricades had thinned to only two or three deep now, with the occasional gap for a kid idly freestyling on a bike or bouncing on a skateboard. Other kids were clustered around the news trucks, gawking at the equipment and chatting up the techs. This was the event of the summer for them, the way the moon landing and the big eastern blackout of '77 were summer landmarks of my childhood.

Most of the remaining adults—the ones who weren't cops or media—were packed into Holly's Tavern, which was doing a once-in-a-lifetime Monday night business. There were Salvatore's Pizza boxes everywhere, piled high around the garbage cans and littering the street in front of the barricades.

"How's it going out there?" Randy said.

"It's mostly kids now. The TV news vans are still here."

"All this free advertising, maybe I'll see a bump in sales."

"Maybe."

"I could use it. Especially if me and Colleen can talk Tyler into junior college."

"You're talking like someone who's expecting to live," I said, still looking outside.

"Habit, I guess."

"If Tyler is still gone missing," I said, "he's going to kick himself for missing the show."

"Yeah, that might be true. Kids love a shoot-`em-up." Trent yawned convulsively. "I wonder if Colleen's out there."

"Could be."

"She's probably not. She probably ain't too worried. She's always said I have more luck than I deserve."

I closed the door and went back to my spot near Randy and sleeping Alice. We sat in silence for a minute or two, listening to the sounds coming from outside, the occasional whoop of laughter, the crackle of police radios, the faintly audible sounds of a Monday night baseball game, cranked up on the TVs in the bar.

"We're gonna be okay, aren't we?"

"Yeah," I said. "I guess so."

"That's good." Randy thought about it. "Except for those yearbook pictures on the TV. We ain't gonna live those down."

"You mind if I ask you a question?"

"Shit yeah, I do." He yawned again. "No more questions."

"Why is it called A&B Auto Parts? What's the A&B for?"

"Nothing."

"What do you mean, nothing?"

"I mean, nothing. I bought the place, two places actually, from Shipper Nugent in . . ." he thought about it, "eighty-nine. I worked for him for six years, going back to high school, then I bought him out when he retired to Florida. Low-collateral business loans were easy to come by, back then. Those savings and loan hustlers were giving 'em out to anybody with a driver's license. Anyway, Shipper named them A&B so's he'd be first listing under Auto Parts in the phone book."

"Oh. So you're the first listing?"

"Fuck, no. There was already an AA Auto Parts back when I first started clerking for Shipper. Last I looked, it's up to AAAAA Auto Parts."

"Shipper?" I said. "With an h?"

"I got no idea why. I never asked him."

"Huh."

I sat for awhile longer, then I got up and crossed to the other side of the room. I picked up my journal and pulled a pen from the twill shopping bag. I sat down with my back to the last row of storage shelves, near the back door, where I'd last left the shotgun. I looked at the last page of the journal.

I looked at the four candles on the floor—north, south, east, and west—and the ring of salt. The candles had burned out; they were just misshapen stubs in pools of wax. Danika's spell for personal protection may not have been intended for instances in which the protection required was protection from yourself. Maybe there's another spell for that. I don't know.

I lifted the amulet from my chest and looked again at the picture of me on it. Me, with a little smile on my face, looking up and off into a future that I probably wouldn't have guessed to include a hard cement floor, a shotgun, two weary hostages, a rowdy audience, and a battalion of law enforcement.

I clicked the pen.

I thought about the things you think about when the remainder of your life can be measured in minutes. I thought about what I'd set out to do, a week before. What I'd done. After a while, I looked across the room. Randy and Alice were snug in their little nest of packing peanuts. Randy was nodding off, his forehead dipping toward Alice's shoulder. Alice, sleeping, had the faintest little smile on her face.

I waited a little longer and then wrote the last nine words in my journal. I set the journal and the pen aside. I lifted the shotgun. As quietly as possible, I put the stock between my legs.

"Huh!" Trent woke with a start, his head popping up, as if from a bad dream.

A shotgun is longer than you'd think. Longer than I'd think, anyway. It's long and heavy. I could have shot myself with the pistol, of course. If I could have found the pistol. But I remember believing at the time that the shotgun would do a more thorough job of removing my head.

Trent was looking around himself, blinking, confused.

I set the cold metal circle of the barrel beneath my chin and started feeling around for the trigger, but I couldn't find it.

"Nate?" Trent said, foggily. And then, very sharply, "Nate!"

So I reversed the process. I grabbed the trigger first and stretched my neck back.

"No! Nate! No!" Randy was yelling. "Don't do it! Jesus, Nate!"

Alice had slipped sideways out of Randy's lap and was facing the wrong way, toward the front of the store, pawing groggily at packing peanuts.

It seemed I had to stretch my neck very far out to slip my chin over the end of the shotgun barrel.

"No! Nate! Not now! Not after all this!" Trent was up in a half-crouch, whipsawing the handcuff chain back and forth across the beam. I heard the staticky rending of the last Olympic flag. "Please! Listen to me!"

Alice turned the right way, took one look at me, and rolled out of the nest of styrofoam. She tried to get to her feet, but her one foot rolled across the pellets and she landed hard on her stomach. "Nathan!" she yelled.

I tightened my grip on the trigger.

By then, Randy was yelling "Help! Help! Help in here!" Roaring at the top of his lungs. Alice was scrambling across the peanuts.

I was astonished. It was quite a send-off, really. Every suicidal fool should have one.

Alice was on her feet and moving, about ten feet from me, when the whole world blew up. It seemed that every window in the place, on both side walls and across the back, was exploding at the same time and great white shafts of light were reaching into the room and the air was filled with flying glass and I was squeezing the trigger.

§

June 30th, 12:45am

Ah, June 30th. Here at last.

Welcome to my 45th birthday party.

Grab a seat anywhere, there's plenty of room. Small turnout tonight, for these festivities under the stars. Just you and me.

Oh, don't feel bad. It's just as well. I didn't want anything gaudy, anything grandiose. The events of later today, nine or ten hours from now, will be gaudy and grandiose enough.

Can I get you a beer? Plenty of cold ones in this cooler under my feet.

You sure? Well, you tell me if you change your mind.

Nice night, huh? I could say that I'll miss the stars, the moon, the nighttime frenzy of crickets and tree frogs and what-all. But that wouldn't be true. I won't miss them at all.

I'll miss you, dear readers. Colleen and Tyler, whom I've never met. Alice, a fleeting acquaintance. And you, Felicia. I've come to know you best of all, a little better than you might think. There's a little of me in you, Felicia. We're not so different, I think. Both a little desperate, a little damaged.

Hang on, I've got to take a leak.

Back again. Sorry I was gone so long. There's something wrong with the float in the toilet tank, here at Mom's place. There was something wrong with it twenty-five years ago, too, if I recall. Sometimes the float gets caught in the handle chain and doesn't rise, so the water keeps running until you jiggle the handle. It's the same float, the same chain, after all this time. My mother must have been jiggling the handle for twenty-five years. Rather than having a plumber in and tossing him forty bucks. Or getting a ten-dollar kit from Home Depot and spending twenty minutes installing it. But that's Huffnagle life in a nutshell for you. Listening to the toilet run through the night for twenty-five years.

So. Where was I?

Ah. Right. The night. The night sky. The dim, distant, indifferent stars, the big blank hole in the sky called the moon, the spaces between things.

Don't worry, folks. I'm not going to insult your sensibilities with any twinkle-twinkle-little-star nonsense. None of that maudlin last-night-on-earth stuff from me. I know you guys aren't on my side.

I've got one story left to tell and then I'm out of here.

I'm making a segue now. Here it comes. Hold on tight.

Once I was staked out beneath a night sky. Left to dangle in the void. I learned then that there's nothing out there, in the night. I learned how long the long night can be. How cold it can be when you're left out in the cold.

I learned that we, that people, that you and me, have nothing to offer each other. Not a thing.

It was March of my senior year of high school. The occasion was our senior class trip. In the days leading up to the trip, my family life had vanished off the map. My father was gone and my mother was gone, too. We—my brother, my sister, and me—had no reason to expect them back. We weren't sure what to do about any of this.

Uh-oh, you're thinking. Here we go again. But no, I'm as tired of hearing about my crappy family as you are, believe me. I mean only to say this, that when the day of my senior class trip arrived, I was happy to go. I was happy to escape that empty house, if only for two days in Mount Lookout Lodge in the Catskills.

Mount Lookout Lodge was a shabby, anonymous, down-at-heels Catskills hotel that billed itself as a "mountain resort." I believe it was a resort at one time. When we got there, it was all gloomy lobby, threadbare carpets, rotting draperies, peeling paint, and surly staff. Everywhere a tacky, clammy March dampness. The room I shared with two other guys—they took the twin beds, leaving me the foldout cot—was lit by one dim ceiling fixture, a yellow globe filled with dead bugs. The bedspreads and drapes and carpet, even the wallpaper, were all the same dirty, beigey no-color, a non-color like phlegm. The twin beds each had "Magic Fingers" massage features, a quarter for ten minutes. We tried them; they were both broken. The closet was nailed shut.

I don't know what kids do on senior class trips these days. Maybe they tour art museums and donate their time to food banks and help save the manatee. I don't know. I know what they did in seedy Catskills hotels in 1985, though. They wandered the hotel grounds in feral packs, getting stupid drunk on cheap beer, cheap wine, cleaning products, anything they could find. And they pillaged and sacked and raised hell and tortured each other.

I was in the game room of the Lookout Lodge—a frigid, cinderblock-walled basement room with a few worn-out pool tables, a ping-pong table, and a handful of battered video games sadly blooping and bleeping away—when they found me. It was about ten o'clock on the first night.

There was nowhere to hide, nowhere to run. Randy Trent and two other guys came pounding down the stairs and into the room, took one look around, and descended on me in a pack. They lifted me up into the air and raced out of the room, howling like B-movie Indians, with me held aloft and struggling over their heads.

And no, I'm not going to cover this ground again, either. As my parting gift to you, Trent fans in the home audience, I'll skip most of the Trent-as-sadistic-oppressor stuff. Most, but not all. So breathe a sigh of relief. Just imagine the usual insults and indignities, given the added twist of drunkenness and novel surroundings.

Randy Trent's reign of terror. See previous. Ibid., op. cit.

Okay?

Anyway, we ended up out on a big field behind the hotel, some kind of playing field or parade ground, near a flagpole. I was on my hands and knees on that big field, naked. Randy Trent had me in one of his efficient holds, one hand pushing my arm very high up behind my back, his chest pressing my shoulders down, his other hand at the back of my neck, grinding my face into the dry, winter-scorched turf.

He was chiding me for my audacity, as usual.

"Who told you you could come on this trip, huh?" He was twisting my arm, by way of punctuation. "Who told you you could show your zit-covered, cock-sucking face on this trip? Who told you you could pretend to be a regular person? Huh? I don't remember giving my permission for you to leave your jerk-off hole in the ground, Nathan."

Or some shit to that effect. I don't remember exactly. My clothes were at the bottom of the tiny duckpond in front of the hotel. I could feel a lump growing on my forehead from where I'd smacked the top of a doorframe on my airborne passage through the lobby. I still remember the weary look on the face of the night-staff guy behind the front desk as we went by. He was no stranger to senior-trip horseplay and shenanigans, that guy.

Trent and I were accompanied on our late-night tour of the grounds by two other guys and a girl. Ned Bradshaw was a special-ed kid, one of those kids in public schools who occupied the gray area between slow-but-functional and mildly retarded. Just being part of Trent's gang for a night would have represented a startling leap up the social ladder for him. I remember that he listened to and followed each of Trent's orders with a solemn gravity befitting his new station in life.

The other guy was a slight, olive-complected kid whose one talent, shoplifting, sometimes brought him into Trent's orbit. He had the rather unfortunate name—unfortunate in 1985, anyway—of Richard Simmons, and was along on this ride mostly to provide war whoops, off-color jokes, and general cheerleading.

The girl's name was Mandi Otto. We'd picked her up along the way. She didn't have any responsibilities. She was on her hands and knees, puking up great gouts of Boone's Farm Apple Strawberry fortified wine into the grass.

Trent had sent Ned and Richard off to break into a gardener's shed at the edge of the field. They were looking for something to tie me to the flagpole with. When they returned, they were carrying a big cardboard box between them.

"What's that?" Trent said.

They set the box down and Ned tore it open. He reached in and pulled out a folded bolt of shiny material. He snapped it open on the night air, revealing a little flag, maybe three feet by five feet. Lake Placid, NY, it said, beneath a familiar, multi-colored five-ring symbol. Home of the 1980 Winter Olympics.

"I said get some rope, ya fucking retard," Trent said. "What the fuck is that?"

"There's nothing in that shed," Ned said, looking sheepish. "Just some tools and some boxes of these."

"And a riding mower," Richard said.

"Send a retard and a klepto on one simple—" Trent stopped. "A riding mower?"

"Oh, god," Mandi gurgled, and let fly with another volley of vomit.

"It's got a key ignition start," Richard said. "And the key isn't there. I checked."

"Huh. Mower, huh. Okay." Trent snagged a fist in my hair and started roughly hauling me to my feet. "First things first."

When I had my feet under me, Trent ran me forward and caromed me off the flagpole. Then he picked me up again and slammed my back to the pole. He went behind me and tugged my arms back, one on either side of the pole. "Put your feet together," he said.

Trent held me, while Ned and Richard tied me to the pole with the flags. When they were finished, I was bound across the ankles and across the midsection, my hands behind me.

"Alright," Trent said. "Put another one across his chest and one across his knees, tight, so he can't get out. I'll be right back."

He went to Mandi, picked up the bottle of Boone's Farm wine beside her and then marched off in the direction of the shed.

Ned and Richard did as they were told.

"He don't like you, does he?" Richard said, as he was tying off the top flag.

"No," I said, "I guess not."

"Tough break for you."

As Ned and Richard were finishing up, a mechanical sputtering sound came from the shed, then a roar. Gears clattered and Trent emerged from the shed, atop an enormous riding mower. The mower had some kind of landscaping rig on a trailer behind it. He wheeled it around and bore down on us. He passed within a foot or so of the pole, causing Ned and Richard to flee, the mower goosed to its top speed of maybe fifteen miles per hour. Then he came back and rolled to a stop.

"That oughta keep him for a while," he said, looking me over. But he'd clearly lost interest in disciplining me. "These Deeres are pussy to hotwire." He looked at Richard and hiked a thumb at the trailer. "Climb on back, klepto. And you, retard." Ned waited expectantly. "Pick up what's-her-face and climb on, too. We got shit to do."

Ned went to Mandi Otto and slung her easily over his shoulder. She moaned and puked down the back of his shirt. Ned climbed onto the trailer.

"You don't look happy," Trent said to me, when everybody was aboard. "I'm not scarin' ya, am I?"

Was I scared anymore? I didn't think so. Weary seemed a more accurate description.

"Good," Trent said. "Because I like to think that I have a smile for everyone I meet."

This absolutely cracked him up, so much so that Ned and Richard laughed too, though they surely had no idea what Trent was talking about. I wondered if Trent believed this last line was an original thought or if he remembered from where it had originated. Insane Steve Tolas in the bathhouse, years before.

"Okay, cocksucker. Enjoy the rest of your senior trip." Trent took a last slug from the Boone's Farm bottle and tossed it away. Then they were off, yodeling and yahooing and puking up the hill.

THE END IS NEAR

When they were gone, I wrestled and squirmed and hyperextended in my Olympic restraints, preferring chafes and bruises to being found by someone out for a stroll. After a while, though, I gave up any pretense of dignity and started yelling. And then, my throat torn ragged, I gave that up, too.

It was cold, that night. It had been warm earlier, with daytime highs peaking in the high sixties. At night, though, the temperature dropped. Not precipitously. Down to fifty degrees or so. Tolerable, if you were, say, ambling about the playing field in a light sweater and khakis and white suede bucks, a croquet mallet cocked jauntily on a shoulder, making small talk with your best girl. Not so tolerable if you were hogtied, naked, to a flagpole in the dark of night.

And then the wind picked up. Just a teasing night breeze, enough to generate something of a wind chill. A slight wind chill, a low-grade wind chill, not even below freezing. Above forty degrees, perhaps.

I could hear snatches of music, of laughter, of shouting and carrying-on, from the hotel. People would wander out onto the balcony, backlit by the tacky ballroom, the winding-down party behind them. I tried to call to them, but they were surrounded by light and sound, and I was out in the dark and quiet. So I guess they couldn't see me or hear me. Though more than once I thought I saw someone waving to me.

I was in a familiar position out there. Isolated from the world of real people and real events. Removed from any real expectations of, if not camaraderie and respect and well-being, at least simple safety. I was outside and looking in. It was a position I'd been in many times before. Though rarely in so literal a sense. Roped like a steer, like a sacrifice, at the periphery of a party.

Eventually, the music stopped and the party petered out entirely. Hotel employees moved back and forth behind the ballroom windows, clearing tables and sweeping up. Then they were gone, too, and a single white-jacketed staffer came out and extinguished the balcony lamps one by one. I screamed myself hoarse trying to be heard. It seemed quiet enough then that he should have heard me very clearly. But the last lamp went out and he went inside. Shortly later, the ballroom lights went out, too.

Then it was just me and the cold and the dark and the chill stars of March. I still heard the occasional shout, the occasional short blare of car-stereo music, the sound of engines racing in the parking lot. As the cold and the damp set into my bones, I lost feeling in my hands and feet. I began to worry that the flags were tied too tight, that my circulation was cut off. I entertained myself with visions of my hands, my feet, being amputated in emergency rooms.

My first visitor arrived just after midnight. I knew this because I asked him what time it was. When he told me the time and I realized I had been tied to the flagpole for less than two hours, I laughed out loud. I had been watching the horizon, wondering, aghast, at what natural phenomenon could account for such a lengthy delay in the normal rise of the sun.

"Thank god you're here," I said, my teeth already chattering. "I was freezing my ass off."

"What happened to you?"

"I got tied to this flagpole."

"Oh." My savior was Michael Adubato. He was carrying a thick paperback book with a plain green or gray cover. Like a bound treatise or research paper. He had been reading it by flashlight. He walked around behind me and looked. "Huh," he said."

"I was starting to think I was going to be here all night."

"Uh-huh." Michael was tugging gently at a knot or two, inspecting. "These are pretty tight."

"Yeah, I might have made them tighter, trying to get loose," I said, eager as always to steal some portion of the blame for myself. "Good thing you brought a flashlight."

"I guess." He'd stopped tugging. "I don't want to get into any trouble or anything."

"What, trouble?" I looked at Michael, trying to anticipate his reasoning. Michael had known from the age of seven on, with perfect clarity and certainty, that he wanted to be a molecular physicist. Not just any physicist. A molecular physicist. He was that kind of kid. "I'm the one in trouble. I'm tied up."

"Yeah. No. I know. It's just . . ." He was looking around us now. "These knots are pretty tight."

"Okay. Maybe if you had a knife . . . or could get a knife—"

"Who tied you up?"

I looked at Michael. "Does it matter?"

He thought about it. "It might."

Michael Adubato was less than three months away from losing his four-year pitched battle with Linda Dubcek, the other class brain, for top academic ranking in our little Class of '85. His gym grades—and Linda's sexless tomboy competence at sports—would be his undoing.

"Randy Trent," I admitted, reluctantly.

"Oh, right. That freak." Michael said this like someone who'd had a run-in or two with Trent himself. He backed a step away from me, then another. "I saw Trent cruising the front parking lot. On a fucking lawn mower."

"You might not even need a knife. These knots look tough, but you might—"

"That guy's fucking certifiable. If you get loose, he'll want to know how. He could be back down here, like, any minute now."

"—be able to . . . Oh, no. He won't be back. He said I was on my own. Down here."

"Uh huh." Michael took another step back. "Look. Knots like that, you'll need a knife. Or a scissor. I'll go up to the kitchen and get one. Hang on." He started hustling back up the hill to the hotel.

"Hey. Hey! You'll be back, right? Michael?"

I watched him go, regretting my needless and ridiculous honesty. My next rescuer would get a different story. A knot-tying exercise gone wrong. A performance-art protest aimed at the International Olympic Committee. Something.

My next rescuer would be a long ways away. By the time she arrived, I would be well on my way to becoming a different person. A person much like the person I am today.

She wasn't someone I knew. Maybe she was a ghost. How real does a ghost look? How real does she feel? I don't know.

She looked ethnic, exotic. She was dark and slim, like a young Jewish girl who'd stepped out of the hotel's more prosperous past to see how the eighties were shaping up. Could it be that rundown Catskills hotels still got that kind of girl? In 1985? I don't know. But that's what she looked like. Like 1960 taking a peek into 1985.

She scampered down the hill from the hotel like someone running away from something, and then slipped and skidded to a stop on the damp grass when she saw me. She had pale, high cheekbones and heavy eyebrows that didn't quite connect in the middle. She was my age, seventeen or eighteen, and dressed in a shiny white blouse and black skirt. She looked at me with luminous eyes for a full minute, then two.

"Hi," I said.

She didn't say anything. She walked a circuit of the pole, stopping in front of me again.

"I'm kind of in a fix here."

She looked at me some more. Maybe, I thought, she's never seen a naked guy before. Maybe she's mute. Maybe I'm experiencing a hallucination caused by plummeting body temperature.

"Could you help me out?" I could already see that this rescue, too, was going to go awry. I just didn't know how or why yet.

She was looking over her shoulder now, back to the hotel.

"My name's Nathan," I said. As if it mattered.

Whatever she saw behind her seemed to satisfy her. She approached me and stopped, her face a foot from mine. Her eyes were big and dark; the moonlight shimmered in the curves of the single strands of hair that stood up, frizzy, all around her head. She had the smallest hint of a smile on her big, fleshy, intricate lips. She wasn't pretty in a way that I could have recognized, then. Young as I was. She put a finger first to her lips, then mine. Shhhh.

"Look, I'm not asking for much. All I need—"

She rose up on tiptoe, set a warm hand on my naked chest, and set her lips lightly on mine. My lips felt cold and forlorn in contact with hers. It was a chaste little kiss—my first ever—out there in the dark and the cold, amidst my fear and increasing despair.

After she ended this kiss, she took a step backward and raised her finger to her lips again. Shhhhh.

And then she was gone, scampering up the hill as quickly as she'd scampered down.

Time passed, the way it does when you've come unsprung out of time, when you're at the end of your rope, at the nub end of your sanity. When the world has turned its back on you and the vast cold void, the vacuum, embraces you. Which is to say, time passed very slowly.

Somewhere out there in that void, I gave up on people. I wasn't giving up much, granted. What had people ever done for me?

I gave up on people, and I gave up, too, the notion that something must be wrong with me, that I could give up on people. People had nothing to offer me. And I had nothing to offer people. I don't know why I hadn't seen it, accepted it, before.

I gave up on people. I gave up on all the things—bonds, connections, shared experience—that keep you tethered to the earth. And in return I got myself back. I kept myself. Whole, entire, and separate. All in all, it wasn't a bad deal. It got me through that night, when nothing else—nothing less—would have done so.

Trent and Ned and Richard Simmons never did come back. Not that they ever said they would. Mandi didn't come back either, though she may never have known she was there in the first place. Trent and Ned and Richard Simmons probably got involved in something else—drinking to spectacular excess, drag-racing mowers, pummeling other unlucky night travelers—and forgot all about me.

Which was surely just as well.

My third visitor arrived sometime before dawn. I don't know what time it was. She was a young girl, maybe twelve. She came down the hill and sat, crosslegged, before me. She sat and watched me like a young girl watches Saturday morning television—passively, blankly, lost in the show.

I didn't mind. I said a thing or two to her in a rusty, teeth-chattering squawk. I wasn't surprised when she didn't answer or offer to help me. I was wandering in and out of consciousness, by then. Sleep or shock, I don't know which. Just lifting my head seemed like more trouble than it was worth. I looked up a few times over half an eternity, and she was there, watching. Then I looked up and she was gone.

I had put my time to good use. I had learned some things under the chill stars of March.

I would never count on anyone for anything again. I would never encourage anyone to put their trust in me, either. To count on me for anything.

We're in this thing alone. Life. Only a fool pretends otherwise.

And this life we're in? It's a dirty, nasty, grubby business. I've talked about it enough.

I was set free, eventually.

"Hey!" somebody said, and I swung my head up, startled, and cracked it on the pole I was bound to.

"What the hell you doin' out here?"

The muscles of my neck were shrieking. My head was ringing. There was a dull gray light coming from everywhere and nowhere, and I was soaking wet. Just raising my head sent water streaming down my face and neck and chest. I was drowning in dew.

"You fuckin' kids."

What, I tried to say, though nothing came out of my mouth.

"This place was a resort. Franklin fuckin' Roosevelt stayed here."

I couldn't raise my hands to squeeze the water from eyes. I was blinking and sniffling and choking. I tipped my head up and gurgled until the gray hotel swam into focus. Then I looked directly before me. An old man dressed in overalls was standing in front of me. He was holding a styrofoam cup in one hand and a lunch pail, the old-fashioned kind with the round lid and big metal clasps, in the other.

"Now we have you shitbag kids, shittin' up the place. It's a goddamned shame."

Help, I said. And then again, audibly this time, "Help."

"Fuckin' sons a bitches." He came closer and peered up at me. "What the fuck you doin' without no clothes on?"

"They took them away," I whispered.

"This place was a fuckin' resort. Franklin fuckin' Roosevelt stayed here."

"Help," I gasped. "Get me off of here."

"You fuckin' kids." He walked around behind me and then appeared again. "What's this shit? These flags are hotel property, you know. I'd call the goddamned director, if he was worth a shit."

"A knife. Do you have a knife?"

"Little bastard he is, thinks the desk makes the man. When I think of the men sat behind that desk I could fuckin' shit. Great men, great days, they were. This place was a fuckin' resort."

"A knife."

He reached into one of his pants pockets and produced an elaborate Swiss knife with scores of attachments. He thumbed out a longish blade. He went around behind me and started sawing.

"You fuckin' kids."

I heard flag material rending and then the ground came racing up and struck me in the face.

"You're still here in five minutes, I won't call the director. I'll run you over with the fucking mower, I will."

Ah. The mower. I didn't want to be around for that.

I was free. I crawled up the hill on my numb hands and knees. I pulled myself to my feet on the frame of the door that led to the back of the main lobby of the hotel. I crept, naked, through the lobby. At that hour—it probably wasn't yet six—there was nobody there. I tottered into the elevator. When I got to my room, my two roommates were asleep, one in a pool of vomit. I crawled onto my cot and fell asleep. Or passed out. Whatever.

Ah, well. Memories. Where does the time go?

Here our party is at an end and I've monopolized all of our time talking about me, me, me. As usual.

Forgive me.

Here comes the new day, creeping up all around us. It's 5am. I've gotta wind this journal up.

So. Here we are. At last.

THE END IS NEAR

I promised this time would come and here it is. Time for goodbye.

How do you wind up your last night on Earth? How do you leave gracefully? How do you achieve closure? How do you say goodbye?

Saying goodbye is hard enough, when your audience is a sympathetic one. But when your audience is a hostile crowd—a crowd bereft of its pride and joy, its beloved father-figure and ex-spouse and stud muffin, its Trent, tragically snatched away in the prime of his life by your narrator—the job becomes that much more difficult.

But take heart, sweet Alice and Felicia, noble Tyler and stoic Colleen. I won't ask anything more of you. I've thought on this, and I think I have a way out. A way that won't be too embarrassing.

I'll leave the last word to Randy Trent.

"What goes around, comes around."

That's what he said to me in the Sail Inn, last night. At last call.

And he was right.

What goes around, comes around.

And now? Let's run.

Take my hand, aggrieved and vengeful readers. Come on. Let's run as fast as we can.

Let's run and not look back.

§

I read all the pages of my journals—front and back, past and present—last night. You said the truth was here. That I'd been writing it all along.

I fell asleep no more enlightened than ever.

And I woke up and there it was. The truth.

It's right here, just as you suggested, on every page. It's so obvious, so easy to see, that I couldn't see it. I was looking through it, past it, for something else. I was looking in the wrong place. In the wrong direction.

Someone else, reading this, might think that there isn't much truth on either side of these pages. That my search for truth wandered off into the briar patch of empty journalizing and died. But it's right here. In between the lines, on every page.

I know now what you meant, when you said that it wasn't the writing that mattered. That the writing was just the way there.

I'm ready for you, Death.

I have an answer.

§

It was all for nothing. There's nothing to say.

§

All along, I've been writing for someone else. Felicia and Alice, Colleen and Tyler, the police, the Angel of Death.

Now I'm writing for me.

Angel's been here and gone. She got what she wanted. She got her answer.

This pen feels odd in my hands. The doctors tell me I've been in and out of consciousness for six days. I don't remember any "in" parts.

My dosages of pain killers have been increased again, though they're killing me. But what isn't, at this point?

THE END IS NEAR

My liver, I'm told, is falling apart like a wet paper bag. As Dr. Croate said to me, days ago, I picked a bad time to remove a large part of my head and require extensive medication. Unshotgunned, I might have enjoyed another three or four years of compromised health.

That's what I hear, anyway.

The Angel of Death entered my room six days ago. She wheeled her cleaning supplies cart over to the window and started Windexing the glass.

"Let's hear it, Nathan," she said.

The door to my room opened again and Dr. Croate entered, followed by another doctor, a gray-haired eminence with ears like droopy, poisonous flowers and a facial expression even more dour than Dr. Croate's usual expression. They were both wearing white coats and stethoscopes. Dr. Croate had a laptop, which she plugged into the jack at the foot of my bed.

"Nathan," Dr. Croate said, "This is Dr. Dunsten."

I was watching Angel polish the glass.

"Nathan?"

I'm ready for you, Angel, I thought.

"Good. I knew you would be." The front of Angel's smock was dusted with some kind of cleaning powder. Ajax cleanser or something.

"Nathan, I'm afraid I don't have good news," Dr. Dunsten was saying. "We're coming to the end of what we can realistically do for you. Nathan?"

Angel finished polishing and popped her rag. "Tell me, Nathan."

"Nathan?" Dr. Croate said. "Are you seeing angels again?"

"Angels?" Dr. Dunsten said.

I have your answer. You were right. It was there all along.

"Hallucinations. Hepatic encephalopathy. Though the buckshot and head trauma probably aren't helping, either."

I want to live, Angel. I've got half a head, no prospects, no home, no money, legal troubles of catastrophic proportions, and I want to live. That's the truth. More than anything I've ever wanted, I want to live.

"If it was just your liver, maybe we could do something," Dr. Dunsten was saying. "If we had a viable organ donor, which we don't. Your spleen is gone. You have bleeding veins in your stomach and esophagus. Your immune system is compromised. And we're losing your kidneys. You have a type of kidney dysfunction called hepatorenal syndrome."

"This is your answer?" Angel said.

Most of it. The rest of my answer is this. Life is good. I have a few friends, a little bit of family. I want to live. Life is good. That's it.

The elderly doctor was winding up his speech, the word "fatal" popping up here and there. "I'm sorry," he said. "There's little more we can do."

"Excellent!" The Angel of Death tossed her rag into her cart. She looked very pleased. "You thought you weren't up to it, but you were. You did great, Nathan."

Dr. Croate was making a regretful face. "We'll make you as comfortable as we can."

"You held up your end. And a deal's a deal." The Angel of Death hung her bottle of Windex from a hook on the side of the cart. She beamed at me happily. "Now you can die."

I gripped the rails and stared back at the Angel of Death.

I don't want to die.

"Nathan?" Dr. Croate was saying. "I know this comes as a shock. Do you understand everything we've said?"

The Angel of Death was peeling off her plastic cleaning gloves. "I hear that a lot, in my line of work."

No, I thought. No. I'm not going. I'm not ready.

She shrugged. "Ready or not, makes no difference to me."

I don't want to die.

THE END IS NEAR

"Nathan?" Dr. Croate said.

That was it. That was six days ago.

And I'm still here, as far as I can tell.

I've had plenty of time to reflect on recent events and my current situation.

What do I know? I know this.

I know that death—or Death—comes for us all.

I know that my situation is not all that different from yours, dear reader. Who is to say how many minutes, how many hours, each of us has left? Who is to say that five minutes are all that different from five decades?

Our time is finite and the end is near. The end is always near.

In the meantime, it's enough to breathe the air. Flirt with a nurse. Let your thoughts drift out a window. See things as they are.

Let it all go. Let people in.

Treasure the day.

That's it. That's the truth. All of it I know.

§

www.ingramcontent.com/pod-product-compliance
Lightning Source LLC
Chambersburg PA
CBHW050539260626
47157CB00002B/367